I0606659

The magic had been an accident, but could they prove it?

Anglaise sat stiffly, hands clenched and propped on the table. Her leg bounced with nervous energy as she stared intently out the window. She looked ready to pounce and fight.

"So we just sit here?" Anglaise glared at Bruleé, eyes leaving the front window long enough to make her point and rub poison on Bruleé's doubts.

There wasn't a lot Bruleé could say. That was, in essence, her plan. Wait and see how angry the townspeople were. If they were in a forgiving mood, Bruleé could explain what happened. If not, their brooms were a few feet away leaning against the bakery case. "We sit and wait," Bruleé said. She reached across the table and squeezed Caramel's hand. "I have a feeling we'll be all right."

The sound of tires squealing made them all freeze. Anglaise flicked another accusatory glance at Bruleé. This was it. The cops could be on their way to arrest them.

Anglaise grabbed her broom, and Bruleé could hear her muttering a power chant to gather and focus—energy she could turn into an offensive weapon.

"Anglaise, stop it!" Bruleé was out of her chair a second behind Anglaise, but it felt like minutes, her sister had moved so fast.

Anglaise was so ready to fight and run, she hadn't noticed the car that pulled up wasn't the police. No sirens tore through the night and no flashing red lights. The magic Anglaise had called blazed in her hand, a ball of glowing white fire as incandescent as her rage. Bruleé felt like she was struggling through molasses as she trailed a few steps behind Anglaise, unable to catch up.

"Stop it! It's not the cops!" Bruleé screamed.

Anglaise either didn't hear or didn't believe her. She kept going not even missing a step. What was her idiot sister thinking? Attacking innocents with a ball of magic that would stun an elephant. The fact that she assumed the car was the cops made it worse. Assaulting an officer would get her jailed for life, if not worse.

When three witches open a teashop in the small Maine town of Midswich, the locals are none too happy. Leading the opposition is Pastor Austin, whose outspoken dislike of the witches hides a private pain.

The three witches, Bruleé, Anglaise, and Caramel, are only looking for a home. A place to start over after the death of their parents. With luck, and a little magic, they will make more friends than enemies and find a place in their new community.

KUDOS for *Tea Times Three*

"This is a sweet, entertaining story with serious undertones, a lot of heart, and some truly hilarious moments. It will also make you want to eat all of the baked things. All of them." ~ Reggie Lutz author of *Haunted*

"Tea Times Three blends small town drama and feel-good witchcraft into a story as sweet and fluffy as one of the pastries the Créme sisters sell. You'll want to have some fresh baked cookies on hand while you read this one." ~ Celia Swift, author of the *Christmas at Kellynch* Regency Romance Series

"A delicious and clever concoction of magic, witches, and dangerous small-town secrets." ~ Suzanne McLeod, author of the *Spellcrackers* urban fantasy series

"The story is cute, clever, and heartwarming, with a strong plot and plenty of surprises to keep you on your toes." ~ Taylor Jones, Reviewer

"*Tea Times Three* is heartwarming; funny; at times, suspenseful; at others, hilarious. It can make you laugh, cry, and bite your nails, sometimes all on the same page." ~ Regan Murphy, Reviewer

ACKNOWLEDGEMENTS

A lot of people helped with this book, and without many of them I would never finished it. Suzanne McLeod cheered me on during the writing of the first draft and even read my hand written pages. My critique group, Jessica Kormos, Miriah Hetherington, and Julia Rios were kind enough to read the later drafts and give suggestions. And special thanks to my mother for her unending support.

By Ché Gilson,

A Black Opal Books Publication

GENRE: PARANORMAL SUSPENSE

This is a work of fiction. Names, places, characters and incidents are either the product of the author's imagination or are used fictitiously, and any resemblance to any actual persons, living or dead, businesses, organizations, events or locales is entirely coincidental. All trademarks, service marks, registered trademarks, and registered service marks are the property of their respective owners and are used herein for identification purposes only. The publisher does not have any control over or assume any responsibility for author or third-party websites or their contents.

DEDICATION

To Sunny Frazier, who said,
"Why don't you just set it in Amercia?"

Chapter 1

At 5:00 a.m., the town of Midswich, Maine, was silent. One person strode through the pre-dawn twilight. Geoffrey Callister kept the tradition of opening Callister's Dry Goods himself every morning, same as his father and grandfather.

Geoffrey liked the hours of quiet he had to himself. He liked seeing Midswich wake up, watching the cobbled streets slowly fill with locals he knew on sight and tourists during the summer.

The old boutique was open.

Geoffrey halted.

He looked up and down the street, as if expecting to see a hidden camera or his friends laughing at him. The Piccadilly Boutique had closed years ago, when the economy went south along with Mrs. Herman's mind. The shop was empty. Or, at least, it had been.

Overnight it had changed. Gone was the "For Sale" sign in the dirty windows. The windows were clean, the old faded awnings replaced by crisp white new ones, and window boxes filled with pink geraniums decorated the outside. A fancy ironwork shingle hung over the front door—a silhouetted teapot embellished by floral cutouts. The words *Tea Times Three* curved around the teapot in iron letters.

Across the street, two girls in their mid-twenties set up a folding chalkboard sign. They looked normal enough. But he couldn't get past the fact that yesterday there hadn't been a teashop in Midswich.

Geoffrey realized he stood frozen in front of his grocery store. *Shut your mouth and man up,* Geoffrey thought. They're just girls. Ordinary young women who had opened a teashop overnight. He swallowed a couple of times, his mouth dry from hanging open.

The two girls finished putting out their sign. The tall, blonde straightened up and turned to Geoffrey. She was almost pretty enough to be a model or maybe an actress. But instead of "glamour," there was a hominess that warmed her good looks.

The girl smiled at him and waved. "Good morning!"

The other girl was a few inches shorter, dressed for work in a chef's coat, sneakers, and beige cargo pants. She looked across the street at Geoffrey, unsmiling, her eyes narrowed in suspicion.

Geoffrey raised a tentative hand and gave a weak hello wave. He couldn't quiet force out a return greeting.

He looked at the chalkboard.

Today's Specials

Oolong
Chamomile Blends
Chinese Blue Tea
Orange Pecan Scones
Butterscotch Brownies
Chocolate Cherry Gateau

The menu didn't look very magical. High in calories, but not actually witchy.

The distinct rumble of the news van's engine drew near. The familiar sound was a relief.

As Geoffrey waited, he kept staring at the two girls. They were going to think he was a perverted old man pretty soon. But he couldn't seem to look away, either. They looked so normal. There had to be some hint of the uncanny. The only thing so far was that the cheery blonde kept smiling and waving.

Geoffrey looked up. Descending from the sky was a third girl. The broom she flew on was loaded with packages, and the broom's bristled end wobbled on descent. Geoffrey inhaled, amazed. This was the sort of thing normally only seen on television, like the Mona Lisa or Ferrari cars. He knew they were out there. But to see it in person was indescribable. A thrill bubbled up in his chest and fear curled in his gut then, like a rollercoaster, wonder rose up and overshadowed the fear.

The news van from Musquash arrived with Geoffrey's morning delivery of newspapers and magazines for the Dry Goods. Geoffrey caught sight of Rob Harris, the deliveryman. Rob saw the witch land across the street. His granite face didn't even twitch. He took in the sight of the girl on the broom, and the van peeled away from the curb, leaving a long black streak of rubber on the street. The van sped past, leaving Geoffrey in an acidic cloud of burnt rubber and exhaust.

"My papers," Geoffrey coughed.

Three blocks away, in front of the town square, the van screeched to a halt. A bundle of papers were unceremoniously tossed out the back of the van.

"Oh, no. Your newspapers."

The voice came from so close beside Geoffrey, he jumped, and his already taxed heart sped up. The blonde girl stood right next to him. He reminded himself he wasn't in a horror movie. She'd just walked across the street while he'd been staring at the van.

"I'll get them for you," she said, and her eyes narrowed in concentration. She raised a hand, pulling back as if tugging an invisible string. The two bundles of papers lifted off the pavement and drifted toward them, landing at Geoffrey's feet.

"There you are," the blonde said. She let out a tired exhale, but her perky smile never faltered.

Geoffrey snapped. Too much was happening too early in the morning. He offered a weak, almost hysterical smile. "I have to go now," he said.

He turned and bolted for the safety of the Dry Goods. Geoffrey hit the door full force, forgetting he hadn't unlocked it. The door shuddered as he bounced off it and his vision went gray. There was a vague sensation of falling, and he knew he wouldn't last long. After all, the pavement was only a few feet away.

"I told you not to show off, Bruleé."

Bruleé gave her sister a sardonic look. The way she carried on, you'd think she was the oldest sister. "He'll be fine, Anglaise."

Bruleé knelt beside the man on the sidewalk. Secretly, she knew Anglaise was right, but she would burn at the stake before admitting it.

She ignored her sister and summoned her magic. A warm feeling rose from her bones, suffusing her body. She always pictured it in her mind as a golden light radiating from within, but there was nothing visible until she released it.

"See the unseen, good or ill, show me what's in need," she muttered.

Her slender hand passed over his light blue shirt and red tie. A white glow left a trail in the air behind her hand. He was fine. He'd bruised his head on the sidewalk, and his nose would be sore from its impromptu meeting with the door, but other than that, nothing was wrong with him. Though, he could use one of her slimming teas to get him back to his ideal weight.

"Well?" Anglaise demanded.

Perhaps she'll be satisfied if I pronounce him dead, Bruleé thought. She could feel steel-gray eyes drilling into her, waiting to be proven right.

"He's fine," she said, "I just wanted to help."

"You've helped us to a lynch mob," Anglaise snapped.

"Don't be ridiculous. That doesn't happen these days." *And wait for it,* Bruleé thought.

"Tell that to Granny Bonbon."

There it was. The one example of modern violence against witches that Anglaise could dredge up to prove her mistrust of people was right.

Never mind that Granny Bonbon had gone senile and started cursing people when she thought she was aiding them. And never mind that a little boy had almost died. Granny had been assaulted by the parents, but then the police came, and now she was in a nursing home for old witches, her powers bound, where she could do no one any harm.

"Oh, look. He's waking up," Bruleé said.

"You should wipe his memory."

"Nonsense. It's not like the town won't know we're witches sooner or later."

The man groaned and scrunched his eyelids in pain. Slowly, he cracked one eye open and looked around.

Bruleé smiled kindly.

"What—uh—" Both his eyes opened and he looked from Bruleé to Anglaise.

"You took a nasty spill, sir," Bruleé said.

Anglaise snorted. "Because you scared him witless."

"That's enough, Anglaise."

He frantically dug into his pants' pocket. "No, no, no. I'm fine." He jumped up and leapt for the grocery store. He thrust the key into the lock, sparing an anxious glance over his shoulder. "Thank you, anyway."

The bang of the door slamming shut rattled the windows, and Bruleé felt a puff of wind in her face. She heard the click of the lock and knew he was trying to lock them out.

Anger radiated off Anglaise, standing stiffly beside her.

"I'm going to start packing," she snarled then added softly, "Again."

Anglaise turned and started stomping back across the street before Bruleé could rally.

"No, you're not!" Bruleé shouted after her sister. "I said we're staying."

Bruleé ran after her. She caught the teashop door before it closed. Anglaise was already stomping past the wooden cottage tables and chairs that were ready for customers. Her baby sister Caramel stood in the middle of the room, holding a stack of menus fresh from the printers. They were what she'd been flying in when the news van drove off. She'd been placing them on the pink-and-white-striped tablecloths next to the porcelain and silver tea services laid out on all the tables. Her wide golden-brown eyes looked searchingly from Anglaise to Bruleé.

"Start packing," Anglaise said, passing the glass display case next to the register. The bakery cases were full of cookies, scones, and golden pastries. Behind the baked goods rose a wall of cubbies, each one holding a glass jar of dried tea, herbs, spices, or flowers. A passage behind the counter led to Anglaise's domain, the kitchen, and a staircase that led to the apartment above.

Caramel pulled the menus to her chest. "A—are we leaving?"

"Yes!" Anglaise disappeared into the kitchen.

"No!" Bruleé crossed her arms. "Don't you dare fold a sock."

Anglaise came back into the main shop. "Is that so?"

"We don't know for sure that everyone will act like that guy. Maybe if—"

"Maybe if what?" Anglaise cut her off. "Maybe if we gave the green grocer a heart attack, they'll really take a shine to us?"

"Um…p—p—please?" Caramel stammered, her voice a tremulous whisper.

"I was only trying to help. We need to make friends here."

From up above came the thump-thump-thump of a small body rapidly descending the stairs. There was the skitter of nails on tile, and Fraiche, their Pomeranian, burst into the teashop, an excited ball of cream-colored fur.

Bruleé walked up to the counter and leaned over it, staring at Anglaise. Anglaise had a point. Witches had always been persecuted, even into the twentieth century. When the Jim Crow laws were abolished in the sixties, the anti-magic laws that punished the use of witchcraft with long jail sentences, and even death south of the Mason-Dixon Line, went with them. "We're here to open a magic teashop. How can we, if we never use our magic?"

Fraiche jumped up and down beside Anglaise, each leap accompanied by a shrill yap. He sprang higher than the counter on his little legs.

Anglaise scowled. "There's a time and a place."

"S—stop fighting," Caramel's voice rose to normal speaking level, which for her was a shout. Caramel blushed bright red and dropped her eyes to the floor. Bruleé and Anglaise waited expectantly while Fraiche ran to her.

"I—I want to stay," she whispered.

Fraiche shimmied and waved his pom-pom tail in support.

"See? Caramel is on my side," Bruleé said.

"No, I—I'm not. I just l—like this town. It's cute…" Her voice trailed off to nothing.

Anglaise looked furious, her chef's temper close to boiling over. Bruleé could see her gears turning. Did she carry on, insist they leave, and crush her little sister, or did she agree to stay?

"Fine." Anglaise spun on her heel and headed for the kitchen. "Just don't say I didn't warn you."

Bruleé let out a quiet sigh. She went to one of the tables and sat down. Head propped on hands, she stared at the china plates.

Caramel sat down beside her. "D—did you really s—scare the greengrocer?"

"Yes." Bruleé nodded, miserable. "I did." Her usual mistake. She'd used too much magic, too soon, hoping she could force people to accept them.

She glanced at Caramel, still hugging her menus. Unshed tears moistened her light brown eyes.

Bruleé nudged her with an elbow. "Want to bop me?" Caramel hit Bruleé on the head with the menus then offered a shy smile. "I deserve that." Bruleé grinned. She looked around suspiciously. "Just don't tell Anglaise."

Fraiche whined at Caramel's feet, and she picked him up. She hugged him and mumbled into his coat, "B—but what do we do n—now?"

Bruleé put an arm around her sister and looked around the teashop. The sparkling crystal, the chintz curtains, and polished hardwood floor—all of it was just as she'd imagined. Midswich had been her choice. They had one last chance to start over and this was it. Their inheritance was almost gone and, despite popular belief, witches couldn't conjure money.

"Don't worry." Bruleé squeezed Caramel's hand. "The Crème sisters will never be defeated."

Chapter 2

Geoffrey stood behind the front counter of the grocery store. He peeped out of the blinds at the teashop. The fancy ironwork shingle over the door swung back and forth in the early morning breeze. The witches had certainly familiarized themselves with Midswich's strict building codes.

He had to tell someone. Claire, of course.His hands shook a little as he pulled his cell phone from his pocket. He told himself he was just shaken by the fall. Claire was speed dial number one on his phone. Geoffrey punched the button.

The phone rang and rang. He was afraid it was about to go to voice mail when a sleepy voice finally answered.

"What time is it?"

"Claire! You'll never guess what happened," Geoffrey whispered softly into the phone. He stayed crouched on the floor, afraid the witches could see and hear him.

"Vegetables not been delivered?"

Geoffrey could sense her already slipping back to sleep.

"It's not the veggies." Geoffrey was shocked by the high pitch of his voice. He coughed. "Sorry."

"Are you all right?"

He took a deep inhale to steady himself.

"Witches own the teashop."

There was a moment of stunned silence on the other end.

Slowly, Claire said, "What teashop?"

"The new teashop. They must have opened it by magic. It's right where the old Piccadilly was, and it wasn't there yesterday," Geoffrey said.

"Oh, my. I have to call Emma."
The line went dead.

Claire Callister pushed a mop of highlighted brown hair out of her face and pulled her friend Emma's number from her cell's address book.

Emma was a good ten years older than Claire, but she was a good friend and client. Claire had been cutting her hair for the last fifteen years.

Unlike Claire, Emma was an early riser, getting up at five to do yoga and go jogging with the God Squad, Pastor Austin's jogging club. She checked the clock. She might be able to catch Emma before meeting the running group.

A chipper voice answered the phone. "Morning, Claire. I was just out the door."

"You'll never guess who's running the teashop," Claire blurted. With gossip this juicy, there was no time for pleasantries.

"What do you mean?"

"There's a brand new teashop in town run by witches!" Claire couldn't keep the note of triumph out of her voice. Being married to Geoffrey had its perks. He was the most reliable gossip in town.

"Witches? Are you sure?"

"Spell-casting, real-life witches," Claire said, trying to keep the glee out of her voice and failing. She blamed Midswich. Nothing much happened in the town, so it was all the better when something did.

"Witches," Emma repeated.

Claire caught the note of anxiety in her voice, and she was glad she was not alone. As happy as she was to have news to spread, she had to admit Geoffrey's call had left her with a growing unease. She'd called Emma, in part, to get some reassurance. Emma was a Christian, too, but she also loved all things metaphysical. She burned sage to cleanse her house on a regular basis and even tried to keep her chakras clean.

Claire's glee faded. "Do you think we should be worried?"

"I think I better call Veronica," Emma finally said.

"Wait," Claire said.

"Thank you for telling me."

"But—"

Emma hung up without answering Claire's question. Of course, that was probably answer enough. Claire flopped back into bed and stared up at the ceiling. Witches were just regular people, right? She chewed the inside of her cheek, trying to push away a growing anxiety now that the thrill of fresh gossip had worn off.

What happened if the town turned into a bunch of spell junkies? Of course, there were already two bars, the fake pub, Rosa's, and the grocery store selling booze. That didn't make the town full of alcoholics. She should be reasonable. She just didn't feel reasonable.

Dani sat at the table in her breakfast nook, looking down at an egg white omelet. She was not a cook, and the egg whites came from a carton with a picture of the perfect omelet.

She hated egg whites. Her mother had been a terrible cook, and Dani remembered vividly the severely underdone scrambled eggs her mother had made her eat. *'Because children in China were starving, Danielle.'* Honestly, what did that have to do with anything? The runny egg whites were slimy, little globs of wobbling snot on the plate. Usually, she drowned it in ketchup. Later, she just refused to eat eggs at all, opting for breakfast cereal and toaster pastries.

Dani had burned the omelet nearly black to make sure the whites were fully solid. She still wasn't sure she could get it down without vomiting.

She picked up her fork and scowled at the omelet, imagining herself as some latter day Dirty Harry. "Go ahead, punk, make my day."

The omelet, too crispy and misshapen, lay on the plate. So far, it was winning the staring contest.

"Think of the last ten pounds," Dani said. She tightened her grip on her fork.

She couldn't take it anymore. How many calories could ketchup possibly have?

Just as Dani stood, her phone rang. She breathed a sigh of relief, glad to have any excuse to put off eating the omelet.

"Hey, Veronica," she said.

"Dani, you'll never guess!"

"No, I won't. Just tell me." Dani pulled open her fridge. A nearly empty bottle of ketchup rattled in the door. She eyed the quarter inch in the bottom.

"Witches opened a teashop. In our town," Veronica said. "Can you believe it? I mean, what are they like in real life?"

Dani straightened up and closed the fridge. "For real? Witches?"

"Yeah. In Midswich, of all places."

A mean chuckle escaped Dani. "God, Aunt Penelope's going to shit a brick."

"You're so mean. You shouldn't wind her up."

"Why not? It's so easy. I mean, the woman vacations in Roswell, hoping for aliens to land."

"Do you think I should be worried?"

"What, like do I think witches are going to lure your kids into their oven with baked goods? It's a teashop. How evil can it be?"

Veronica laughed. "That's just what I said. But do you think it's a problem?"

"I don't care, but I know plenty who will. Pastor Sunshine for sure."

Pastor Austin had never had a kind word for anyone that Dani knew. His sour demeanor was nothing a candy bar couldn't fix. How a grown man survived on rabbit food, she couldn't guess. Low blood sugar might explain a lot.

Dani could hear Liz and Jordan fighting in the background.

"Hang on," Veronica said. "Hey, put that back! I'm taking the last Twinkie!"

"Sorry," Veronica told Dani. "I gotta get the little monkeys to school. Wanna meet for lunch?"

"Sure," Dani said.

"Rosa's at 12:30?"

"I'll be there."

Veronica hung up and Dani turned back to the now cold omelet. She picked up the plate and took it to the garbage. The omelet bounced into the trash.

Penelope Owens stood in the kitchen, staring thoughtfully at her backyard. The sight of new buds and purple crocus poking out of the brown grass couldn't cheer her up. She had been standing there, a can of dog food in one hand, the can opener in the other, for ten minutes. She was trying to calculate how long it would take Pastor Austin to get back from his morning jog. He didn't take a cell with him, and he forbade the others in the running group to bring anything electronic as well.

The phone rang and she started. Prince Albert whined at her feet, looking up hopefully at the can. His slender tail whipped back and forth.

She looked down at him, "Sorry," and answered the cordless phone hanging from the kitchen wall. "Hello?"

"Aunt Penelope, guess what? There's a new teashop in town run by you'll never guess who owns it," Dani said gleefully.

Penelope frowned. "Witches."

"Damn it," Dani swore under her breath. "So you already know."

"Of course," Penelope said. "As if witches could pull anything over on me. I know all about their tricks."

Penelope had seen the teashop when she took Prince Albert for a walk that morning. The new shop and its sudden appearance meant only one thing. Her heart had squeezed so tight in her chest she thought she might have a heart attack. Penelope had turned around and gone straight back home to try and calm down.

"They might actually improve this town."

"I wouldn't get attached if I were you."

"What are you planning, Aunt Penelope?"

"Just wait 'til Pastor Austin hears about this."

"Come on, they're just witches, not terrorists," Dani groaned.

"There's no such thing as *just* witches, Danielle," Penelope held the phone in the crook of her shoulder and opened Prince Albert's dog food. The beef bits in gravy plopped into his bowl.

"I feel racist even having this conversation. Look, I gotta get to work," Dani said.

"It's not racist to protect yourself or your family," Penelope countered. Her hand tightened on the empty can of dog food. "Promise me you won't go to that teashop."

Penelope waited for Dani's reply. She tossed the can into the recycling. Why did Dani have to be so stubborn? She was bull-headed, just like her mother. When Dani was little, she would pout and ball her fists, sticking to some ridiculous point. Just like her mother had at that age.

A frustrated noise came from Dani's end of the line. "Maybe. I don't know," she said at last.

"I would appreciate it a great deal. You are, after all, the only family I have left."

"Nice guilt trip, Aunt Penelope. I'll think about it."

Penelope smiled. She bent down and gave Prince Albert a scratch behind the ear as he scarfed down his breakfast. "Thank you, dear."

Dani hung up with one last grunt of exasperation.

Penelope looked at the clock on the microwave. Quarter to seven. Pastor Austin should just be getting back to his house.

After last night's rain had washed the world clean, this

morning's jog had been particularly glorious. Pastor Austin had once heard that the Navajo ran five miles in the direction of the sunrise every day and when dawn broke, thanked the great Creator. He understood perfectly. It was good to have the earth beneath your feet, see the beauty passing by, and feel the workings of your body. He often felt jogging and appreciating nature was as much a communion with God as going to church.

Austin walked the last few blocks to his Tudor-style. He went around the side gate and entered the backdoor. In the mudroom, he took off his running shoes. The kitchen was pristine and little used. Oscar Austin was one of those rare, tidy bachelors who immediately washed, dried, and put away any used dish. He ate sparingly to begin with, so there was rarely much mess to clean. Austin ate the recommended seven small meals a day, supplementing them with protein shakes and power bars.

He pulled a strawberry-flavored electrolyte gel from the fridge and went to his office to listen to his phone messages and stretch out.

The message light on his answering machine flashed twenty-two. Austin frowned as he propped a foot on the desk to stretch is hamstrings.

The phone rang as he folded himself over his leg. For a second, he thought about ignoring it, but duty won out over self-indulgence. He picked up the receiver.

"Pastor Austin speaking."

"Pastor Austin, I'm glad I caught you."

Austin grimaced at the sound of Penelope Owens's voice. She was a dedicated parishioner and a good woman, but she was prone to hysterics. As her clergyman of choice, he often ended up on the receiving end of her outbursts. He frequently wished he could pass her off to Pastor Clark at the Baptists.

He switched legs on the desk to stretch the other one. "What can I help you with?"

"There's a new teashop in town. It's run by witches," she said.

Austin froze mid-stretch. Witches had come to Midswich.

He felt a flare of territoriality. How dare witches come to his town? And worse than that, open a teashop. They might as well have opened a bakery. Surely, this was a test. Not just of the town's character, but of his own.

"Thank you for telling me, Penelope."

"Can you imagine?" she said. "Witches in this town."

"Don't worry. I don't think they'll be staying."

"I can't tell you how relieved I am to hear you say that," Penelope said.

"Goodbye, Penelope."

"Er, goodbye."

Pastor Austin hung up. Obviously, Mrs. Owens had wanted to say more, but Austin had plans to make, starting with this Sunday's sermon. There were two days left to work on what he wanted to say.

Chapter

idswich sparkled in the afternoon sun. A few
puddles in the gutters reflected the clear, blue sky
and scattered white clouds.

The sign in the window of the teashop may have said
Grand Opening, but Caramel was feeling less than grand. Her
nerves still jangled from the fight that morning and, so far, not
a single customer had come in. Half an hour ago, Bruleé had
ordered her onto the sidewalk with a stack of menus.

Caramel wasn't sure why Bruleé wasn't out here too. She
knew how shy Caramel was, but as the youngest. she always
ended up with the jobs no one else wanted.

When they had decided on opening their own teashop, each
sister had taken the job that most suited them. Anglaise could
bake, and she could add spells to the pastries and confections
she made. She could make a chamomile and lemon balm
shortbread that cured insomnia, ginger biscotti for digestion,
and a hundred other things, each one tasty and powerful.
Bruleé blended teas and tisanes, herbal infusions imbued with
magic to do everything from soothing migraines to inducing
prophetic dreams.

Caramel, on the other hand, was assigned the job of
waitress. She wasn't even good at it. Caramel didn't seem to
be good at much. Not magic, not baking, and certainly not tea.
That left her with waiting tables, cleaning up, and, on very bad
days, standing on the sidewalk, handing out flyers.

Caramel glanced up at the sound of footsteps. A woman
and a little boy, too young for school, headed her way.

Bruleé had given Caramel a tea for her nerves before pushing her out onto the sidewalk, but Caramel's nerves were winning the battle. Her hand shook as she pulled a single flyer from the stack. She glanced back up. The woman was only a few feet away from her.

Caramel held up the flyer without looking at the woman. She kept her eyes locked on the sparkling pavement.

"T—t—tea T—t—times Three now open," she stuttered.

A small chubby hand reached for the pink sheet of paper and Caramel sighed in relief. Finally, success. The boy's round face smiled up at her. A tentative smile formed on her lips.

"Hurry up, Andrew," came his mother's sharp voice. She yanked him out of range of the flyer.

Carmel felt her face freeze then overheat with a deep blush. She felt shamed and embarrassed then angry that she felt that way. What did she have to feel embarrassed about?

"Mom!" The little boy drew the word 'mom' out for at least fifteen seconds. "Smells good."

"Decent people don't support their kind."

"But, Moommm." Andrew dragged his heels on the sidewalk, giving the teashop a longing look over his shoulder.

Caramel couldn't take it anymore. The woman's words rang in her head, stirring up the fear already there. Tears welled up in her eyes, then spilled over. The world blurred and wobbled as she dropped the flyers.

Half blinded, she fled inside the teashop, her footsteps tapping hollowly on the polished hardwood.

She ran behind the counter, ignoring Bruleé's surprised shout. Caramel turned left and hurried through the kitchen, where Anglaise was sitting idle in the corner. She looked up as Caramel burst in, but Caramel made an immediate right. The stairs up to the apartment were right next to the kitchen door. Anglaise opened her mouth, but Caramel didn't stop. She threw open the door and pounded up the stairs.

The stairs led up to a little living room, still full of boxes from the move. Down a short hall was her new bedroom. The smallest bedroom in the apartment, barely big enough for her bed. She slammed the door behind her, and cast a quick locking spell. Then she threw herself down and cried.

She didn't care if Bruleé was mad. She wasn't going out there again. Bruleé could hand out flyers if it was that important. It wasn't like she had customers to serve.

Seconds later there was a knock on the door. Caramel heard the doorknob rattle.

"Carmel, what's wrong?" Bruleé asked through the door. She could have easily dismantled Caramel's spell, but was nice enough not to.

"I—I can't do it," Caramel raised her voice.

"What? Why not?"

"T—they're too m—mean," she wailed, burying her head in her pillow.

Anglaise shouted from below, "Just leave her alone! You shouldn't have sent her out with flyers, anyway. You know how sensitive Caramel is."

"Go back to the kitchen, Anglaise," Bruleé shouted back.

"Never left it," came the fainter reply.

There was a heavy silence. Caramel pulled the pillow over her ears. Anglaise was right. She was too sensitive. Too sensitive to do anything.

"I'll come back later with some tea and maybe a muffin or cookies, all right?" Bruleé said.

Caramel could feel her sister waiting on the other side of the door, but didn't have the energy to reply. After a few minutes, Bruleé's footsteps faded as she went back downstairs.

Why couldn't she ever seem to do anything right? Caramel curled up into a ball. She studied spell craft and crystals, tarot and astrology, but she was hopeless. Her sole talent seemed to be taking spells apart. Which wasn't helpful when you were trying to *cast* them. She cracked open an eye. On the floor, next to an empty bookshelf, was a box of books. She hadn't been practicing much lately, but she didn't really see a point when her casting was so hit or miss.

She choked back a sob. To think, just this morning, she had voted to stay in town. She wanted to go home. She missed the familiar Boston streets, the noise, and the witch neighborhood they'd lived in.

Caramel hugged her pillow. She suddenly missed her stuffed rabbit, Moony. She'd put him away only last year, finally deciding that fifteen was too old for plush toys. Even though she was sixteen, she still missed the comforting presence of his soft, cotton felt.

For a while, Caramel just lay there, hoping Bruleé made the right choice. Midswich had seemed ideal. A quiet New England town with a lot of tourism. The picture-postcard good-looks of the town had done a lot to soothe Caramel's fears. Surely a town that cute couldn't be anything but welcoming. Caramel had tentatively suggested staying in Boston, but the truth was, they couldn't afford to open up a teashop in a big city, no matter how many prosperity spells Bruleé cast. Their parents had left too much debt behind. More than anyone had known.

So, Midswich it was. If they failed this time, their family would also break apart. Aunt Licorice wanted to take in Caramel. She'd been after Bruleé to give up custody since their parents died. Anglaise always seemed to have one foot out the door. Bruleé was working hard to keep them all together, and Caramel couldn't even hand out a single flyer.

Fresh tears pricked her eyes. She pushed them down, trying not to feel sorry for herself.

She heard Bruleé's voice outside. Caramel stood and took two short steps to the window. Her bedroom had a panoramic view of Stratford. She looked down, just past the awning. Bruleé was on the sidewalk handing out flyers, or at least she was trying. The locals hurried by, ignoring her. Some of them even crossed the street to get away from her.

Caramel vowed that, tomorrow, she would try again. Tomorrow would be Saturday, and maybe there would be some tourists. Although it was too early in the season, she could still hope.

The Dry Goods was as full as Geoffrey had ever seen it. Today, no one was bothering with the pretense of buying anything. Just about the entire town had come to hear about his harrowing encounter with the witches. A story he told and retold, relishing the attention.

Claire had come in at lunch so she could stand inside and look out the window at the teashop, until a hair appointment finally took her away.

Still, most everyone in the whole town came into the store, staying long enough to hear Geoffrey's story and to observe the witches from behind the safety of the Dry Goods' plate glass windows.

Mrs. Owens frowned as she stared daggers across the street. "I can't believe witches had the nerve to come here."

The blonde witch he'd met that morning was trying to hand out flyers, replacing a young girl with brown hair Geoffrey guessed to be a little sister. Mrs. Bradford had said something to the young woman and sent her fleeing.

"Well, maybe they'll turn out to be all right," Geoffrey said.

Penelope Owens shot a black look at Geoffrey. "You should be the last one defending them."

"I wasn't defending them," Geoffrey said hastily. He didn't have to justify his opinion to her, but something in her self-righteous tone threatened consequences if he didn't agree with her. Another hazard of the church crowd.

"Didn't they threaten you with magic?"

Geoffrey scratched his head. He had the uncomfortable feeling he should have pulled himself together before calling Claire this morning. Or just kept his mouth shut.

"Threaten is too strong a word," Geoffrey said.

Penelope didn't listen. She had already turned her attention back to the window.

"Look, are you going to buy anything?" Geoffrey asked her.

Mrs. Owens had been in the store nearly two hours, and he was getting sick of her.

An imposing figure in black caught the corner of

Geoffrey's eye. Pastor Austin was coming down the sidewalk. Penelope Owens perked up like a terrier greeting its master at the sight of him. Geoffrey felt his stomach wither. He frowned as the pastor headed for the grocery store.

The store bell chimed pleasantly as Austin came in. Considering the look on the pastor's face, a death knell would have been more appropriate.

"Geoffrey, Penelope," Austin said.

Penelope lit up with righteous vindication, but Geoffrey just nodded. He'd never much liked Austin. The pastor had the habit of calling everyone by their first names, but never let anyone call him Oscar. Geoffrey found it patronizing, and he made it a point to stay out of the pastor's way as much as he could.

Penelope nodded at the teashop across the street. "Pastor Austin, look."

Austin joined her at the window. "Yes, I saw the witch on my way here."

He turned to Geoffrey. "Do you know their names?"

"No," he said.

"Well, that's fine," Austin said. "I don't think they'll be here long enough for it to matter."

Geoffrey frowned and busied himself behind the register. He never should have panicked this morning. He had smelled them baking all morning, and he'd been tormented by the scent of cinnamon, browning dough, and cookies. If only he'd had the nerve to go back over there. He'd made such an ass of himself before, when they helped him with the newspapers, and he couldn't bring himself to cross the street. The unfortunate truth was that Midswich was a small town. His livelihood depended on the good opinion of his neighbors. Get on the wrong side of this witch issue and he'd see a sharp downturn in customers.

"I'm planning a special sermon on Sunday," Austin told Penelope.

"I'll be there," she said.

Austin turned to Geoffrey. "And will you be there, Geoffrey?"

Pastor Austin knew very well Geoffrey would not. He hadn't set foot inside church since his wedding, which had been presided over by the former minister, Pastor Carlson.

"I have to take inventory," Geoffrey lied.

That earned him a tight smile from Austin. Good opinion was one thing, but Geoffrey wasn't rearranging his entire life to suck up to the town's largest denomination and least pleasant clergyman.

At lunch, Eddie Piñero locked the door of the Jefferson Elementary School Library and walked down Greenwich Avenue, his step a little lighter than usual.

He was meeting Matilda for their weekly lunch date. *Don't call it a date*, he reminded himself, over and over, even as the anticipation grew.

Eddie was a relative newcomer to Midswich. His family had moved from Providence when he was nine—a bookish, skinny kid with a pronounced widow's peak. By the age of twenty-four, it was sharply receding. Eddie had never made friends easily. He still remembered those first few days at Midswich Elementary. Everyone in town had grown up together. They had made friends in kindergarten or earlier, and there was no room for a new kid. Eddie's entire class had ignored him.

He'd spent every spare minute in the school library, sometimes to avoid the other kids, but mostly because he loved books.

One day, Matilda had come in looking for a book-report book. Mrs. Danby, the librarian, had been busy copying something in the office, and had left Eddie in charge.

Eddie would never forget the sight of Matilda standing in the fiction section, hair blazing red, lit by theafternoon sun slanting down from the high windows.

She'd come down the aisle to the front desk where Eddie was sitting.

"What's a good book?" she'd asked. "I have a report to do."

"*Mrs. Frisby and the Rats of NIMH*," Eddie had said, thrilled she was speaking to him, even if it was just business.

"All right, where is it?"

Eddie hopped down from the big chair and went straight to the fiction aisle. He pulled the book off the shelf and handed it to Matilda.

"I hope it's good," she said.

"It is. Trust me." Eddie had read it three times already.

Matilda had nodded, waiting for Mrs. Danby to return from the office so she could check out the book.

The next day at lunch, Matilda did the greatest favor any nine-year-old could. She put in a good word for him with her friends. She had told them he was nice and had given her a good book.

After that, the ice began to melt. The boys in the class said, "Hi," once in a while, and he started to get invited to basketball games and on bike rides.

Now, they were good friends. They had been all through junior high and high school.

And she has a boyfriend, he reminded himself for the hundredth time as he turned right onto Strafford at the town's square.

As much as Eddie enjoyed their weekly lunches, it was becoming painful to be around Matilda. He wasn't sure when his feelings had changed, but maybe he'd always loved her. Instead of changing, perhaps they were just getting more acute. He should find an excuse to be busy next week. Of course, he'd been thinking that same thing for months now, and every week, he showed up.

Matilda was there on the patio of Rosa's, spring sunshine caught in her strawberry-blonde hair. Big sunglasses masked her blue-green eyes. For a second, Eddie couldn't breathe.

She was staring down the street, head turned. Then she looked back and saw Eddie. Matilda smiled and waved.

He hurried around to the front of the restaurant and ducked in the front door. The dining room was all but deserted.

Everyone was outside, trying to get a better look at the teashop.

He waved to Consolata, who was taking a tray of food from the kitchen. She nodded, but was too busy to stop.

"Hey, Eddie," Matilda said as he sat down.

"It's crowded today," Eddie said. All the patio tables were occupied by locals. The other diners were all staring down the street in the same direction Matilda had been.

He followed their gazes. Everyone was fixated on the teashop. He should have known. News of the shop and its witchy proprietors had spread like gasoline on fire throughout the elementary school.

"Can you believe witches came here, of all places?" Matilda leaned across the table. "Maybe we should have gone there for lunch."

"I don't know," he said.

He watched as someone crossed the street to avoid even walking in front of the shop. As an outsider, Eddie had come to understand two things about small towns. Anything new was automatically distrusted, and it never paid to go against the grain.

Small towns had long memories. To Eddie, it looked like Midswich had already made the decision to get rid of the teashop as soon as possible.

"I want to go," Matilda said.

Eddie noticed she stayed seated. "I don't know," he repeated and cringed. Such witty conversation. That was really going to win her over. *Remember she has a boyfriend.* Eddie changed the subject. "Did you order already?"

Usually, the food was on the table when he got to Rosa's. He only had forty-five minutes for lunch and Matilda had eaten all the chips and salsa before he got there.

He picked up the empty chip basket and held it upside down over the table. A few crumbs fell out. "Thanks for leaving me some chips."

She grinned. "I thought about leaving you some."

"Oh, well, as long as you thought about it."

They both chuckled.

"So, what do you think the witches are like? Did you know any in Providence?" Matilda kept looking back at the teashop, unable tear herself away.

Eddie tried to recall. "Well, there were some witches, but I never met them. My grandmother went to one for some kind of arthritis cure."

"And did they?"

"No. I mean, cure isn't the right word. She had some potion or something that helped the pain. 'Better than aspirin,' she said."

"I wonder why everyone's freaking out?" Matilda propped her head on her hand. "I love this town, but it's so stupid sometimes."

"Not stupid," said Eddie. "More like provincial."

"Is there a difference?"

"Yes. There has to be."

"You don't think angry villagers will show up with pitchforks and torches, do you?"

Eddie laughed. Matilda never failed to make him smile. "I think the witches must be thinking the same thing."

Matilda sighed and looked back over her shoulder at the teashop. "It makes me sad. Maybe I'll go over there later."

"I—uh—" Eddie paused. He wanted to tell her she shouldn't go, but realized it wasn't his business.

She turned back to him and pushed the sunglasses up on her head. "You what?"

"I just—" He didn't want to say. He wouldn't risk it. Despite having lived in Midswich for fifteen years, he still felt like a newcomer, and he was keenly aware that his position in town was precarious. Matilda's family, on the other hand, had lived here for generations. She could do what she wanted.

"Edward Piñero, are you afraid of what people will think?"

There was no good answer to that. If he tried bravado, she might challenge him to go to the teashop right then. If he said he did care what people thought, he was a coward.

Eddie looked at his wristwatch. "I think I am going to have to get lunch to go. Mrs. Mackey's third-graders are coming in next period."

Matilda burst out laughing, a surprisingly loud, warm laugh that gave Eddie a pleasant chill.

"Wow, are you really that lame?" she asked.

"I'm going to go with 'yes.'"

"And that's your final answer?"

"Where is the food?"

They looked at each other. For just a second, they both kept a straight face. Then they crumbled into laughter.

"Fine," Matilda snorted. "Be that way. But you, of all people, should know what it's like to be new in town."

That stung. He was saved by the arrival of Consolata and the food.

"Hey, guys. Sorry it's late," she said as she put the tray down. "I put yours in a take-out box."

Consolata put a brown, waxed paper take-out box in front of Eddie. Rosa's refused to use Styrofoam containers.

"Thanks," Eddie said.

"Just bring the silverware back whenever."

The restaurant also let people take their silverware, so they didn't have to hand out plastic forks and knives. The return of silverware meant five percent off the next meal. They got most of it back, but they also got other people's silverware back as a result. Still, Rosa never said anything, and the restaurant now had an eclectic collection of dinnerware.

Matilda had ordered his favorite lunch for him: chicken mole and chili relleno on the side. She had the carne asada steak salad.

Eddie took a few bites and then checked his watch again for real. "I gotta run. I wasn't lying about the third graders," he said. He was pleased to see the look of disappointment on Matilda's face. *Maybe someday—*

He didn't let himself finish the thought.

"All right. See ya later," she said.

"Bye." He took the silverware and his take-out box, went back through the restaurant, and walked back to school.

Alyss sat on the edge of the fountain, holding court in the town square. Gathered around were the other Midswich goths. Normally, they gathered after school, in order to glare at the normies, the ordinary citizens of Midswich, as they went about their dreary, sheep-like lives.

Today was special. The group huddled together in a tight knot to discuss Tea Times Three. A storm of text messages and phone calls had swept the town that morning as everyone discovered witches had come to town and were running a teashop.

Each of the five teens had been forbidden to enter the teashop, but was considering it anyway. Alyss' mother, Rosa, wanted to make sure that going into a shop run by witches wasn't going to be endangering her family's souls. Alyss had been forced to swear on *abuelita* Nina'a grave not to go to the teashop until Father Halloran had cleared it. Not every witch was a good witch, Rosa said. In Texas, no Catholic would come within spitting distance of a witch who wasn't approved by the local priests.

Not that there were too many witches in Texas. Alyss had never seen one before. Mexia may have been bigger than Midswich, but it was still tiny.

Alyss looked down Stratford. She could see the wrought iron teapot hanging over the sidewalk. She pushed her long, black hair out of her face and frowned. Caroline sat dejected in the grass, hiding behind a veil of white blonde hair, twirling the green dyed streak around her finger, then letting it fall. Morris kept pacing.

He'd settle for a minute on the ledge of the fountain then get up and walk a few mindless steps. Tyler sat on the ground, his back to the fountain, toying with the chain on his jacket.

"We should just walk right into that teashop, in front of everyone," Morris said, as he walked a circuit around Caroline.

None of them moved. No one seconded the idea or shot Morris down. There was a fine line between rebellion and being disowned.

"It doesn't matter," Alyss said. "The place isn't going to

stay open." She nodded in the direction of the teashop. "The whole town is against them."

"Besides, it's all pink and frilly," Caroline said in a soft, dreamy voice.

Four pairs of eyes fixed on Caroline.

"Did you go in?" Tyler tried to keep the awe out of his voice, but Alyss heard it, anyway.

That was Caroline. Shy, quiet, unassuming, and supremely brave. Alyss frowned and caught herself. She should have been the one to check out the shop, and a spark of resentment that Caroline had beat her to it flared. She ignored her feelings, pushing aside the petty thought.

Caroline shook her head. "I peeked in the window."

Tyler laughed. "That's more than anyone else."

"I bet Pastor Austin's gonna scare everyone away." Morris sat down again, but his leg jittered.

"I think everyone's already scared," Alyss said.

"When I went by this morning, the teashop smelled like my grandma's cinnamon rolls," Caroline said. She sighed. "No one made cinnamon rolls like Gam-Gam."

Silence followed Caroline's very un-goth-like nostalgia. Caroline did as she pleased and either didn't care what other people thought or didn't notice. Again, Alyss felt a familiar twinge. She wished she cared less about other people's opinions, but the snide comments from the other kids at school stung.

"Maybe we'll go on Monday. Get tea and cookies and stuff," Alyss said. She might have Father Halloran's verdict handed down to her by her mother by then. Alyss wasn't sure how this worked. Maybe the Father would have to investigate the teashop, do an exorcism or something. Still, there were ways around obeying parents, and Alyss knew she'd come up with something.

Chapter 4

The Presbyterian Church sat on a little parcel of land just off Sussex Avenue. Years ago, the church had been backed by a pine forest, which gave its graveyard room to grow. The forest had been tamed, trimmed back into a tidy city park, and the old graveyard was now fenced and closed to new residents. The churchyard received plenty of tourists, who came to take pictures of the tombstones and statues, some of which dated back two hundred and fifty years.

Many tourists were surprised to find that the church was still in use. The church itself dated back to the early 1800s and, while additions had been made, the original granite edifice still stood. The protestant utilitarianism was evident in the church's plain lines and solid squatness. The late Victorian period had made an attempt to pretty up the church, but the stained-glass windows brought from New York and the fancy stonework looked like an afterthought.

The modest parking lot was full of cars, and more spilled along the street for blocks around. Normally, nothing but a funeral or a wedding drew that sort of crowd.

Today, Pastor Austin was going to address Tea Times Three. All weekend, the town had buzzed like a shaken beehive. So far, none of the townsfolk had had the nerve to set foot in the teashop, and Austin meant to keep it that way.

Austin had an excellent memory. He wrote most of his sermons days in advance and memorized them. He practiced them a few times in the privacy of his home, to get the emphasis down. Being a good preacher was like being a good actor. All you had to do was know your lines, then make everyone believe.

After today, no one would dare give the witches their business. With no sales, the witches would soon be forced to leave.

The week of pleasant spring weather they had enjoyed turned gray and windy. Austin sat by the window in the vestry. He glanced up from his index cards every few seconds, going over the words in his mind. Outside, it was overcast, the clouds black with rain. Cold wind bent the tree branches, making them scrape along the roof and windows of the church.

Austin smiled tightly. All he needed was some lightning for dramatic punctuation, and the scene would be complete.

The runner's watch he wore beeped. Time for services to begin. Austin left the index cards behind.

Parishioners squeezed in shoulder to shoulder. Austin was pleased to see that not only were the holiday Christians there, but even a few people, who either never went to a church or attended other denominations in town, were here. A slight compression of the lips was all the smile Austin allowed himself as he stepped up to the pulpit. A low insect drone of conversation filled the church. Then the first row noticed Pastor Austin, and they quieted. Silence moved over the crowd, dampening their speculation. Eyes turned to Austin, hundreds of pairs, all wondering what he would say when he delivered the sermon.

Pastor Austin stood at the antique carved pulpit. He felt the cool wood and worn polish under his palms. He always gripped the pulpit for a second before he began his sermons. He didn't like to admit it, but his hands sweat, and the lower temperature of the pulpit helped to cool him.

There was utter silence in the church. Distantly, the stormy winds of the spring day howled through the treetops and whistled through the church bell tower.

He softly cleared his throat so no one could hear, then began services with the church announcements. He followed the typical order of services, going through the hymns and readings that were the backbone of Sunday worship. "Today, I would like to talk about temptation and its myriad forms, both mundane and other worldly. Temptation can be as innocent as, say, sugar. But how innocent is sugar really, in a nation suffering an epidemic of obesity? More Americans are morbidly obese, stricken with health problems like heart disease and diabetes than ever before.

"Of course, temptation alone is not what's responsible for this crisis. Cookies and cakes and pies don't jump into people's mouths. People yield to temptation. And they yield because it is easy. Why make dinner when you can pick up a pizza? Why eat a balanced breakfast when it's so much easier to get a doughnut or a bagel or coffee cake?

"What is easy is often false. A mirage. If I can save myself the time or the effort, doesn't that make my life easier? Isn't that what you tell yourselves? But how much easier is that pacemaker? How much easier is the extra ten, twenty, a hundred pounds?

"The same holds true for magic. For those gifted with it, magic is an easy way out of having to do the things the rest of us have to do. A way to be lazy and fix whatever goes wrong without putting in the effort. And without reaping the personal reward of growth and hard work. What sort of people do you think embrace magic as a quick fix? Don't bother doing your homework. Here's a spell to ace the test. Don't worry about getting a job, here's a spell for money. You get people who have not only given in to the ease of temptation but those who would also lead you and your children into the same trap.

"As you go out today and tomorrow, conducting business, going shopping, spending time with your family, I'd like you to contemplate temptation and decide what sort of person you want to be. What sort of example you want to set for others."

Pastor Austin surveyed the parishioners. Penelope Owens stared up from the front row, glowing with admiration. Her niece, Danielle, who never came to church, shifted in her seat and frowned. Face after face looked justified, nodding in agreement, and turning to their neighbors as if to say, "You see, I was right." Even those who appeared uncomfortable still looked thoughtful. Austin had gotten to them. The sermon was a success. Claire Callister looked faintly approving, and she and Emma exchanged knowing glances. Austin scanned the ranks for dissenters. Matilda Hartwell scowled at the pew in front of her, her lips pursed. Beside her, Hugh was nodding off, head drifting toward his chest. Some of the teenagers, Tyler and Caroline, the two goths whose parents were members of the church and were dragged in each Sunday, failed to look convinced.

The doubters didn't matter. Once word spread of Austin's disapproval, people would shun the witches' teashop. Fear of their neighbors' disapproval would reach even those who didn't care, and they too would keep clear.

Mass droned on, given by Father Halloran, who looked like a weather balloon in his white vestments. Alyss picked at her flaking black nail polish. She was bored and anxious, eager to tell Father about the teashop, but she had to wait until after Mass, which made the entire service feel like unending purgatory.

Alyss envied Consolata. She was twenty-three and, after a year-long war with their mother, had managed to get out of church. She was back home, still cozy in bed. Alyss had tried the same thing, and she'd been grounded for a month, all her electronics taken away, and all visitors banned. Even her cell phone had been locked in a cupboard at the restaurant.

She might not have been so bored if Mass were in Spanish or Latin. She missed hearing Spanish all the time, a rarer language in Maine than it had been in Texas. Once, her mother had taken them to a special Latin Mass. It had felt mysterious, more like a magic ritual than the usual repetitive ceremony she'd been going to since birth. Of course, it had had only seemed more interesting because she didn't understand the language. It had still been the same old stuff, just in a different wrapping.

Alyss sighed loudly, hoping her mother would take the hint. She'd tried negotiating Rosa down from church every week to once a month, then to every other week, and then she'd given up under threat of further groundings. Her mother said when she was eighteen, she could do what she wanted, which was a lie. None of her other sisters had "done what they'd wanted." Consolata was stubborn enough to get away with more than the others. But Alyss was determined to take her up on that. She planned to get a tattoo, move to New York, and quit going to church.

Beside Alyss, her little sister, Juana, sat straight, paying attention to Father Halloran's every word. Or at least faking attention. The little suck-up Juana, baby of the family, could do no wrong.

Alyss slumped in her seat with another dramatic sigh and elbowed Juana hard in the arm. Juana scooted over and crossed her arms.

Mass ended, and at last Alyss was free. She sighed in relief, thinking about the hours of her life she'd never get back. Church would be fine if it only lasted ten minutes and dropped all the stupid rules.

"Mom, I want to talk to Father Halloran," Alyss said, as she stood up and stretched.

"The teashop," Rosa said.

Alyss figured her mother already knew exactly what she wanted to ask. Alyss also figured her mother was as curious as she was.

They let the church empty, while Juana waited impatiently, rolling her eyes and complaining about how long they had to sit there. Rosa hushed her, letting almost everyone leave before stepping into the aisle. On the concrete steps of the church, Father Halloran stood shaking hands and chatting up his flock. His laugh boomed over the parking lot, and his jelly-donut-made gut shook under his vestments.

"Father Halloran."

"Mary-Alice, good to see you. Nice nail polish," he said.

Alyss stuck her hands in her pockets. "Um, I wanted to ask you to check out the new teashop in Midswich."

"Oh? A new teashop?" He grinned. "Gluttony is my favorite sin."

Alyss couldn't entirely squash a laugh, as much as she wanted to stay cool. "Thing is, the shop is owned by witches, so Mom won't let me go."

Rosa gave her a narrow look. "I just want to be sure. That's all."

"I imagine Austin is having kittens by now."

A genuine laugh escaped Alyss. "Everyone in town is afraid of the witches. No one will go to the shop. It sucks."

"Mary-Alice," her mother warned.

"Well, it does."

"Don't worry," Father Halloran cut in. "I'll pay them a visit. I'm sure you've nothing to fear."

"You better make it soon. The whole town is, like boycotting, or something. No one has gone in." Alyss gave her mother a sidelong glance.

"I promise, I'll get there this week. If they turn out all right, I may try having a talk with Oscar," Father Halloran said brightly.

Anglaise's light brown hair whipped in her face as she flew back from Musquash. The two nice days of spring they had enjoyed evaporated with a capricious New England change in weather. When Anglaise had left Midswich, there'd been a chill breeze and a gray overcast, but the weather had worsened during her outing.

Now, the bleak charcoal-gray clouds threatened rain, and the wind beat against her. A sudden gust threw her to the left, and Anglaise pulled up just in time to avoid plowing into a pine tree.

All this for a coffee run. Anglaise pursed already thin lips. Bruleé hated coffee and refused to allow it in the house. She claimed even the smell gave her a headache. Anglaise thought she was just being melodramatic. Anglaise lost that battle years ago, but she also liked having an excuse to get away from her sisters every week.

Early that morning, she'd gotten on her broom and flown to a coffee shop called Mean Joe's in Musquash. The coffee was excellent. Anglaise drank her frothy, sweet cappuccino there, but when she saw the weather worsening, she'd gotten a double espresso to go.

Big mistake. Anglaise thought she could outrun the weather on her broom, and now she was in danger of wearing the espresso.

Every time she tried to fly higher, the wind pushed her down. She was skimming the treetops, trying to dodge the taller pine trees, coffee in one hand, broom handle in another.

A sudden ferocious gust hit Anglaise from the side, sending her spinning. She dropped the espresso, and both hands clutched the broom.

"Dammit." Anglaise watched as the paper coffee cup plummeted into the forest, disappearing before it hit the ground. Money well spent.

A blast of icy wind hit Anglaise, tugging her clothes. Her broom spun out of control, and she crashed into the top of a pine tree. Branches slapped her in the face, clawing at the black rain slicker she wore. Anglaise grabbed at branches, but the slippery evergreens slid out of her hands.

After a heart-stopping drop, she finally hit some branches that held her weight. Anglaise pulled herself upright, unhooking her legs from the tangled boughs, managing to perch on a sturdy branch. Her broom had settled a few branches below. She sat there for a couple of minutes, steadying her breathing and calming down. A few curious birds flitted among the branches, twittering at her. This never happened in Boston. The air currents around the buildings were tricky, but at least there was the bus if all else failed.

Anglaise looked up at the gloomy, flat sheet of sky and sighed. Sometimes she wished she came from a normal family. A normal family would have a car. A normal family could *afford* a car.

She held out her hand and silently called to her broom. It

twitched, then gently floated up to her. Anglaise climbed back on and lowered herself through wind-bent pines to the forest floor.

Looking around at the dense Maine forest, Anglaise realized she had no idea what direction to go. She had been heading for town before the wind forced her down, but now she was turned around. She tried to think. Midswich had just been coming into view. She had seen the rooftops and the church steeple in the distance.

She could either strike out in a random direction, head back up above the treetops and take her chances with the wind, or wait for it to die down. Anglaise didn't like any of those choices. She should have just stayed home. She could be in her kitchen right now, warm and eating the pile of leftovers from their less-than-grand opening. Instead, she was hovering a few feet off the mulch of the forest floor.

A sound echoed over the woods. The church bells rang from the spire Anglaise had seen.. She listened closely, gauging the direction of the sound.

She leaned forward and nudged the broom with her mind. The broom eased ahead, as silent as the woods. The dense foliage—ferns, and bushes, saplings struggling for light, and the thick tree trunks of their parents—meant she could only go walking speed on the broom. Anglaise felt better with a task to concentrate on. The forest was creeping her out. She and her sisters had lived in the city their entire lives, and the idea of being lost in the woods was uncomfortable. She had to keep reminding herself that she could fly above the trees, and it was impossible to be lost with a bird's eye-view.

Anglaise was pondering heading up again when the church bells rang out, so close and loud, they made her heart leap in sudden fright.

A few yards away, she saw the trees thin and sped up, commanding the broom to go faster so she could get out of the dark woods.

She burst out of the forest and found herself on the edge of a wide expanse of spring green grass. She saw a playground up ahead, and beyond that, the church and the town.

Civilization. Anglaise breathed a sigh of relief. She looked over her shoulder at the wall of dense forest behind her and stuck out her tongue. She'd conquered the woods and hopefully she'd never wander them again.

Broom in hand, Anglaise struck out across the park on foot. Bruleé had cautioned them against overt displays of magic, only after her own titanic mistake. If Bruleé hadn't been so eager to show off, they might have gotten some customers, building up a clientele before revealing they were witches. But how angry would their patrons be to find out, after the fact, that the sisters were witches? Anglaise looked up at the stone church and the rows and rows of cars parked along the street. Maybe Bruleé was right. If their customers thought they'd been spelled without their knowledge, all hell would break loose. The words "frontier justice" came to mind. Anglaise shivered. It was against the law for a witch to spell or dose another person without their knowledge, and the witch could be arrested for it. People didn't always wait for the cops though, and then it usually ended badly for the witch.

Anglaise changed course halfway through the park. She had been heading for the street but angled left instead. Her eyes darted all around, making sure she was alone. The street, sidewalk, and park were all empty. The town may as well have been deserted.

When she reached the church, Anglaise remounted her broom. She flew over the cemetery wall, then flew up along the side of the building. The wind tried to pull her in different directions, but she stayed close to the stone cliff of the church's outer wall. Her head was cocked, ears alert for a trace of sound.

The stone gave nothing away, but Anglaise guessed the stained glass windows weren't so secretive. She moved on to the window. The mumble of a voice could be heard inside, but she couldn't make out the words.

"Give me sight and give me sound." Anglaise traced a rune for clarity on the white robe of a saint. The glass brightened, becoming transparent enough to see through, and she could hear the sermon.

The tall, skinny priest glowed with righteous indignation as he proselytized, "But temptation alone is not what's responsible for this crisis. Cookies and cakes and pies don't jump into people's mouths. People yield to temptation."

Anglaise's whole body went rigid. Her face burned and red-hot anger ignited in her chest. She listened on through the whole sermon, as the preacher struck at and insulted everything she was and everything she did. Clearly, he didn't like witches. She was used to that, but what on earth had pastry ever done to him?

She was so preoccupied with her own thoughts of what she'd like to do to the pastor that Anglaise didn't realize the sermon was over until she noticed the ringing silence. She looked down into the church, neck stiff from tension. The priest smiled benevolently at his flock. Do they applaud if they like it? She could only see the backs of the congregation's heads.

A general murmur went up, but Anglaise's spell wasn't powerful enough to amplify the words. No doubt they all agreed with the sermon, though. The preacher was their leader after all. Even if they didn't, fear of their neighbors' disapproval would keep them in line.

Their teashop, on which they'd pinned so many hopes and dreams, was done for, only two days after opening.

Anglaise felt unshed tears sting her eyes. She pushed them down with rage and felt the tears subside even as her lip trembled. This was exactly what she'd known would happen.

She felt hollow. Defeated. Anglaise tried to let go of the broom handle to rub her eyes but her hands had cramped, white-knuckled, around the wood.

With conscious effort, she worked her hands loose. They tingled as blood flow returned.

Home. She very badly needed to go home. She flew around the back of the church, over the cemetery, and disappeared into the forest that edged the park. She landed safely under the cover of the trees.

She would walk back, keeping to the forest and then the side streets. Hopefully, she could make it home in one piece.

"Flora! Flora! Come here, quick!"

Flora Barton had been counting out her younger sister's arthritis pills for the week when Anne called out.

Fearing something terrible had happened, she rushed to the bedroom as fast as her age allowed.

Her sister, Anne, crippled by rheumatoid arthritis, sat up in her inclining bed, the eyepiece of a telescope glued to her face.

Flora had bought the telescope so her sister would have a window on the world. She'd had her sister's bed moved to the half-moon turret room of their third-floor apartment. From there, Anne could see the park, the church, the woods, and a generous portion of town. The telescope was intended for birding, but Anne watched the people of Midswich instead.

Relieved nothing was wrong, Flora assumed her best disapproving air, honed by fifty years of teaching. She could make a nun squirm.

"You aren't supposed to be peeping in windows." Flora noted the downward angle of the telescope. Quite a few homes were in view of her sister's gaze.

"I'm not, I'm not," Anne protested. Her voice was the last firm thing about her. Anne's rheumatoid arthritis had started in her hands in her thirties. By her forties, the disease had crept into her knees. Now, at sixty seven, she was bedridden, the arthritis creeping up and down her spine, invading her hips and shoulders. Heating pads and pain pills were her only salvation.

Anne gestured with a clawed hand. "I saw one of the witches!"

"What?" Flora went to the curving bank of windows. "Where?"

"She came out of the woods, flying on a broom! Flying!"

Flora squinted out the window with the best view of the woods and park. "Where?"

"You can't see her now. She walked behind the church."

"Walked? You said she was flying."

"She landed, just after coming out of the forest."

"Why was she in the woods?"

Anne giggled. "How should I know? Hunting mushrooms for potions? I like that."

"Potions, huh?" Flora hadn't given much thought to the witches or their teashop, since she assumed the town would boycott them into leaving.

Anne was back at her telescope, trying to spot the witch again.

"Oh, where did she go? Why isn't she flying her broom? Flora, you have to go to the teashop. I want to know all about them."

"I don't have time for that nonsense," Flora protested. But she was already shifting her schedule around in her mind. "If you'll excuse me, some of us have work to do."

Flora left her sister spying on the town and went back to the tiny kitchen, which had probably been a linen closet before the grand Victorian house had been chopped up into apartments. She carefully counted Anne's pills out, getting them into the blue plastic organizers, each labeled with day of the week and a.m. or p.m. Anne had a pharmacopeia of candy-colored drugs.

Back when the arthritis had first started eating away at Anne, she'd tried natural cures, herbs and tonics, joint compounds, and acupuncture. None of it had worked. Anne finally started taking the prescriptions the doctor gave her.

Flora smiled. About the only thing she hadn't tried was a witch. The nearest witches were down in Vermont and Massachusetts.

Her hand froze as she reached for a Prednisone. There were three new witches in town. Maybe they could help Anne. She could go and ask. What could it hurt? Flora frowned, feeling a touch of uneasiness. What would people think if she went?

L iving with two sisters meant time alone was a treasure. Anglaise got up at five a.m. Monday morning, like she always did, but instead of cooking, she watched the sun rise, pink and pale blue over Midswich, then went down to the kitchen to catch up on her food magazines.

Two hours later, Anglaise was copying down a hazelnut torte recipe from *Bon Appetite* magazine and adding it to her *Book of Shadows*, with the addition of magical notations. With some trial and error, she felt she could turn the torte into a powerful spell to draw true love to whomever ate it.

She was jotting down her final notes when she heard Bruleé's tread on the stairs. Bruleé had the quick light steps of an external optimist, aided by high heels in every color known to fashion. Anglaise knew the sound of both her sisters' steps, not that Caramel made any noise. She crept soundlessly everywhere she went.

Bruleé popped into the kitchen, a question written all over her face.

Anglaise said, "You want to know why you don't smell anything baking."

Bruleé frowned. "So, what's the answer, smarty pants?"

Anglaise shut her Book of Shadows. "There's no point."

"No point?"

"None whatsoever."

"Did you put the sign out with the specials at least?"

"There aren't any specials," Anglaise snapped. "There aren't going to be any customers."

"You don't know that," Bruleé said.

She crossed her arms and tried to look authoritative, which Anglaise found funny. Her sister was only two years older, looked like a dumb blonde from a movie, and dressed like she still lived in California, all pastel, all the time.

"Think about this, Bruleé. Everyone in town shunned the shop on Friday, right?"

Bruleé nodded.

"So, what makes you think they'll come flocking, once the local clergy has got through with them on Sunday?"

Understanding sparked in Bruleé's eyes. Anglaise could see Bruleé making an effort to shake off her words.

"Well—well, we can't have an empty shop, no matter what," Bruleé stuttered. "And…" Her eyes searched the ground for an answer. She smiled up at Anglaise when she hit on something. "…I want to hand out free samples."

Anglaise frowned. "I'm not letting more work and ingredients go to waste. You can cast an illusion spell on the bakery cases, and I'll make a couple dozen cookies, but that's it."

"Thank you." Bruleé smiled triumphantly. She ducked out of the kitchen before Anglaise could say more.

Alone again, Anglaise went to the pantry and pulled out the essential ingredients of any pastry chef. Sugar and flour. She liked to bake primarily with brown sugar, because it imparted a richer flavor than white sugar, which had none. Cake flour gave just about anything a silkier texture. She also kept confectioner's sugar and organic powdered sugar on hand at all times. Organic ingredients always had better flavor than non-organic and, as a witch, Anglaise reasoned she ought to do something for the environment.

Next, the cold ingredients. The tiny kitchen had a huge stainless steel fridge with double doors. Bruleé had protested the size of the fridge but Anglaise had refused to budge. Even though it took up almost one entire wall, she still felt it was too small.

Anglaise looked over the ingredients she had in the fridge and changed her mind about the cookies. She'd make one batch of cookies and two batches of scones. Tea Times Three was a teashop after all, not a bakery. Cream scones for the timid pallet and strawberry basil scones for the adventurous. She compiled her chilled ingredients—eggs; butter, both salted and unsalted; cream; and milk. Then she added fresh strawberries and sweet, Thai basil.

As Anglaise started cooking, she felt her cares and worries start to slip away. She knew the recipes she was making by heart, and it was a great comfort to sink into a world of measurement and action. Mixing and beating had their own rhythms, just like chopping. The measurements kept time and, during lulls in the symphony, she cleaned her station.

Soon, the smells of her labor began to fill the kitchen. The smells crept from the double oven—warm dough, melting butter, and sugar first. The cozy scent moved from the kitchen to fill the teashop, and finally spilled into the streets of Midswich. The light, floating scent of baking herbs and spices then followed, enriching the air.

Anglaise kept a close eye on the clock while paying attention to the smell of the baking. She could tell from the fragrance when things were done, but she liked to double check with a clock. Pastry was a precise business, and it wasn't in Anglaise to do less than her best, so she double-checked everything.

Caramel came downstairs just as Anglaise took the snickerdoodles out of the top oven. Fraiche followed on her heels. The little fuzz ball bounced over to Anglaise. His entire backside wagged back and forth, as hopeful brown eyes begged for a treat.

"Th—those smell good." Caramel shut her eyes and inhaled the warm cinnamon scent of fresh cookies.

"They're free samples." Anglaise slid the heavy-gauge baking sheet onto a cooking rack. "That means we'll be the ones to eat them."

Fraiche barked excitedly at that announcement, bouncing up and down.

"Take Fraiche out, will you? He can't be in the kitchen."

Caramel scooped up the little pom and grinned. "Come on,

time for walkies." She pulled a purple nylon leash out of her skirt pocket and clipped it to Fraiche's rhinestone collar. They left through the back door, which led from the kitchen to the alley.

Alyss, Caroline, Tyler, and Morris clustered together, a knot of black crows on the town square. School started in twenty minutes, but it only took ten minutes to walk there, so they had plenty of time for a conference.

"I don't care what Pastor Austin says. He's not boss of the world," Morris sneered.

Word of Pastor Austin's sermon had spread through the town via phone lines and texting. Church goers or not, word had gone out of his condemnation of the witches and baked goods. A small town, wary of strangers, readily accepted the clergyman's disapproval of magic. His rant against dessert had raised a few eyebrows. But that could be ignored. The witches in their midst could not.

"I don't like Pastor Austin. He's too healthy," Caroline said.

Tyler laughed. "Seriously! I think he does his grocery shopping at GNC."

"Father Halloran hasn't weighed in yet," Alyss said. "Not everyone in town listens to…" Her sentence died out. She raised her head and sniffed the air. "What the hell is that smell?"

A sweet fragrance, at once comforting and mouthwatering, drifted over the group. All four of the teens lifted their heads, trying to find the strongest whiff. Caroline closed her eyes and smiled faintly. Even Morris held still for a minute.

"Cinnamon." Alyss was always aware of cooking smells, having been raised in a restaurant.

Caroline grinned. "Smells like cookies."

"But—" Alyss paused. She took a few steps in the direction of the smell. "Basil? Strawberries? What is it?"

"The teashop," Tyler said.

At the same time, they all realized they were facing down Stratford, noses to the wind.

"Snickerdoodles!" Caroline cried out. "Oh, my God! Oh, my God!"

Before anyone could stop her, Caroline was running down the empty main street toward the iron teapot hung over the witches' door.

Taylor ran after her. "Caroline, you can't!"

Morris grinned and took off. "Finally."

Alyss quickly caught up to them. She pulled up to the jogging Caroline, who was getting winded after a block.

"My Gam-Gam always made snickerdoodles." Caroline slowed as the group neared the teashop. She pulled an inhaler from her hoodie pocket and took a hit for her asthma.

Tyler looked around nervously, "Your mom will kill you."

"Don't be such a baby," Morris told him.

Caroline ignored them all. She pressed her face to the window, cupping her hands around her eyes. She slumped in defeat. "Aww, I don't think it's open. The bakery case is empty."

Alyss frowned. So the witches were giving up. She looked at the specials board sitting on the sidewalk. *FREE SAMPLES* it advertised. That was better than going out of business, but Alyss doubted anyone in town would take the samples. She was dying to know what the strawberry scent was coming from. Tarts? Cupcakes? And how did basil fit in? Or was that from something else?

"Let's come back after school. We can go around back," Alyss said.

The group relaxed and nodded.

"Come on." Alyss led them down the street. She turned the corner on Brighton Street. An alley ran behind all the shops. She pointed down the alley. "There, we can see if they'll answer the back door."

They peered into the depths, which held several big dumpsters, crates, garbage cans—and one of the witches.

Alyss and her friends stared. The youngest witch, a girl

who looked to be about their age, stood wide-eyed and fearful a few feet away. Her little Pomeranian jumped up and down excitedly, straining on his leash, eager to meet new people.

"Uh, hi," Alyss said.

The witch let out a squeaky cry of fright and scooped up her dog. She ran down the alley and pulled open a door set in the brick wall. The door slammed shut behind her. The sound echoed off the narrow walls and quickly died away.

No one moved. Alyss was too surprised.

Morris broke the silence. "What the hell was that?"

Alyss blinked. "I think we scared her."

"*We* scared a witch?" Tyler said.

"They haven't exactly gotta warm reception," Alyss said dryly. "We gotta go."

Slowly they drifted in the direction of Midswich High School.

"She looked about our age," Caroline said.

Morris kicked at a juniper bush they passed. "Yeah, how come she isn't in school?"

Tyler rolled his eyes. "They've only been in town three days, dumb ass. It takes time to get registered."

"Maybe she's too scared to go to school." Caroline looked over her shoulder, even though they were blocks from the teashop.

"You still wanna go after school?" Morris asked.

"Yes." Alyss couldn't help following Caroline's gaze. She hoped there would be free samples left. The memory of the delicious smells still lingered.

The four of them tightened their formation as the red brick school came into view. The four-story high school was another relic of the past, built during the turn of the century. The school was designed to look like a medieval castle, but Alyss always thought it looked more like a prison. The school felt like one, too. She put on her best angry face and steeled herself to make it through one more day.

Bruleé carefully combed her long hair yet again. Anglaise would accuse her of primping, but really, what was wrong with putting your best foot forward? She clipped a section of hair back with a silk flower hair clip, before checking her outfit in the bathroom mirror.

Her frilled blouse had a Victorian look, but she found it at a thrift shop. The full knee-length lavender skirt had been on the sale rack at a department store. She smoothed her hands over the clothes. Everything was pressed and wrinkle-free.

Ready to meet the public, she practiced her most winning smile. Lip gloss. She needed lip gloss. Bruleé dug in her cosmetics drawer. She was the only one who used any, so she kept her make-up in the bathroom without fear of her sisters using it.

Anglaise didn't care about make-up or clothes. She wore whatever was comfortable and utilitarian. T-shirts and cargo pants were her standard uniform. The only thing she did with her hair was pull it back into a sloppy bun. Bruleé liked to make an impression.

She put on shell-pink lip-gloss and decided she was presentable enough to hand out free samples.

Bruleé went downstairs to the kitchen. Anglaise was idle again, reading the current issue of *Saveur* magazine. There were three trays set out on the kitchen island. Each tray had a mix of scones and cookies, all cut to bite-size samples and put in little paper cups.

"You could at least pretend to be busy," Bruleé said.

Anglaise looked daggers over the edge of her magazine. "Why?" she asked flatly.

"At least work on your spell casting or something. You are a witch."

Anglaise went back to her magazine.

Bruleé picked up the first tray. Witches or no, she was hoping people would take a sample. After all, what could be better than free? She left the kitchen and went to collect Caramel.

The girl was moping in a back corner of the teashop, supposedly dusting the teapots for sale. Caramel was taking down a small Chinese teapot designed to look like a dragon. The mouth of the dragon was the spout, its snakelike tail the handle. She gently wiped the surface with a dust cloth.

"Come on," Bruleé said. "Time to face the world."

She gave a reassuring smile even as Caramel hung her head. Caramel had run into some local teenagers when attempting to take Fraiche for a walk. She had locked herself in her room, until Bruleé had finally had enough and dismantled her locking spell. Poor Fraiche got only a short walk, escorted by Anglaise, and he was sulking upstairs.

Caramel nodded without looking up and took a stack of flyers from a table in the back.

Caramel hadn't always been this bad. True, she was nervous and shy, but back in Boston, she had been much more outgoing. Of course, Boston had a witch community. That meant she could leave the house without curious stares, and she'd had a place to fit in. When their parents died, Caramel retreated into herself. Bruleé alternately wanted to shelter Caramel and to shove her out the front door. She couldn't hide away her whole life, running from ordinary people, afraid to step outside. But how hard could Bruleé push before Caramel broke?

"Don't worry. I'm right beside you today." Bruleé kept smiling as Caramel joined her by the front door. The young witch nodded, but didn't lift her eyes from the floor. She opened the door for Bruleé, and they stepped into a sunny, breezy day with just a hint of chill.

Bruleé was relieved to see people out on the streets and specifically on their side of it. Either the townsfolk had gotten braver, or they were too lazy to cross the street in order to avoid the teashop.

"Big smiles, big smiles," Bruleé murmured, as much to herself as to Caramel. Even Bruleé needed encouragement once in a while, and she'd had to do it herself. Her sisters looked to her for strength and optimism. She couldn't let them down. They never knew how often the world ground her down, or how much she wished they would spare her a kind word.

With her best and most practiced smile firmly planted on her face, Bruleé held out the tray of neatly cut cookies and scones.

"Free sample? Free sample?"

A few people walking by eyed her suspiciously, as if an insect had just spoken to them. Others lowered their heads or dodged onto the street between parked cars, so as to avoid having to take or refuse a sample.

Her practiced retail eye could tell that some of the pedestrians were at least tempted. A certain pause in their steps as they hovered in indecision, a sidelong glance or a lick of the lips. Not one was brave enough to take anything from her, but for the first time in days Bruleé felt a spark of hope.

Caramel hid behind Bruleé, shrinking back every time someone approached. Bruleé let her. At least she'd managed to coax her out of the building. Bruleé had hoped she'd try and hand out the flyers highlighting the extensive list of goods and services they offered. But, so far, Caramel kept the bundle of papers clutched to her chest.

"Free sample?" Bruleé held out the tray to a tall, young man, good looking enough to be a model.

Unlike the others, he gave Bruleé an appraising look, blue eyes roaming the curves of her body, his gaze lingering on her chest. He snorted with amusement and kept walking.

She frowned as she watched the guy walk away. "Jerk."

"C—can I go in now?" Caramel whispered.

Bruleé turned to look at Caramel, a confident smile she didn't feel on her face. "We haven't even been out for fifteen minutes."

"B—but that g—guy."

"Don't worry. It's what happens when you're as pretty as we are."

Caramel made a soft, mewling noise of disappointment as Bruleé turned back to her job.

Another man headed their way. He was even taller than the jerk that had checked her out, and his intense dark eyes were fixated on the tray.

A customer at last. Bruleé could feel it in her bones. Her

smile widened. He didn't look like the teashop type, if the stained, mechanics' overalls were anything to go by, but Bruleé had learned that occupation could never stand in the way of a sweet tooth.

The man slowed as he approached Bruleé, feet stumbling a little, as if insisting he stop whether he wanted to or not. His broad nose flared as he took in the smell of the cookies and scones.

Bruleé could hardly contain herself. Here was a true gourmand. Every gourmet knew that all good food begins with sight, then smell. A refined palette could identify ingredients and cooking methods from scent alone.

"Free sample, sir?" She held the tray out to him. He slowed to a stop in front of her. She had him.

"Today, we have—"

"Don't tell me." He held up an elegant long-fingered hand and pushed his short dreads out of the way as he leaned over and inhaled deeply. "Snicker doodles for sure, the cinnamon is unmistakable," he said.

"Correct," Bruleé chirped.

Caramel tugged Bruleé's sleeve but she shrugged the girl off. "Not now, Carmel."

"B—b—b—b—" Caramel sputtered.

"Just a minute," Bruleé said.

"Cream scones. I can tell those by sight." The man was still studying the tray. "But am I crazy, or are these strawberry-basil?" He pointed at a scone flecked with pink and green.

"You're right! My sister, Anglaise, is our pastry chef and she made them fresh this morning."

"So, do I only get one sample?" he asked, and gave her a canny smile, ready to negotiate for more.

Caramel's tugging became more insistent and her stutter worse. "B—b—b—b—b—b!"

"What is it?" Bruleé turned to Caramel, hoping her youngest sister didn't ruin the sale.

Caramel, white as paper, pointed at something just behind the man who reached for a sample of the strawberry scone.

A skinny, black shadow materialized on the sidewalk.

"Good afternoon, William," said a cold, resinous voice.

Startled, William pulled his hand back as if he'd stuck it into a fire.

"Pastor Austin." William looked guilty. His eyes darted from the pastor to Bruleé and then lingered on the tray before going back to the pastor.

A terrified squeak, like a strangled mouse, and the tinkle of bells let Bruleé know that Caramel had fled to the safety of the teashop's interior.

William opened his mouth as if to say something, but nothing came out.

"We missed you on Sunday," Pastor Austin said smoothly.

"Yeah, well…bye," he said. William took off down the street, speed-walking like he was trying out for a team.

Spirits sinking, Bruleé watched her only potential customer make a break for it. She turned back to the pastor Austin, forced a smile, and held up the tray. "Free sample, Pastor?"

The priest gave her an equally brittle grin. "What a shame. I just ate. And to think this may be my last chance to try one."

A flush of anger burned in Bruleé's face. Of course, the pastor had already spoken out against them. Of course, everyone was afraid of them. And, of course, Anglaise was right. A bitter taste rose in back of her throat. Bruleé swallowed.

"What does that mean?" she asked. She already knew the answer, but she wasn't about to give the man the satisfaction of caving to veiled threats. If he wanted them gone, he'd have to come out and say it.

Pastor Austin took a step closer and leaned over, the tray wedged between them.

"This is a town of decent people, who know better than to submit themselves to the wiles of your kind."

"My kind?" Bruleé echoed hollowly. This was the same ignorant attitude she had run into before. As if witches were somehow other than human. Her flash of anger dwindled to something close to despair. When would people realize witches were just like everyone else? Gifted in a unique way, yes, but no more so than a great painter or a skilled surgeon.

Bruleé pushed the sample tray into Pastor Austin's solar plexus, forcing him back a step. She rallied and said, "My *kind* are a lot more like normal people than you'd think. We certainly eat like normal people. Are you sure you wouldn't like a bite of scone, Pastor?"

"Are they made with eggs?"

"Yes, organic."

"Sugar?"

"That's organic, too."

"Butter?"

"Of course."

"Cream?"

"The cream scones, of course, since it's in the name," Bruleé swelled with pride.

"Then, no."

She deflated like a left over party balloon.

"Fat, calories, and more fat," Pastor Austin said.

Bruleé looked down at the samples. How else were pastries made? Those were basic ingredients. But he said them like he was naming street drugs. Bruleé wondered if it was really the fact she and her sisters were witches that bothered Austin most.

"Good day to you, miss." Pastor Austin looked smug as he walked away.

The cancerous chemical smell of perm solution, acrylic nails, and hairspray wrinkled Hugh's nose. Barely Hair was loud with music and chatter. Claire Callister was setting the curls on an old lady, while three more withered bags read magazines under massive blow dryers. The owner of the salon, Lorelei O'Donnell, was giving Officer Frank Connolly, one of only three Midswich policemen, a trim.

Matilda leaned against the reception desk and paged through a magazine all about haircutting. She had spent a year and a half in beauty school in Connecticut, before dropping out for reasons she refused to disclose. Hugh found it ironic that a beauty school dropout worked at a hair salon. He liked to joke about it once in a while, just to get Matilda riled up.

He grinned as she glanced up. "Guess what?"

"What?"

"One of those witches tried to give me a free sample." For once, he had her full attention.

"What was it? Did you get me one?" she asked eagerly.

"Get you one? I didn't take anything from a witch." Hugh drew back, surprised at the thought.

"Why not?" Matilda pressed.

"They're witches, duh. And plus, no one in town would speak to me again. And plus, how's that going to look on my image?"

Matilda rolled her eyes, a sure sign she was about to go into lecture mode. Hugh checked the clock on the wall. He regretted telling her anything. Lately, it was getting harder and harder just to have a conversation with her.

"First of all, stop saying 'And plus.' They practically mean the same thing. Secondly, your image? Really, Hugh?"

"Hey, I have to uphold the family honor and stuff."

"Your dad is the mayor, not President of the United States."

"Whatever. I still don't wanna be shunned."

"Is she still out there?"

"Who?"

"The witch." Matilda stood up. "I'm going to get a free sample."

"Whoa, Nelly." Hugh grabbed her upper arm. "No, you're not."

"Why not? You don't own me."

He used to think it was cute that she was feisty. Now, he was just getting tired of it.

"Because I don't want you getting shunned either." *And me by extension*, he added silently. "Do you really wanna piss off the town?"

Matilda paused, brow creasing just between her eyebrows. He could feel the tension go out of her, and he let go.

"You sound like Eddie." She frowned as she resumed her station behind the reception desk.

"Eddie's a smart little guy."

"He's not little," Matilda said.

"He's five-six. You wanna fight about that now?"

"No," Matilda said. "I just don't think the witches are bad. If someone would just give them a chance, I think the town might come around."

Hugh squashed the laugh that wanted to escape. He couldn't remember the last time Midswich had "come around" on any issue.

"Well, keep dreamin', kiddo." He gave her a gentle chuck under her chin.

She batted his hand away and gave a soft, genuine laugh. "Not funny," she said through a smile.

He grinned back. "We could always move, you know. Go to New York. They have witches there."

Matilda sighed. "No, you know I don't want to move."

Hugh nodded and let it drop. The problem was, he did want to move. Midswich was too small for him. He was tired of working at town hall as his father's gopher. An idea had been forming in the back of his mind lately, so ridiculous and so fragile, he dared not name it, even to himself. But that dream was getting bigger and, as it grew, Midswich got smaller and more chaffing.

Unlike Matilda, Hugh had never really gotten out of Midswich. Not unless community college in Portland counted. Which it didn't. He was itching to get out of town and see something of the world before it was too late.

"Well, I'll see you at dinner. Right?" Hugh said.

"Yeah," Matilda said. The phone rang and she had to answer it. She mouthed, "I'm sorry," to Hugh then said, "Barely Hair, how may I help you?"

"I gotta go," Hugh said.

Annoyed, he left the salon without a backward glance. Lately, Matilda seemed to be getting more and more distant. Perhaps she wanted to break up with him. A small, traitorous part of him wondered if that would really be such a tragedy.

Then he'd be free. He could move to New York and pursue his dream.

Hugh crushed every stray thought he could find and buried them deep. He should just concentrate on work. After Hugh had graduated from Portland Community College, with a useless associates degree in liberal arts, he decided school wasn't for him. Hugh's father, Nathan Kelly, had insisted he go into the family business of politics. As far as Hugh could tell, politics in Midswich involved fifty percent paperwork, twenty percent sucking up, and thirty percent golf. After three years of filing papers, fetching coffee, and playing golf with the other town luminaries, Hugh had had enough. He couldn't bring himself to quit, so he just performed worse and worse, hoping his dad would fire him.

Midswich Town Hall was three blocks away from Stratford, down on Oxford Street. The two-story Victorian stone building was another feat of historic preservation. In the fifties there had been a brief campaign to tear down the building with its Greek portico, Corinthian columns, and malfunctioning clock tower. Instead, an ugly modern addition had been added to the rear, providing space for offices.

Hugh headed around back to the glassy box-like single-story office block at the back of the building. He had his own office and title of Executive Assistant to the Mayor. Which Hugh knew, basically made him a fancy secretary. Not that he did much. But he did have a computer and an online poker game he was eager to get back to.

Long shadows crossed the street as the sun lowered in the sky. Only two establishments stayed open later than six o'clock before tourist season kicked in. Rosa's and Fiddler's Moon, which, even if the food was bad, still had a full bar and cocktail hour.

Other than that, the main street was deserted, the shops locked up, and the parking spaces empty.

Alyss and her friends had arranged to meet at the alley running behind the teashop. Alyss thought she'd be the first to arrive, but when she showed up, Caroline was already waiting. Morris showed up next. Last to arrive was Tyler.

"I hope they didn't run out of samples," Caroline said, as the four of them ducked into the premature night of the shadowed alley.

"My mom said no one stopped for a sample, but she only watched 'em for a few minutes," Alyss said.

"Hey, maybe we can get all of them," Morris said.

"Greedy, much?" Tyler asked.

"No! I just…like food," Morris finished lamely.

Alyss gave Tyler a warning a glance, and he looked away. Morris never got enough to eat. He lived with his neglectful older brother while their mother was in jail. There was more booze than food around, and Morris was always bumming extra sandwiches, chips, and candy.

Tyler didn't press his point.

Alyss knocked on the back door marked *DELIVERIES*. Nothing happened. The group waited and looked at each other.

"Knock louder," Morris urged. Then, "I'll do it." He pounded a fist against the door. The spiked wristbands and chains he wore amplified the sound.

"Maybe they think we're angry villagers," Tyler said, once the echoes died.

Alyss stepped away from the door and craned her neck. She could see lights in the upstairs window.

"Stop knocking!" Tyler said as Morris's hand rose to strike again.

Morris put his hand down. "Just trying to help."

Caroline patted him on the back. "Just help a little less."

Morris had never in his life encountered the word moderation. Everything he did was full throttle.

High-pitched, excited barking came from the other side of the alley door. They heard little claws scraping the door at different heights.

"Aww, it's their doggy," Caroline said.

Above, Alyss saw a window open and a head poked out.

She could see a girl, maybe twenty-three or so, frowning down at them.

"Go away," the witch yelled.

Everyone looked up. Then they looked to Alyss as their leader.

"No," Alyss yelled back.

The witch leaned farther out the window, her scowl deepening. "I'll curse you."

"No, she won't!" came a lighter voice from the apartment. The speaker remained unseen.

The witch ducked back in the window, and the kids heard the sound of a brief, heated argument, but they couldn't make out the words.

The girl poked her head back out the window. "I'm coming down."

The window slammed shut and, a few minutes later, the delivery door swung open.

The witch's golden-brown hair was pulled back and she wore a T-shirt that read *NEW YORK FOOD FESTIVAL*. She held a struggling ball of cream-colored fuzz under one arm. The Pomeranian yipped, legs paddling the air and tail pumping back and forth.

"What do you want?" the witch asked.

For a second, none of the kids spoke. What had seemed like a good idea this morning now seemed completely stupid when faced with an angry witch in an alley.

Alyss summoned up her courage and said in a weak voice, "Free samples?"

"We're closed." As the witch started to close the door, Alyss heard the second voice from earlier.

"Anglaise!"

"Fine," Anglaise said to Alyss. "You want some free samples?"

The door closed in Alyss's face. She stood blinking at it and looked at her friends. "Was that a yes?" she asked.

Caroline shrugged.

"Maybe," Tyler said.

Before anyone suggested leaving, the door opened again.

Anglaise was there, sans dog. She thrust three-quart-sized plastic baggies at Alyss. "Here's the free samples."

"We can have all of that?" Morris asked, with unmistakable hope.

"Take 'em before I change my mind."

Morris and Alyss reached out at the same time. She grabbed a baggie of scones, and he snatched the other two.

Again, the door slammed in Alyss's face. "Thank you," she said to the gray metal.

"Well, come on. Let's go eat." Morris was sniffing the contents of one of his baggies. The aroma of strawberries and sweet basil wafted out.

Alyss nodded, and they headed slowly to the mouth of the alley. Halfway down the alley, Alyss heard a window slide open. She turned and looked up. Leaning out the window, was the young witch from that morning.

Alyss waved up at her. "Hi!" she called.

The others turned, wondering whom Alyss was talking to.

The witch ducked back inside without a word, and Alyss heard the window close.

"Weird," Tyler said.

"I still think she's shy," Caroline observed.

The four of them left the alley, heading to the fountain in the town square. Once settled, they opened all three baggies and started passing around the contents.

Alyss took one of the pink and green-flecked scones, excited to see what they tasted like.

"Oh, my God," she said, through a mouthful of scone, her eyes wide with surprise. The subtly sweet, bread-like scone melted in her mouth. Strawberry chunks, chewy and delicious, added texture, and the hint of basil complemented both better than a savory herb ought to. Alyss found herself rethinking herbs entirely. In her mind, they had always been divided into sweet and savory. Sure, there were a few crossovers, but they weren't used for much.

She remembered her mother making Swedish meatballs one time and the shock she'd gotten at their taste. Nutmeg and cloves in ground beef and pork had been a disquieting taste combination. Alyss hadn't liked them much at the time but suddenly she wanted to give them another try.

Caroline had a stack of cookies in her hand and a look like rapture on her face.

"How are the cookies?" Tyler asked around a mouthful of scone.

"Just like my Gam-Gam made, exactly!" Caroline stuffed an entire snickerdoodle into her mouth.

Alyss took a cookie from the bag. She took a bite. The cinnamon was fresh, the cookie buttery and flaked in her mouth. She could taste the rich flavor of brown sugar.

"This is what heaven tastes like." Morris had a scone in one hand and a snickerdoodle in the other. He took alternating bites of each.

Rosa was one of the best cooks in town, and everyone flocked to her restaurant, but she wasn't big on desserts. The restaurant had a few—Mexican hot chocolate floats, fried ice cream, and fresh churros with a cinnamon dipping sauce. Alyss liked her mother's desserts, but even Rosa said, 'Pastry is an art!' And this, Alyss thought, as she ate another scone, is art.

"They have to stay in business," Caroline moaned, as she ate her seventh cookie.

"Well, it'd be nice," Tyler said and eyed her curiously.

"No, you don't understand. My Gam-gam died in a fire, and all her recipes burnt with her."

Everyone stopped eating and looked at Caroline.

"I didn't know. Sorry," Alyss said. Her own grandparents on both sides were dead before she was born, so she never knew them.

"Thanks. It was a long time ago. But I remember her food. The cookies she baked whenever I came over. Her house always smelled yummy."

"Maybe you can get the recipe," Tyler suggested.

"Well, if we buy stuff, maybe they'll stay open awhile," Morris said.

"We'd have to buy an awful lot." Alyss should have asked for one of their flyers. She was curious about what other pastries they had and how magic figured into the teashop. Of course, good food had its own magic.

The group broke up soon after, each one heading home. By unspoken agreement, Morris was given the leftovers to take home and eat.

Chapter 6

The two-lane blacktop of the highway ribboned out behind Father Halloran's pickup almost a week after Mary-Alice had asked him to investigate the new witches. He felt bad it had taken him this long, but a priest's life was a busy one. Still, he was glad to get away.

He planned to arrive in Midswich exactly at teatime, four o'clock, hoping the teashop offered high tea. Once, on a trip to Canada, he had gone to high tea at a fancy hotel, and he'd never forgotten the experience. The tiered serving trays, piled with finger sandwiches, slices of teacakes, petite fours, and a variety of cookies they called biscuits, the like of which he'd never seen before or since. Just thinking about it made his stomach rumble, and he pressed the gas pedal.

Driving into Midswich was always pleasant. He enjoyed coming over the small hill and seeing the British style village come into view. Soaring trees made it a green and lively place. Shady in summer, picturesque in winter. He knew the town was kitschy, but somehow the charm remained. After all, what else could a Maine town without a lighthouse do?

The first building Halloran passed that announced civilization ahead was William Sheppard's Garage and Gas. He passed the well-kept 1920s building and pressed a little harder on the accelerator. The pickup zoomed past, gaining speed as Halloran climbed the last hill.

The town spread out below—a quilt of evergreens, spruce, pine, and larch, and the mandatory dark brown shingles of the houses. Father Halloran found a parking spot on the main street, right in front of Tea Times Three, which already looked promising. He wondered if the entire town was too skittish to even park in front of the witches' shop.

He climbed out of the pickup and looked around. There were about half a dozen people on the street, and all of them had stopped in their tracks. Father Halloran felt their keen attention on the back of his neck. He smiled and waved to the gawkers. Across the street, he saw Mr. Callister actually run out of the grocery store, presumably to get a better view.

Waiting to see if I come out a toad, he thought. Still smiling, Father Halloran turned and went into the teashop.

The inside was every bit as charming as the outside. Gleaming silver tea services sat empty on each table.

Father Halloran hated all the new tea and coffee shops that popped up everywhere, like overly aggressive mushrooms. The blaring music, ugly glass-topped tables designed for easy clean up.

Those places were always loud, and the staff seemed to be in a hurry to get people out the door. The customers were pushy and rude or oblivious to the world, plugged into their computers and phones.

But here was a real teashop. A place to sit down and enjoy, not order at a counter while on your way to the bank. In a corner of the shop was a girl, so still and quiet, he hadn't noticed her. One of the witches.

She stared at him, eyes round and brown as a doe's caught in headlights. She wore a ruffled apron over a cream-colored T-shirt and brown skirt.

"Uh, good afternoon." Father Halloran took a step toward her. She scooted sideways along the wall in alarm. "I'm here for tea?"

The girl gave a mute nod and fled the tearoom.

Unsure if he should sit or leave, Father Halloran eyed the bakery case and decided to seat himself. He chose a table near the pastry display but away from the windows. He didn't want to look out at curious villagers, staring at him like a fish in a bowl. As he was getting settled, the girl with the apron came back followed by a taller witch with a welcoming grin.

"Welcome to Tea Times Three," the tall girl said. "My name is Bruleé, and this is my little sister, Caramel."

Caramel put a leather embossed menu on the table and ducked behind her sister.

"Oh, my." Father Halloran opened the menu and started reading. There were two pages of teas alone, broken into three categories: black, green, and white. One section was labeled tisanes and a list of magical spells the teas could have cast upon them, for added health benefits. "What's a tisane?"

"A tisane is what people mistakenly call herbal teas. Only tea is tea from the tea plant," Bruleé said.

"I see." Halloran raised his eyebrows. "You learn something new every day."

He flipped a page of the menu. "Ah! Dessert. This is what I was looking for. Do you offer high tea?"

Bruleé's customer service smile faltered. "Um, by appointment? Yes, we do by appointment. That may change if we get a lot of customers though."

Halloran saw Caramel look at her sister with surprise.

"So, what do you have today? Everything in that bakery case looks awfully good." Father Halloran was looking at a particular Napoleon he was thinking about ordering.

The older witch's smile turned brittle and finally faded altogether. "We don't have anything, Father. We don't have any customers."

"But, the bakery case..."

Bruleé went over to the case and tapped the glass three times. In a burst of gold sparks everything disappeared. All the scones, the shortbread, the muffins, and that particularly good-looking Napoleon.

"An illusion. I'm sorry, Father."

Father Halloran couldn't quite hide his disappointment. If that Napoleon had tasted as good as it looked, he was sure to have had a little fore taste of heaven.

"So, there's nothing to eat?"

Bruleé shook her blonde head. "Nothing, unless you want to wait while Anglaise makes something." She sighed. "And that's if I can talk her into it."

"What sort of something?" Halloran prompted.

"Well, Scottish shortbread doesn't take long and we have all the ingredients for several flavors."

"Flavors? Of Scottish shortbread?" Intrigued, Halloran scoured the menu. "What flavors?" he asked, just as he found them on the menu.

"We can make plain, lemon thyme, chocolate lavender, orange zest, traditional oat flour, brown sugar, pecan, and poppy."

Father Halloran had never heard of such a variety of shortbread before. There were a dozen more listed on the menu. It all sounded wonderful, and with effort, Halloran settled on one, which he thought showed great restraint. He was tempted to order one of each.

"I'll try the chocolate lavender." Halloran felt very adventurous. Perhaps the illusory Napoleon wasn't such a great loss.

"Wonderful! And would you like some tea while you wait?"

"Of course." He turned back to the lists of teas at the front of the menu, chuckled, and patted his ample stomach. "How long does the slimming tea take to work?"

"Well, you have to drink it daily, and it only really works with magic applied to it. And you still have to exercise some."

"Oh." He was disappointed. His doctor had been after him for years to lose at least forty pounds.

"But it works better than any diet pill," Bruleé assured him.

"For now, how about Earl Grey."

"Excellent choice with the chocolate lavender shortbread. Would you like it spelled to be soothing?"

Father Halloran thought about that. "Best not to the first time. I have to drive home."

She nodded. "I'll be back with your tea."

Bruleé disappeared around a counter behind the antique cash register. He heard a brief exchange and then she came back. She pulled a glass jar labeled Earl Grey from the wall of cubbies behind the counter. Father Halloran watched with interest as she scooped out a measured portion of dark black teas leaves with a wire mesh tea ball. She turned on an electric teakettle that was on a counter just below the wall of cubbies.

"Caramel, pick out a teapot."

He had forgotten about the young witch who'd given him the menu. Halloran looked around. She'd retreated to the back of the store.

There were shelves and shelves of teapots on display, porcelain and iron, some plain, some fancy. There were floral and Wedgewood, solid color, and raku. He'd never seen so many teapots: round, square, short, tall, squat, some sculpted to look like animals, while others resembled fruit.

Caramel pulled down a green, celadon, Japanese-style pot with a woven handle, and took it to Bruleé.

"Excellent choice," Bruleé told her.

Halloran thought so, too. The simple teapot was graceful, but not floral or feminine. He liked the pot's understatedness, too. The clean lines and unfussy design were something he might have chosen himself.

Bruleé checked the temperature of the teakettle. The digital display was easy to see from where he was sitting, and Halloran noticed she shut the kettle off before the water reached boiling. Halloran was surprised. He always waited for his teakettle to whistle loudly from the stove before he took it off the heat.

From under the counter, Bruleé took two mugs. One was plain white, shallow, and small. The other was a match to the celadon teapot, green and handleless in the Japanese style.

Bruleé put the tea strainer over the white mug and poured the steaming hot water over the leaves. She swished the tea ball around in the mug, then pulled it out and put it into the teapot. Then she filled the pot from the teakettle, before putting the mug and teapot on a silver tray.

"Go see how Anglaise is doing," she said.

Caramel took the white mug back to the kitchen with her. Halloran expected Bruleé to bring the teapot right over but, instead, she let it steep. She checked her wristwatch against the antique clock on the wall. Halloran looked down at his own watch. Exactly four minutes later, Bruleé took the mesh tea ball from the teapot. She put it on a silver tray with the mug, and brought them over.

"Would you like cream, milk, or lemon with your tea?" she asked him as she set the tray in front of him.

"You serve real cream?" Halloran was surprised. Not many people these days risked the calories of real cream. He always saw people using those horrid non-dairy creamer powders.

"Yes," Bruleé said. "We only serve all-natural food here."

"What about sugar?"

"That, too." She pulled the china lid off a little white sugar tub on the table. "Sugar cubes." She took the lid off another one. "And raw sugar. We also have honey, by request, in three flavors."

"My word." Father Halloran was dizzy with options. So much to choose from, he wanted everything. Too many condiments would spoil the tea, though. "Just cream, please."

While Bruleé went to go get the cream, Father Halloran poured out a cup of tea. The Earl Grey gave off a citrus perfume from the oil of bergamot used to flavor the tea. He inhaled deeply, feeling the hot, liquid warmth of the cup. He'd never cared for plain tea. He liked to mellow the bitter with cream or milk, but he had the urge to try this straight.

He took a sip of Earl Grey, expecting the familiar strong, black tea he often brewed at home. He'd noted the much lighter brown of the tea Bruleé had brewed and feared the tea would be weak. He couldn't have been more surprised. The tea was perfect. Instead of the bitter tannin-rich brew he had drunk for years, the effervescence dance across his palate. He could actually taste the tea and the bergamot. There was the bitter undertone he was used to but, instead of overwhelming the flavor of the tea, it enhanced the natural richness of the leaves.

Looking to make sure the sisters were out of sight, Halloran crossed himself. He'd never tasted better tea in his lifetime. It was a revelation, like the time his mother forced him to try butternut squash.

As a child, he'd refused on the basis of squash being mushy and looking like baby food. At long last, when he was seventeen, he broke down and took a taste. The sweet, melt-in-your-mouth flesh of the squash had stunned him. To think, he could have been eating butternut squash all those years. And to think, he'd been drinking fifty-years' worth of bad tea.

Bruleé came back as he was pondering his cup of tea, a white porcelain creamer in her hand. She set it down on the table.

"Anything else I can get you, Father?"

"You have to tell me how you made this tea. I've never tasted anything like it."

Bruleé grinned hugely, and a blush touched her cheeks. "It's good then?"

"The best."

"Well, some of it I learned from a Chinese tea master and some of it from reading."

"Please, sit." He gestured to an empty chair. "This sounds interesting."

"Oh, it's not really," Bruleé protested as she sat down. "First thing is, don't let the water boil. I know that's what it says on tea bags and such, but it's wrong. Boiling water scorches the leaves. Then, and I learned this from my master, Mr. Woo, rinse the leaves in hot water first. If you go to a Chinese teashop, you'll see them do this. Pour hot water over the leaves, then toss out the water. Doing this opens the leaves and readies them for steeping. Lastly, steeping, most people just leave the tea in the pot the whole time, and by the second cup, it's bitter, right?"

"Exactly."

"The Chinese teas aren't steeped long. Some steep only thirty seconds."

"I had no idea. Are they flavorful?"

"Many are very delicate, but also very aromatic. I've worked with the western teas and tisanes for years to find the best length of time to steep them."

"That's very…" He searched for a word. "…dedicated?"

Bruleé laughed. "Anglaise calls it fussy, but she likes coffee." She shivered and made a face of exaggerated disgust.

Father Halloran laughed. He poured a tiny amount of

cream into his tea. Normally, he drowned it in milk, but this time he didn't have to. He took a sip.

"Perfect!"

"I'm so glad you like it. The shortbread is in the oven and should be done in a few minutes." Bruleé stood up to go.

"So soon? I've no one to talk to." Halloran looked around the empty tearoom. Even the ghostly quiet Caramel had disappeared.

She looked around the shop as well, and her smile died.

"I think I've made a terrible mistake moving us here," she said softly. "You'd think we were storing nuclear waste, for all the welcome we've gotten."

"Mary-Alice told me to hurry over and check you out, before the shop closed."

"Mary Alice?" Bruleé cocked her head. "I haven't really met anyone in town."

"She's Rosa's daughter," Halloran supplied.

"As in Rosa's? The Mexican restaurant?"

"Yes, indeed. You'd know her if you met her. Dresses all in black, lots of jewelry."

Bruleé gasped. "I have! She came to the back door the other day, asking after free samples."

Halloran chuckled. "She seems very eager to get Papal approval."

"And do we have the church's stamp of approval?"

"Most definitely," Father Halloran said enthusiastically.

A buttery, chocolate smell drifted in from the kitchen. Halloran lifted his head and inhaled deeply. "My word," he muttered. "You're sure the shortbread isn't enchanted?"

"Positive," Bruleé said.

"Your sister must be very gifted."

"We try not to fuel her ego." Bruleé winked. "I should check and see if it's done. And, please, don't be surprised if the shortbread is crumbly. Normally, it should be room temp before serving."

"I think I'll survive warm shortbread."

Bruleé headed for the kitchen and Father Halloran finished his first cup of tea. He poured himself another, adding just a bit of cream. The empty shop was depressing. The place should have been filled with people and lively conversations. Instead, he sat all alone, wondering if he could do anything.

He could recommend the teashop in the church bulletin, but most of his parishioners lived in Musquash, and he wasn't sure they'd make the trip just for a teashop. Midswich only had a handful of Catholics, and even they may not want to break town convention by coming in. The problem was that old Puritan, Pastor Austin.

At least Father Halloran had set an example of tolerance for Midswich by coming here today. Hopefully, others would follow and give the teashop a fighting chance. He would be sorry indeed to see it closed the next time he came to Midswich.

The delicious chocolate smell hanging in the air intensified, and Halloran's stomach rumbled. How could anything as simple as shortbread smell so good? Maybe the witches used a spell to intensify the scent of their baking. If that was the case, the taste may not live up to the promise. He'd certainly run into enough bakeries where the pastries looked better than they tasted.

The uncharitable thought vanished as Bruleé reappeared with a white porcelain plate in one hand and napkin-wrapped silverware in the other. He could see the pride in her smile as she set the plate down in front of him.

The chocolate shortbread let off a wisp of steam so fragrant, he could almost taste it. The shortbread was cut into uneven, brown diamonds, the pastry so delicate when warm that the edges crumbled on the plate. Father Halloran could see the delicate lavender buds sprinkled throughout and could smell the floral undercurrent, now that the shortbread was in front of him.

He leaned over for a better whiff. "This smells incredible," he said.

"I hope you like it. I'm a little embarrassed to serve it hot," she said.

"Nonsense," he assured her. The shortbread smelled so good he would have eaten it under any circumstances.

He tried the fork, but the shortbread crumbled to powder, so he got the spoon Bruleé had brought.

She hovered nearby, a faint blush coloring her cheeks when he resorted to the spoon.

The first warm bite of chocolate-lavender shortbread not only lived up to the smell, but shot past all his expectations like a comet. He could taste the simplest of ingredients: butter, sugar, flour, cocoa, and lavender, all perfectly balanced, all working together in harmony to produce something far greater than the sum of its parts. The shortbread melted into the sandy texture all good shortbreads shared.

"This is wonderful. Better than wonderful. Perfection"

"I'm so glad you like it."

"Like is a very small word, Miss Bruleé." Father Halloran picked up another spoonful of the delicate cookie.

"Would you like to take some home?" Bruleé asked.

"Can I?"

"Well, buy some, I mean. There's a whole pan of shortbread in there," she waved in the direction of the kitchen.

"I'll take it," Father Halloran said, spraying crumbs. He swallowed his mouthful of shortbread. "Excuse me." Enthusiasm at the prospect of take-out had gotten the better of him.

"I'll go wrap up the rest of the shortbread."

The Earl Grey tea was the perfect accompaniment to the chocolate shortbread, and Father Halloran poured himself the last cup to sip as he ate. While he might not have gotten the high tea he was hoping for, he hadn't been disappointed.

When Bruleé returned, she had two small cardboard boxes, one white and one blue. "In honor of our first customer, I spelled the shortbread in the blue box." She set the box down. There was a gold sticker on it as well with an embossed S. "Lavender is known to be soothing, and these will help you sleep."

"The spells are non-habit forming, I take it?" Father Halloran said.

"Of course. We would never do addicting spells!" Bruleé looked shocked at the very idea.

"Sorry, bad joke." Father Halloran cringed. He'd meant to reference the ads on TV for sleeping pills, but he should have known better. There were witches, now jailed, who added an addicting factor to their spells to insure repeat business. There were also a few people who became hooked on spells due to their own folly, much like drug addicts.

Bruleé looked relieved, but Halloran could see he had spooked her terribly.

"I really am sorry."

She shook her head. "It's all right. I guess I'm just used to the worst. Ugh," she said with disgust. "I'm starting to sound like Anglaise. There's a reason we keep her in the kitchen."

Halloran chuckled. He took the two boxes of cookies and stood. The street outside had grown noticeably darker and Father Halloran glanced at the clock on the wall.

Ten after five. He blinked, surprised that he'd been at the teashop over an hour.

"Perhaps I can schedule a high tea next week? Bring a few people with me, maybe the choir?" Halloran said.

"That would be lovely. Call a few days ahead, though, in case—in case, we've closed."

Halloran shook his head. "Don't think like that. God provides, and He really does. I've been wanting a good teashop for years and here one is. Ten minutes down the road."

He saw the doubt in Bruleé's smile. Perhaps she wasn't religious. The few witches he'd met had been mostly pagans or atheists, but Father Halloran didn't care. Good company and good tea were rare enough in the world. He certainly wasn't going to turn his nose up at them.

"Well, good luck," Father Halloran said. "And if you don't mind, I'll put in a prayer to Saint Homobonus, the patron saint of small businesses."

"I don't mind at all, Father."

Bruleé walked him to the door and held it open for him as he left.

Father Halloran felt somehow refreshed. As if a little of the business of his life had fallen away in the quiet of the shop, and he was lighter in spirit for it. He looked up at the sky as he stepped out of the shop and saw that clouds thick with rain had crowded above. Even the overcast couldn't bring him down. Halloran felt sure that the rain was needed. He thought nothing could dampen his good feelings.

"Afternoon, Jon."

He was wrong. Halloran froze as he reached for the car keys in his jacket pocket. With a heavy sigh, he turned around.

"Afternoon, Oscar."

Staking out Tea Times Three had finally paid off. Penelope Owens had spent a long week sitting in her car across the street from the teashop. She had been using Callister's as her headquarters, until Geoffrey threw her out. Apparently, he wasn't worried about saving the town's soul. That job fell to Penelope and Pastor Austin. Her knees hurt and her lower back was on fire, but at last someone had dared break the invisible blockade around the shop.

Penelope was surprised to see Father Halloran from Musquash. She hesitated to call Pastor Austin. Maybe the priest was there to tell the witches to leave town. There were a number of Catholics in Midswich who all went to Saint Mary's. After all, it had once been the Catholic Church that had led the Inquisition. The Church had softened a lot since the Dark Ages, so Penelope remained suspicious.

She looked at the time on her cell phone. If Father Halloran didn't come out in five minutes, she'd call Pastor Austin.

The five minutes came and went. Penelope fiddled with the car radio and wondered how Prince Albert was doing home alone.

She squirmed in her seat. She hadn't realized how uncomfortable the seats in her Mercury were until now.

She waited. Maybe Father Halloran was arguing with the witches. He might need ten minutes to tell them off. Penelope took her cell phone out of her purse. She clicked through the numbers and stopped on Austin's name. Still, she didn't call him.

For some reason, Penelope felt odd about snitching on one clergy to another. Matters of God should be left to those in His service. On the other hand, Pastor Austin had been asked to be informed in the event someone went to the teashop, so he could have a chat with them about their immortal soul.

Penelope noticed she wasn't the only one who was watching the teashop. Geoffrey stood on the sidewalk, his boyish face all open curiosity. Flora stood a few feet away—a keen, hawk-like expression sharpened her spare features. Down the block gathered the four little Satanist kids, all dressed in black, led by Rosa's daughter, Mary-Alice. At least Rosa was concerned enough about her daughter to take her to church. What kind of church had a priest who visited witches? Maybe Mary-Alice's soul wasn't the only one in danger.

Her cell phone showed 4:30. Penelope hit the call button.

"Hello?"

"Pastor Austin, it's Penelope Owens. Someone went into the teashop."

"Who?"

"Father Halloran, of all people," Penelope told him.

There was a moment of silence on Pastor Austin's side.

"I'll be right there," he said and hung up.

She nodded in agreement, even though he couldn't see her. Penelope was sure she'd done the right thing.

A few minutes later, she saw Pastor Austin come around the corner onto Stratford. He was dressed for business in a black blazer, shirt, and slacks. The white of his clerical collar stood out even brighter in the gray overcast that was creeping over the town.

Getting out of her car, Penelope waved at him. He waved back and headed toward her. Austin nodded to Flora and Geoffrey as he passed. They returned the greeting feebly, and Penelope noticed they both regarded the preacher with suspicion.

"Pastor Austin, I'm glad you came," Penelope said as he walked up.

"Thank you for calling. How long has he been in there?"

"Almost an hour."

Austin frowned. He squinted at the shop across the street. The reflections on the window made it hard to see in.

"Has anyone else gone in?"

"No."

"That's a relief."

"Should we…should you go in?"

"Don't worry, Penelope, I'll have a chat with Jon when he comes out."

Penelope nodded. She kept reminding herself the witches would be gone soon, but she feared she was wrong. People always succumbed to the easy promises magic made. What would happen if Father Halloran gave Tea Times Three his seal of approval?

Another fifteen minutes went by, and the crowd on the sidewalk had grown. Mary-Alice and her friends loitered in front of Callister's Dry Goods. Geoffrey's wife, Claire, still wearing her Barely Hair apron and carrying a pair of scissors, had joined her husband. Beside them was Matilda, who must have followed Claire right out the salon's door.

Of all of them, Mary-Alice Ruiz had the biggest stake in Father Halloran's visit. With the priest's seal of approval, she could go to the teashop in defiance of the town and her mother, who ought to know better than to let an impressionable teenager anywhere near witches.

She was just about to suggest going into the teashop when Father Halloran came out. The portly priest had a smile on his face, and he looked up at the sky as if welcoming the overcast.

Pastor Austin trotted across the street toward Halloran, and Penelope followed.

"Afternoon, Jon." Austin gave Father Halloran a tight smile.

The genuine smile on Halloran's face faded, replaced by an obvious fake one.

"Afternoon, Oscar," Father Halloran said. He pulled a key from his jacket pocket and gave them a jingle. "I was just heading out."

Austin managed to insinuate himself between Father Halloran and the priest's truck.

"I was just wondering what you were doing in Midswich, Jon."

Halloran glanced from Austin to the teashop. "That seems pretty obvious, Oscar."

The tight smile on Austin's face stretched to breaking. "And what were you doing there?"

"Holding Mass. What do you think I was doing? Having tea."

Penelope glanced at the two preachers as they squared off like a clerical gunfight. She waited for one of them to say, "Draw."

"The tea met with your approval, then?"

Halloran's eyes narrowed. "In every way. Best tea I've ever had."

Austin colored furiously. He took a deep breath, coughed, and got himself under control. Penelope wondered if this confrontation would come to blows, and she had the sick feeling she was responsible. They're grown men, she reminded herself. They could take care of themselves.

"The witches aren't welcome here, Jon—"

"Nonsense."

"—and," Austin ignored, the interruption. "I would have thought you, of all people, could appreciate that, given the Church's history."

"You know very well, the Catholic Church offered an apology for the Inquisition to witches worldwide in 1966."

"That doesn't mean you're best friends."

"No, it means that each witch is judged individually, as a person, like everyone else."

"Then, what's your verdict of them?" Austin gestured at the teashop.

"Two of the nicest young ladies I've met in a while."

Pastor Austin loomed over the smaller man. Penelope saw Austin's jaw clench, and he was rigid with anger. Father Halloran stood his ground, a faint look of triumph on his face.

"How can you say that?" Penelope burst out. She couldn't

keep silent any longer, especially when Father Halloran seemed determined to condemn them to Hell. "They'll ruin everyone in this town. It doesn't matter if they're nice!"

Father Halloran gave her a concerned look. Pastor Austin looked approving.

"Exactly," Austin affirmed. "Their characters aren't the issue. It's the charms they peddle."

Penelope nodded emphatically. If they were normal girls who'd opened a teashop, there wouldn't be a problem.

Halloran frowned, shifting the boxes he carried under one arm. "There's no arguing with a mind made up," he said. "I need to get back to Musquash, so if you'll excuse me."

He reached around Austin toward the truck door, forcing Austin aside.

"What are you telling your congregation, Jon?"

Father Halloran climbed into his pickup and gave a last, almost sad, look at Penelope and Austin.

"Well, Oscar, opinions are like assholes. We all have one." He shut the cab door and the truck roared to life.

Penelope and Austin stepped up to the curb as the truck pulled out. She watched Halloran leave and felt her hands squeeze into tight fists.

"How dare he undermine me—er—you?" she hissed.

"Don't worry, Penelope. He's only one man with a handful of parishioners here." Austin started walking away. No doubt he had work at the church to get back to.

Maybe Pastor Austin was right. Even those who didn't attend any of the churches in town hadn't gone to the teashop. Still, she didn't like to think the witches could stay.

She looked at the teashop and then did something she'd never done in her life. She spit on the sidewalk then took off across the street to her car.

Prince Albert would be hungry and she needed to get home.

"That old bitch just spit on our sidewalk." Anglaise sat at one of the empty tables, eating a piece of shortbread she'd saved from the priest's order. They were scratch-end, triangle-pieces, left over from cutting the cookies into diamonds. She stood up, ready to give the old biddy a royal tongue-lashing. Her and that Pastor Austin. Unfortunately, he'd left already.

"Stop right there," Bruleé said.

"Oh, come on," Anglaise snapped but she halted anyway.

Bruleé put the jar of Earl Grey back into its cubby. "Let's just celebrate our first customer."

"Like that ten dollars is going to save us from bankruptcy."

Bruleé turned around so Anglaise could see her roll her eyes. "He's a priest, and he'll tell his congregation we're okay."

"Whatever," Anglaise grunted. Witches were about the only business that needed clergy approval, and she just wished people would think for themselves.

A loud bang echoed through the kitchen. Anglaise and Bruleé looked at each other.

"Kitchen door?" Bruleé asked.

"Again," Anglaise said. She headed for the back. "I'll go see what they want."

Anglaise yanked open the delivery door just as the knocking started up again. The same brown-skinned, black-haired girl from the other night was there with her friends. Her eyes were startled, and her fist was poised to knock once again.

"Oh," she said and put her arm down.

"What?" Anglaise looked over the group. Four pairs of eyes stared back nervously.

"Uh," the girl said again. She coughed. "What did Father Halloran say?"

"About what?"

"Whether it's safe to eat here," said the boy with the mohawk.

"You the Catholic Emo League or something?" Anglaise leaned against the doorframe. If she looked bored enough, would they leave?

"Goth, not emo. Emo's for pussies," the boy said. "And only Alyss is Catholic." He punched the lead girl's shoulder.

"I am not," she shot back.

"And so not caring," Anglaise cut them off. "Ask your priest if you want to know if he gave us his super special seal of approval." She stepped back, ready to slam the door in Alyss's overly made up face.

"Wait!" Alyss stuck her foot in the door. "Did he say people couldn't come here?"

"He drank tea, he ate cookies, and he left. That's all I know."

"Uh—uh—"

Anglaise heard a soft choking noise behind her. Caramel, trying to spit something out.

"'Scuse me," Anglaise said to the goths.

Behind her, Caramel peeked around the wall that blocked the stairs to the second floor from the kitchen. The fluffy head of Fraiche also poked around the wall, and he gave an excited, "Yip."

"What?" Anglaise asked, one eye on her sister and one eye on the door. She didn't want the vampire brigade to steal anything.

"Th—the p—p—priest was nice."

"Why don't you tell them that?" Anglaise marched over and yanked her little sister down the steps. She dragged Caramel over to the back door, ignoring her squeaky protestations.

Fraiche needed no encouragement to meet new people. As soon as he saw Caramel head for the door, willingly or not, he zipped over to the visitors, furry flag of a tail waving happily. He bounced up and down as if spring loaded, yipping with each bounce.

Anglaise shoved Caramel in front of her and put her face to face with the lead goth girl. They looked about the same age, Anglaise thought, and who else in town was going to befriend a witch but a bunch of freaks dressed in black?

"Hi," said the goth girl.

She stuck out a hand with black painted nails and studded

rings shaped like snakes, bats, and dragons. Ever so slowly, Anglaise saw Caramel's hand rise and held her breath as Caramel reached out for the other girl's. Even Fraiche seemed to realize something momentous was happening. He stopped jumping and stood still, pointed ears perked.

The two girls' hands met, and the goth saw her chance. She gently seized Caramel's hand and pumped it a few times.

"I'm Alyss."

"C—C—C—C—C—C—"

"Caramel," Anglaise supplied. Otherwise, they'd be there all night.

"Caramel?" Alyss repeated. "That's pretty."

"She was waiting tables when the priest came in," Anglaise said.

"Really? So, what did he say?"

"H—h—he talked t—to Bruleé and h—h—he drank t—tea and h—h—he knew we're w—witches."

"That sounds like approval to me," said the kid with the mohawk.

The other two finally spoke up, a boy with spiky brown hair with red tips and a pasty-faced, thin girl with unfocused eyes.

"My mom's not going to care what a Catholic priest thinks," said the boy.

"Mine either. They care way too much what Austin says," added the girl.

"Don't worry," said Alyss. "We'll work it out." She turned her attention back to Caramel, who was still rooted to the threshold, staring at the ground. "Nice to meet you, Caramel."

Caramel managed a nod. Anglaise could see the deep crimson blush on Caramel's cheeks through a veil of long, brown hair. But Anglaise also caught what she thought was a faint smile.

"See you 'round," added Mohawk, as the four departed.

When they were gone, Caramel came unstuck. She scooped up Fraiche and bolted for the stairs before Anglaise could blink. Had she pushed Caramel too hard, making her meet people? Anglaise felt a twinge of uncertainty. Caramel had to get out more, though. She'd never been outgoing, but what sixteen-year-old was a total recluse? The girl didn't even have an e-mail account.

Anglaise shut the door and went back to the main shop. Bruleé had flipped the *OPEN* sign to *CLOSED*, and she was dusting the teapots for sale.

"So, who was that?" Bruleé asked. She took down a tiny iron teapot with a red glaze and wiped it with her dust rag.

"Bunch of goths."

Bruleé waited a minute for more information, and Anglaise let her.

"And what did they want?" she prompted at last.

"To know what the priest said."

"I think I can safely say we have Father Halloran's approval." Bruleé nodded to herself, glowing with optimism.

Anglaise rolled her eyes and stuck out her tongue at Bruleé's back. "Yeah, whatever. Unless the priest can eat a thousand dollars' worth a week, we still aren't gonna break even."

"You're negativity bounces right off me, " Bruleé replied. She turned and gave Anglaise a megawatt smile.

"You make me sick." Anglaise took her half-eaten plate of shortbread ends and headed for the kitchen.

"It's a shame you find happiness so unbearable!" Bruleé called after her.

Geoffrey went back to the grocery store after a word with his wife, then Claire and Matilda crossed the town square on their way back to Barely Hair.

Flora lingered. She couldn't quite bring herself to move. She watched, incredulous, as Penelope Owens spit on the sidewalk. Spit! A grown woman. Flora opened her mouth to say something, then realized she was slipping back into teacherly behavior, ready to chastise errant children.

Somehow, two years of retirement didn't make up for the

nearly fifty years of lecturing gum-chewers and tattletales.

A chill breeze swept over town. The low clouds promised rain. Anne's arthritis would be aching, and Flora had been gone two hours already. She needed to get home, make dinner, and give Anne her pills.

Slowly, she turned and walked away, back to Greenwich, where she hooked a left, heading north. Flora, like just about everyone else in town, walked to her destination, unless there was heavy lifting involved or multiple errands to run.

She passed the alley that ran behind Callister's and the other shops on the block. The heavy smell of diesel coated her nose and throat. Flora glanced down the alley, and saw a large refrigerated truck idling beside the Dry Goods loading dock. A couple of men were wheeling dollies loaded with crates of ice cream and frozen entrees into the back of the grocery store. Her nose wrinkled. Deliveries could be made earlier so they didn't stink up all downtown.

Quickening her steps so she could reach fresh air, Flora held her breath until she was past the alley. She then settled into a more sedate pace and thought about Anne as she walked.

How to get Anne to the witches? Or rather, how to get the witches to Anne? For some reason, Flora still couldn't bring herself to stroll in the front door of Tea Times Three. Not with the entire town set against them. The weight of public opinion in a small town could be crushing. She'd seen it drive out a number of former students, mostly the sensitive types and artists. Some whose only crime was a love of musical theater. Once the rumors started, almost nothing could stop them. Proof was never needed. Just a sense of righteousness and small town values.

But, how long would she have to live with the town's ridicule and silent treatment? She wasn't getting younger. Her knees creaked. It took forty-five minutes to walk the length of Greenwich. When she was twenty, she could do it in half that time. Nothing in her body worked right. She had to think on things longer and couldn't eat half the foods she used to.

She came from a long line of long-lived women. Her

mother had died peacefully at the age of ninety-nine. Her grandmother, aunts, and cousins—all the same story: vital women until the day they dropped dead.

That gave the town another twenty years or so to shun her. If she walked into the teashop now, only the second person to walk in that front door, the rumor mill would overheat. Flora had no doubt that she would destroy her reputation, past and present. A distinguished teaching career spanning nearly fifty years would be dragged through the mud.

These felt like such petty concerns in the face of Anne's suffering, and a large and disquiet part of her soul rebelled against town "opinion" as well.

Flora stopped in her tracks. She blinked and looked around. The afternoon seemed brighter, even though the sun was still covered in a blanket of clouds. The image of the Dry Goods' loading dock came back to her so strongly, she could taste the diesel.

Alleys ran behind all the shops on Stratford, and that's where the back door would be. Flora had never thought to check for a literal back door. She just thought she could find the teashop's phone number or something. But this could work out even better.

Matilda waited on the sidewalk for Claire to say good bye to Geoffrey. She'd followed Claire out the door after Geoffrey had called his wife. Claire told her Father Halloran had gone in to the teashop, and Matilda wanted to see it firsthand.

If Midswich still had a newspaper, that would surely have been on the front page tomorrow: *Priest Defies Teashop Cordon!* in three-inch-high letters. Matilda grinned at the mental image.

Claire waved at Geoffrey as she joined Matilda. "See you tonight."

"Bye," he said.

They started walking. Claire had left Emma with her hair

half cut, and Matilda was sure no one was answering the phone. Not that there was that there was so much business the answering machine couldn't handle it. If she'd remembered to turn it on. Matilda felt bad for running out, but she was dying to see what happened to Father Halloran. No one from Midswich had braved the teashop yet. Not that she expected Halloran to exit a different species than he entered, but part of her wondered if he'd end up enchanted in some way. All the father had left with was some take-out.

Matilda checked her silver wristwatch. "My God, we were standing there for, like, an hour."

"Are you serious?" Claire grabbed her wrist to look at the rhinestone-studded face herself.

"Poor Emma," Claire groaned. "I'll give her half off. I hope she didn't leave."

"Looking like that?" Matilda was pretty sure Emma would be where they had left her. In the chair.

"Lorelei might have finished the cut."

"Emma doesn't like Lorelei."

Claire nodded. "I just wanted to tell her about Father Halloran. He has some nerve going in there."

"I wish I had his nerve," Matilda said. She'd been trying to work up the backbone to go to the teashop all week and failing miserably.

The older woman grabbed Matilda's arm making her miss a step. "You can't be serious!"

"I am," Matilda said.

She looked at her arm then at Claire. Taking the hint, Claire removed her hand.

"I want the witches to stay," Matilda went on. "Don't you think it's even a little bit interesting? This stuff only happens in big cities. Now it's happened here. Midswich could use the…" Her hands fluttered in the air. "…excitement!"

"Did you not hear a word Pastor Austin preached Sunday? You're starting to sound like Geoffrey."

A big grin split Matilda's face. "He supports the witches?"

Anger-tinged exasperation colored Claire's face, momentarily emphasizing her crows' feet as her eyes narrowed. "He does not! And anyway, are you insane?"

"No." Matilda started walking again. Claire followed. They crossed the patchy green and brown grass of the town square. "This town could use some spicing up, though."

"But, Pastor Austin—"

"Pastor Austin isn't God. He doesn't know everything."

Claire shook her head. "You can do what you want, Matilda, but at least consider your reputation. Your family's reputation."

Emphasis on the family, Matilda noted. The Hartwells had been one of the founding families of Midswich. No less than eight family members were neck-deep in local politics. Her father was the sole district judge, her aunt sat on the town council, her oldest brother was the chief of police, yet another aunt was school superintendent. The list kept going. She loved them, but she hated being stuck with their reputation.

"I think they'll live," she said, with a bitter note. She hadn't meant to sound so petulant.

Claire shook her head again but didn't say any more.

After a few seconds of silence, Matilda said, "Geoffrey likes the witches?"

A groan escaped Claire. She slumped dramatically.

Matilda laughed at the performance. "Is it the pretty blonde one getting you down?"

Claire straightened. "No, I mean, not that he's not a man, but Geoffrey's starting to feel sorry for them because they're a struggling small business. It's weirdly dad-like or something."

"Well, that's sweet."

"It's disturbing. I keep trying to tell him what Pastor Austin said, but he hates Austin and doesn't care about God."

Religion was, as far as Matilda could tell, the one small bone of contention in an otherwise happy marriage. Most of the time, Claire and Geoffrey worked around the problem, each agreeing to go their separate ways on Sunday morning.

"I hope you don't let the teashop come between you." Matilda patted Claire's shoulder. "You're such a cute couple."

Claire frowned. "Cute always means old."

"No. I mean you work."

"Oh, please. You and Hugh, now there's a cute couple. That Hugh." Claire's eyes glazed over as she roamed the peaks and valleys of Hugh-land.

Matilda just about wanted to vomit. Not that Hugh didn't deserve the lingering looks he got from women, young and old alike. She just wanted to run around behind him shouting, "He's not all that. He's condescending and ignorant and he owes online poker five thousand dollars" Not that it mattered. No one was into Hugh for his personality. Not even Matilda. She was ashamed to admit, even to herself, that if Hugh were ugly, she'd have dumped him a year ago instead of moving in with him. Once, when passing a mirror in a restaurant, Hugh had pulled her close and said they were the two best-looking people in Midswich. She'd been flattered at the time, but a few weeks later, she started wondering if looks were the only reason he was with her.

She hated to think about it, but the time may have come to have a chat about their relationship. The dreaded, "We need to talk."

Chapter 7

U nlike the most of Midswich, William Shepherd did most of his grocery shopping at Good Earth Organic Market in Musquash and the rest online.

He was looking for organic strawberries and sweet basil, in the hopes of recreating the scones he didn't get to sample at Tea Times Three. They had been haunting him for a week.

The only strawberries in the store were greenhouse grown, neatly packed in clear plastic, punctuated with holes so the delicate fruit wouldn't rot. William fondly remembered his trip to California last year for the Sonoma Food and Wine Festival. The strawberries had been in season and some of the best he'd had in his life.

Hot house berries or not, at least they were fresh. He picked up a full container and put them in his basket. They'd better be perfection in a berry, because the price was nothing short of extortion.

Next was basil. If it were later in the year, his herb garden would be sprouting a forest of basil, but the Maine springtime was changeable and slow to warm up. Another cold snap was expected before winter finally gave way.

A small bunch of fresh basil went into his basket with the other groceries. He had a week's worth of meals planned in his mind. The scones would be for breakfast. Curried lamb stew cooked for lunch could be eaten the whole week, since stew only got better with age. Then, for dinner, he'd purchased a huge crown roast of beef. Roast on night one, then make a perfect roast beef sandwich with ciabatta bread, Gorgonzola, and sun dried tomato pesto the next day. A shepherd's pie would do for the last two days.

No one in Midswich knew William spent more time fixing gourmet meals than he did repairing their cars. His father had told him, over and over, cooking was woman's work, with the exception of barbeque, and he'd never managed to completely shake off his early sense of shame. Besides, no one else in Midswich could tell a sun choke from a green onion or spell *fois gras*, let alone competently use it.

Shopping accomplished, he drove to Mail Boxes R Us to check the postal box he kept there. Only his regular mail went to his house in Midswich, the electric and gas bills, flyers from political candidates, and catalogues of gas station-related paraphernalia.

The public mailbox in Musquash received his subscriptions to *Saveur, Food and Wine, Bon Appetite*, his online purchases of truffle oil and asafoeteada, artisan cheeses, and balsamic vinegar from Italy.

Today his mailbox contained the latest issue of *Saveur* he'd been hoping for and the more humble *Taste of Home*, which always included the best recipes for comfort food.

After all, man could not live on black truffles alone. There was also a small box with a customs stamp and a label from Spain.

William smiled. The little box weighed nothing, but inside was gold. Saffron from his friend Rodrigo's farm. He'd met Rodrigo at the Aspen Food and Wine Classic six years ago, and they exchanged packages of food items on a regular basis. Once the season began, William was going to send Rodrigo an express shipment of fern heads he planned to harvest, fresh from the woods behind the gas station. The last thing he wanted was a running commentary from J.J., his mail carrier. A package had come from Japan one time, and she'd hounded him for weeks until he finally told her what it was. A part for Mr. Rimbaldi's Toyota.

Small town nosiness wore thinner than a used rag, but he was as guilty as his neighbors. He found himself walking or driving up and down Stratford, for no good reason other than to eyeball the teashop. William wanted to meet the chef. but he couldn't tell which sister it was, and he'd only seen two of the three so far.

He took the magazines and packages to his Jeep. There was one last stop he liked to make on the way home. Mean Joe's for a cappuccino and a bag of whole bean Ethiopian coffee, which he ground himself.

Mean Joe's was packed on Sundays. The post-church crowd was in need of some caffeine, particularly those who went to the earlier services. William cringed a little as he parked three blocks away. Church was something he'd been avoiding lately. William had been raised Baptist but, as an adult, he'd tired of hellfire and brimstone, and he'd drifted over to the Presbyterians. Mostly for camaraderie. Now he found himself drifting again. Pastor Austin meant well, but his Puritanical austerities didn't agree with William. Perhaps it was time to start shopping. The Methodists seemed tolerant enough, but it meant driving to Musquash for church. Or maybe it was time to quit altogether. He could believe in God without going to church.

William turned the corner and a blast of icy wind smacked him in the face. His scarf whipped behind him and he almost lost it before wrapping the woolen tail around his neck one more time.

The glass door with Mean Joe's logo—a coffee mug with an angry face and a puff of steam coming out the top—opened just as he arrived. He smiled and stepped aside as a girl carrying a broom came out. He wondered if Phil had hired some new help.

"Morning," he said.

Her gray eyes flicked over him. "Morning," she said automatically, voice devoid of welcome or enthusiasm.

She zipped up her puffy down coat and shifted her cardboard carryout container to one hand. Then she climbed on the broom. William froze, his hand holding open the door. He heard some distant protest from inside the shop about the cold air coming in, but didn't shift his attention long enough to really listen.

She rose off the pavement. The third tea witch. He'd finally met her. William released the door.

The witch's feet left the sidewalk and she hooked them over the bristles. Leaning forward, she adjusted her grip so she could steer and carry coffee.

She was leaving. The broom drifted higher, and he saw her pushed sideways by another sudden gust of wind.

His chance was slipping away. "Miss Witch!" William took a few steps down the sidewalk, waving his arms like a madman. "Miss Witch! Miss Witch!"

She turned to him, fury etching lines in her face. She wasn't much younger than he was, but in that moment she looked older. "What?" she snarled and drifted down a few feet.

William swallowed before he could answer. "Are you the chef?"

"What's that to you?" Her face softened from anger to puzzlement.

He was glad she'd relaxed, if just a little, or he didn't think he'd have been able to get the next sentence out. "The strawberry basil scones. Can I get the recipe?"

The witch's eyes narrowed to flinty slits. "No."

The girl and broom ascended quickly to about forty feet then accelerated toward Midswich. Not over the roads of course, but over the woods. As the crow flies, William thought. He realized his arms were still in the air, like he was flagging down an imaginary taxi, and he dropped them.

Her blunt refusal didn't surprise him. A lot of chefs refused to reveal their recipes. But he had been hoping to talk cooking with her. Then there was the fact that he had been about as welcoming as the rest of Midswich.

Ever since he'd smelled the witch's handiwork, he'd been dying to go to the teashop. He just wasn't dying to be the first through the door. Judging from the smells that wafted from the teashop, someone in town was bound to crack.

Mass and communion over, Father Halloran made the community announcements. The usual litany of rummage sales, changes to Sunday school, and congratulations floated past Alyss without her notice.

"And lastly, I'd like to say that a wonderful new teashop has opened in Midswich called Tea Times Three. The shop is run by witches, and in case you were wondering if the Church approved, it does. Or at least, I do." He chuckled at what he must have imagined to be a joke. "Anyway, they have very good tea. Just don't abuse the spells and we should all be fine."

Alyss looked at her mother.

Rosa sat listening calmly. "I don't know," she said at last.

"Come on, Mom," Alyss groaned. She turned to Juana hoping to recruit aid. "You want to go get tea, don't you?"

"I don't know," Juana parroted their mother.

"It'll be like the princess tea parties you have, but with real tea and cake."

"Everyone at school says the witches are bad."

Alyss kicked the pew in front of her. "Well, everyone at school is a narrow-minded idiot."

"Mary-Alice, you're going to confession."

"You oughta go for lying," Alyss shot back. She stood up, ready to go to the parking lot and wait and her mother yanked her back down. "You said we could go when Father Halloran approved."

"Sit down and be quiet," Rosa hissed.

Juana, the little traitor, sat quietly, holding Rosa's hand. Alyss got the unbreakable upper-arm clench for the next twenty minutes while Mass wrapped up. Was it Alyss, or was church getting longer? She was ready to follow Consolata's lead and start sleeping in. She was sixteen and, if she was old enough to learn to drive, she was old enough to skip Mass.

When the service was over, Rosa marched Alyss and Juana out to the parking lot. Alyss struggled free as they neared the car.

"The problem isn't Father Halloran," Rosa said as she let Alyss go.

Alyss crossed her arms. "I know. It's the dumbass townies."

"I don't appreciate that kind of language."

Alyss dropped her gaze to the pavement. "Sorry," she mumbled.

"I just need you to wait until someone more local than us goes into the teashop."

"Like that'll happen."

"It just might."

"No, it won't!" Alyss looked up at her mother, pleading. "No one will go and the witches will leave, and we'll be back to being stupid, boring Midswich, where nothing ever happens."

"I want them to stay, too." Rosa looked at Juana. "Don't tell your friends I said that."

Juana nodded gravely and crossed her heart silently.

Rosa looked back at Alyss. "But I also don't want to lose my customers. Do you understand? This isn't an easy decision, but all our money, our livelihood is sunk into the restaurant."

Alyss bit her lip. She couldn't refuse when her mother invoked the restaurant. Each Ruiz daughter knew that everything from the mortgage payments on their house to the clothes on their backs came from the restaurant.

"What if I could go with no one seeing me?"

Rosa laughed. "Then I guess you'd be a witch yourself."

Alyss spent the drive back to Midswich texting her friends. She sent the same message to each of them to meet her at 6:45 a.m. in the town square. They texted her back a collective "Yes," with the only complaint about the hour coming from Morris.

Frost glittered on the tips of the newly greening grass in the town square. A few more days of frost, and the town lawn would struggle to recover. The bright yellow daffodils planted in the borders were unaffected by the cold, their sunny heads held high on green stalks.

Alyss stood shivering by the fountain in an oversized *Nightmare Before Christmas* hoodie, striped scarf, and sunglasses to cut the glare of the sunrise. There were a few other early risers on the streets. Shopkeepers for the most part. A delivery truck bringing fresh produce to the Dry Goods, commuters who had to leave early for work. Alyss watched the God-squad jogging club run by. Her lip curled as Pastor Austin passed. If the witches left, it'd be his fault.

Caroline showed up first, wearing a long, black frock coat that looked as if it had come from a period film. "It's early," she said. "What are we doing?"

"Wait for the others," Alyss said.

Caroline sat down on the edge of the fountain, hands in pockets. She coughed in the cold and pulled an asthma inhaler from her pocket. She sucked in a dose of the medicine and put it back.

Tyler and Morris arrived simultaneously from opposite directions, Tyler from the upscale neighborhood on Sussex Street and Morris from the southern edge of town.

"Why am I conscious?" Morris asked.

"We're going to the teashop." Alyss tried to sound grave.

Caroline hopped off the edge of the fountain. "Finally."

"What, like, now?" Tyler asked.

Alyss smiled her best, most wicked smile. "Right now."

Tyler didn't dare protest too much, or everyone would think he was a coward, but Alyss could see the doubt in his eyes.

"We're going to go around back and place an order at the delivery door."

Tyler relaxed, grinning. "Oh."

"I'm kinda short," Morris said.

"I want spells," Caroline declared.

"I don't…isn't that extra?" Tyler asked.

"I've got fifteen," Caroline offered.

"I've got about thirty-five dollars, but I wanted to buy a game," Tyler said.

"First, let's just go look at the menu." Alyss started across the town square.

They arrived in the empty alley behind Tea Times Three. Today, there were no baking smells coming from the shop, only the mild stench of garbage dampened by cold greeted them.

Alyss raised her hand to knock when Caroline said," I want to talk to them this time."

Shrugging, Alyss stood aside. "Go ahead."

Caroline made a fist and banged on the door.

"You don't suppose we're gonna piss 'em off showing up like this?" Tyler asked. "I don't want to end up a toad or something."

"Too late," said Morris. He laughed along with the others. Only Tyler was unamused.

The delivery door whipped open and their laughter died.

"Goddamnit, what now?" asked the witch.

It was Anglaise, the one who always answered the door and by now, Alyss was used to her temper. The witch's default mode seemed to be anger.

"Morning," Caroline said. "We would like to see a menu."

The witch frowned. "What for?"

"What do you think?"

Alyss was impressed with the size of Caroline's cajones.

"Nothing's ready," the witch said.

"We can wait."

"Nothing's going to be ready. How about that?"

"We have seventy dollars," Caroline said brightly.

"Aww, man," Tyler moaned.

"We have thirty-five dollars," Caroline corrected.

Anglaise eyed them. "Spend fifty and you've got a deal."

"Deal!"

"Come in. I'll get you menus." Anglaise held the door open as the four teens filed in.

"Don't touch anything, don't steal anything, and don't move," the witch ordered. She went to the base of the stairs leading to the second floor. "Caramel! Bruleé! Get down here!"

Alyss smothered a laugh. She did the same thing every time her mother asked her to go get her sisters—yelled for them, instead of actually going to them.

Two pairs of footsteps clattered down the steps, and the older sister appeared first. A sunny smile lit her face, and she waved at the small group into the kitchen.

"Good morning," she said.

The shyer Caramel trailed behind. She flashed a weak smile in Alyss's direction then arranged herself along the back wall. Seconds later, excited barks could be heard from above.

"Fraiche, stay," Bruleé commanded.

There was a whine and then the patter of little paws as the dog retreated.

"There now," Bruleé said. "Up to health code."

Alyss, Caroline, Tyler, and Morris all exchanged amused glances, but none of them could bring themselves to laugh out loud.

Anglaise hooked a thumb at the kids. "They want menus."

"Of course." Bruleé turned to Caramel, but she was already ducking out of the kitchen.

"They've got fifty to spend."

Bruleé frowned at her sister then turned to the group. "You're our second customers."

"Sorry we didn't come in the front," Alyss said.

"Our parents would kill us," Tyler added.

"Sure you should be here?" Anglaise asked.

"It's quite all right," Bruleé snapped. "Nothing wrong with tea and cookies."

"I want a spell," Caroline said.

Bruleé looked nervous. She was saved a reply by the reappearance of Caramel, who had four leather-bound menus in hand.

"You'll have to pick the order up later. I'm presuming you all go to school?" Anglaise said.

"We could come back at six or something," Morris said. "Like for dessert."

"Sounds good to me," Alyss said. The others nodded in agreement.

"We'll have your order ready for pick up," Bruleé said.

Alyss and her friends looked over the menus, forming up into a huddle to discuss the collective order.

The pages of tea, pastries, detailed explanations of spells, and the properties which certain ingredients could be imbued with were amazing. Alyss glanced at the cookies and, while they all sounded good, she didn't want fifty dollars' worth of cookies. She was looking for teacakes and she found them on page five.

The cakes hovered around three dollars a slice, and she guessed they could afford an entire cake.

"Guys, look at the cakes. We could split a full one."

The other three flipped through the menu until they found the cakes.

"Holy crap," Morris said with deep appreciation. "What's a gat-ow?"

"It's gateau. They're French cakes," Anglaise answered.

"What's a Charlotte?" Morris pointed to an item halfway down the page.

"You slice up a sponge jelly-roll, line a bowl with the slices, fill it with custard, and let it chill. It's a little like an ice cream bombe but I don't make those for tea."

"I want the Charlotte," Morris said.

"I want the German chocolate," Tyler said. "That's what I get on my birthday."

"Well, it's not your birthday," Morris shot back.

"Green tea gateau with adzuki bean paste and vanilla frosting," Caroline said.

"That sounds nasty," Alyss said. "I don't like Asian food."

"The Charlotte, the Charlotte," Morris bounced up and down.

"Can it at least be a chocolate Charlotte? Is that possible?" Tyler looked at Anglaise.

She nodded.

"I'm game for chocolate Charlotte," Alyss said. She looked at Caroline.

Caroline sighed. "Fine, but next time I pick."

"We want an entire chocolate Charlotte."

"You want it totally chocolate or you want something else in there?" Anglaise asked.

"Chocolate cake and chocolate filling and vanilla custard," Alyss said. She looked over her friends and received a collective nod.

"That's thirty-five dollars right there."

"Tea for all of us."

Bruleé stepped forward. "Would you like that to be spelled?"

"Yeah, if we can afford it," Alyss said.

"What would you like then?"

"Money," said Morris.

"I need an 'A' in algebra," Tyler said.

"Spells don't really work like that. I could give you something for focus and memory, though."

"Nah, just gimme plain chai with milk."

"For you," Bruleé said to Morris. "I can do a charm for fortune. It won't last long but you'll find yourself lucky for a few days."

He nodded. "Sounds cool. I've never been lucky."

"I want good health," Caroline said. "I have bad lungs."

"Easy. And you?" Bruleé turned to Alyss.

"Maybe just the luck thing to start with."

"Your order will be ready to pick up at six."

"I wouldn't recommend not coming," Anglaise added.

"Uh…" Alyss said.

"Stop it." Bruleé poked her sister with an elbow. "She's kidding."

"No, I'm not. I'm not wasting a Charlotte."

"Nothing will happen."

"We can pay now," Alyss answered them.

That won smiles from both the witches. Or at least Bruleé. Anglaise's looked more like a smirk.

"Your total is forty-eight dollars and ninety-two cents," Bruleé said.

A moment of pocket mining later, and they produced the fifty dollars. Alyss handed the cash to Bruleé.

"I'll be back with your change." Bruleé headed to the shop.

Once she was gone, Caramel detached herself from the wall and came forward. Alyss had forgotten she was in the kitchen with them.

"Y—your m—menus," she whispered and held out her hands.

"Sure." Alyss handed hers over. The others did the same.

Before Caramel could melt into the background again, Alyss said, "So, have you registered for school yet? We could show you around, so you don't get lost."

Caramel turned pink and clutched the menus to her chest.

"Witches don't go to school," Anglaise said. "Not your kind anyway. Caramel's getting home-schooled."

"Oh," Alyss said. "That sounds better than high school."

Alyss thought she saw Caramel's mouth twitch, like she wanted to say something, but the girl left before Alyss could be sure.

"Here's your change." Bruleé bounced in, all smiles. She handed Alyss the two dollars and eight cents, which Alyss handed to Tyler.

"We'll be back," Alyss said, as her friends exited the back door.

Alyss paused at the deliveries door and turned back. "Say bye to Caramel for us."

"I will." Bruleé grinned and waved.

Nearly six o'clock, and Flora was walking down Oxford, half blinded by the enormous pair of Yoko Ono sunglasses she was wearing. As if no one was going to recognize her. She was more liable to fall and break a hip than fool anyone with her ridiculous disguise. If sunglasses and a floral head scarf could be called a disguise.

She was being silly and she knew it, but felt helpless to stop. For starters, the disguise did render her harder to identify, but Flora also found herself enjoying the thrill of sneaking around. She felt like a spy.

Flora stuck to the creeping shadows, made long by sunset, as she made her way to the teashop. She'd picked a good time to go. People were preoccupied with driving home, and most of the shops downtown were closed.

She passed Stratford and immediately found what she was looking for—the alley running behind the shops. The shadows were denser there, the fading rays of sun blocked by buildings on both sides. If she were still sneaking around later in the year, she'd have to come after the sunset. The summer sun would be high enough to reach the alley.

The alley felt a few degrees cooler than the cold snap that had settled over most of New England. What was she thinking, going to see witches when no one was around? Flora shivered in her vintage camel-colored coat. *No one can hear you scream*, she thought.

Shaking off the melodrama, she squared her shoulders and pulled off the sunglasses. There. Things were brighter already.

Now to find the backdoor of the teashop. She walked down the alley, visualizing the shops from the front. Tea Times Three was sandwiched between Pickett's Antique Attic and One Pearl, Two, the knitting and fabric store. She knew from staring at the teashop all week that it was right in the middle of the block, which meant the backdoor ought to be in the middle as well.

She passed two doors marked with *NOT AN ENTRANCE*, then saw one stenciled with *Pickett's*. Good, the next door should be the teashop.

Flora stopped at a gray, metal door with *DELIVERIES* painted in black. Her gloved fist rose to knock on the door. She knew from watching the sisters that they lived in the apartment above. A good, loud knock ought to bring one of them downstairs. Before Flora could talk herself out of it, she knocked on the solid door.

Her fist thudded dully on the metal, and she felt her bones vibrate with the impact. Who could hear that all the way upstairs? She needed something sturdier than her aging flesh to knock with. If she knocked again, she was afraid her hand would shatter.

She was looking at her feet for a rock or something when the door swung open.

"I swear I'm putting in a freaking doorbell."

Flora stood face to face with a young girl in a chef's jacket.

"You're new," the witch said. She looked Flora up and down. "What do you want?"

Flora felt herself gawping like a fish drowning in air. She rallied quickly. "I need a witch."

"For what?"

"My sister."

"What does she need one for?"

"Are any of you good at healing?" Flora looked down the alley. This was taking far too long.

"Yeah, hang on."

The door closed in Flora's face. She reddened with anger. *The customer is always right. Some measure of politeness ought to be present.*

The door opened. The taller, slightly older witch stood there. "I'm sorry," she said.

"What are you sorry for?" Flora asked.

"Anglaise, I'm sure." She smiled. "What can I help you with?"

"My sister, Anne," Flora began. "She has rheumatoid arthritis, bad, and the doctors can't do anything."

Flora felt foolish. She took a step back. If the whole of modern medicine could do so little for her sister, what could a skinny wisp of a girl do? "Sorry," Flora muttered. "This was stupid. I should go."

"What? Why?"

"There's nothing you can do," Flora said bitterly.

"You don't know that. And I won't know until I see her."

Flora pulled back another step. Had she really put on a disguise and made a fool of herself for nothing? It had taken two hours of digging in the hall closet to find the ugly sunglasses.

"You'd have to come to our apartment. Anne can't get around anymore." Flora assumed that would be the end of it.

"Give me the address."

Flora blinked in surprise. "No one should see you come."

The witch's smile turned brittle. "Fine."

"And you have to bring your broom." Anne would kill her if a witch showed up without one.

"My broom? How far away do you live?"

"Not far—it's for my sister—" Flora couldn't bring herself to say more. At times, Anne's enthusiasm bordered on childish.

"Tomorrow night, say nine o'clock?"

That was a bit late, but Flora nodded. The witch would have to come after dark if she wasn't going to be seen, and Midswich wasn't exactly hopping at nine on a Tuesday.

With the details settled, Flora started to leave.

"Wait, I need your name and address."

Turning back, Flora said, "Of course, how stupid. Flora Barton, apartment 3A at 512 Plymouth Avenue."

"I'll see you then, Flora. And my name is Bruleé."

Flora's cheeks burned, and she was glad she was outside the light cast by the open door. All good manners had escaped her, and she hadn't even thought to ask the witch's name.

"Nice to meet you, Ms. Bruleé," Flora said. "Good night."

The witch smiled and waved from the doorway. Flora nodded a goodbye and turned to go. The delivery door closed behind her, leaving the alley lit only by the sulfurous security lamp of the antique store. Halfway down the alley, Flora almost collided with four black silhouettes that materialized out of the darkness.

She managed to hold in her scream, but her heart clenched painfully, and she could feel at least five years of her life being shaved away.

Squinting, Flora snapped, "What are you doing here?"

"Mrs. Barton?" one of the shadows asked.

They took a few steps closer. Children, Flora noted, irritation chaffing in her chest.

"It's Miss Barton." They all looked far too young for her to have them in her classes. Or she was too old to remember. Flora couldn't tell which. She recognized them all from around town, and they, of course, knew her the same way.

"What are you doing here?" countered the boy with the mohawk.

Flora couldn't remember his name, but she'd had his older brother in her class. Even in third grade he'd been a delinquent. She wondered if she was going to meet her death by hooligans, every old lady's fear.

"Did you buy something from the witches?"

Flora recognized Mary-Alice, who sometimes helped out at her mother's restaurant.

"No," Flora said, hoping she didn't sound too guilty.

"Then what are you doing?" the second boy asked.

"None of your business." Flora could hear a note of smugness in his voice, as if he'd caught her out in a lie.

"But you did go see the witches, right?" Mary-Alice was a little too sharp for her own good.

"I have to go," was the only response Flora could think of that wouldn't incriminate her further. She tried to look dignified as she strode past the only witnesses to her misdeeds.

Flora was a few feet away from the mouth of the alley when she heard Mary-Alice's voice again.

"Don't worry, we won't tell anyone," she called out.

There was a chorus of chuckles from the other three kids. A chill slithered up Flora's spine. She was at the mercy of a bunch of children. A position she'd never been in once in her entire teaching career.

Her steps slowed, and she said over her shoulder, "Neither will I."

The laughter from the peanut gallery abruptly stopped and Flora kept walking.

The TV was on in Alyss's living room, but no sound came out. A commercial for IHOP had come on, and Alyss hit the mute button.

She and Caroline wallowed on the couch in a food coma, and if Alyss had to look at anymore, she'd vomit.

It was all the Charlotte's fault. "Let's go to my house," Alyss had suggested. No one was going to be home until eight, and as long as the huge cake box from Tea Times Three was out of the house, by then no one would be the wiser.

Alyss, Tyler, Morris, and Caroline had walked the five short blocks to Alyss's house on Thames Avenue. Morris carried the cake box, which weighed somewhere upward of three pounds.

Anglaise had handed the box to Alyss first, but after a few minutes, her arms became tired. Morris had stepped in, always eager to have anything to do with food. They opened the cake box on the kitchen counter. Alyss swore the cake was the prettiest thing she'd ever seen in her life. Angels should have sung when the lid came off. Who knew? Maybe somewhere in heaven, they were.

The cake was a perfect dome made of chocolate spirals filled with darker chocolate filling. Alyss stared at the cake along with the others. She was reminded of a tortoise shell or millifiore glass beads, like on her mother's favorite necklace. She knew it looked more complex than it really was, but that alone was an art.

"Should we cut it?" Caroline had asked.

"I'm not here to stare at it," Morris said.

Morris neatly cut the cake into fourteen slices. The first slice revealed the creamy, golden vanilla filling.

Alyss took a picture of the cake with one perfect slice taken out with her cell phone so she could use it as a wallpaper for her computer monitor.

Then they ate. The first slice was consumed in stunned silence, broken only by the occasional moan of "Oh-my-God-this-is-so-good."

The jellyroll was chocolate sponge cake made with bitter-dark chocolate only lightly sweetened. The chocolate filling was a thick ganache made with a lighter, sweeter chocolate. The custard was where most people fell down. Most custard cake filling was wobbly and thick, overpoweringly sweet, and tasted of too much artificial vanilla. The custard at the center of the Charlotte was smooth and creamy, soft but firm. Alyss could see the dark speckles of real vanilla bean seeds. By the second slice, the reverence had worn off a bit.

"I want to hollow this out and live in it," Morris said.

They worked on the cake for a full two hours, washing it down with the tea they had ordered. Alyss was a little surprised to find thelucky tea tasted like any other herbal tea. The flavor was delicate, and left a long aromatic hint of nutmeg at the finish, so it was still better than tea from a teabag.

After the Charlotte, she had been expecting mind-blowing tea, and instead, had gotten pleasant.

The two remaining slices of Charlotte were sent home with Morris. The four of them had over eaten without realizing what they were doing. The cake was almost physically painful to stop eating and, even after three slices, Alyss found herself nibbling crumbs.

Tyler had followed Morris out the door, clutching his stomach, and vowing to walk it off.

Caroline opted to stay at Alyss's to let her stomach settle and hope for a ride when Rosa got home.

The IHOP commercial was over when Alyss opened her eyes. Ghost Hunters was back and Alyss unmuted the TV.

At first, she and Caroline had tried watching South Park reruns, but there was way too much vomiting, so Alyss settled on *Ghost Hunters*.

She stared glassy-eyed at the screen as a bunch of idiots green with night-vision lenses ran around some kind of asylum/jail/hospital.

"That was, without a doubt, the best thing I've ever put in my mouth," Caroline said. "I didn't even know cake could do that."

"I must have put on five pounds," Alyss said.

"So worth it, though."

"No kidding."

"I think I'm gonna get fat. I'll go to the teashop every day and eat nothing but cake and cookies."

"Stop talking about food." Alyss wrapped her arms around her stomach, just in case the Charlotte made a run for it.

"I'm serious. Who cares about boys when there's cake like that? I'm going to eat everything on that menu."

Alyss laughed, ending with groan. "So, can you breathe better?" she asked.

Caroline inhaled deeply. "I think so. I hate these spring cold snaps. They always make me sick. Do you feel luckier?"

"I don't think that's something I can tell. The tea was good, though."

"Super good. Mine had eucalyptus and mint and some other stuff."

Ghost Hunters cut to commercial, and the fifty two-inch plasma screen filled with a greasy hamburger patty being loaded with onions and cheese.

Both girls moaned in pain and averted their eyes. Alyss hit the mute button again.

"Still worth it," she said through clenched teeth.

"Totally," Caroline said.

All the way home, Flora was nervous. She hadn't thought anyone else would be at the back of the teashop. Would the kids tell? She couldn't think why they would, except to be mean to an old lady. They were old enough that there had to be something in it for them, like money or a chance to increase status. If she didn't say anything to anyone, chances are they wouldn't either.

Flora walked up the mountainous three flights of stairs to her apartment. By the top flight, her left knee was twinging. She thought again about moving. There were independent senior living centers, which was what they were calling rest homes these days. She'd looked a few up on the Internet at the library. There wasn't a decent one near Midswich, which meant moving to Augusta or Portland.

Her knee would straighten out in an hour or so. If it gave her too much trouble, she could stick a Salonpas medicated plaster on it before she went to bed.

At least the hall was short. Flora did her best not to limp, pulling out her key ring from her purse. "I'm home," she said as she came through the door.

"Did you see the witches?" asked Anne.

Despite the sudden drop in temperatures, Anne was having one of her good days. She'd been able to get out of bed, and made it into the living room with the help of her walker. Anne sat on what Flora had always scorned as old people furniture, until she'd been forced to buy one—an easy chair with a mechanism that raised and lowered the chair, making it easy to sit down and get up.

"Well, I saw two witches."

Anne used a crabbed finger to push the stop button on the oversized universal remote. Flora had a media center that a spaceship would envy. Not that she knew how any of it worked.

Eddie, a former student living on the first floor, had put it together for her. Anna had been listening to a mystery novel on CD because she couldn't hold a book anymore.

"Which witch?" Anne giggled. "You know what I mean."

"The one who would talk to me is named Bruleé, of all things. She's young and blonde and likes her pastels a little too much."

"Darn, not the one I saw in the park. I really wanted to know *her* name."

"I'm sure we can ask." Flora tossed her coat over the back of the sofa.

"Oh, I'm all giddy," Anne said. "Did you ask about the broom?"

Anne's enthusiasm was catching, and Flora found herself smiling. "I did, and she'll bring it."

"Oh, good!" Anne clapped her hands. "I wonder if there's enough room to fly in here."

The ceilings were a good twelve feet high. Flora looked up at the cracked plaster. A medallion circled the Victorian lighting fixture that hung in the middle of the living room.

"There might be. I don't really know how it works." Maybe the witch could hover a little, just to give Anne a demonstration. Even a few feet off the ground would make Anne happy. "Anyway, I'm ready for supper," Flora said, heading for the kitchen.

"What are we having tonight?"

"I don't know yet."

There was still too much basil in the scones. William could tell by the smell before he even took them out of the oven. The first batch had the same problem as the last dozen he'd tried to make.

Now he was out of strawberries. He smelled the scones as he pulled them out of the oven. He put the pan on a cooling rack next to scone attempt number one. The first batch was green with basil. The herb taste overwhelmed the strawberry. He might eat them anyway, although the sweet finish of the quarter cup of sugar was a bit off-putting.

He broke off a steaming piece of the fresh baked scone and blew on it. When the temperature was less than burning, he popped it in his mouth. The second batch was better than it smelled. William chewed thoughtfully to analyze the flavor.

The basil was much subtler than he had thought. The problem this time was too little strawberry. When he had a chance, he could go back to Good Earth for more. Or he could break down and see if Geoffrey stocked anything other than frozen berries this time of year. He drew a star beside the scone recipe he'd written down in one of his recipe notebooks. The first attempt was crossed out, and William erased the half cup of strawberries and changed it to three fourths of a cup, making a note to try freeze-dried strawberries as well.

He drummed his fingers on the stainless steel counter top. William looked around the stark, modern kitchen that would do any restaurant proud. Every surface was steel except for the marble slab for tempering chocolate. The equipment was professional grade, too, from the Vitamix to the walk-in freezer to the mixers.

He was annoyed he hadn't been able to make the scones on the first attempt, especially with so much gleaming technological help.

Not that he had any right to be irritated. He thought of the witches and their empty shop. That was where he should be getting scones. He shouldn't be trying to steal their recipe.

William tore both the scone recipes out of the spiral bound notebook and tossed the sheets into the garbage.

One of the perks of owning the sole gas station in a small town was that everyone had to stop there. Those pit stops inevitably brought a wealth of information, speculation, and idle gossip to his doorstep.

He'd heard from Matilda that Geoffrey Callister of all people was soft on the witches. William hadn't really believed her, since it was Geoffrey who had spread the rumors of their arrival in the first place. Although, gossip didn't necessarily mean condemnation.

The phonebook sat in a little cubby built into the wall, underneath where the cordless phone was mounted to the wall. William had a cell phone, but no one in town had the number. He kept it reserved for his private life. Only chef friends and fellow foodies had that number.

William pulled out the phonebook and found Geoffrey's home number, then dialed it on the cordless.

After two rings, a man answered. "Hello?"

"Hello, Geoffrey? It's William."

"Oh, hello. What can I do for you?"

William raised his voice. He could hear a TV playing in the background. A laugh track suddenly blared. "I wanted to talk to you about the witches."

"The w—" Geoffrey cut himself off. "'Scuse me," he said, probably to Claire.

William waited. He heard a shuffling then the TV faded away.

"That's better," Geoffrey said. "Now we can talk. I don't like to mention them in front of Claire. It's been a bit of a sore point lately."

"Sorry," William said. "Maybe I should let you go."

"No, no," Geoffrey said. "What did you want to ask?"

"Hmm, well." William wasn't sure what to say or how to say it. He wandered over to the breakfast nook next to the kitchen and sat down. "I was wondering if, as fellow business owners, we ought to do something for them." William rubbed his forehead, irritated at his own in-articulation.

"I've been wondering, too," Geoffrey said.

William straightened up in his chair. "Yes, it doesn't seem fair that a legitimate business can be chased off by a few superstitious people."

"I did some reading online about witches and, well, I think I overreacted."

"It's not your fault," William said. The blame lay squarely on Pastor Austin's shoulders as far as he was concerned. Austin's sermon against the witches was now town legend.

"Did you know they could heal people? Not everything, of course, but they use herbs and magic, and sometimes it works better than medicine."

"Huh," William grunted. "I just thought their pastries smelled good."

"You should've smelled today. All downtown smelled like chocolate for hours."

"Awwww." Most days all William got a god whiff of was gasoline and engine grease.

"I think the witches could bring in tourists. Lots of them."

"That's kind of why I called," William said. He could tell Geoffrey was building up a head of steam, and he didn't want to spend all night on the phone. "I was thinking we should give Dan a call, see if we can call a meeting of the Chamber of Commerce, and maybe help the witches out."

"I can give a presentation."

William cringed. Geoffrey had learned PowerPoint a few years ago, and he jumped at every chance to use it.

"Sure, maybe a short one on boosting tourism," William said.

"You know, I wanted to bring this whole witches thing up with Dan myself, but I just didn't want to be the only one. You know?"

"I know how that goes."

"Safety in numbers, right?"

"Exactly."

"Let me talk to a few other people, too," Geoffrey said. "I might be able to sway some fence sitters."

"All right, let me know what happens."

They said goodbye, and William put the cordless back in its cradle.

For once he was glad of the rampant town gossip. If people started taking a stand, Pastor Austin would have to back down.

The cell phone jingled with Matilda's ring tone as Eddie was letting himself into his apartment. His heart skipped a beat and his key missed the lock. He took a second to breathe deeply then pulled his cell from its pocket in his messenger bag.

"Hey." His voice was neutral but he couldn't help grinning like an idiot, and he was glad she wasn't there in person. He managed to insert the key into the lock on the second try and hurried in.

"Lunch, tomorrow," Matilda said.

"But it's Wednesday." Why was he protesting? Eddie mimed slamming his head into the plaster wall of the front entry.

"People eat on Wednesday."

"No, I know, just not us." Eddie dropped his bag to the floor and rested his forehead against the cool surface of the wall.

"Come on, it's not like you have a date," she chuckled.

Irritation squeezed his chest. Was it so inconceivable a woman could be interested in him? "You don't know that."

Three seconds of dead air and then, "Oh, come on, no, you don't."

"Yes, I do," Eddie said.

"With who?"

He could hear the doubt in Matilda's voice but it was wavering. Eddie flipped through a mental list of the single women in town.

He came up with, "I guess you'll find out on Wednesday."

"You're serious? If you're kidding, now would be a good time to tell me."

Eddie felt the words, "I'm joking" form in the back of his throat. He could hear the doubt in her voice, the mild distress that her good friend was unavailable. His first urge was to sooth her, tell her he was kidding, and go to lunch with her tomorrow. But he was tired of being "just a friend."

"Maybe we could do lunch later, like Thursday or Friday."

"I guess, maybe," Matilda said. "If you aren't busy." She sounded as unmoved as he felt.

"Yeah. I'll see you later," Eddie said. The cold casualness of his tone surprised him.

"Okay, then. Bye."

"Bye."

His hand shook a little as he pressed the end button on his cell. The display glowed, telling him how long the call with Matilda had lasted. One minute and forty two seconds.

Eddie felt very heavy, the weight of his gambit pressing down on his limbs like lead shackles. He let himself slump into the plaid recliner he kept by the window for reading.

He took a minute to stare up at the hairline cracks in the ceiling plaster. Why had he lied? The cell was still in his hand. He could call her and say, "Psych!" and they would laugh. And nothing would change. She would be with Hugh, and he'd be alone in his apartment every night.

The cell phone clattered to the floor. He had less than twenty-four hours to find a date. A believable date.

The Chamber of Commerce was housed in two rooms of the town hall.

Geoffrey and William had arrived early so they could wheel a TV cart in from the town council conference room. The town council got uppity about the Chamber using their meeting room, so they were relegated the smaller conference room. Geoffrey had put together what he felt was his finest presentation yet. The last one he made hadn't been shown because no one could figure out how to hook his laptop up to a TV. This time, Geoffrey put his video together in Moviemaker and he'd been able to burn it to a DVD.

"There, all plugged in," William said. He stood up and brushed his slacks.

Geoffrey pushed the open button on the DVD player. "Is there a remote for this?"

"I didn't see one."

The DVD tray slid open with a mechanical whir. Geoffrey pushed the power button on the TV. The screen faded in to solid blue. The blue standby mode was replaced with a piece of Halloween clip art that Geoffrey had downloaded just yesterday. Muzak played softly behind the opening titles, also downloaded and inserted as background music for the video. Geoffrey had wanted to add voice over but didn't know how.

"Witches, Tourism, and You…" faded in over the clip art of a cartoon witch.

Geoffrey grinned. He'd stayed up all night, working on the video, and he was pretty sure it had paid off. He pushed the stop button.

William nodded and leaned against the conference table.

"So how hard was the video?" William asked.

"Oh, not too bad. And you can use pictures and video from your camera, too."

"Nice," William said.

" Goddammit. I'm not watching another presentation."

Geoffrey and William both jumped at the gruff voice.

Geoffrey whirled around. Dan Harding had just come in. He looked like he'd come straight off the job. He wore a yellow vest and hardhat. Dan ran a construction business and liked to be hands-on, even though he was the boss.

"It's Moviemaker this time," William said in defense of Geoffrey.

Dan banged his scuffed briefcase on the conference table. "I don't care if it's a dancing robot. It better be under ten minutes."

"It's only four minutes long."

Dan sat down heavily, a frown etched into his jowls. "Wake me when everyone's here." His chin dropped to his chest and shut his eyes.

Geoffrey looked at William, and they both shrugged.

As head of the Chamber, Dan always took the seat at the head of the table, and the rest were first come, first served. Geoffrey took the seat closest to the TV and William sat opposite. The only sound was Dan's harsh breathing.

Next to arrive was Rosa. She took a seat quietly at the far end of the table, beside Geoffrey and William.

Henry Pickett, trailed by Junior Pickett, arrived next.

"I don't see why we have to have a special meeting. It's not right dragging a man out this late at night. Especially not when it's so damn cold. This better not take long." Henry grumbled all the way to his seat halfway down the table. He pulled off a furry cap with ear flaps, and tried to pat down an unruly mass of silver hair.

Dan took his feet off the table with a grunt. "Nice to see you, Henry."

"Are we going to start soon?" Henry asked.

"Not everyone's here yet," Geoffrey said.

"What's this about anyway?" Rosa asked. She looked at Dan, but Geoffrey answered.

"The witches."

"What about them?"

"That's it. I'm going home," Henry said.

"Dad, come on," Junior said.

"You're already here," Dan said. "Might as well stay for the show."

"Not more computer crap, is it?"

"I used Moviemaker this time," Geoffrey said.

The conference room door burst open and Lorelei O'Donnell fluttered in, bringing the heavy smell of her floral perfume and perm solution.

"Sorry, sorry, sorry," she said and sat next to Rosa. "What did I miss?"

"You're on time for once," Henry said.

"We've been late before," Junior said.

Henry crossed his arms and muttered.

Lorelei, grinning, took a seat next to William. "Evening."

"Evening to you."

Dan looked around the room. "Is this all who's coming?"

"Veronica said she'd try," Lorelei said.

"Let's just get this over with." Henry looked at his wristwatch and checked the time against the clock on the wall.

Geoffrey looked at Dan, who nodded. He stood up and cleared his throat.

"I wanted to talk to you about the witches," Geoffrey said. He inclined his head toward William. "William and I think they may be good for business. I did a little research on the Internet, and we think tourists would love a magical teashop."

He pushed PLAY on the DVD console and sat down while the video played. Geoffrey wished he'd had more time to spend making it. He could have downloaded better music and spell checked the text.

The video started with a brief explanation of witches' powers, adding that witches were ordinary people with a lot of psychic ability. Geoffrey had fudged that a little. Science didn't fully understand witch's powers yet, but he doubted anyone else in town had bothered to do any research, so this was the easiest explanation. The video went on to some statistics he'd found about the number of people who sought out witches for love potions, cures, fortune telling, and charms of all sorts.

The best bit of information he'd found were mystic bus tours. The video showed photos of busloads of happy tourists he'd taken from the website. The tours bussed people to witchy establishments in places like New York, Boston, and Salem. Sometimes, the tours even pulled in international customers wanting a look at exotic magic systems.

The video ended with a montage of cake, cupcakes, pies, and cookies. The last title superimposed over a picture of a teapot surrounded by tartlets read, "After all, who doesn't like desert?"

The TV screen went blue, and William clapped until he

realized no one else was joining in. Geoffrey smiled with gratitude. At least someone appreciated his efforts.

"That's it? Can I go?" Henry said, puncturing Geoffrey's triumph.

"Huh," Dan said. "Wasn't too bad. You spelled dessert wrong."

Geoffrey stood up. "I think the Chamber of Commerce should support the witches. We should look into getting the witch tours to come. Maybe they could come up in July, time it so the Victorian Faire is going on."

William stood up, too and Geoffrey was grateful for the support. "I think he's right," William said. "Plus, the town hasn't had a teashop in ages. They fit right in. The last travel magazine we were in said Midswich didn't have enough eating establishments."

"I don't care what some magazine says," Henry banged a liver-spotted fist on the table. "If those Satan worshippers stay, I'll pack up and move. See if I don't"

"Don't be ridiculous, Dad. You can't afford to move."

"I don't care. I'll sell off the shop. I'd be gone already if I thought they were staying."

"They don't worship Satan," Geoffrey said. He could see the meeting was spinning out of control. Maybe it was hopeless to try and change anyone's mind, but he'd thought at least the promise of tourism would appeal to their pocket books.

"People have a lot of wrong ideas about witches," William put in.

"You don't tell me what I believe."

"I have to agree, no respectable place should have witches. Let them go back to the city," Lorelei said.

"Father Halloran is satisfied the witches are safe."

"Like I listen to that Papist," Henry said, just loud enough to be heard.

"Care to speak up, Henry?" Rosa asked.

The old man grumbled under his breath then said, "No."

Geoffrey cringed. "Can we please just stick to the witches?"

Dan nodded once, then pointed to the TV. "You may have a point, Geoffrey. I've never known Midswich to turn its nose up at a busload of tourists. The town council ought to see this, and the rest of the Chamber at our regular meeting."

Geoffrey nodded. Finally, someone had shown some reason. It wasn't much, but Geoffrey allowed himself a moment of pride.

"Pastor Austin is going to hear about this," Henry said.

"I hadn't expected otherwise," Dan said. "Geoff, you may want to call around, take the temperature of the other shops around town. I think we all know where Henry stands."

Rosa snorted and rolled her eyes.

Henry stood up. "Well, I'm not listening to a second more of this crap." He walked stiffly from the room.

Junior let out a sigh when he was gone. "I'll try to talk to him," he said and stood up as well.

"I wouldn't waste my breath."

"For the record, I wasn't sure about the witches either, but whatever they're doing over there smells awful good," Junior said. He followed his father out the door, giving everyone a final wan smile and brief wave.

"All right, Geoff, you got your say. Emergency meeting adjourned." In the absence of a gavel, Dan tapped his hard hat on the table.

Without so much as a "Goodbye," Dan got up and left.

Geoffrey, William, Rosa, and Lorelei stared at each other for a second.

Lorelei's perma-smile didn't falter. "Much as I hate to agree with Henry, he has a point." The red and gold tip of her acrylic nail traced the fake wood grain.

"Even knowing the business the witches could bring in, you're still against them?" Geoffrey asked. He thought his movie had been pretty convincing.

"Look," Lorelei said, "Where I come from, decent people just don't have anything to do with witches. I doubt there's a publicly practicing witch south of West Virginia. Except New Orleans and Miami, and they don't count."

"That's just the kind of ignorance I'm talking about,"

Geoffrey said. Not that he was so much better, having only recently even bothered to learn a little about witches and witchcraft. Maybe if he'd known more, he could have welcomed them when they arrived instead of panicking like an idiot.

"I will ignore that because I'm a lady," Lorelei said. She gathered up her purse to leave.

"Has anyone here even talked to the witches?" Rosa cut in. "Maybe if people met them, they wouldn't be so scared. Father Halloran said they were very nice girls."

Geoffrey nodded. "We should give them a welcome party."

"I'd be willing to host it," William said. "The dining room's going to waste since Mom moved."

"Perfect." Geoffrey grinned. "The more of us who come out in support of the witches, the more Austin won't have a leg to stand on."

"Well, that's about as much nonsense as I can take for one night. I'll pray for all of you," Lorelei said from the doorway. "Good night."

When she was gone, Geoffrey said, "I hate it when people say that, like you're doing something wrong."

William and Rosa laughed.

"You can't expect to win everyone over," William said.

"You also can't argue with anyone whose made up their mind," Rosa added.

"Good enough we got Dan on board," William said.

Rosa got up. "We'll have to wait and see what happens. I'm not sure the mayor will cave. He's a member of Austin's church. *Buenos noches* and good luck," she said as she left.

In Geoffrey's elation over getting the president of the Chamber on board with keeping the witches, he'd forgotten about the mayor. Simon Kelly was a staunch Presbyterian and, while his religion didn't usually cross over into city affairs, the witches could be an exception.

Geoffrey looked at William and saw the same frustration on his face.

"I guess we'll just have to see what happens," Geoffrey said. His poor attempt at optimism received a nod.

"I guess so," William said.

Tuesday night was cold and moonless, the darkness relieved only by street lamps below. Bruleé had thought to get to Flora Barton's apartment by a short high arc, beginning at the teashop and ending at the address Flora had given her. Turned out she was wrong. At an altitude of seventy five feet, Bruleé looked down at the tidy grid of Midswich and realized she had no idea where anything was. She'd been too afraid of the villagers to take a walk around and familiarize herself with the town she'd insisted on moving to.

Bruleé had a map with her, but she was too high up to read a house number.

No help for it now. She descended until she was level with a streetlight at an intersection. The map was in her jacket pocket. She pulled it out and shook it open. The street signs put her on the corner of Greenwich and Manchester, four short blocks from Flora's house.

If she knew her way around town, she'd have been there already. Bruleé rattled around in her memory. She hadn't even taken Fraiche for a walk. Not a real one. Once, she'd walked him around the block a few times.

No wonder Anglaise hadn't bothered unpacking. Despite all her bluster and assurances, Bruleé hadn't tried to make herself part of the community at all. She was supposed to lead by example, and she barely left the teashop.

Bruleé dropped to the sidewalk. At this rate, it was taking her longer to fly to Flora's than it would have to walk. She tucked the broom under her arm and started up Greenwich.

The bitter chill nipped at her cheeks and, in the light of the street lamps, she saw her breath puff out in a cloud. After four blocks, her face was numb, and she was glad to find Flora's building.

The huge Victorian manor had been split into apartments sometime in its past, but it must have been a grand house in its day. Three stories, trimmed in gingerbread, climbed to the gabled roof. There was a tower with a witch's cap and a porch that wrapped around the side of the house. Lilac bushes, already green, were planted in the yard, and a row of blueberry bushes had been planted below the porch. A tall pine soared left of the path, and a circular bench ringed its trunk.

The only thing that looked out of place was a big metal mailbox, divided into nine smaller boxes, that sat next to the porch steps.

The porch light over the etched glass front door was on, and Bruleé could see a lit foyer beyond. She pulled open the front door, and a rush of warm air folded over her. To her left was a hall of closed doors, each one numbered, and to her right were wooden stairs with a scrolling banister.

Bruleé took the stairs to the third floor, keeping her broom upright so it wouldn't bang on the walls.

Flora's apartment was easy to find. There were only three apartments per floor and 3A was at the end of the hall.

Bruleé unwound her scarf from her face and took off her gloves. She felt underdressed in a pair of jeans, but since she'd mistakenly thought she was flying over, she'd worn pants. At least she'd ironed them before she left.

Since she was as tidy as she could get, she knocked.

Excited exclamations came from inside.

Flora answered the door. Her white hair made a braided loop around her head, and she looked impeccable in a loose, gray wool cardigan, with a belt tie and charcoal skirt that hit mid-calf. Very stylish, Bruleé thought. She was definitely the sort of old woman Bruleé hoped to be someday.

"Good evening," Flora said.

"Hi. Nice to see you again," Bruleé replied.

Flora peeked out the door and looked down the empty hallway.

"Anyone see you arrive?"

"No." Bruleé felt her stomach twinge. Disappointment settled in like bad meat loaf. She should have expected the question, but it still stung. She had gotten used to warmer receptions in the city.

"Come in before someone does." Flora stepped aside and Bruleé entered.

The apartment was a nice size for one person, but Bruleé could see it was straining under two occupants. The living room was spacious, with nice Victorian details, waist-high wainscoting, and a high ceiling. The apartment was in the front corner with the witch's cap, so they had a circular nook just off the living room. The nook held a twin bed and a telescope pointed toward the windows.

Sitting on the couch in front of one of the fanciest TV set-ups Bruleé had ever seen, was another old woman. Unlike Flora, she was in obvious disrepair. The woman wore a loose lavender housedress beneath a fuzzy bathrobe. Pink fake-fur slippers and socks kept her feet warm. But unlike Flora, she smiled, her big, warm grin of excitement matching the twinkle in her eyes.

"Ms. Bruleé, this is my sister, Anne," Flora said.

Bruleé held out her hand. "A pleasure to meet you."

Anne took it in both of her clawed, frozen hands.

"The pleasure is all mine," Anne said. "So, you're a witch."

"Yes, I am."

"Sit, sit." Anne patted the red velvet couch cushion beside her.

Propping her broom against the arm of the sofa, Bruleé sat down. She looked from Anne to Flora, who was still standing. Anne looked older, bent with disease, the wrinkles on her face deeper, but she still had brown in her bobbed hair.

"You must be the younger sister," Bruleé said.

"I am," Anne giggled. "Most people think I'm older."

"Men and children age you," Flora said. "Especially bad ones."

"Be sweet," Anne said.

Flora harrumphed, settling into a wing chair next to the sofa.

"What do you need me to do, dear?" Anne asked.

Bruleé sat down beside Anne on the couch, shifting to face her. "Just sit quietly. Try to clear your mind, but don't worry if you can't. I'm going to take your hands, and you'll probably feel a warming sensation. That's the magic. For now, I just want to see for myself how advanced the disease is. Sort of feel it out."

"I thought you'd need a circle or something."

"Casting circles aren't used for everything. For now, I'm not going to do much. Think of it like an initial exam. Once I know the state of the disease, I'll know more what I can do."

"All right, that sounds simple enough." Anne closed her eyes and took a deep breath.

Bruleé took her hands and did the same. She reached inside, calling up her magic. She focused on her physical connection with Anne, letting the energy flow into the older woman. Anne stiffened when she felt the psychic touch. Bruleé felt her defenses rise then relax to allow her in.

Immediately, Bruleé felt the disease. The inflammation, the overtaxed immune system fighting what it thought was an invasion of foreign tissue, all the while eating away at Anne's joints. The disease had begun in her hands. Bruleé could feel the cold quiet there, a deserted battlefield without a winner. The joints were stripped to the bone. Her hands would never recover.

There were other places, her spine, knees, hips, and toes that were still under attack. They still had cartilage and joint fluid, and may yet be saved.

Working magic on such a microscopic scale was difficult. Bruleé had read about it, but never tried it. What she wanted to do was soothe Anne's immune system. Get it to back down and return it to normal. She couldn't speak to the cells individually. Her consciousness was too large and their awareness far too small. She needed to balance the system somehow. The cells needed a healthy example.

Bruleé shifted her focus to herself, to get the feel of her own healthy immune system. She kept that feeling of her own, calmly functioning cells, imprinting that feeling into the energy she poured into Anne. Anne's immune system settled down. Bruleé didn't need it to start functioning perfectly right away. She just needed the attacking cells to back off.

As Bruleé pulled her energies back, she realized she'd spent too much magic without noticing. She'd gone too far, and done too much in one session. Bruleé had thought she could manage it. Now, panic tore at her, pulling her focus farther from her immediate problem. If she didn't get herself together, her dislodged consciousness could dissolve. Her body would be left alive, an empty shell doctors would declare comatose.

No one would know what had happened. She'd die of stupidity. If she'd had a mouth, she would have laughed.

This was Healing 101. Don't spend too much energy. Don't lose yourself in the healing process. Bruleé had come within months of completing her certificate for the healing arts. But then she'd gotten the call about her parents, and she'd left San Francisco two days later. Except for checking over the grocer, it had been over a year since she'd healed so much as a bruise. And now, to make such a rookie mistake? She hadn't thought she'd be so out of practice that she'd put herself in danger. And this time, there was no instructor to bring her back.

Bruleé forced herself to calm down, centering her energy. She needed to find the connection back to her own body. No matter how faint it was, it would still be there.

She felt a faint pull and, when she concentrated, the sensation grew stronger. Relief buoyed her. She now had a direction to go in. She wasn't back in her body yet, but Bruleé was certain she could make it now. Healing was her specialty after all.

Pulling her energies together, she hadn't realized how thin her energy reserves had grown. It was like shoveling water with her hands. The energy infusion might do Anne some good, but Bruleé would suffer for it.

Forcing herself in the direction of her body, she found the going hard. Bruleé fought her way upstream, unwilling to die from her own idiocy. Regret and anger fueled her journey. Then, with a surge of strength, she broke through, her consciousness once more back in her own body.

Her eyes fluttered open.

Anne's face, lined with concern, leaned close to her. Bruleé was slumped against the back of the couch. A crabbed hand with unbending fingers brushed hair out of her face.

"Are you all right, dear?" Anne asked.

Bruleé's head felt stuffed with cotton. Anne's face swam, appearing far away even though it was only inches from her. She blinked hard, but that didn't help.

"Could you help me lie down?" Bruleé whispered. Her eyes slid shut.

"Flora, help," was the last thing she heard.

The pungent stab of ammonia woke Bruleé. Her nose wrinkled, and she tried to wave away the terrible smell.

"Thank God! Miss Bruleé?"

She opened her eyes. Bruleé looked up at Flora and Anne. They hovered over her, concern etched on their chalky faces.

"We thought you might be dead," Flora said.

"Well," Anne said, "comatose maybe. But you gave us a real scare. You wouldn't wake up."

Bruleé stretched, relieved all her limbs were moving, even if they were weak.

"What happened?" Flora asked. She put the smelling salts down on the coffee table.

"Don't interrogate her," Anne told her.

"No, it's all right." Bruleé sat up. Blood rushed to her head, making her wobble. The room spun before settling down.

"I just used too much magic. I'm not in as a good a shape as I thought." She gave a weak laugh. "I need to practice more." She wasn't about to tell them she almost died on their couch. They didn't need to know, and she didn't need to embarrass herself.

"Will you be all right?" Anne asked.

"Yes," Bruleé assured her. "I just need rest. And a ride home."

Anne frowned. "You can't fly now? At all?"

Flora leaned over, catching Bruleé's eye. "She only cares because she wanted a demonstration."

"That's not fair."

"I can show you next time," Bruleé said.

"You mean, I'm not cured?"

The fading hope in Anne's voice struck Bruleé's heart, but she couldn't lie. She would have loved to tell Anne that she'd be fine, but this was only the beginning of a course of treatment. "Far from it, I'm afraid."

Anne wilted against her walker.

"But I can help," Bruleé said in a rush. "There are teas that will help, some foods, too, and more sessions like tonight. I can't fix what's done but I think I can prevent more damage. And you'll feel a lot better, I'm sure."

"Don't trouble yourself on my account," Anne said.

"What she means is, we don't have much money," Flora said.

"That's not it." Anne pointed at Bruleé. "Look at the poor girl. She can barely sit up. It's not worth putting someone in danger to help me."

"I'm not in danger," Bruleé lied. She was determined to make it true. She could brush up and practice her healing. Next time, she'd be prepared.

"If she can help, let her help," Flora said.

"No."

"No isn't an option, Anne. Either you get better, or we have to move to a nursing home."

Anne looked sharply at her sister.

"I'm old, too." Flora's face blushed with angry red spots. "I can't take care of you by myself. You can't even get downstairs anymore. What if there's a fire?"

Anne leaned heavier on her walker, a drying vine held up only by the trellis. Her feet shuffled and didn't seem to know which way to go. She looked at Bruleé, her eyes shiny with unshed tears. "You can really help?"

Bruleé hesitated. She looked from one sister to another. She hadn't known how important this was to them. "You won't be completely healed. I can't restore the joints, but I can do something. Give me time. How much improvement there will be, I don't know. But if you can wait a few months, we'll see what happens. If it isn't enough, then you can move. I'm sorry that's the best I can do."

"Stop apologizing to us," Anne said.

"I'd like you do what you can," Flora said. She glanced at her sister. Anne was silent. "How much is tonight going to cost?"

Bruleé hadn't come with a fixed notion. The teas and spells had set prices and she'd apprenticed in healing but had never done this on her own before, let alone charged. She knew a Boston witch who specialized in Reiki and charged $300 a session. If the two old ladies could afford that, they wouldn't be sharing a one-bedroom apartment.

The drug dealer option then.

"The first one's free," Bruleé said with a smile she hoped was wining and not too exhausted-looking.

Anne brightened. Flora's face scrunched with suspicion.

"How much after that?" she asked.

"Well, that depends on how much I help."

"Thank you so much, dear," Anne said.

Flora opened her mouth, but it was Anne's turn to silence her with a daggered look. Flora snapped her mouth shut.

Bruleé searched for a clock. There was a decorative wall clock hung over the entertainment center. Nearly eleven p.m. How long had she been unconscious? Bruleé wasn't even sure how long she'd been in the healing trance.

"Can I get a ride home?" Bruleé looked at Flora.

Flora nodded. "Of course."

Flora had a much smaller car than Bruleé anticipated. The little sedan was parked behind the apartment building. Bruleé thought she would drive a titanic land yacht from the sixties, not a compact economy model.

"Can you make it a block if I drop you off at the town square?" Flora asked as she unlocked the car. "I know that sounds horrible but—"

"You can't be caught with a witch," Bruleé finished for her.

She nodded. "I'm sorry to put you through all that and come out so ungrateful."

Bruleé put her broom in the backseat. The handle stuck out the window. Flying brooms were longer and heavier than ordinary cleaning brooms. The bristles were thick and long, made of dried broom, rowan twigs, and a core of dried lavender that wasn't very traditional, but lent the broom speed and maneuverability. Every witch liked to tweak their broom for performance.

Flora drove slowly, but they arrived at the town square faster than if Bruleé had walked. But just barely.

Bruleé opened the passenger side door.

"Wait," Flora said. She pulled a wallet from her purse and produced two, twenty- dollar bills.

"I told you, it was free," Bruleé said.

"You passed out on my sofa. I pay my debts."

Bruleé wasn't sure that made sense. She looked at the money, then at Flora's stone hard expression.

"All right," Bruleé said. "I'll come by tomorrow with a tea I think will help."

Flora nodded. "Thank you."

Bruleé took her broom from the back seat. "Good night." She waved as Flora drove off.

Forty more dollars for the till. A total of almost eighty dollars for the week, and it was only Tuesday. Perhaps her prosperity spells were working after all. She decided to go home and burn a green candle tonight, and to drink some clove tea for success. If she could stay awake. Maybe she'd had enough prosperity for one day. Her eyelids were drooping by the time she crossed the street.

Hillary Johnson was a new teacher at Midswich Elementary, and she was the prettiest non-date Eddie could find at short notice. She wanted to put together a sort of book-reading scavenger hunt for her third-graders, and she'd been after Eddie to help her with the list for a week.

They had the same lunch hour, so Eddie suggested Rosa's. He needed witnesses, and he was hoping Matilda would drop by and see them.

It didn't hurt that Hillary was attractive. Petite and dark skinned, she had high cheekbones and a warm smile that disarmed even the naughtiest kids at school. If she didn't make Matilda jealous, then it was time for Eddie to give up on her and start trying to find a girl who liked him as more than just a friend.

Eddie poked his head into Ms. Johnson's classroom.

"Ready to go?" he asked.

"Yup." She took her purse from a desk drawer then grabbed her larger paper-stuffed school tote from underneath. "Are we walking?"

"Yeah, bring your coat if you get cold."

Her leopard-print fur jacket hung on a peg behind the desk. She slipped it on, joining Eddie at the door. She locked the door and they left.

Consolata gave Eddie a long, smoldering stare of disapproval when he walked in with Hillary. Despite being an outsider, Consolata had fit right into the Midswich social circle, and she was now one of the town's more outspoken busy bodies. If Matilda didn't come in today, it wouldn't matter. Consolata would no doubt give her an earful. More than once, Consolata had joked about what a cute couple he and Matilda made. Matilda laughed it off, but Eddie could tell Consolata was sincerely trying to sway her.

"Table for two, please," Eddie said.

"Yeah, it'll be a minute," Consolata said.

Eddie looked around. The lunch rush hadn't started yet, and there were a dozen empty tables.

Consolata left her post at the hostess podium and disappeared into the kitchen.

"Is she kidding?" Hillary checked her watch.

"I hope so," Eddie said.

From the kitchen, there was a heated exchange of loud voices firing off rapid volleys of Spanish.

Eddie thought he caught something like, "I don't care, just seat them," coming from Rosa. His Spanish was getting rusty.

Consolata reappeared. She grabbed two menus from the hostess podium.

"This way," she said.

Eddie and Hillary looked at each other. The service was normally better.

Consolata was heading to a table in the back close to the door to the restrooms.

"I was hoping for a window seat," Eddie said.

"They're reserved." She gave him an arctic look, colder than a nor'easter. She threw the menus down and said, "Here's your table, anything to start?"

Eddie and Hillary both said, "Water." Best not to poke the bear.

Consolata left and Eddie looked at Hillary.

"Do you think it's safe to order lunch?" Eddie whispered.

Hillary laughed, covering her mouth so Consolata wouldn't hear. "I don't know," she whispered.

"I hope they don't keep poison in the place."

Hillary's shoulders shook with silent laughter. "We'll be leaving feet first."

Eddie snorted. They took a minute to get over the giggles. Finally, Hillary said, "You brought the reading list, right?"

Eddie pulled four printed pages from his jacket pocket.

"There's a list of below-level books for the kids not up to speed, some for those on level, and a few higher-level books for the adventurous. I'm pretty sure they have study guides you can get online, too, so you don't have to make up your own questions."

"Perfect." Hillary took the list and started reading.

Consolata came back with their water. She saw Hillary reading the papers and looked puzzled.

"What do you want?" she asked, order pad in hand.

"Lobster taco, please," Hillary said.

"I'll have chicken tamales with salsa verde."

She wrote the order down. "Got it." Consolata left again, still looking troubled.

"Well, that went better," Hillary said.

"Yeah." Eddie might have to have a talk with Consolata before he left. If she figured out it was just a business lunch, she'd reassure Matilda nothing was going on.

"The school library has all these books?" Hillary asked.

Eddie tried to remember what they were talking about.

"Yes, but not always at the same time. Your kids may have trouble getting all the books if the whole class will be wanting to check out the same things."

"Maybe this wasn't such a good idea," Hillary said. "I hadn't thought of that."

"The public library has most of these books, too. Do they have to read in a specific order?"

"No."

"Then you should be all right."

Consolata brought chips and salsa. She had a knowing snicker on her face, and Eddie's heart did a sudden gymnastic move.

"Here's your starter. The chips are hot out of the fryer." She gave Eddie a wink as she put down the basket of chips.

"Thank you," Hillary said. She was still pondering the reading list and didn't see the wink.

Cold sweat filmed over Eddie's forehead. She left before he could think of anything to say. Of course, he couldn't say anything in front of Hillary, anyway.

"Um, I forgot to get extra salsa verde for my tamale," Eddie said. He stood up. "I'm just going to tell Consolata now."

"Okay." Hillary didn't look up.

Eddie caught Consolata as she was heading to the kitchen.

"Hey, um." He couldn't think where to start.

"It's okay. I know what you're doing," Consolata said.

"And what am I doing?"

"Making Matilda jealous, duh," she said.

"Oh. How did you—"

"I watch movies."

"But—"

"And TV."

"All right, I didn't say it's a good plan," Eddie said. "Or original. But what am I supposed to do?"

"Man up and tell her you like her."

"Aside from that."

Consolata let out a low whistle through her teeth and shook her head. "Well, you're in luck. Claire called in the lunch orders for Barely Hair, and your girlfriend's coming to pick it up."

"That's perfect."

"Guess I should shut up and enjoy the show then."

Eddie started back to his table then remembered his cover. "Uh, and can you bring extra salsa verde?"

Hillary was on the last of the reading list when he sat back down.

"This is a good list," she said. "Thanks for putting it together."

"No problem."

"Don't be modest."

"I went to a ton of trouble, late hours, working by candlelight."

"Sorry about that."

"I'm kidding," he told her. "I know the books really well, and there are recommended reading lists online."

She smiled and joked, "Don't scare me like that. I was getting worried for a second. Next you'll tell me you got consumption staying up so late. "

They chatted about school and the other teachers until the food came. Then they fell silent as they ate. Eddie kept glancing at the door.

The bells over the door jingled when Eddie wasn't looking. His head snapped up. There was Matilda.

She spotted him immediately in the near empty restaurant. Her pale face went stiff, and Eddie could have sworn the red spots on her cheeks were from more than the cold.

Just to drive the point home that he was here with a woman, Eddie gave her a friendly wave.

Her hand did little more than twitch in his direction.

While she was standing there, Eddie had one last card to play. He turned to Hillary.

"That bracelet you're wearing is amazing. I've been noticing it all lunch."

"You like it?" Hillary held out her wrist.

"May I?"

"Sure."

Eddie took her hand with his. He traced the bold lines of the gold metal.

"It's heavy," he said. "It's not real gold, is it?"

"If this was real gold, you think I'd be teaching?" She laughed. "Nah, I would be, but I'd own my own school. It's just brass. I got it in Lagos."

"Where—wait, Lagos, as in Africa?"

"Nigeria."

"You've been to Africa?" The farthest Eddie had ever been was Puerto Rico with his parents.

"Twice. But I want to go again."

"Wow. Tell me about it."

Her face lit up. "Seriously?"

"Yeah."

"All right, but remember you asked for it. You're just lucky I can't show you the slide show."

Hillary started in on the story of her first trip to Africa. Eddie listened, and he was so engrossed he didn't even notice when Matilda left.

The Presbyterian church's meeting hall was a separate building, half a block from the church, across the small parking lot. The church was too historic to build an addition, and the basement rooms were small and used for storage. The meeting hall had been built in the sixties by a local architect who liked modern architecture a little too much. Or maybe, he just liked pancakes. The steel and glass A-frame building looked just like the old IHOPS, and tourists still pulled into the church parking lot looking for their daily carbo load.

Today, half a dozen cars were parked close to the front entrance. Pastor Austin was presiding over the first meeting of the newly named Midswich Anti-Magic Coalition.

Pastor Austin sat in front of a small group of parishioners

whom he considered his most dedicated at the moment. Ever loyal, Penelope Owen, Emma, Henry Pickett, Councilwoman Jillian Hartwell, Kim Bradly, and Lorelei O'Donnell, who was a Baptist but a good Christian anyway, and the one who alerted Pastor Austin to the plans of the Chamber of Commerce.

"Now that we've decided on a name, we should get to the matter at hand," Pastor Austin said. He looked around the table, making sure there were no dissenters. They had already spent forty-five minutes on the name.

They all nodded.

"Very good. Suggestions?"

"We should protest with signs in front of town hall," Kim Bradly said.

"I'm no damn hippie," Henry said.

"I work there," Jillian said, "I don't want to have to cross a picket line."

"The entire point is you wouldn't go to work," Kim told her.

"The protest has merit." Austin raised his voice to put an end to a conversation sure to derail them. "We will need a show of numbers. How many people do you think we can get before the next meeting of the Chamber of Commerce?"

Emma shifted in her plastic chair.

"Emma, do you have something to say?" Austin looked at her.

"I don't feel right about this. I don't want to come out against anyone in town."

Lorelei nodded. "The Chamber is full of reasonable people. They'll listen if we present our side."

"The problem is the witches." Henry slapped the tabletop to get everyone's attention. "Get rid of them, and it won't matter who colludes with 'em."

Kim chuckled. "Why don't we picket their shop? No one can accuse us of interfering with their business,"

"I'd be happy to do that," Penelope said. "I think I've even got poster board left over from garage sale signs."

The group nodded. Austin knew agreement when he saw it.

As long as someone was taking an active role against the witches, he was satisfied. For two weeks in a row, his sermons had focused on the evils of magic, witchcraft, and obesity, but there had still been the alarming smell of chocolate hanging over downtown last week, like high caloric doom. Someone must have ordered a cake. If even one person in town was brave enough to break the ban, then the floodgates would open.

"Good," Austin said. "We'll protest the shop itself. Penelope, you should be in charge of making signs."

"I'd like to help with that," Lorelei said. "Any chance to break out the glitter."

"Very good. I'll e-mail the congregation and see if we can't get more volunteers. When we have enough people, we can organize into shifts, and protest during their business hours."

Jillian raised her hand. "I think we'll need a permit from the police."

Austin frowned. What had become of the Constitution? "Could you see to that, Jillian?"

"Sure."

"Permit or no, I believe we need to send a message and start protesting now."

"If it'll get rid of the damn witches, you have permission to march in front of my shop," Henry said.

"Thank you, that should help," Austin said.

"Couldn't we just, I don't know, maintain the boycott?" Emma asked.

"The boycott isn't working. Unless they're just baking for themselves, which I doubt," Penelope said.

"I'd also like to present our side to the Chamber, protest or no," Lorelei told them.

"All good plans," Austin said. He turned to Emma. "I wish the boycott had worked as well, but obviously, they're getting customers somehow."

"I haven't seen anyone go in," Penelope cut in.

"Perhaps phone orders. Whatever the method, it means they are making money." Austin saw her wavering commitment, and he hoped to bring her back. Maybe she'd tasted the witch's wares. Whatever the cause, he must bring her back or cut her loose.

"But, surely not enough to pay the rent," Emma said.

"I'm not taking the chance," Henry said. "You do whatever you want out front."

"If it soothes your soul, Emma, you don't need to take part. But you will be sorely missed."

He didn't want Emma pulling down morale, but he needed every soldier he could get for the crusade. If morality couldn't win her over, guilt might.

She smiled gratefully. "I'll think about it."

Austin returned the smile, but he was annoyed she'd shown up, only to let him down. What was the point, if she was already on the witches' side? "So we all know what we're doing?" He surveyed the group. They nodded. "Very good. Meeting adjourned."

"I brought refreshments," Emma said. She got up and went to the meeting hall kitchen. She came back a minute later with a plate of homemade chocolate chip cookies.

Austin was dismayed to see everyone's eager looks. Even Henry perked up. He was reaching for a cookie—calories— before Emma even set down her plate.

"Well, I should go start on that e-mail," Austin said. He shuffled his notes, tapping the sheets on the table.

"I didn't forget about you, Pastor." Emma gave him a wink. She pulled a Cliff bar from her purse.

Austin blinked a couple time, then set down his notes.

"Thank you. How thoughtful."

He was used to being left out of the social bonds of eating. He had intended to leave and get some work done. Instead, he found himself chatting with his parishioners for another forty minutes, long after the cookies were gone, most of them having disappeared into Henry's pocket.

Chapter

F raiche's pom-pom tail mopped the floor in front of the delivery door. He let out a little whine and looked around the kitchen.

Caramel sat at the kitchen island, reading *Food and Wine* magazine. She wasn't really that interested, but the only magazines around the house were either food, which were for Anglaise, or fashion magazines that Bruleé brought home for the seasonal collections.

"Just a minute, Fraiche," she said. Caramel was waiting for Bruleé to finish blending the arthritis tea—made of dong quai, white willow, fever few, and a generous dose of real cinnamon.

They had all of one regular client now. Not that Caramel wasn't grateful, but the shop was still empty, and the cash register gathered dust and spider webs. If this business failed, they'd have to go live with Aunt Licorice. After that, there was nowhere to go.

"That dog better not be in the kitchen," Anglaise yelled from upstairs.

"C—come on."

Caramel got up and scooped Fraiche off the floor. She went into the shop. Bruleé had spent all afternoon adding healing spells to each separate ingredient in the arthritis tea. Normally, she would have done it after hours, but with no customers to wait on, Bruleé had taken over the big square table in back of the shop for her workspace. Caramel had been left to sweep up the salt circle Bruleé used for casting.

Caramel always wondered why she couldn't just use a chalk circle like everyone else. The least she could have done was vacuum it up herself.

Bruleé had come back down after dinner to blend the tea, and now she was packing measured amounts into tea bags.

"A—are you a—almost done? Caramel asked. Fraiche whined, eager for another walk. That was the only reason Caramel had agreed to go with Bruleé to meet the client. Bruleé had suggested combining business with walkies, and Caramel had agreed. She was regretting it. She could have taken Fraiche twice around the town square and been in for the night. Bruleé had firmly insisted this would be *fun* and that Caramel *needed to get out more*. It was the same refrain she heard, day after day.

"Only three more tea bags to pack," Bruleé said.

"I—it's g—getting late."

Bruleé looked at her as if she'd announced the moon had turned into flashing neon.

"It's only 8:30. How is that late?"

"I—it's d—d—dark out."

Bruleé paused and her jaw tightened. "You should have said how nervous you are earlier. I could have given you some calming tea. It'll take too long to cast the spell now. But you agreed, and you're going."

Caramel sat down at the table and hugged Fraiche close. She knew Bruleé and Anglaise were trying to help, but they didn't understand how hard she found it to do things other people did all the time, like talk to strangers, and make idle conversation. Bruleé and Anglaise had never been shy. Bruleé charged ahead, saying, "Everything will be all right." And Anglaise just charged ahead with whatever popped into her head.

Bruleé filled another teabag with a narrow ended scoop. She folded the teabag closed and sealed it with a food safe staple.

"You'll like Anne," Bruleé said. "She's a sweet lady. Flora is more forthright, but she means well."

Caramel said nothing. Obviously, Bruleé wasn't going to

let her back out now. She pulled Fraiche's leash from her pocket and clipped it to his collar.

"There, all done." Bruleé finished the last tea bag. She put it into the folded paper box with the others. Bruleé had made two neat rows of handmade tea bags. She folded the box lid down. Printed on the lid was the Tea Times Three teapot logo.

"Get your broom," Bruleé told her.

"I th—thought we w—w—were walking."

"We are. I want to be able to make—" Bruleé stopped. "Anne wants a demonstration of flying."

Caramel pursed her lips. That wasn't what she'd been about to say. Her mind filled in the blanks. 'I want to be able to make a quick getaway' was where that sentence had been heading. There was a saying among witches, "One month, then free and clear." If the locals hadn't driven you out of town by then, they weren't going to. Until then, no witch could rest easy.

Bruleé carried the box of tea, and Caramel followed her to the kitchen. Their brooms were kept in a closet under the stairs. Bruleé grabbed hers first, then Caramel took hers.

"I c—c—c—could just cast a s—s—see-me-not spell," Caramel said.

Bruleé shook her head. "Anne wants to see one of us fly, and if we're going to live here, we ought to be able to walk the streets."

"Th—then why aren't w—we d—doing this in the day time?"

Caramel received a sharp, narrow-eyed look from Bruleé. "Is that sarcasm, little sister?"

"N—n—n—o."

Bruleé laughed and slapped Caramel on the back. "You're too smart for your own good."

Caramel relaxed when Fraiche whined and struggled in her arms. She'd been clutching him too tight.

They left the teashop from the back door. Bruleé locked it behind them, still grinning. "I know. I'm a total hypocrite," Bruleé told her. "But our one dear patron, Flora, doesn't want to be seen with us, so we have to go at night."

Caramel nodded, setting Fraiche down. He immediately started running, only to be yanked to a stop by the end of his leash.

Gloomy silence settled over them as palpable as the spring chill. Only Fraiche was unaffected. He strained at his leash, dashing ahead, then stopping abruptly to smell every lamppost and corner. This was his longest walk to date, and the territory was brand new.

Caramel stared at the gray sidewalk that glittered in the streetlights. For the hundred, thousand, millionth time in a year, she missed her parents. Her home.

A touch on the arm startled Caramel out of her reverie. She jumped, accidentally yanking on Fraiche's leash.

"Sorry," Bruleé said. "We're here. You were about to walk right past."

Caramel looked up to see an extravagantly frosted Victorian manor, dripping with fancy shingles. The house was made to be rendered in gingerbread. Come Yule, Caramel decided to do just that. Provided they were still here.

The third floor hallway was quiet and smelled overwhelmingly of pot roast. Caramel stood behind Bruleé as she knocked on the door.

An old woman with sharp eyes answered the door.

"Good evening," she said. "Sorry for making you walk, er, fly over."

"We walked," Bruleé said. She stepped aside and Caramel was visible.

Caramel froze, body going rigid, like an exposed animal.

"Evening," said the woman.

"Flora, this is my little sister, Caramel. Caramel, Flora."

Fraiche yipped, tail waving and Caramel wished she had his confidence.

"N—n—n—n—n—n—n," was as much of "nice to meet you" as she could squeeze out.

"She's shy," Bruleé said.

Flora nodded. "Please come in."

They went inside. Fraiche lifted his nose in the air, taking in the new smells of the apartment.

The place was small, made smaller by the bed in the turret nook. Caramel saw another old woman in the bed.

"Anne, hi." Bruleé waved and stepped over to her. Flora followed. Caramel hung back, sticking close to the door. Fraiche wandered to the end of his leash, sniffing the corner of the heavy old Victorian sofa.

"Hello, Bruleé," Anne said. "I see you brought a guest."

Caramel felt their eyes on her. She shifted. The words of her favorite *see-me-not* spell leapt to mind. She'd cast it, if only there weren't all these people looking at her.

"Caramel, this is Anne," Bruleé told her.

She nodded in Anne's direction, but couldn't bring herself to do more. Caramel let her long, straight hair fall over her face and peered out from behind it.

"You two brought your brooms and a third little visitor," Anne said.

"Sorry, Fraiche, I forgot to introduce you. Caramel, let him go," Bruleé said.

Caramel dropped the end of the leash, and Fraiche darted away, short legs pumping. He leapt into Bruleé's arms.

"This is Fraiche."

Anne chuckled, petting Fraiche as well as she could with her unbending fingers. Fraiche licked her hands, happy for the attention.

"Today, you'll get your flying demonstration, too."

Bruleé handed the box of tea to Flora. "I wrote down the instructions, but I'd like to go over them with you. They need to be followed exactly." Bruleé took a folded sheet of paper from her jacket pocket.

Flora and Bruleé huddled up as Bruleé explained, "Don't microwave the water. That just kills it. Bring it to just under a boil on the stovetop. Do you have an electric kettle?"

"No."

"I recommend getting one. Anyway, bring the water to almost boiling and then let it cool before using it. You don't want to pour boiling water over tea."

Bruleé went on like that for another ten minutes. She was a tea-brewing textbook. Flora listened patiently, nodding here and there. The tea had to be taken in the morning and evening so the dozen teabags Bruleé had spent all day spelling was only a six-day supply.

Caramel took a few steps toward the bed. She kept an eye on Fraiche, who was basking in Anne's attention. She envied the little dog. He was better with people than she was.

Anne looked up and smiled at Caramel. "Do you mind showing me how you fly?"

Caramel shook her head. Flying was about her only skill, unless fading into the background and breaking spells counted.

"You're so lucky. I wish I could fly." Anne turned to look out of the night-black windows.

Everyone, who wasn't a witch, envied flying the most. A faint smile tugged at the corners of Caramel's lips. Flight was wonderful, but sometimes she thought she'd trade all magic just to spit out a complete sentence.

"I've never seen a witch fly before," Anne said. "I don't think I've lived anywhere big enough to have witches."

Caramel shook her head. She took a few more steps toward the bed. "Th—th—that m—m—might not be true."

"Hmm?" Anne cocked her head a little. "What was that?"

"Some w—witches don't m—m—make a living a—at m—magic, so y—you m—might n—n—not know." She got her voice slightly above a whisper.

"I didn't think of that," Anne said. She smiled. "Well, if I could fly, I'd never put my feet on the ground—"

"All right," Bruleé said, cutting in. "Anne, you'll take the tea twice a day for the next six days and then I'll be back for another healing session. I'll be ready this time."

Caramel eyed Bruleé from under a veil of hair. Bruleé had come home hours late last time, falling asleep in her clothes on the couch.

"How does the tea taste?" Anne asked.

Bruleé screwed up her face in an attempt to find a diplomatic way to say it tasted awful. Caramel had seen that look a hundred times herself. She shook her head.

Anne noticed. "Caramel says it tastes bad."

Caramel felt the wildfire spread of a blush. She quickly

retreated two steps backward. Bruleé looked at her wonderingly. Anne laughed. "It's all right. I don't mind. I've taken so many unpleasant medicines, what's one more?"

Bruleé was still looking at Caramel. Her questioning look had faded to a good-humored twinkle in her eye. Then she turned back to Anne. "Caramel's right. It doesn't taste very good. But you can't add sugar or sweeteners. Just let it cool and drink it as fast as possible."

Anne nodded. "I can do that."

Bruleé grabbed her broom from where she'd left it leaning against the kitchen counter. "Now, would you like to see us fly?"

Anne's already bright face lit up a few more watts. "Oh, yes!"

Bruleé nodded. "Caramel?"

Caramel's broom was propped against the sofa. She picked it up. Lying still, the broom weighed a good ten pounds. The solid carved rowan shaft was four inches around and the bristles dense and heavy. The dried plant materials were far weightier than synthetic bristles. No witch she'd ever heard of could fly on plastic bristles.

When Caramel touched the broom, it became light as a twig. Her magic infused the wood, bringing it to life. She held the broom parallel to the floor, tucking her skirt between her legs. Normally Caramel would wear biker shorts under her skirt, but she was wearing tights today, and she didn't intend to get more than three feet off the floor.

Bruleé had changed her clothes before they left, from skirt to jeans, so she could fly to the ceiling if she wanted to.

Caramel closed her eyes and used her magic to gently push against the floor. She always felt a bit like a buoyant cork in water. She wanted to soar up and up and up, but the point was balance, maintain altitude, and direction. She hooked one foot over the broom handle and lifted about three feet off the floor. Anne and Flora gasped. Indoor flight was touchy because of ceilings and furniture. So Caramel let her leg dangle, in case she needed to jump off.

Anne laughed and clapped her hands. She sat on the edge

of the bed and stared up at Caramel, eyes wide as a child's. Then Flora joined in. She looked amazed as well, but more as if what she was seeing went against the laws of nature than because of pure delight. Bruleé grinned at her, pride shining plainly on her face.

Caramel's magic shriveled. Too many people were looking at her again. A flurry of fear, expectations, and embarrassment swept through her. She dropped quickly and landed on her feet.

The applause rose as Bruleé joined in.

"Well, I never," Flora said

"Now, you, Bruleé," Anne said.

Bruleé stepped to the middle of the living room and Caramel gratefully retreated against the wall.

Bruleé rose quicker and higher than Caramel had. Flora and Anne probably couldn't tell the difference, but Caramel could see her confidence and power in the way she controlled her broom. Bruleé hovered for a second, two feet below the ceiling, then turned in a tight circle to fly once around the room.

Caramel peeked out from behind her hair. Anne and Flora looked up, faces rapt. Even Flora seemed to be warming up to magical flight.

After her circuit of the room, Bruleé set down, drifting gently to the floor as she pulled her magic from the broom, making it heavier and heavier. She slid off the broom and took a bow.

Anne clapped as hard as she could with her crabbed hands. Flora whistled through her teeth.

"I'm so glad I lived to see this," Anne said.

Flora glared at her. "You'll live to see more."

"Anyway," Anne said, ignoring Flora. "Thank you so much."

"Our pleasure," Bruleé told them. She joined Caramel by the door. "We should be getting back."

She rubbed Caramel's back, and Caramel knew Bruleé was leaving early so she could get home. She was grateful to leave, but sorry Bruleé was cutting the visit short. Caramel's grip tightened on the broom handle. She had the feeling Bruleé would stay longer if she weren't there.

"Good night," Anne said from the bed. She waved at them. "Please come by anytime, both of you, or either one."

"We will, I'm sure," Bruleé told her. "I'll check in with you this week."

Bruleé opened the apartment door.

"Hang on," Flora said. "You haven't been paid yet. Wait there."

Caramel saw Bruleé frown with discomfort. She could tell Bruleé liked the two women a lot, and didn't want to charge them. Caramel looked around the tiny apartment. She probably worried that their standard rates would bankrupt Flora and Anne, who obviously lived on the dreaded senior curse of a fixed income.

Spells weren't cheap, though. The salt Bruleé cast her circles with was Hawaiian sea salt. She'd spent their entire day spelling the ingredients, and if the teashop had customers, she'd have had to do it after hours.

"You really don—" Bruleé started, but Caramel stopped her with a tug on the arm.

"What?"

Caramel pulled her down. Bruleé stooped so she could hear Caramel whisper.

"F—F—Flora's p—proud and w—we n—n—need the money."

Bruleé's sigh was heavy with resignation. "You're right."

She straightened up as Flora came back with her purse.

"How much for the tea?"

A dozen spelled, custom blended teas cost a hundred dollars. Anglaise would be pleased, or at least less snide when they got home.

"Forty dollars, same as last time," Bruleé said.

Caramel cringed. She looked up at Bruleé. Bruleé kept her eyes fixed on Flora. Caramel tugged Bruleé's sleeve again, but Bruleé kept smiling at Flora and shook her off.

Even Flora paused at this news, frozen with her hand reaching into her purse.

"Are you sure?"

Caramel yanked her sister's sleeve again.

Without looking at her, Bruleé said, "Why don't you take Fraiche and wait in the hall?"

That was the end of it. Caramel had seen that fixed wall of a smile on Bruleé's face before. The expression was more implacable than her rare shows of anger.

Caramel let go of her sleeve and clipped the leash back onto Fraiche's collar. "C—c—come on."

She didn't have long to wait. Bruleé appeared a moment later, presumably with forty dollars in her purse. That would bring their total income for the day to exactly forty dollars.

Caramel stared at her as they walked down the hall. "B—B—B—"

"All right, I know, we're going broke. We've been living on bologna sandwiches for weeks now, but I can't bleed two old women dry."

"I—it's n—n—not—"

"I know that, too," Bruleé said. She sighed and, for just a second, Caramel saw Bruleé's optimism slip and fall.

Her stomach lurched. If Bruleé was losing heart, then disaster was closer than she thought.

Caramel and Bruleé skimmed over the ground on their brooms at an altitude of three feet. Caramel wanted to get home quickly, but Bruleé still wanted to tempt angry locals to make a move. At least, that's what Caramel thought must be happening.

So far, not much had happened. A few people had seen them fly by, running outside for a better look, but no one had thrown anything. Even at the best of times in Boston, kids, teenagers, and the occasional gang of drunks would try throwing rocks, or shoes, or something worse at a flying witch. Every witch in the city knew better than to fly at street level, unless taking off or landing.

Still, Caramel was relieved when they arrived at the town square, just a block from home.

"Caramel!"

The voice startled Caramel and Bruleé. Caramel lost her

one-handed grip on Fraiche, who had been struggling to get down the whole broom ride home.

Bruleé looked for the sound of the voice. Fraiche made a dash for the open green of the square.

"See me not, see me not, wrapped in shadow—"

The words of the spell popped out of her mouth unbidden. They were a reflex action she'd been using it so long.

"Wait." Bruleé touched her arm. "It's your friend."

The spell died, incomplete and uncast.

"I d—d—don't have a f—friend," Caramel said. Then she looked where Bruleé was pointing.

Across the street was the goth girl that kept coming to the bakery with her friends. Caramel hadn't seen her right away because of her standard-issue black outfit. Fraiche had noticed her, however, and he ran straight to her, an creamy blur under the streetlight.

Alyss caught Fraiche as he yipped and jumped into her arms.

"Why don't you go talk to her?" Bruleé said. "I have to get back and clean up."

Caramel shook her head, but Bruleé just smiled and took off on her broom. Caramel was tempted to flee as well, but she couldn't abandon Fraiche.

She gripped her broom and flew across the street. She was glad there was no traffic at night in Midswich. Otherwise, Fraiche would have been in real danger when he'd made a run for it.

"Your dog is really cute," Alyss said.

Caramel dismounted on the sidewalk. "Th—thanks."

The girl set Fraiche down, handing the end of his leash to Caramel. "Were you walking him?"

"S—sort of."

There was an awkward silence as Alyss waited for follow up from Caramel, who remained silent.

"We could walk him around the park. That is, if he hasn't done his business yet."

Fraiche had done his business on the way back from Anne and Flora's, but he hadn't been getting walked much lately, so

Caramel nodded. They started a slow circuit of the town square. Caramel kept a hand on her broom so it remained ready to fly away.

Alyss kept glancing from the broom to Caramel. If only Caramel could be normal, she would have told Alyss all about witches' brooms. Not that she didn't want to. But every time she thought to say something, her throat closed up and her jaw locked.

They walked quietly for half a block, while Fraiche paused to sniff the flowerbeds and mark a lamp post.

"So, what brings you to Midswich?" Alyss said in a mock grownup voice.

"Um." The question caught Caramel off guard. "Ch—cheap rent."

Alyss laughed. "What? Seriously?"

Caramel nodded.

"That can't be all."

She shook her head, but she wasn't sure she should say more. Silence stretched out again, getting thinner until Alyss broke it.

"We moved here after my dad died."

Caramel looked at Alyss through her hair.

"He died a while ago. Mom freaked out a little and moved us here. I'm originally from Texas."

"S—s—s—s—sorry," Caramel said.

"About my dad? Yeah, it sucks, but I don't know. The hurt kind of faded. We still have lots of memories." Alyss shrugged, thrusting her hands into her jacket pockets. She looked up at the night sky. "It's pretty nice here, too. At first, the other kids were mean, but it got better."

Caramel's feet stopped working, which was good, because her vision was too blurred with tears to see. She halted on the sidewalk and tried not to cry. Squeaking little sobs kept escaping anyway, and her stomach started to hurt from holding them in.

Alyss turned to her. The concern on her face was more than Caramel could bear. Her sobs shook loose full force.

"Oh, my God," Alyss hugged her before she could even

think about making a run for it. Caramel blubbered on Alyss's shoulder, while Alyss muttered soothing words in Spanish.

Caramel could feel Fraiche pawing sympathetically at her pant leg and whining.

"I'm sorry," Alyss said.

Caramel shook her head. She pulled away from Alyss, wiping her face with the sleeve of her jacket. "I—I—I—it's n—not y—y—you." She took a deep breath and let it out. If only there was a spell to cure pain and stuttering. "M—m—my p—p—parents d—died."

"What? Oh, my God." Alyss hugged her again. "Now, I'm really sorry."

"Th—th—thanks," Caramel said when Alyss released her.

"Recently?"

Caramel nodded. She felt relieved to talk to someone. Especially someone who could understand. Even if Alyss was practically a total stranger. "A—a—about a y—year ago."

"Wow, that is recent."

They walked again, while Caramel sniffled and tried to get herself together. She didn't want to go home, only to have Bruleé interrogate her as to why she was crying. Bad enough knowing Bruleé was probably hanging out in the kitchen, waiting to see if her awkward little sister had finally made a friend.

"If you ever want to talk or just hang out or anything, I live on Milton."

"Th—th—thanks. B—b—but I'm n—not sure h—how long w—we'll be here."

"Don't say that," Alyss told her. "I'll make sure you stay. I will."

Caramel blinked in surprise. She didn't know anyone cared that much about a teashop.

They reached the spot in the town square where they'd started their walk, and Caramel slowed to a stop.

"I sh—should go," she said softly. For the first time in a very long time, Caramel felt torn between going home and talking to someone who wasn't her family.

Alyss nodded, "Me, too. But it was cool talking to you.

We'll come by again and buy more. Your spells totally worked. Morris found a twenty on the sidewalk, and his brother left him alone a whole week. Caroline hasn't needed her inhaler, and I managed to get all the limited edition Lip Service clothes I wanted off eBay."

"I—I'm glad. B—Brule does the t—tea spells. A—Anglaise only d—d—does the food."

"Tell her that Charlotte was insane. We ate practically the whole thing in one sitting."

Caramel glanced at her in wonder. "A—and you d—didn't get s—sick?"

"Not that sick, but we did eat too much."

A giggle slipped out before Caramel could stop it. Her hand flew up to smother the sound.

"All right. I'll see you 'round," Alyss said. She waved as she cut across the frost-burned spring grass.

Caramel returned the wave. When Alyss was out of sight, she turned and headed home.

Wednesday's sign-making for the protest had gone very well. Pastor Austin smiled as he and the other picketers unloaded the signs made by Penelope and Lorelei. He wasn't entirely sure about the amount of glitter outlining slogans like *Witches Go Home* and *Magic is the Devil's Work*, but he could live with it. The sun was out, the cold snap had dissipated, and the weatherman predicted a glorious day. A sign from God, if ever Austin had seen one.

Austin waved as Mrs. Bradley pulled into the public parking lot behind the bar. She parked next to Penelope.

"Good morning, Penelope, Pastor," Kim Bradley said, as she got out of her car. Her youngest, Andrew, pressed his face against the back-seat window.

She came over to look at the dozen or so signs. "Very nice."

"Thank you." Penelope handed her a large square of poster

board painted with *Witches Are the Devil's Servants* in red paint with gold glitter accents.

"Very…colorful." Kim examined the poster board. "Where's the handle?"

"Unfortunately, we didn't have the budget to get anything from the hardware store," Austin said. "But they should work just fine."

"Look what I made." Penelope whistled through her teeth. Prince Albert jumped out of the back seat of her car. The Chihuahua wore a tiny sandwich board sign slung over his back. On one side it read, *Witches*, and on the other was *Go Home*. The whole thing was covered in gold-star stickers.

Thankfully, another one of Austin's parishioners arrived before he was obliged to remark on Prince Albert.

Shawn Kelly, Mayor Kelly's older brother, pulled up in his latest, rusty, vintage pick-up that he was restoring. With the mayor's brother on board for the protest, Austin was sure the Chamber of Commerce wouldn't have a leg to stand on, no matter how many presentations Geoffrey whipped up on his computer.

"Morning, Shawn," Austin said. "Grab a sign."

"Morning, Pastor." Shawn helped himself to the least glittery sign he could find.

"No handles?"

"None," Austin said. "But this is just a start. If we don't raise our objections now, the witches may be here to stay." He held a hand up to get everyone's attention. "All right, everybody. Thanks for donating your time to this worthy cause."

They gathered around him.

"I've scheduled shifts, so in a few hours we'll have replacements. This way, there will be a constant presence, and no one will get tired.

The group nodded. All except Andrew, who just looked bored, and Prince Albert, who wagged his tail.

"Try to stay in front of Pickett's Antiques. I've been told by the police that we aren't allowed to interfere with anyone going in or out of the witches' shop. Not that that will be a problem." He was pleased with the round of chuckles this garnered. Austin pulled a set of printed index cards from his pocket. He passed one to each of the protestors. "I've also printed up a list of hymns to sing during the march. We can keep these rotating, or throw in a few more."

Penelope nodded. "Very thorough."

"All right, let's get started."

At 8 a.m. there wasn't much to protest. The only thing open on Stratford was the Dry Goods. Nonetheless, they formed an orderly circle in front of the antique shop and started to march. Every time a car drove by, they held the signs high, waving them at the passersby. Some of the cars honked as they went by, drivers or passengers waving. Austin waved back, glad to have community support.

It took Bruleé a while to realize she kept hearing singing. She was in the teashop, polishing the empty glass display case, too lost in thought to pay attention to the noise coming from the street.

She wondered if there was a festival going on. Bruleé had decided to wait a month before presenting herself to either the Chamber of Commerce or the Recreation Department to get a list of local activities.

Before moving to town, she'd looked up Midswich on the Internet, and found a list of fairs held during the year. She didn't recall there being one in May.

Bruleé poked her head out the front door. Her stomach clenched and fell through the sidewalk at the same time. In front of the shop next door were protestors holding signs and singing "Onward Christian Soldiers."

The warm spring day turned arctic, as icy fear froze her blood. That skinny Pastor led the group. The only others she recognized were the rude woman who had refused her free sample and the older lady, who was with the pastor, when he confronted Father Halloran.

"There's one!" the free sample woman screamed. "Witches, go home!"

The knot of protestors took up her cry and started chanting.

Bruleé recoiled, eyes stinging. She slammed the front door and stood there a minute as the chant rose over the sounds of traffic. Her hands shook as fear gripped her, refusing to let go. Then she fled through the teashop to the public restroom under the stairs.

She locked the door, grateful Caramel and Anglaise were upstairs. Bruleé collapsed on the toilet and let loose her tears. Wracking sobs shook her body, but she cried silently so her sisters wouldn't hear her. Bruleé unrolled a thick wad of toilet paper and covered her face.

She had been so sure they could make it in Midswich. Just two more weeks and it would be June, the start of the tourist season.

Bruleé tossed the crumpled ball of toilet paper into the wastebasket. Her tears had soaked it through. She pulled another pile of toilet paper off the roll.

Now she was going to have to call Aunt Licorice and make arrangements for her and her sisters to move into her Philadelphia townhouse. The shop would have to go back on the market, and if it didn't sell…

Bruleé coughed out a hard sob and pressed the tissue to her face harder.

If the teashop didn't sell, she couldn't pay the lease, and she'd have to declare bankruptcy in order to legally default. And Anglaise.

She came up for air long enough to choke back a loud moan and get a refill of toilet paper.

Anglaise would stay long enough to apply to Le Cordon Bleu in France, and then she'd be gone. Bruleé would have to go to work for Aunt Licorice's potion business, and Caramel would have to go with her.

There was a loud knock on the bathroom door.

"Bruleé, you in there?" Anglaise yelled through the door.

She took a deep, steadying breath, forcing her voice not to crack. "Just a minute, I'm using the bathroom."

"Have you seen what's going on outside?"

"Yes, I have." Bruleé was surprised at how normal her voice sounded.

"Are you worried? Should we do something? I'm thinking an itching hex."

"Don't you dare!" Bruleé screamed. She caught herself and took another breath to try and calm down. "Just ignore them. I don't need you throwing gasoline on the fire."

Bruleé could feel Anglaise's rage through the door. She stood up and wiped away her tears with the wet toilet paper. Then she washed her face in the sink with cold water. Her eyes were puffy and red.

"My face is smoothed, no marks to mar, no puffy eyes, the redness soothed."

All evidence of her crying jag was gone. Eyes clear, skin smooth. Bruleé wiped away one last tear and opened the bathroom door.

She gave Anglaise a bright smile. "We still have two weeks to see what happens. You never know."

"How much more evidence do you need that this isn't going to work?" Anglaise asked.

"You agreed to the full month, like we all did," Bruleé told her. "Now go bake something. Something that smells really, really good."

Bruleé looked up at the clock on the kitchen wall.

"Have it ready by ten. Everyone gets hungry around that time."

"But—"

Bruleé held up her hand and Anglaise shut her mouth.

Bruleé smiled. "How about cookies?"

Anglaise threw her hands up in surrender. "Fine. Whatever. Chocolate chip and candied orange, spicy peanut butter, and coconut pineapple. I hope you like 'em, 'cause we'll be eating them for weeks."

Bruleé gave Anglaise a gentle shove toward the kitchen island. "I don't care, just as long as they smell like heaven."

"Where is Caramel?" she asked, even though she had a pretty good idea.

Anglaise pulled open the walk in. "Crying in the living room."

"I'll leave her be," Bruleé said.

Geoffrey finished ordering the restock online, wanting to get out of the office. He'd been in there four hours, and the closet-sized office, stuffed with filing cabinets, desk, and computer, always made him a little stir-crazy. There wasn't even a window to look out. Even Claire's attempt to make over the room hadn't helped. The sky blue paint and backlit animated tropical scene looked tacky. His favorite wall was the one with the framed vintage food labels.

Looking at the clock in the corner of his computer screen, he saw it was almost ten. He put the computer into sleep mode andwent to help get ready for the lunch rush.

He walked through the crowded shelves, making a mental note of what items seemed to be doing well. He'd have to start stocking for the summer people with the next order. Gourmet foods, more specialty items, and high-end brands. The locals liked to save and the vacationers liked to spend.

Geoffrey got up to the front register. Rob, the cashier, was helping a customer and staring out the front window. He wasn't doing either very well. Geoffrey was about to tell Rob to get his mind back on work, but he noticed the customer was staring out the window, too.

Across the street, Pastor Austin and his best cronies were shaking anti-witch signs at passersby. They stood in front of Pickett's Antiques.

Henry Pickett, that narrow-minded, old son-of-a—bitch, must have told the Reverend about the Chamber meeting.

"Rob, mind the store," Geoffrey told him. He marched outside and crossed the street.

Henry Pickett had dragged a cane chair outside and sat with the protestors, holding a sign saying, *Magic: Brought to You by Satan*, festively outlined in red glitter.

Geoffrey was half way across the street, when he yelled, "Henry, what the hell are you doing?"

The protestors looked at Geoffrey. Geoffrey was not surprised to see Penelope, Kim, and Austin, but he was disheartened to see Mayor Kelly's brother, Shawn in the mix.

"I'm protesting, like a damn hippie," Henry shot back.

"No, I mean, you didn't even give the Chamber time to do a real presentation for the City Council."

"That's not going to be necessary, Geoffrey," Austin said.

"I wasn't talking to you, Oscar," Geoffrey snapped.

Pastor Austin's face stormed over. "Now, you just listen here—" he started.

"No, you listen, Pastor. You have no idea what an asset the witches could be to this town. I'm talking busloads of tourists, a whole market we never thought to tap." Geoffrey fixed his gaze on Shawn. Maybe he would be so good as to tell the mayor what he was missing out on. "Not a bad deal in a recession, huh? Especially after the last two years' steady decline."

He saw the signs waver. Kim Bradley and Shawn Kelly exchanged guilty glances. A flicker of triumph sparked to life, then died.

"'For what does it profit a man to gain the whole and forfeit his soul,'" Austin said, the steel in his voice sharp enough to cut down further debate.

Penelope shook her sign at Geoffrey. "Hear, hear! There's more than money at stake, Geoffrey."

He pulled a crumpled dust rag from his apron and threw it on the ground.

"No, there isn't. No one ever lost a soul to tea! You're running a perfectly good business into the ground. Shut up!" he said as Penelope and Austin opened their mouths.

"You can get off my sidewalk, now," Henry said. "You made a fool of yourself enough for one day."

"I suppose it was too much to ask for you to let the Chamber of Commerce decide for itself, Henry."

"Oh, it wasn't me who told the pastor about your scheming. Lorelei did it for me."

"Fine." Geoffrey drew himself up. "I'll go have a talk with her."

He marched away from the protestors, anxious not to look defeated. There was no way he could just go back to his store now, like a chastened child. He'd said everything he had to say to Austin and Henry, and he felt himself losing steam as he crossed the town square.

The stinging chemical reek of acrylic nails and hair products smacked Geoffrey in the face as he walked in the door of Barely Hair.

"Hey, Geoffrey," Matilda said. She put down her *People Magazine* as he came in. "Claire's with a customer right now, if you want to wait."

"I'm here to see Lorelei," he said.

He spotted her across the salon just as she saw him. Geoffrey leveled a finger at her. "You told Austin about the Chamber meeting. They're out there now picketing the teashop. Do you have any idea what you and Austin are costing this town?"

The entire salon went silent. The blow dryers switched off. The buzzy clippers stopped. He saw Claire, a pair of scissors in her hand, staring at him, along with a wet-haired client.

Lorelei fidgeted and looked around her shop.

"Now, now, Geoffrey, no need to go all *j'accuse*. Austin would have done something sooner or later, whether I told him about the Chamber's little meeting or not—"

"Picketing the teashop?" Matilda threw down her magazine and bolted from the reception desk.

"You didn't even give the witches a chance," Geoffrey said. "The very least you could have done was let everyone vote."

In the ten years Lorelei O'Donnell had lived in Midswich, Geoffrey had never seen her get angry. He'd heard stories though, that her temper, once aroused, was as fiery as her Irish last name and orange dye job. She strode across the salon floor, heels clomping like a runway mode. Everyone in her way hurried to get out. "Now you listen here, Geoffrey Callister. Don't you dare come into my shop, trying to lecture me about right and wrong. Not when you're the one who called everyone up, crying witch like it was Armageddon. You ain't set one foot in that teashop since the day it opened, and you know why? You're yellow." Lorelei made a complicated pattern of snaps in the air.

He had no idea she went all Southern when pissed. "You know what? You're right."

She looked triumphantly around the room, hands on hips, nodded, and gave a loud, "Mmm-mmm."

"So I think I better go have tea and meet the witches."

"Geoffrey," Claire exclaimed, "You don't mean it!"

He turned and headed for the door. "I do."

"Then you're sleeping on the couch," his wife yelled.

"Couch it is," Geoffrey said as he left the salon.

For the last few weeks, he'd wanted to go into the teashop, but he'd been too afraid of public scorn to do it. Now that he'd announced his intention to a crowd, he had to go in or be branded a coward. Nothing like the threat of ridicule to motivate a man.

The protestors in front of Pickett's had gotten louder. The ranks had swollen too. Three more people from what Geoffrey considered the churchy crowd had joined Pastor Austin.

If he caved now and went back to his own store, no one would be left to stand up for the witches. Someone had to set an example. Determination swept through him. He marched passed the picketers, daring them to try and stop him. He flexed his biceps ready for a fight. Geoffrey would bet money he could take Pastor Austin down. The man was in shape, but he was a runner. The last heavy thing he'd lifted was a Bible.

Geoffrey marched past Pickett's Antique Store, head up, and fists ready.

"Don't do it, Geoffrey! We'll boycott the Dry Goods," Penelope yelled.

There was a chorus of agreement.

He paused long enough to fire back, "Have fun driving to Musquash then."

People might boycott for a while but the first time they were out of milk or diapers, they'd crawl back.

Geoffrey's hand tingled as he touched the doorknob of the witches' teashop. The first to enter the most feared shop in town.

He pushed the door open. Bells tinkled overhead. He looked around.

"Wow, it's really pink in—Matilda?"

Seated at a large, square table in the back corner of the shop was Matilda. She waved at Geoffrey and offered a weak smile. He matched her smile in both strength and enthusiasm. But while Matilda looked nervous, Geoffrey felt himself deflating. All the energy whooshed out of him. So much for bravery and being the first.

"Hi," she said. "Care to join me?"

"Sure," Geoffrey said.

His retail experienced gaze traveled around the room. The layout was open and there were only seven tables, each draped in pink, striped linen. The rest of the shop was done in wood. Lots of cubbies for teapots and teacups. A nice display of tea accessories for sale. Strainers, cozies, infuser balls, and spoons.

"It is kind of girly, isn't it?" Matilda said.

"Not as bad as I first thought." Geoffrey pulled a chair out from the table. The seat was upholstered in pink. "Brown or gold would be a lot more neutral."

"We can change the colors."

Geoffrey nearly toppled over as he was sitting down. He clutched at the table and steadied himself.

The blonde witch stood a few feet away, a menu in her hand.

"Oh, hello, how's your head?" she asked Geoffrey and stepped over.

He sat down. "Fine, just fine," he coughed. He was hoping she wouldn't mention that. Not in front of Matilda.

"His head?" Matilda looked at the witch then at Geoffrey.

Geoffrey dropped his gaze to the tablecloth. "It was nothing."

"I startled him when we first met. He ran into a closed door. But there was no concussion," Bruleé supplied.

"Really? I'm so glad to hear that," Matilda said.

He could feel her eyes on him and hear the playful mocking in Matilda's voice.

"Imagine that, big strong Geoffrey is scared of a—"

"Is that the menu?" Geoffrey snatched the thick leather bound menu from the witch. "Good God, this is thick as a phone book."

"Well, normally we have a lot to offer. Some of it you can special order, a lot of it is tea and spell combinations," the witch said.

"Oh, and I should introduce myself. I'm Bruleé and I'll be taking care of you today."

"Bruleé, like the dessert?" Geoffrey had heard the witches talking when he'd hit his head, and the name felt familiar.

"Yes, the same," Bruleé said. "I'll go get another menu."

Geoffrey read his menu.

"That is a thick menu," Matilda said. She leaned over the table to read over the edge.

He put it down on the table so she could see it.

"There's four pages of tea blends with optional spells broken down by category," he said.

"I wonder what Father Halloran ordered. Are you okay, Geoffrey? You look red."

"Fine," he said. In all the excitement, Geoffrey had forgotten Father Halloran. He'd been the first to set foot in the teashop. *So much for all my bluster.*

Bruleé returned with another menu and gave it to Matilda.

"We don't have much to offer today, but if you'd like to wait, Anglaise is baking three varieties of cookies and I can recommend a tea to go with each one."

"Cookies sound good. What kind are they?" Matilda asked.

"Spicy peanut butter, chocolate chip with candied orange, and macadamia pineapple."

"Wow," Matilda said.

"Those," Geoffrey said, "I'll have those."

"Which ones?" Bruleé asked.

"All of them."

Matilda put her hand up. "Seconded."

"How many?" Bruleé looked alternately confused and happy. As if she couldn't believe her good luck at finding hungry customers.

"I want two each to start," Geoffrey said.

"Just one each." Matilda looked down at her trim figure. "I don't want to get fat."

"Have you decided on a tea? Spelled or un-spelled?"

"I don't know." Geoffrey looked over the menu again. "Do you have a spell for an angry wife?"

Bruleé laughed then caught herself and gave him a sympathetic look. "I do have love spells but they're general in nature. To draw the love someone wants into his or her life. They aren't for catching specific people."

Geoffrey had been joking, but he didn't want to hurt Bruleé's feelings by telling her. Not after such a sincere answer.

"Peeved or not, Claire's stuck with me. For the foreseeable future anyway." He held up his hand and waggled his fingers showing off his wedding band. "So, um, sencha sounds good."

"Cinnamon-orange for me," Matilda said.

Bruleé nodded. "Excellent choices." She reached to take their menus, but Geoffrey held on to his.

"I'd like to read the whole thing if you don't mind. It's practically a book."

"Me, too." Matilda had been handing her menu to Bruleé but pulled it back halfway there.

"All right," Bruleé said. "I'll go check on the cookies. Anglaise should be putting them in the oven."

Bruleé headed back to where the kitchen must be. Geoffrey turned to the first page of his menu.

Matilda's cell phone rang. She put the menu down and pulled her cell from her jeans' pocket. She frowned at the display and clicked a button. The cell's musical ring tone cut out mid-chorus.

Geoffrey tried to keep his eyes on his menu, but when the cell rang again, he peered over the top edge. Matilda ended the call before the ring tone got three bars into the song.

"Sorry," Matilda said.

With the speed of redial, her cell rang a third time. Matilda gave a frustrated grunt.

"You should probably get that," Geoffrey said.

Matilda put the cell up to her ear and pushed the accept button. "Yes, I'm at the teashop, and no, I'm not leaving."

"Uncle Shawn called me. Do you have any idea how pissed he is?"

Geoffrey clearly heard Hugh Kelly on the other end of the line.

"Why do I care about your uncle?"

"He's calling your dad, Matilda!"

"So, let him."

"How do you think this looks?"

"Oh, my God. I don't care, Hugh."

"I'm coming to get you."

"Set one foot in this teashop and we're over. Do you hear me? You don't tell me what I can do or where I can go."

"This is different and you know it."

"And still not caring." Matilda hung up then shut her phone off. "Sorry about that."

"I'd offer you my couch, but I'll be occupying it tonight."

After Matilda's phone went to voicemail the fifth time, Hugh gave up.

He hurriedly cashed out his hand in the online poker game he was playing. No great loss, since he wasn't winning anyway. He knocked on his dad's office door then opened it before waiting for an answer.

"Dad—" Hugh interrupted the meeting Mayor Kelly was having with Dan Harding.

Dan gave him a cross look. "What the hell?"

Hugh gave Dan what he called the "super-model-thousand-yard stare." It meant he could see Dan, but didn't care.

"I'm going to join the protestors, so I'm knocking off for the rest of the day."

"What?" Simon Kelly asked.

"See ya later." Hugh shut the door and ran for it, before the mayor could pull rank and order him back to executive assisting.

Pastor Austin welcomed Hugh with a sign and a smile. When Hugh had received Austin's e-mailed bulletin about the protest, he'd laughed it off. An actual picket seemed redundant since no one had gone to the teashop since it opened. He'd certainly had no intention of wasting his time standing around outside, waving signs at people.

Leave it to Matilda to make him actually do something.

Hugh took a spot next to his uncle.

"She still in there?"

"Her and Geoffrey," Shawn replied.

"You've gotta be kidding. What's he doing?"

"He wants the witches to stay. Says we're turning down money, but I'm not convinced."

Midswich economics didn't interest Hugh enough to have an opinion, and he was crap at math. He did know that his dad chased every tourist dollar he could with the determination of a beagle after a fox.

"Are we?"

"What?" Shawn raised his sign at a passing car.

"Turning down money."

Penelope cut in before Shawn could answer. "It doesn't matter if we are. Tourists or not, we have to think of our souls and the souls of our children."

As little as Hugh cared for economics, he cared even less about the souls of children. Penelope's words got a round of approval from the others, and she swelled like a feeding tick on their approval. The crackpot had found her cause at last.

Hugh edged closer to the teashop. He wanted to peek in and see what Matilda was doing. He leaned over, trying to look casually over his shoulder.

The shop was dim inside, and he had to squint past his own ghostly reflection in the plate glass. There she was. Most of Matilda was hidden by Geoffrey's bulk, but that was definitely her shoulder. He wondered briefly what Geoffrey was doing, there then realized he didn't care. He pulled his cell from his pocket and tried Matilda again.

She picked up. "What is it, Hugh?"

He could hear her eyes roll. "What are you doing?" he asked.

"Getting tea with Geoffrey," she said.

"I can see that. What I mean is why?"

"You can see?"

He saw her lean over to get a better look out the window. Geoffrey turned around in his seat. Hugh waved at them.

"You're protesting?"

The pasty-white fury of Matilda's face was unmistakable, even at this distance and seen through plate glass, floating with reflections of the street behind.

"I'm not," he said.

"There's a sign reading 'Temptation Comes in Pleasing Forms' leaning against the window."

Hugh had stuck the poster board down in a planter. He turned it around.

"Better?"

She made a frustrated squealing noise. "No, Hugh. It's not better."

"Look, I'm only here because I'm worried about you."

"What's to worry about?"

He wasn't sure. Not when she said it like that. A few minutes ago, he'd felt strongly about something. He was sure of it. But now, with Matilda staring at him, eyes all hard and flinty, he wasn't so sure. "It's, like…" He searched around, trying to articulate his concerns. "Why do you have to be like this?"

"Like what?"

Panic was setting in. He recognized the too-calm tone of her voice, knowing nothing good could come of this conversation. For some reason, though, he was never able to stop himself. "Like flaunting society. If no one wants the witches here, it's not your job to prove everyone wrong." Nothing was coming out right. He'd somehow swung wide of everything he wanted to say. "I mean, are you trying to rebel?"

The phone went dead in his hand. Matilda had gone from pale to waxy. Hugh half expected her to hurl the phone at him and was thankful for the glass. Geoffrey had wisely scooted down the table, so he was no longer between them.

Hugh mouthed, "I'm sorry." Seeing no change in Matilda's face, he threw his hands up, took his sign, and went back to the protestors.

Matilda had the nearly overwhelming urge to hurl the phone at Hugh. She'd played softball in high school, and her arm was as deadly now as it was then. He was lucky to be in public and behind glass. She looked at Geoffrey. A few minutes ago he'd been sitting across from her. Magically, he was now several feet away.

Geoffrey gave her a smile, hovering between sympathetic and embarrassed.

Matilda shut her phone off. "Serves me right, trying to update Twitter." She had meant to try and laugh, but the words came out so bitter, she decided not to bother. "Why does he have to be like that, anyway? At least I'm not the one too scared of my parents to quit a job I hate. It's none of his business if I want to have tea and cookies. How is that rebelling, anyway?"

Geoffrey looked like he was trying to swallow something that wouldn't go down.

"What?"

"Well, I thought I was being rebellious," he said. "I mean, there are protestors outside."

Matilda thunked her head into the surface of the table. The porcelain tea cups rattled on their saucers. She let her head rest. She didn't think she'd live to see the day Hugh was right. No, that wasn't fair. He was a born people pleaser, and to pull that off required an observant nature. Hugh had known her all her life, and he'd seen her defy every high expectation her parents had for her. Get good grades, go to college, become a doctor, lawyer, or executive. She'd squeaked through high school with straight C's and then dropped out of beauty school. Her siblings had all excelled in school, in sports, and in life.

Her head popped back up. "Fine. I'm such a rebel. Wanna go smoke cigarettes behind the bleachers after this?"

Geoffrey grinned. "I used to do that. I thought I was cool. But, uh—" he leaned forward. "They weren't cigarettes," he whispered.

Matilda gave him a conspiratorial wink. "Wow, you are a rebel."

"Ah, those were the days," Geoffrey said. He opened his mouth to say more but paused to sniff the air.

Matilda inhaled deeply. She could smell the cookies baking. The chocolate chip-orange cookies were strongest, followed by the peanut butter. Her stomach rumbled loudly.

"'Scuse me," she said.

Geoffrey wasn't listening. His eyes were glassily fixed on nothing, staring toward the front of the teashop.

"What is it?" she asked.

"The peanut butter cookies." His eyes focused again. "They smell like my mom's, but not. I wonder if she still has the recipe. I should call her."

"My mom doesn't bake," Matilda said. She inhaled again. The enticing cookie smells were getting stronger. "She just bought cookies for us." She couldn't help one more deep breath then another, and another. Her fight with Hugh dissolved under the blissful erosion of fresh-baked cookies.

"If there's a heaven, this is what it should smell like," Geoffrey said.

"It better," Matilda.

Bruleé came back to the front of the shop. "The cookies are almost done," she said.

A wave of fragrant baking smells washed over the

protestors. Their signs lowered and noses lifted into the air. Austin inhaled the scent of fresh-baked cookies. For a second, he forgot why he was out on the sidewalk in the middle of the morning, recalling the smell of his mother's kitchen. She used to bake for everything. Church raffles, school bake sales— when she felt good and when she felt bad. There was always something in the oven when he was a boy. Pies, cakes, cookies. She was ready with a treat every time he skinned his knee or came home crying, because the other boys had teased him. died in a diabetic coma when he was twenty-two.

Austin's eyes refocused. He heard the collective rumble of stomachs around him. His own stomach made a hollow gurgle that was sure to be heard by his nearest neighbors.

He checked his watch: 10:30 a.m. Of course. Time for a morning snack. Austin's jaw tightened as he grit his teeth. Those witches. He'd bet they planned to be baking at this time.

The protestors all turned toward the teashop and the scent of temptation.

Andrew Bradley sat down on the sidewalk. He beat his mangled, folded sign against the concrete.

"I want cookies. I want cookies," he chanted.

"Andrew, get up." Kim pulled at her youngest son's arms, but he resisted by going limp.

"Cookies, cookies, cookies," he wailed.

Red-faced, Kim finally tore the sign from his hands. "Andrew Bradley, get up."

"No."

Austin needed to act before the protest could deteriorate or be called on account of the munchies.

"I brought snacks." He tucked his sign under his arm. "Just let me run back to my car."

He took off at a light jog. A few minutes later, he returned with a box of chocolate caramel protein bars. He opened the box and handed them out.

Everyone took one, even Andrew. There was a chorus of crinkling wrappers as each opened their protein bar. Not everyone looked thrilled with the snack, but judging by the average weight of those present, it wouldn't do them any harm.

Kim opened Andrew's bar for him. The boy took a small distrustful bite, chewed slowly, his face screwed up in serious decision-making.

At last, he threw down the bar. "I want cookies."

Kim hoisted her son off the sidewalk. She looked around apologetically. "I've got to get him home," she said. "I'll come back this afternoon if I can."

Austin patted her arm. "Of course."

"Thank you. Sorry." She hurried off with the sniffling Andrew in her arms. The boy looked like he was working himself up to a full-blown tantrum.

The protein bars helped settle everyone's stomach, but nothing could be done about the smell of baking cookies that filled the street. The chocolate, sugary scent was a constant distraction. Their hymns faltered and heads kept turning to the teashop.

Surely the smell couldn't last forever? Austin chewed his lower lip. The witches could have done something, a spell to make the smell of cookies last. All to thwart him. He wasn't sure if he should be angry or flattered. If they were really threatened by the protest, all the better.

Matilda knocked on the door of Eddie's apartment. She couldn't keep a huge grin off her face. He must know by now. The entire town was talking about the protest and how she and Geoffrey had crossed the picket line to get tea at the teashop.

She held a blue bakery box under her arm with three of each cookie the witches had made. The chocolate chip-orange cookies were rapture on a plate. She would have brought the entire remaining batch, but Geoffrey had more cash on him. He'd bought all the leftover cookies she couldn't. He said he was going to try to prove to Claire that the witches weren't evil, and no cookie that good could be the work of the devil.

Matilda pointed out that it might prove the opposite. Geoffrey shrugged and said he'd eat them if she didn't want them.

Matilda heard Eddie's voice from inside the apartment. Her grin stretched wider.

"Eddie, it's me," she called out before he could get to the door.

The door opened. Eddie gave her a friendly but tense smile. Not his usual warm welcome.

"You've been to the teashop," he said.

"I so have." She bounced her heels a little. Her grin got wider and stupider.

"Oh? How was it?"

The voice came from behind Eddie. A woman was in his living room. Matilda leaned to the right and looked over Eddie's shoulder.

Hillary sat on Eddie's beat-up, second-hand couch. There was a laptop on the coffee table in front of her. What was she doing here? Matilda felt an injection of icy cold jealousy. Not that she didn't already have a boyfriend. But Eddie was her best friend. Her feelings had nothing to do with Hugh.

Hillary waved at her.

Matilda's jaw locked, her smile froze into a rictus. She waved back. "Hello…"

"Hillary."

"I know. I'm just surprised." Matilda searched Eddie's face for some hint about what the schoolteacher was doing in his apartment.

Was he blushing? Sweating? Shirt buttons done up? She scanned his clothing. Shirt buttoned normally. That was good. No hanky panky she could discern.

"We're looking at the slide show of Hillary's trips to Africa," Eddie said. He paused then added, "You want to come in?"

The pause was too long, his invitation too hesitant.

"No. I just…" Matilda didn't know why she was there anymore. She had come over to tell him all about the teashop and give him cookies. Her grip tightened on the box. He wasn't getting any now. Not with Hillary sitting there.

"I should go," Matilda said. "So, bye."

She turned and hustled down the hall. A feeling of being lost swept over her. The hollow ache of being unable to find home. She found herself cut off from all the people she would normally talk to. Hugh was mad at her. Lorelei had been positively arctic when she returned to work. Her family, never her biggest cheerleaders, would no doubt be pissed yet again at her laughably minor defiance. And her last steady rock, Eddie, seemed to have a girlfriend.

Matilda left the apartment building and crossed the street to the park. She sat down on one of the picnic benches and opened the box of cookies. They still smelled fantastic. The aroma of orange and chocolate, with the peanut butter undertone. They smelled like they had just come from the oven, even hours later. Maybe there was some enchantment on them after all.

Chapter

Geoffrey found himself sitting in his car, idling in the circular drive in front of William's house. The fight with Claire replaying in his mind…

"Hello."

"How could you do that to me today? Show up where I work and start yelling at Lorelei."

"I'm sorry. I wasn't thinking. But I didn't—"

"I don't show up at the grocery store and yell at the baggers."

"I know. I brought you cookies."

"Are those from the teashop?"

"They aren't Satanic cookies."

"I won't have any. How could you even buy them?"

"The witches are nice girls. You haven't even spoken to them."

"You're the one who called all in a panic when they moved in, remember?"

"Well, I was wrong."

"No, you weren't. Pastor Austin says—"

"I don't care what Austin says. The man is a fruitcake."

"He's a man of God."

"His job doesn't make him special. He hasn't talked to the witches any more than you have. You're all prejudiced."

"Sorry we're such ignorant peasants."

"Claire—"

"No, really. I don't know how you could stand it all these years, being the only enlightened man in our quaint village."

"Claire, that's not what I meant. But really, what's happened since the witches came? Nothing. No hexes, no curses, no one has died, no milk cows have run dry."

"That's not funny."

"I wasn't trying to be."

"I think you need to leave for a while."

"What?"

"And take the cookies with you."

William's house was set a good hundred feet behind the gas station, camouflaged by a couple of ancient pines and half a dozen gooseberry bushes that nearly qualified as trees. William wasn't exactly Geoffrey's best friend but, when he stopped to think about it, Geoffrey realized he didn't have any close friends. He knew everyone in town and was friendly enough. But most of his high school buddies were busy with their own lives and kids. His best friend was Claire, which was the problem right now.

It was a bit of a sore point for Geoffrey that William did most of his grocery shopping at that frou-frou organic market in Musquash, but it was a minor enough complaint. William always stopped at the Dry Goods for various sundries, so it was a forgivable offense.

He stood on the porch and rang the doorbell then positioned himself to best display the offerings he had brought—box of cookies in one hand and beer in the other.

Geoffrey hoisted them up as William opened the door.

"Claire is unhappy. Can I, uh, stay for…I don't know…a while?" Geoffrey tried to think. He figured a few hours should do it. In a little over fifteen years of marriage, he'd only had to vacate overnight twice.

"Sure," William said. He stepped aside so Geoffrey could come in.

Geoffrey almost sighed in relief. He grinned and stepped inside, handing William the beer. He'd picked a six-pack of imported beer, knowing William had a fondness for fancy food. "Let's get drunk."

William looked from the beer to Geoffrey. "It's the middle of the week. We both have to go to work in the morning."

"Fine," Geoffrey said. "Mildly buzzed. Sometimes I miss being a teenager."

"If we were still teenagers, you would have had to bring more beer."

Geoffrey laughed. "Sucks to get old."

"I'm not that old," William protested.

William poured the beer into proper beer glasses. Then they settled down at the kitchen table.

It was strange for Geoffrey to realize that, for all the years he'd known William, he had never been inside the man's house. Not that Geoffrey had ever had William over, either. Maybe it was the age difference. William was a good eleven years younger than Geoffrey, so they'd gone to school at different times.

William was single, and while he was on the receiving end of the town's best gossip, he rarely spread it.

"So, you went into the teashop," William said. He looked over the bakery box as if it was a treasure chest.

"I did."

"And, come on, how was it?"

"The shop is nice. A little on the pink side but, except for me, most of their customers are women."

"Lots of people drink tea, not just women."

Geoffrey scratched his head. "No, I know, but the fancy tea party thing. You don't see men running around in red hats, eating dainties en masse."

William cracked up. When he could talk again, he took in a shuddering breath and managed to say, "You have a weird idea of tea parties."

"Whatever."

"And are those the dainties?" William let out another laugh, his voice cracking on the word dainties.

"Since you ask." Geoffrey opened the blue box printed with the Tea Times Three logo, an art nouveau inspired teapot and flowers inside a circle, surrounded by the name. "They made cookies. Not for us, just in general. I had to fight Matilda to buy the leftovers."

The cookies smelled as good as they had when they first came out of the oven. William waved a hand over the box, fanning the smell toward his face.

"Wow."

"I know, right?" Geoffrey said. "I don't know how the protestors could focus on anything with that smell next door."

"I heard about that." William frowned, a deep crease forming between his eyebrows as they drew together. "I wanted to come down today but Nell called in sick and Rick is out of town."

Geoffrey nodded. "I hate vacation time."

They clinked beer glasses to toast the inconvenience of employees.

"Have a cookie," Geoffrey said. "Try the pineapple-macadamia first. It's good but the others will blow your mind."

"Then why am I starting with it?" Will picked up the pale blond cookie, chunky with macadamia nut halves and candied pineapple. He thought he caught the tropical scent of toasted coconut as well.

"It's the most delicate flavor. The others are really bold. I ate the chocolate-orange first and then everything kind of tasted like it."

"Sage advice." William took a bite of the cookie.

Geoffrey couldn't help smiling at the stunned surprise on William's face. He had felt the same expression on his own that morning.

"Holy shit," William said softly.

"Have you ever had a better cookie?" Geoffrey said.

"I hate to say it, and nothing against my mom's, but damn. No, I have never eaten a better cookie."

"We have to keep this shop open," Geoffrey said. Then he added, "Eat the peanut butter cookie next."

They both took a dark, golden-brown cookie from the box.

William paused before biting in. "Are these spicy?"

"Yes, but not too hot. There's some kind of chili in it, though. I had my doubts, but you have to try it to believe it."

William was already eating before Geoffrey finished. "Oh, my God." He finished the cookie in a single bite and took a drink of beer. "Hey, try it with the beer."

Geoffrey ate a peanut butter cookie, the low heat of chili burning his mouth. Then he took a sip of beer. The cold beer cooled the fiery spice and pleasantly cut the sweet of the cookie.

"Huh," Geoffrey said. "I think you just discovered the perfect drinking cookie. Weird. But good."

William tried the chocolate-orange and pronounced it even more amazing than the other two. He spent a while slowly chewing, trying to guess the ingredients. "How bad a trouble are the witches in?" he asked as he finished his glass of beer.

"I asked Bruleé about that. She's the oldest sister. She didn't say much, but I could tell from her face they aren't doing well. The bakery case in front of the shop is empty, too. Austin and his cronies are just the final nail in the coffin."

"With cookies like these, I don't want to lose them. I don't think Paris had better cookies."

Geoffrey nodded. "People need to buy things, though."

"I think you and Matilda set a good example."

"Or a bad one."

William chuckled and helped himself to another peanut butter cookie. "I'll go tomorrow. If more people see other people going in, maybe they'll go in, too."

"Hear, hear."

William got up and took two more beers from the fridge.

Geoffrey was grateful for the refill and the company. Tomorrow he'd see if Claire had forgiven him.

"And do what?" Flora had asked.

Short of a business loan, Flora couldn't imagine what she could do to save the teashop.

"Just go in," Anne had shot back. "And I mean, through the front door."

Flora had no response. She wasn't sure she could do it. Go in the front, cross Pastor Austin's picket line. She wasn't even sure what she was afraid of anymore. Everyone seeing her? Ruining her reputation? The town riding her out on the rails?

Surely none of that would happen. But the thoughts still paralyzed her.

"If you won't go, I will," Anne had said.

Anne had slowly pushed herself off the sofa, levering herself forward through sheer will power and the support of her walker.

"Anne, don't be silly," Flora had said.

Anne ignored her and clawed open the front door, wincing as she forced her fingers around the doorknob. She hobbled out into the hallway.

Flora was stunned. She stood in the doorway, watching Anne inch her way to the stairwell at the end of the hall. She wasn't moving fast, but she was moving. More than she had in years.

Was it working? Were the teas and spells really working?

"Anne, Anne, come back," Flora called out before her sister could try for the stairs. "I'll go over tonight and find out if there's anything I can do."

Anne had stopped and turned around. "Promise?"

"Yes."

Anne made her agonizingly slow way back down the hall. "I guess that's as good as I'm going to get from you."

Flora stared, still amazed at the sight. Anne had walked a good ten feet down the hall then made the return trip. She wanted to shout, but she didn't want to point out to Anne what she'd done in case that broke the spell. Flora just waited as Anne came back to the apartment and closed the door behind her.

And now, Flora was making good on her promise. Navy

blue twilight covered the town. The decorative Victorian style lampposts glowed brightly in the late spring evening.

Flora pulled on a sweater. The weather had warmed, but temperatures still dropped below comfort at night. She decided to walk. She wanted the time to think, and she didn't want people seeing her car parked down town. She said goodbye to Anne then started off at her briskest pace.

The witches were staying. All day long, her mind had gone back to Anne walking down the hall. The weird creaking gate of her walker-assisted trip. Flora was a little sorry she had stopped Anne before the stairs. Could she have gotten down?

Shaking her head, Flora dismissed the thought. Stairs were a good way off still. But there was improvement. Thanks to Bruleé. The doctors hadn't done so much in years as that girl had done in a week.

Flora went straight around to the back of the teashop. The gossip lines had been burning today. After she and Anne got word that there was a protest, the phone rang again. Geoffrey Callister and Matilda Hartwell, of all people, had gone into the shop and apparently drunk tea and eaten something. Flora had asked sourly what else they would do. And hung up.

At last, someone had taken a stand, and here she was, sneaking back over like a coward. She was ashamed, but helpless in the face of her emotions. Tomorrow. Tomorrow she could come back and purchase something. Some kind of tea biscuit.

Flora knocked on the *DELIVERIES* door. Now it was almost as familiar as her own front door.

The door was pulled open mid-knock, and the purse held tightly in her hand nearly hit Anglaise in the face.

"Watch it," the witch snarled as she ducked.

"Sorry. You should wait for people to finish knocking," Flora said.

"And maybe you should try the front door when we're actually open."

"Next time," Flora said.

Anglaise looked suspicious of that remark, but let it slide. "You here to join the party?"

"What party?" Flora asked. She was getting an excuse ready when Anglaise threw the door wide.

Seated around the kitchen island, drinking teas from fine china cups, were the crow-black goth contingent and the other two witches.

Anglaise waved Flora in. "Well, come on then. I don't have all night."

Flora came right to the verge of turning and leaving. The only thing stopping her was paralyzing indecision. Without meaning to, her feet started forward, and Flora found herself inside.

The four teens, hunched over their tea like vultures, eyeballed her over the rims of their tea cups.

Bruleé smiled and stood up.

"Flora, welcome! What are you doing here?"

"I just—" She kept her eye on the kids. "I came to see if there was anything I could do to help."

"Come in." Bruleé took her elbow, guiding her to an empty chair at the island. "Would you like a cup of tea?" she asked.

Flora nodded. "Sure."

"I have something I think you'll like, even though you don't take your tea sweet." Bruleé disappeared into the darkened front room of the shop.

Flora sat and surveyed her company. Anglaise was on her left, then Mary Alice Ruiz, the mousy witch, the Bradley boy, rake-thin Caroline something or other, and across the stainless steel counter, Morris of the mohawk. Flora remembered his brother. She'd taught him years ago. The boy had been a bully, foul mouthed and cruel, even for a third grader.

Flora nodded stiffly to each of them. "Kids," she said.

"Ms. Barton," they chorused.

"So, what brings you here?" Flora tried to sound causal but it came out stiff.

Anglaise answered for them, "Same thing that brings you here." She reached into the side pocket of her olive green cargo pants and pulled out a tiny silk pouch then opened it. Onto her palm slipped a square tarot deck, an inch and a half by an inch and a half. She mixed up the cards without shuffling them. Then Anglaise cut the deck and pulled three cards.

Bruleé returned before she could turn over the cards.

"Oh, you started without me," she said.

"I wasn't going to turn them over."

Bruleé put down a fragrant mug of steaming-hot green tea in front of Flora.

"Try it."

Flora picked up the mug. She blew on it a second and took a sip. The mellow bitterness of the green tea was cut with a sweet lemony herbal taste, but there was no hint of the sourness lemon gave.

"Amazing. What's in it?"

"A syrup of lemongrass and lemon verbena. It adds the tart of lemon, without having to load the tea with sugar to cut the citric acid."

Flora looked at the mugs each of the kids also had in hand. "You get the same thing?"

They shook their heads.

"Rosewater," Mary Alice said.

"Eucalyptus syrup," said Caroline.

"Ginger syrup," Tyler told her.

"Cinnamon," Morris said. "It's super hot."

Bruleé sat and waved at Anglaise to continue. "Go on."

Anglaise reached for the first miniature card. "This is the current situation." She turned the card over, careful not to disturb the orientation. The card had a solid black background with folk art drawing of a greedy-looking dragon surrounded by four coins. The fifth coin was its eye. "The five of pentacles. This is our impending and current poverty. Hard to believe there's farther to go, huh?" Anglaise said, sarcasm giving way to bitterness at the end. "This is the problem, what stands in our way." She turned over the second card.

The second card was upright as well. It showed a hand with oak leaves coming from a sleeve, with an infinity sign on the cuff.

"The Hierophant," Anglaise said. "Literally, it represents members of the clergy. Not much of a leap to figure that one out." She turned over the last card. The picture was a sad-looking man with his knees drawn to his chest. The ten swords poking out of his back probably had something to do with his depression. "The ten of swords means ruin. Failure. Defeat. Again, not much of a stretch."

"The teashop is going to close?" Flora said.

"We're circling the drain," Anglaise said.

"No, you can't leave," Mary Alice said.

That's my line, Flora thought. Anne had made such progress in so short a time. Bruleé had told her it might be months to learn the real outcome of the treatments, and Anne would always need some kind of maintenance.

Flora should be the one begging the witches to stay. What stake in this did Mary Alice Ruiz have, that she was so passionate they stay?

"How do we help?" Flora asked.

"Buy stuff during business hours," Anglaise told her.

Bruleé held up a hand. "That's part of it. We need people to come to the shop. We also need other people to see people coming in."

"I can do that," Flora said.

"Me, too." Mary Alice didn't want to be out done.

"I will," added Morris. "But I don't have any money."

"I should call Father Halloran, too," Mary Alice said. "Maybe he could bring some friends or something."

Flora glanced at the Bradley boy and Caroline. They were deep in thought. She'd heard that Kim Bradley, a little know-it-all if ever Flora had met one, was one of the lead protestors.

The blonde girl's head jerked up. "I want more of whatever fixed my lungs before. I'll come back for that. If my mom notices I'm not using my inhaler, I can tell her why."

The only ones who hadn't offered to help so far was Flora and Tyler.

"I can come in for something, maybe sweets this time. You're already doing so much. Anne walked down the hall today."

Bruleé reached across the table and grasped Flora's hands. "I'm so happy for you."

Flora let out a tight smile. "Thank you. I don't think she could have done it a week ago."

Mary Alice gave Flora a long, sideways look. "So you've been coming to the witches, too."

"So have you," Flora said.

"What do you buy?" Morris asked.

"None of your business."

"Just asking. Jeez."

Flora took a sip of her tea to cover her look of regret. Not that it really was any business of the boy's. She just didn't want to air Anne's dirty laundry. Or was she just ashamed to have turned to superstition over science?

Bruleé stepped in. "We are all really grateful for your patronage. But the point is not that you continue to come, although I sincerely hope you do."

"We need new business," Anglaise said. "Not just repeat offenders."

There was a heartbeat of silence before Flora, and the kids, realized Anglaise had made a joke. Another beat passed before Flora ventured a laugh. Then everyone laughed. There was even a squeak from Caramel, so quiet Flora had forgotten she was there.

"We thought we might have a tea tasting, but didn't want to do it with the protesters out front," Bruleé said.

"Is that like wine tasting?" Flora had never heard of a tea tasting.

Nodding, Bruleé went on. "Yes. I'd make little sample size cups of tea for people, and Anglaise would make sample size teacakes. Caramel could hand out coupons."

"But where would you have it? And who'd come?" Tyler asked.

"I don't know."

Thoughtful silence muffled the room as everyone stared into their mugs, drank tea, or examined the steel tabletop.

Flora drank her tea with its lemony herbal snap. She almost wanted to suggest the park by the old church. The tea tasting could be on Sunday. That'd show Pastor Austin. Any move that confrontational, though, would destroy any hope the witches had of staying. "Wherever you go in town, the protesters will just follow you," she said.

"I told you, we should just start packing," Anglaise said.

"Not yet," Bruleé said. "We'll move if we have to."

Anglaise just frowned harder and picked up her tarot cards. She put the three she'd drawn back into the deck and shuffled them again.

"Why not the Town Square on Saturday?" Flora suggested. "It's public."

"But the protestors," Mary Alice said.

"To hell with them."

Everyone looked at Flora, surprised by her language. Her face hardened. She was no prude, whatever the town thought.

Morris chuckled softly. "Awesome. Like you said, it doesn't matter where or when you do a tea tasting. They'll be there, anyhow. Might as well not have to walk far."

"Why not?" Bruleé agreed. "We can take over iced tea, our samples, and a folding table."

"I don't like it," Anglaise said.

"It's better than doing nothing," Mary Alice said. "We'll come and help. What time Saturday?"

"Why don't we start at ten?" Bruleé said. She turned to Flora. "Will you join us?"

"Yes," Flora said. She gripped the teacup so tight she thought it might shatter. But she meant it. She would show her support publicly at last, though it may take her last nerve to do it.

The kids all grinned at each other then at Flora, in what seemed a silent dare.

Flora downed the rest of her tea, setting the cup down with enough force to clink loudly on the countertop. "I'll be there bright and early."

"Thank you," Bruleé said.

Flora nodded. "Least I can do, I suppose."

She stood up and checked her wristwatch. It was only seven, but she still had to get home and fix Anne's tea. She'd need more tea soon. The doses were by the week. Flora wasn't lying when she told Bruleé it was the least she could do. She knew she wasn't paying anywhere near what the tea was worth, and it seemed she owed them a debt she wasn't sure she could ever repay.

She nodded to them all in turn. "I should be going. Thank you for the tea. I'll see you all later."

"Bye, Ms. Barton," the kids said in unison.

She squinted at them then decided the chorus had been un-intentional. She shook off her thoughts. She was too used to insolence and had gotten paranoid in her old age. She gave the room a tight smile and picked up her purse. "Good night."

Saturday morning, Bruleé was up early. She wanted to make sure she had the tea brewed and iced by ten. She made three of her favorite spring brews: jasmine green with a touch of honey, ginger passionflower, and lemon mint.

She'd had a quick look at the tealeaves to make sure the weather would be nice and, sure enough, the spring day promised to be kind.

Bruleé even made three flavors of ice cubes the same as the teas, so that as the ice melted, it wouldn't water down the tea. She figured she could serve at least fifty people with the three big batches of tea. There were six pitchers in the fridge. She'd bring one of each and send one of the kids back for refills as needed.

In the back of her mind, Bruleé knew she might not come close to serving fifty. She might not serve any people, other than the promised helpers. But she tried hard not to think of that. Maybe if just one thing could go right, she'd feel like she hadn't made a total mire of their lives.

With the ice cubes in the freezer, her work was done. Bruleé left the kitchen for the shop itself. Anglaise would be down soon to frost the teacakes she'd made the night before.

Bruleé busied herself in the shop, dusting stock that was as pristine as the day she'd put it on the shelves.

She couldn't stop checking the clock on the wall. It wasn't

even nine a.m. She had hours of busywork to do because, if she stopped, she might combust from nerves.

She swept the floors, brushed the crisp new table clothes clean, and polished the bakery case to hospital sterility.

From the kitchen came the whir of the mixer and clang of baking sheets. Bruleé itched to check on Anglaise, but knew better than to try. Instead, she dusted the tea cubbies for a third time, checked the clock, and waited to see if their "friends" showed up at ten.

The bell over the shop door rang. For an instant, the sound drowned out the protestors next door. Day two of protest had gotten a late start, but working to the sound of their constant racket was painful.

Bruleé turned, half hopeful and half full of dread that the protestors had decided to come in and terrorize the shop. She smiled when she saw Flora. "You came," she exclaimed.

"Well, I promised," Flora said and looked around the shop. "It's cute in here."

"Thanks," Bruleé said, though the sour expression on Flora's face meant it might not be a compliment. Then again, Flora sort of looked like she was sipping lemon juice all the time, so it was hard to tell.

"Am I the first one here?"

"So far," Bruleé said. "Please, have a seat. The tea is in the fridge and Anglaise should be done baking soon."

"Those protestors—" Flora waved at the door. "—threw some Bible quotes at me as I came in."

Bruleé cringed. "Sorry. But thank you for coming."

"If you last, I don't think Geoffrey and Matilda will be your only customers. I saw Penelope's niece staring at the tea-shop from across the street."

"I hope you're right." Bruleé sat down across from Flora. In the distance, the oven timer dinged, and there was another clatter as Anglaise readied the frosting. Probably the frosting knives or bowls.

"So what's on the menu today?"

"Jasmine-scented cake filled with coconut curd and vanilla passion fruit," Bruleé told her.

"I'm going to have to take some home to Anne," Flora said.

The front door chimed again, and Bruleé saw Alyss and Caroline, red-faced and angry, come in.

Alyss blew a raspberry at the protestors down the block, and Bruleé heard angry shouts. She stood up and pulled the girls inside. "Don't make them angrier," she pleaded.

"Well, it's not their business and they can tell my mom if they want, I don't care!" Alyss said.

"That's no way to get what you want," Flora said.

"They started it," Alyss shot back.

"Just go sit down," Bruleé said. "We'll be ready to go in a minute."

Caroline tugged Alyss's T-shirt, and the two girls joined Flora at one of the tables. They kept looking at everything: the tea jars in their cubbies, the pots for sale, and the teacups hanging everywhere.

"Wow, it looks like a family magazine," said Caroline.

"Maybe it could be less pink," Alyss said.

"No, I like it," Caroline told her.

"Oh, Morris and Tyler set up a folding table in the Town Square." Alyss grinned and gave a thumbs up.

"Thank you," Bruleé said. "Let me go see if the cakes can be packed yet." She couldn't help smiling as she went into the kitchen.

Anglaise glanced at her grin, but didn't return it. "Well?"

"Well, the help has arrived."

"Spectacular," Anglaise said, without a twitch in her grim expression.

"Are the cakes done?"

"Yeah, but don't expect a lot of decoration."

"Let's just pack them up. I'm sure they look fine.

Anglaise's version of "not decorated" would still be fancier than she let on. She always complained loudest that her presentations were too simple, when they were decoratively frosted with every technique except fondant, which Anglaise hated.

"Start packing," Bruleé said.

"We should leave through the back door if we want a few minutes of peace before the Jesus freaks catch up to us."

"I suppose." Bruleé had thought to leave through the front door, but Anglaise's idea was better. Her paranoia was useful once in a while. Bruleé clapped her hands. "Chop, chop. We leave in five."

They managed to carry everything to the Town Square in one trip. Anglaise took the cake boxes because she didn't trust anyone else not to drop them. Flora, Alyss, and Caroline each took a pitcher of ice tea, and Bruleé carried the cups and paper plates.

They formed a curious parade, with Anglaise leading the way through the alley, and Bruleé bringing up the rear.

Caramel had been relieved of duty. Bruleé thought she could stand a break after so much socializing, and the locking spell on her bedroom door was more involved than usual. A clear sign she wanted nothing to do with the tasting.

She was sorry to see Alyss's look of disappointment, but it couldn't be helped. The protestors had infected their household with a fear that Caramel couldn't shake off. Bruleé wasn't even sure how she herself managed, but somehow she had to.

Morris and a very nervous looking Tyler met them in the Town Square. Morris waved both arms in the air, as if the company could have missed the table.

Alyss and Caroline darted ahead. "We couldn't just put out a table. It'd look like a garage sale," Alyss yelled over her shoulder.

The table was covered with a summery quilt in bright floral patterns. Two teapots on either end, stuffed with flowers, weighted the blanket against stray breezes. A poster board sign with *Tea Tasting* in bright red marker was safety pinned to the blanket.

Bruleé felt tears sting the corner of her eyes, but she

blinked them back. She barely knew Alyss and her friends, but they had gone to so much trouble.

"It's beautiful," Bruleé said, setting down the paper plates and cups. "You didn't have to decorate. But thank you so much."

"Very nice," Flora said.

"Yeah, not bad," Anglaise agreed.

"It wasn't any trouble," Alyss said. "Caroline brought the blanket, and I made the sign."

"The teapot and flowers were Morris's idea," Tyler said.

Morris flushed red and punched Tyler in the arm. "I told you not to tell them that."

Caroline rolled her eyes. "An eye for details doesn't make you gay."

"I stole those flowers," he said.

Bruleé wished he hadn't pointed that out. "Uh…thank you?"

Anglaise snickered. "Awesome."

"Let's just set up," Bruleé said.

Anglaise unpacked the petit-four-size sample cakes, each one in a little paper cup with a swirl of icing and a candied flower on top. She lined them up by flavor, making sure each one faced front.

When she stepped aside, she gestured at Bruleé to arrange the tea. Bruleé just put the pitchers in back where she would stand, ready to pour.

Flora looked around the town square. "Now what?"

They were getting some surprised and cautious looks, but no one approached the table.

"Now this." Alyss took a picture of the teacakes with her phone and began tapping on it. "And send," she pronounced.

Bruleé looked around. Alyss had sounded so firm, she expected a crowd to gather instantly. Nothing happened.

They milled about, then Flora went to sit on the edge of the fountain. A minute later, she was joined by Caroline.

Alyss bit her lip. "Just give it awhile."

"Would everyone like a teacake while we wait?" Bruleé said.

Morris raised his hand. "Me! Yes!"

She poured tea and handed the boy one of the samples. He eyed the table hungrily, and Bruleé looked around. A small crowd was gathering on the edge of the town square, but no one approached. At this rate, Morris would get to eat all of the samples.

"There." Alyss jumped up and down, pointing at the street. "I told you so."

A white van with Saint Mary's painted on the side pulled into a parking place at the edge of the square. Bruleé frowned in momentary confusion, afraid Austin had called in reinforcements. Then Alyss waved enthusiastically at the van.

"Who is that?" Bruleé asked.

"It's okay," Alyss said as she ran toward the van.

"Is she crazy?" Anglaise asked.

"Hang on." Bruleé saw the van doors open.

Out stepped Father Halloran. She laughed, glad to see her first customer again.

He had brought a van full of gray-haired women in coats far too heavy for springtime.

Father Halloran spotted Bruleé and waved at her. Bruleé waved back, but Alyss ran up to greet him before Bruleé could shout hello.

Bruleé turned to Anglaise, "Let's start filling glasses."

Anglaise grunted but nodded and started with the nearest pitcher.

Halloran, Alyss, and the brigade of church ladies approached the table.

"Welcome back, Father Halloran," Bruleé said. She held out a plastic cup of tea.

"It's good to be back," he said and took the cup. "I intend to sample everything."

"That's what it's all for."

Halloran picked up a sample cake. "Come along, ladies, it looks wonderful."

"How are you here?" Bruleé asked as she handed out another cup.

"I told him," Alyss said.

"She told me about the trouble you've been having. I just wish Austin would listen to reason."

"I don't think you have to worry about that," Anglaise said with a grunt. "You only have a few minutes before the protest gets wind of our tea tasting."

"Don't worry. That old Puritan can't scare us off, can he, girls?" Halloran asked the ladies.

"Of course not," they chorused and hoisted their cakes in the air.

Halloran chuckled. "You see?"

"Hey, we got incoming." Tyler pointed across the square.

Bruleé whipped around, stomach dropping, expecting to see Austin and the protest. Instead, she saw a couple of the townies, two women she had seen passing the teashop, day after day, but who had never ventured in.

She quickly smiled but steeled herself. "Hello," she said. "Welcome to Tea Times Three's tea tasting. We have three sample teas and teacakes for you to try."

The oldest of the two women gave a shaky smile and hovered on the edge of the crowd.

The other woman looked close to Bruleé's age, maybe a year or two older. She looked at the tiny cakes like a cat eyeing a slow-moving mouse.

"So is any of this magic?" she asked.

"No, just regular."

"But tasty," Halloran chimed in.

"Well, since you're witches, I thought it'd be magical."

"That costs extra, Miss…"

"Dani."

"Nice to meet you, Dani."

"Yeah, yeah. Do you have any weight-loss spells?" she asked.

"Are you sure you need one?" Bruleé looked Dani over. She didn't look fat. Maybe a bit overweight, but nothing diet and exercise couldn't fix.

"It's for the last ten pounds. You have no idea."

Bruleé saw the sharp look in her eye and knew Dani was sizing up her figure.

"Have you tried—"

"Diet and exercise? Duh. That's all I do," Dani said.

"Danielle," the other woman said, a note of almost motherly correction in her voice.

Dani just laughed. "This is Emma, a friend of my mom's. She's still not sure you aren't going to turn us all into toads."

Emma blushed a deep pink. "I never said that." She turned to Bruleé and repeated, "I never said that."

"But you won't let Veronica bring the rug rats for tea."

The older woman's blush turned from pink to crimson. "I—I never forbade it. Veronica's a grown woman."

Dani barked another laugh. Bruleé felt bad for Emma, though she didn't doubt Dani's words. If this Emma woman had kept her daughter from the shop, she may not have said anything as outrageous as the witches turning people into toads, but she'd surely helped the pastor without even knowing it.

Bruleé decided to rescue the floundering Emma. Maybe she could bring the woman and her patronage over to their side. "I'm sure Mrs. Emma just doesn't know what we have to offer." Bruleé took a teacake off of the table and handed it to her.

Emma stared at the proffered cake with a frozen, brittle smile. Dani covered her mouth and snickered.

Bruleé kept a careful neutral expression—pleasant smile, hand out. She was sure Emma couldn't refuse forever.

With her hand in slow motion, Emma reached out for the cake. Bruleé saw the doubt on her face, but she waited patiently. It was hard not to be a little insulted. She knew people feared and mistrusted witches, but so much of that mistrust was created and perpetuated by regular people, just like Emma, who had probably never met a witch in their whole lives.

Emma took the pastry and looked around, as if to make sure no one else eating them had turned into an animal. Bruleé looked around too, following her darting glances. There was only a group of happy, chatting women and Father Halloran, who laughed loudly at something Alyss said to him. Nothing Emma could object to.

"Go on," Dani urged. She reached past Emma and took a sample of her own. The bite sized cake disappeared whole. "Oh, my God!"

"What? What is it?" Emma looked around, alarmed by Dani's outburst.

"This is so good," Dani said, around a mouthful of cake. She swallowed. "We're all going to get fat with you guys in town."

Bruleé couldn't help but laugh. "I hope not," she said. "We'll add some low calorie options, won't we, Anglaise?"

Anglaise snorted. "Not likely."

"Yes, we will," Bruleé said firmly.

Emma looked at the cake in her hand before trying a tiny bite. "Oh, my," she said. "Oh, my."

Dani nudged her with an elbow. "Amazing, huh?"

"I've never—" Emma took another bite instead of finishing her sentence. She chewed, her face lit with concentration. "It's so floral, so flavorful. I didn't know cake could taste like this. Is that jasmine?"

Bruleé nodded. "It's meant to be eaten with this tea." She handed a plastic cup to Emma, who took it without hesitation this time.

"Danielle!"

A shout echoed through the square, and everyone turned at the noise. Penelope Owens, protest sign waving in the air, charged toward the tea tasting. Straggling behind her, marched the rest of the protest group, including a red-faced and furious Pastor Austin.

"Tyler! Get away from those witches!"

"Leave them alone, Mom," Tyler yelled back.

"You get away now or you're grounded all summer, mister," his mother shot back.

Tyler looked torn but he didn't move.

"Danielle, I asked you not to have anything to do with the likes of them."

Bruleé had the feeling if fewer people had been watching she would have spat again.

"It's just a tea tasting." Father Halloran stepped forward to meet the oncoming mob. "There's no spells, nothing uncanny, just tea and cake."

"You don't get to decide for me and mine, priest," Penelope snarled.

Halloran's jaw dropped. "Excuse me?"

Dani gasped. "Oh, my God, and you don't decide for me either, Aunt Penelope. I'm a grown-ass woman."

Penelope leveled a shaking finger at Bruleé. "You don't know them like I do."

"You don't know us at all," Anglaise said.

"I know your kind," Penelope screeched.

The crowd froze. The church ladies clutched their throats. Halloran backed up a step. Even the teens stopped and waited.

"Witches ruined my family when I was just a little girl. My mother was a spell addict. She spent all our money on her own vanity and even kept Papa spelled, so he never asked any questions. So, don't you tell me I don't know what witches can do. They'll ruin you like they did my mother."

A tear rolled down Penelope's face, following the lines and wrinkles, until it dropped from her chin.

Bruleé's mind was blank, swept clear by Penelope's rage and loss. She should say something in their defense but she couldn't begin to form a sentence or a thought.

"Penelope," Dani whispered. Her voice carried perfectly in the silence. "You never told me. Mom never told me."

"Katy was just a girl then. That's why our parents divorced, why your mom and I moved to Maine with Papa. Mother bankrupted us, left us alone, the whole family. Abandoned her own children." Penelope's voice broke over a harsh sob.

Pastor Austin was the only one to move. He came up beside Penelope and patted her shoulder. Despite the compassionate move, Bruleé could see the burning triumph in his eyes.

"There, there, Penelope," he said.

Bruleé could feel eyes on her and a shameful heat flushed her cheeks. After that display, there was nothing she could say. Any denial would sound hollow and guilty.

"You see, Tyler? You see what they do?" Kim grabbed her son's arm and tried to yank him away.

"They haven't done any of that," he said and wrenched himself free from her grip. "All they've done is help Caroline's asthma. Why can't you just listen to them?"

Austin smirked, still comforting Penelope. "'And lead us not into temptation, but deliver us from the evil one.'"

"'This is how you can show your love to me: Everywhere we go, say of me, 'He is my brother.'" Father Halloran stepped in front of Bruleé. "You really think this vindictive persecution is God's will?"

"That's right," Flora said. "These girls have done more for Anne than the team of doctors ever has."

"Why don't you march your protest back to the sidewalk, or, better yet, straight to Hell?" Anglaise said.

Bruleé whipped around to glare at her. Just when they'd made friends, just when people had stood up for them, she had to mouth off.

Alyss snickered first, then Flora, and finally, a hearty baritone guffaw from Halloran echoed over the square.

Anglaise looked smug, and Bruleé stuck her tongue out briefly, for the childish joy of it. Then she turned back to the confrontation.

Pastor Austin was livid. Veins in his neck throbbed, straining against the skin. An air of violence came off him, dark and heavy as storm clouds. He looked like he was readying to punch Father Halloran in the face. Halloran just stood there, gut thrust out, hands on hips—a still calm that met Austin's rage face to face.

"If I were you, Austin, I'd turn the other cheek," Halloran said.

If only Bruleé had some of Anglaise's bravado, she could say something to end a fight before it started.

A shrill whistle sounded over the brown grass of the park. Hustling toward them was a police officer with a black buzz cut and business-like sunglasses.

"Just in time," Austin crowed. "Now we find out if this little picnic is aboveboard."

Bruleé turned to Anglaise with a cocked eyebrow. Anglaise shrugged. She looked at the others, Flora and the kids. They all exchanged wondering glances.

"Hey, Pastor, what's going on?" the officer asked.

"Ah, Officer Connolly, these witches are a public nuisance."

"Are not," Alyss said.

The officer pulled his shades off. "What sort of nuisance?"

"They're handing out free samples. Probably enchanted to lure back repeat business," Penelope said.

"We'd never do that!" Bruleé had had enough. She pushed to the front of the crowd, "There's no law against handing out free food."

Officer Connolly scratched his face with a gloved hand. "Well," he said, "yes and no."

"Ha!" Austin shouted.

"What?" Bruleé asked.

"It's fine to do it on your own property. That's no problem," Connolly said carefully. "But out in the town square, it constitutes an event, and you need a permit to have an event. Sorry, ma'am."

"Now, fine them." Austin looked so pleased, Bruleé was sure he'd break out in a jig.

"I'm sorry, Officer," she said, voice hardly more than a whisper. She hated that Austin won. And to her shock, she realized she just plain hated him.

"It's okay. The chief said just to pack it up." Connolly looked at Austin. "No fine."

There was a chorus of disappointed noises from the church ladies, and Halloran deflated, gut sagging back over his belt buckle.

"That's not fair," Alyss said.

"Yeah," Caroline and Morris chimed.

"It's more than fair," Austin growled.

With the showdown averted and no punishment forthcoming from the law, Bruleé rallied."Well, if you'd all like to take your tea and cakes back to the shop, I'm sure we can send you all home with a little box of treats," she said.

"That sounds lovely," Halloran said. Bruleé caught his wink at the still-raging Austin. "Doesn't it, ladies?"

Bruleé twirled her finger at Anglaise in a "clean this up" motion. Anglaise nodded and put the remaining goths and Flora to work packing up the sample cakes and the pitchers of tea. Tyler still waffled beside his mother, weighing obedience against punishment. Morris took his centerpieces, and the others took up the rest.

Father Halloran herded his flock in the direction of the teashop and Bruleé was left in the park.

"I'm sorry, Officer Connolly. We didn't mean to cause a problem."

He shook his head. "It's all right."

"Would you like to come for tea?"

He had been eyeballing the departing cakes as Halloran's group had shuffled past.

"No, thanks. I have to get back to work," he said.

Bruleé nodded. Even if it was a brush off, it was a polite one. She turned to Dani and Emma. "And would you two like to join us?"

"No, she wouldn't!" Penelope snapped. "Take me home, Danielle."

Dani's narrowed eyes darted from Bruleé to her aunt. She gave a heavy sigh and her shoulders slumped. "Fine, Penelope, let's go," she said.

Penelope took her arm, and they started off down the sidewalk leading out of the town square.

Emma looked guilty and edged away from Bruleé. "I—I should go now," she said and fled the square at a swift walk just short of a jog.

"I'm going to the teashop," Tyler announced.

"No you aren't. Not unless you want to be grounded forever." Kim made a grab for her son, but he dodged her hand.

"Fine. Ground me forever," he said and took off.

"Tyler Bradley, you get back here!" Kim rounded on Bruleé, eye twitching. "You better send my son home this instant. This is all your fault."

"A rebellious teen is no one's fault, Mrs. Bradley," Officer

Connolly said. He nodded to Bruleé. "Why don't we carry that table back to your shop?"

Bruleé was about to refuse and say she'd pick it up later, but then realized that he might be offering an unofficial escort.

Looking around, Bruleé saw she was alone in the park with Austin's irate cadre of protestors.

"Thank you. I could use the help."

Together they folded up the legs and carried it back to the shop. Austin's crew followed them, singing all the way back. They parked themselves in front of the antique store.

When the teashop door closed behind Bruleé, it shut out the protestors completely. A few days ago, she'd cast a spell designed to block sound. Officer Connolly put the table down and leaned it against the front counter. He looked around the shop and grunted. She waited for further comment, but he didn't offer one.

With a nod, he said, "Ma'am." He left before she could thank him again.

Anglaise was waiting on the guests who were filling the tables. Even Flora sat stiff-backed at one of the round tables with the goth kids.

"Austin still out there?" Anglaise asked.

"Followed me all the way back," Bruleé said. She went to help wait the tables.

"Don't worry about that dried up Puritan," Halloran said. "Bullies like him don't have the stamina. He doesn't have a leg to stand on. All he has on his side is prejudice. You'll see."

Anglaise frowned and opened her mouth, but Bruleé caught her eye with a cautionary glance and shook her head. She didn't want Anglaise's bad attitude dampening the faint air of festivity left from the town square.

"I hope you're right," Bruleé said with a smile.

She was just happy to have customers in the shop and hear the buzz of conversation. Such a warm sound after days of silence and infrequent late-night visitors. Bruleé took a second to survey the shop. The full tables. The customers. A few had even abandoned their chairs in order to price teapots on the shelves. She noticed Caroline reach for Tyler's hand under the table and hold it briefly. This was what she'd always imagined the teashop to be. Lively and full of happy customers. She wanted to remember this moment, in case it never came again.

"Excuse me, miss?" one of the church ladies called from the back wall. "How much is this teapot?"

Bruleé put on her retail smile and went over. Maybe the cash register would see some action, after all.

Chapter

ean Joe's Coffee House was crowded, but William hovered at the front window. He waited until the pretentious couple in designer sunglasses left then took their table.

He ordered a grandé latte and nursed it. The Sunday crowd was steady, but William was looking for one person.

Eyes glued to the blue sky above, he waited for the witch he'd run into last week. He couldn't be sure she'd show up again. She would have to, if she wanted the best cup of coffee within a radius of twenty miles.

An hour and a half of dirty looks from patrons wanting a window seat later, William saw the witch. She descended from the sky on her broom, dropping quickly, until braking somehow the last few feet.

William wasn't the only person watching her arrival. The entire shop paused to watch. He wondered if that, in part, explained the crowd.

Once she landed, the witch tucked the broom under her arm and came into the coffee shop.

Instantly, everyone who had paused their activities went back to drinking coffee, reading the newspaper, or surfing the Internet.

The witch went up to the counter to order. After a short wait in line, she turned around, two large paper take-out cups in hand.

For the hundredth time, William assured himself this wasn't a terrible idea.

Before she could exit the coffee shop, William waved and smiled. He gestured at the empty seat across from him.

The witch looked at him as if he'd turned into a giant lobster. Her expression pinched.

"Miss Witch, um, please, have a seat." William stood, unsure if it was politeness or if he would actually run after her if she refused.

She looked at him closely. "I'm not looking for a date," she said. The witch looked around the coffee shop as if checking for witnesses, then came over.

William sat back down. "I'm not going to hit on you."

She sat down opposite him. "Oh. Because you're not getting anywhere."

"I promise. I just wanted to talk," William said.

She pulled the plastic lid off one of the coffee cups. A sugary mocha smell, heavy on the chocolate, steamed from the mug.

"So, what do you want? A tarot reading? Spell of some sort? Curses are illegal, people know that, but you'd be surprised how many try and ask."

"Nothing like that," William said. "I just—you're a chef right? I wanted to talk food."

She rolled her eyes and started to get up. "If you've got some weird fetish, you can go—"

"No, it's not like that," William protested. "Have you ever been to the Aspen Food and Wine Classic?"

The witch sat back in her chair. "No. Have you?"

"The last six years." He stuck his hand out. "My name's William Shepherd. I own the gas station just outside Midswich."

She shook his hand briefly. "Anglaise Créme. If you live in Midswich, you know all about us, I suppose."

"I heard about the tea tasting in the park. If I hadn't had to work, I'd have been there. That's twice I've missed out on your food, and I'm kicking myself."

"So, you like food," Anglaise said. "But you haven't been in our shop."

"Guilty."

"Are you going to?"

William had to think about that. He didn't want to look like a coward, and he didn't want to offend her either. "Sure, when I get some time," he said.

Anglaise snorted in disbelief.

He couldn't blame her.

There was a stretch of awkward silence. William didn't try to justify his remark and Anglaise didn't embarrass him by pressing the point.

She took a sip of coffee and put it down.

"So, Aspen. Is it everything I hear?" she asked.

"It's amazing. The finest chefs are there, the atmosphere is incredible."

Nodding, Anglaise said, "I've been to a lot of east coast food festivals. Boston of course, New York, Atlanta, and Miami, but not Aspen."

"Have you participated in any?"

"No." Anglaise took another sip of coffee. "Unless you have the recognition or the money, it's hard."

"You still have plenty of time. You'll get there," he said. William was trying to be reassuring, but realized he sounded like some trite old fool. He was only a couple years older than her and had no right to lecture.

Anglaise gave a bitter snort. "Yeah. I've gotten as far as the backwoods of Maine." She waved her hands in the air. "Yay."

"Maine's coming up in the world. We get a lot of tourists in Midswich for the Victorian Faire and stuff. Plus the summer people."

"Bruleé showed us the website before moving us here," Anglaise said.

"But you don't want to be here," he said. "I get it. I wanted to leave too."

"Why didn't you?"

"My dad died and I had to take over the family business."

"A gas station is your family business? Goddess, why not just sell it?"

"It doesn't sound like much, I know, but it's a big deal.

The gas station was the only black-owned business in Midswich for the longest time. My great granddad opened it in 1921, and back then, it was a miracle. And it's still important, because this state isn't exactly the most diverse."

A faint blush tingled Anglaise's cheek. "Oh."

"But, yeah, it's not really my calling," William said. He hadn't meant to sound so harsh.

"Sorry," she muttered.

"So, where did you go to pastry school?" William changed the subject.

"At home."

"For real?"

"Yeah."

"How'd you do that?"

"Well, I watched a lot of cooking shows and spent all my allowance on magazines and books. I worked my way through pastry cookbooks cover to cover."

"Wow." William whistled in appreciation. He couldn't imagine the dedication that would take.

She shrugged. "I started when I was nine. I'd make two or three things a day."

"When did you go to school?"

"Witches home school. I had all day except when I went to my tutors and study groups. I made them eat the food. Until they started complaining they were getting fat."

William laughed and was surprised when Anglaise joined in. It was the only spark of levity he'd seen from her so far.

"If you're foodie enough to go to Aspen six years running, come to the shop."

"I know," William said. He pressed down a sigh. "I almost got a free sample." Maybe this wasn't the best time to bring it up.

"Chicken out?"

"Yeah. Pastor Austin was standing right behind me."

"You should have tried the strawberry basil scones."

"I was just about to."

Anglaise shook her head. "I told Bruleé we'd never make it in a small town. Freakin' backwoods rubes."

William felt bad for a moment then annoyed at the town he called home and Anglaise's assessment of them.

"I tried out my own version of those scones," he said.

Her eyes narrowed. "Trying to steal my recipes?"

"No, I just wanted a taste."

"And?"

"Took me two batches to get anything that tasted good and by then I was out of strawberries."

"Good. Buy them next time."

He chuckled. "I won't steal your recipes anymore, I promise."

Anglaise drained her take out cup. "I always wanted to show at Aspen, but the booths are twenty-five hundred dollars," she said, wistful for a moment. "Bruleé promised we could go if the teashop took off—"

"Give it some time. Maybe you'll be surprised."

Anglaise shook her head, eyes sharp again. "Doesn't matter. Another month and we're flat busted." She stood up, grabbing her broom and second cup of coffee. "Well, if you don't want a reading, I better go." She turned before he could say anything.

"Wait," William said.

"What?"

"I got you something," he said. He reached under the table.

Suspicion flashed across her face. "Look, I don't need a stalker. Defensive magic is allowed by law."

"No, no. It's nothing weird," William said. "It's for safety. You've never lived anywhere rural, have you?"

"No."

He put a bag from Forte's Sporting Goods on the table. "I saw you fly over the woods the last week. You'll need this."

Slowly she reached for the bag as if waiting for it to sting her. Anglaise pulled out an orange Day-Glo vest.

"It's super ugly," she said.

"It's for hunting. So you don't get shot. If you're going to fly through the woods, you gotta be careful."

"Oh." Anglaise studied the vest for a second then tried it on. "Thanks. I guess I didn't think of that."

"There's a lot of deer hunting around. Ducks, too. Even moose. I don't hunt myself, but you can't be too careful."

She gave him a brief smile. "I'll stay above the treetops. And wear the vest. Thanks."

"No problem."

Anglaise gathered her broom and coffee. She inclined her head. "Bye."

"Bye."

The coffee shop quieted as she took off from the sidewalk. The orange hunting vest was brightly visible against the clear spring sky. When she was out of sight, William looked around the quiet coffee shop. A few of the patrons gave him envious sidelong glances. He smiled at them until they looked away.

"Back in a second," Flora said as she headed for the door to check the mailbox downstairs.

Anne was watching TV. She gave a nod, but no reply.

Lately, the mail had become a chore. Every time Flora left the apartment, she received a lot of sideways glances from people she'd thought were her friends and neighbors. They whispered as she went by.

She had begun to regret going in the front door of the tea-shop, and she was ashamed of her regret. She thought she didn't care about what the town thought of her. They had no idea what the witches had done for her, for Anne. But their stares and mumblings still made her face burn.

At four o'clock in the afternoon, the only person Flora was likely to meet at the mailbox was Eddie, and he was a good boy who hadn't said anything about the witches.

Flora walked the length of the footpath in the front yard and opened 3A's mail slot. The electric bill was there. So was the gas and water. She shuffled them to the bottom of the stack. There was a letter from Anne's no-good son. Anne had three children spread across the country, all of whom were too busy and important to either visit or care for their mother. Flora always wanted to toss their letters into the bushes, but inevitably there was a check enclosed. Guilt money, Flora called it, and so she didn't discard the letters.

The last piece of mail was a festive envelope with confetti and balloons printed in the corner. *You're Invited* was printed just above her name. Flora couldn't remember the last time she was invited to something. The return address made her eyebrows raise.

Geoffrey Callister?

Flora opened the envelope. Inside was an invitation to a party. The paper matched the envelope's rainbow of balloons and confetti. For a second, Flora tried to recall the name of Geoffrey and Claire's children before she remembered they didn't have any.

She read the invitation. Geoffrey and William were giving a party to welcome the witches to Midswich. Flora thought her eyebrows would fall off if they rose higher, and she wiped the surprise off her face.

So, Geoffrey, the original whistle blower on the witches, was trying to repent. She looked for an address. William Shepherd's house was given. "An odd pair to give a party."

"What's that, Ms. Barton?"

Flora started, her heart pounding alarmingly for a second. She caught her breath and glared at Eddie. "Don't sneak up on an old lady."

"Sorry." He put his hands up and looked genuinely apologetic. "I was just wondering what was so interesting."

Flora held up the invitation. "A party to welcome the witches."

"What? That's more than my family got."

"Don't be silly. No one gets this sort of welcome," Flora said.

Eddie readjusted his pork pie hat, not quite tipping it to her He wore his usual '50s homage, pork pie hat, sport jacket and skinny tie. "Sorry, ma'am."

Flora then noticed the invitation was three sheets long. She looked at the other pages. Extra invitations on the bottom. *Bring Friends* was printed in bold lettering and underlined.

"Would you like to come to the party?" She held up an extra invitation. "It says bring friends. You could bring that girl you're spending so much time with lately."

Eddie blushed. "We're just friends."

"That's fine. That's what it says," She pushed the invitation at him and he finally took it.

Ten minutes to five. Matilda couldn't remember how late Tea Times Three stayed open. When they hadn't had any customers, the witches had cut their original hours back. Now that a few more people were becoming regulars, they were almost back to normal business hours. Nowadays, the bakery case always had some stock. Tartlets, mini-muffins, butter cookies, slices of teacake—all with Anglaise's unique stamp of interesting flavor combinations.

The bell over the shop door tinkled as Matilda stepped in.

"Good afternoon," Bruleé said promptly, her smile of greeting warm and genuine.

The first time Matilda went into the teashop, it had been empty. For a minute, she had thought it was closed and the door left open by mistake.

"Hi," Matilda said, her voice faint.

Bruleé gave her a second look, blue eyes attentive and piercing.

"Would you like to have a seat?" Bruleé waved Matilda over to a round table.

Nodding, Matilda followed. The pink, taffeta tablecloth and striped upholstery had been changed to a more neutral golden brown. Matilda wondered where they had gotten the money for new linens, before she remembered Bruleé was a witch. She had probably cast a spell to change the color.

Matilda sat down and was surprised when Bruleé took the chair next to her.

Could Bruleé know why she was really here? Again, she *was* dealing with a witch.

There was silence as Matilda tried to think how to begin this conversation. She wasn't even sure exactly what she was after.

"Can I help you with something?" Bruleé asked softly.

Matilda exhaled with relief. A nervous smile twitched her lips then faded. "Yes. But I'm not sure with what," Matilda said. She slumped in her chair and put her head in her hands.

"Would you like a reading?"

"Could you do it for other people?"

"No."

Matilda took a deep breath and sat up. "It's about Hugh, my boyfriend. I doubt you've met him. He's outside with Austin's groupies once in a while. Tall, really, really good looking."

Bruleé nodded. "What about him?"

"We don't mesh anymore. I have no idea what he wants out of life, except that he never shuts up about New York. I want to know why. Maybe if I knew what he was looking for, what his goals are, I'd know for sure if we were over." The thought of Eddie flashed through Matilda's mind. She felt her face get hot, and she pushed the disloyal thought aside.

Bruleé was silent a long moment. Then, she said, "You want to know his dreams."

The words struck Matilda to the core. "That's exactly it." Bruleé had hit on what she wanted better than Matilda herself.

"A reading, cards, or tea leaves, won't tell you that," Bruleé said.

Matilda slumped again. "Oh."

"But Anglaise can make you something."

She gave Bruleé a sidelong glance. "What?"

"It's a spell. And a food, since that's what Anglaise does."

"I don't get it."

Bruleé's hands fluttered. "That's because I'm not explaining it well," she said. "Anglaise can make you dream puffs."

Matilda shook her head, still lost in the conversation.

"Dream puffs are sort of homemade marshmallows. They have a spell on them that allows you to enter someone else's dream, a dream of their heart's desires..." Bruleé hesitated a second. "You'll get that or something they're scared of. Either way, it's enlightening."

The perky glare of Bruleé's smile almost wiped all questions from Matilda's brain. Almost.

"Is that safe? What if I get the fear dream? Could I die?"

"No," Bruleé said quickly. "The whole, 'Die in a dream, you die in real life' is just in movies."

"It's in a lot of movies."

"That's because it's more dramatic. This is real life," Bruleé assured her.

"As long as I don't die, yes, I want to know," Matilda said.

"You won't die."

"So, how much will it cost?"

"It's twenty dollars per dream puff. You won't need more than one."

"Great, I guess. Never spent that much on a marshmallow." Matilda reached for her purse.

Bruleé held up her hand to stop Matilda. "A magic marshmallow, and I'll give you some cocoa to go with it. You can pay when you pick it up. They'll be done in a few days."

Matilda reached out and squeezed Bruleé's hand. "Thanks." The witch looked startled for a second, her body going rigid with confusion. Then Bruleé relaxed. "Sorry," Matilda said. She pulled her hand away. Were there rules against touching a witch? Maybe she just didn't like to be touched.

"No," Bruleé said, although she pulled her hands under the table. "Most people are nervous around witches. I've never had many…non-witch friends."

"Well, if you stay, I think you'll make a few," Matilda said.

Bruleé looked at the tabletop, her face soft and wistful. Matilda had to remind herself, Bruleé was only a few years younger than she was. She looked vulnerable and very, very young.

"That would be nice."

Dream puffs were a complex spell, and Anglaise wished Bruleé would quit promising things without asking.

Anglaise used her broom to sweep the kitchen. She couldn't really sweep a circle for the spell casting, because the kitchen was a long and somewhat narrow rectangle.

After she swept the area, she cast a squareish area, making a circle with sea salt. All her affinities were food related, and she found chalk circles weak.

At least, a circle for casting didn't have to be too literal. It should be a circle, but any sanctified area would do. Anglaise wanted access to the stove cupboards and refrigerator. She had put out everything she needed on the kitchen island, but had learned the hard way to include major appliances when working food spells. Once a circle was broken, the entire spell had to be started over from the beginning.

Once Anglaise had poured the salt circle to include the stove, she set the four watchtowers. There were the four elements: earth, air, fire, and water.

Fire and water were easy. Anglaise had a little bowl of water she set at the direction and she turned a gas burner on the range for fire.

Earth was typically a pinch of soil, but she couldn't have dirt in the kitchen, so she used a clean, smooth block of pink rock salt.

Air was the most difficult one. Covens and most other witches used incense, but the smell would throw off a chef, confusing the palette with the cloying odors. After long years of trial and error, Anglaise had discovered a can of air, made for making food-based foams, worked decently. Sadly, it was more inert than the incense, and any witch looking to break her circle and do her harm could easily get past the can of air. The chances of that were low, and Anglaise had yet to find a better substitute. With the circle cast, Anglaise could get down to making the dream puffs.

Normally when spell casting, an athame or wand would be used to direct power into the spell ingredients, but Anglaise kept to her kitchen tools. She had an antique iron ladle, used by her great-great-grandmother and handed down to her.

She circled the ladle over the marshmallow ingredients clockwise and recited:

"Dream to dream the soul does travel
Fate to find, time unravel
Insight to gain
Or heart to shame."

A faint wispy glow rose off the ingredients as she said the words of the spell. The items were ready to be used.

Gelatin and ice-cold water went into the stainless steel bowl of her heavy-duty stand mixer. Then she was ready for the stove. In a saucepan, Anglaise added more ice water, sugar, and corn syrup, with a pinch of kosher salt, just to bring up the flavor. She covered the mixture and set her kitchen timer for three minutes. While the mix heated, she grabbed her ladle and continued the spell:

"For one who wants to see
Homes and dreams and secrets hid
Truth to see with closed eyelid
So mote it be."

When the sugar mix was hot, Anglaise took off the pan lid and clipped on a candy thermometer.

Cooking and spells were all very precise. That's what she liked about them. The measuring, the ritual, the concentration. For that span of time—when combining ingredients, watching the boil on a pot, making sure the heat wasn't too high—that's all the mind focused on. No worries surfaced, no fears, no anxieties. Everything in her focused on that one thing, clearing the mind of junk.

Anglaise watched the digital readout on the thermometer. The numbers crept higher. The pot was on medium heat, because she didn't want the mixture to boil.

There. Two hundred and forty degrees. Perfect. She pulled it from the stove immediately. The stand mixer whirred to life, whisk attachment beating the water and gelatin.

Slowly, Anglaise poured the syrup down the side of the bowl. Too much too fast, and the syrup wouldn't integrate, leaving the gelatin hard and the syrup runny. A little at a time was the key.

As the two clear liquids melded, they turned white and frothy. When the syrup was gone, Anglaise turned the beaters to high.

The marshmallows would beat for another fifteen minutes, giving her a chance to prep the pan. The sticky foam of not-quite done marshmallows was a nightmare. They adhered to and made everything they came into contact with sticky. To contain the marshmallows, a mix of confectioners' sugar and cornstarch was be needed. She mixed those two in a bowl, using more sugar than starch for a nice, sweet coat on the marshmallows.

Next, she buttered a cake pan. Anglaise didn't like the non-stick sprays normally recommended. They tasted of chemicals more than anything. With the pan buttered, Anglaise coated it with the powdered sugar mix, being sure to get the corners and sides.

Then she went back to the stirring stand mixer to wait and watch. Once the marshmallows stiffened, she would add the Madagascar vanilla extract, during the last minute of mixing.

Five minutes later, she saw the change in texture she was looking for. Anglaise let it beat another minute, then added the vanilla, and let it beat one minute more.

Anglaise took the fluffy, white candy from the mixer and poured it into the prepared pan. If these were regular marsh-mallows instead of dream puffs, she could walk away and let them cool. Dream puffs required her to keep the circle unbroken and needed a little help to cool or she'd be stuck all day.

A tiny bit more magic would move things along. Anglaise circled the ladle counterclockwise over the pan of dream puffs. She pulled the heat from the candy to cool it quickly.

She sprinkled more of the sugar and cornstarch mix on a sheet of wax paper before turning out the pan of marshmal-lows. Now that they were room temperature, she had to work even more quickly. More sugar and cornstarch went on top and she greased a pizza cutter.

The pizza cutter sliced the sticky candy quickly, but even so, she had to pause and regrease at the end of each slice.

Once Anglaise had one-inch squares, she separated each

dream puff and gave it a quick roll in the sugar and cornstarch.

She had one eye on the block of dream puff squares and one eye on the glass jar she put the finished puffs in.

The puffs on the counter twitched. One marshmallow separated from the others and floated upward.

Anglaise grabbed it from the air and gave it a roll in the powder. She made sure the jar lid was closed, to keep the finished puffs from escaping.

Dream puffs were mischievous things when left alone. They would float up and dissolve into air, then look for a person to attach themselves to, and start swapping dreams at random. The puffs had to be contained. Glass jars, tins—anything with a solid lid. Plastic wrap wouldn't do it. They could squeeze under.

As the other dream puffs lifted off, Anglaise plucked them, one by one, from the air, gave them a final roll in the mix to seal the sides, and added them to the jar. She kept a careful count of them in mind so she wouldn't miss one.

Every puff was accounted for, but she glanced up at the ceiling to be sure. Her circle would keep it contained until broken. None had gotten away.

Anglaise closed the jar. It was airtight glass with a rubber ring to seal it, and clasps on the side to hold the lid on. Escape proof. She closed the clasps and let out a small sigh of relief.

Matilda could pick up the two she'd purchased after the welcome party Bruleé was forcing Anglaise to attend.

The jar of puffs went into a tall cupboard where Anglaise stored her more magical ingredients.

The day of the party, William came by and picked Geoffrey up early. The Callisters only had one car, and Geoffrey wanted to be sure Claire had it.

The invitation he left on her nightstand had disappeared, so he knew she had read it. Geoffrey had checked all the garbage cans and wastebaskets in the house to see if she'd thrown it away. He hadn't seen it and took this to be a sign Claire was considering attending.

At dinner the night before, he'd wanted to ask her outright, but he knew better. They kept to carefully neutral subjects all evening and turned in separately.

He was nervous all day. Distracted at work, and when he was gathering supplies for the party, he kept forgetting things. He wandered the aisles of his store, lost, as if he'd never been there before, looking for paper plates and ingredients.

Geoffrey was glad when William arrived, so he had something to do. "Never get married," he said as he got into William's car.

William barked a short laugh. "Still fighting with Claire?"

"Worse. We've gotten civil."

"What?"

"Polite." Geoffrey gave the box of party supplies a last minute once over to make sure he didn't leave out something obvious, like plastic party cups.

"Oh," William said knowingly. "It'll blow over."

"Or end in divorce." Geoffrey gestured at the road. "Let's just go."

William looked at him. "Are you sure? Maybe you ought to…I don't know, give in?"

"It's too late. And it's the principle. This sort of thing leads to lynch mobs." Geoffrey cringed and glanced at William. "Sorry."

"I know what you meant."

The early Saturday streets of Midswich were almost deserted. In another month, the early tourists would be coming, cluttering the streets and taking all the parking.

They reached the gas station in a few short minutes. The rest of the day was for cooking. William had planned most of the menu, but he needed help with the execution. Geoffrey also had a couple items planned. He wasn't much of a cook, but he had a couple items in his back pocket that he pulled out for special occasions.

William had pulled all the Christmas lights from storage and decorated his house for the party. Two ropes of white lights lined the driveway, leading guests from the entrance beside the gas station, through the thick screen of trees to the house.

The porch had more strings of lights dripping down from overhead, twinkling in the spring night.

He hadn't done much to the inside of the house, except air out the formal dining room, where he set up the buffet. The sterno flames burned underneath the chaffing dishes. The hot food should stay warm throughout the night.

William had made his mother's prize-winning macaroni and cheese recipe, as well as a simple lasagna that he'd learned to make while in Italy. Geoffrey contributed a hot dish that a friend of his in Wisconsin had given him years ago. It was so calorie-rich, Claire only let him make it on special occasions. The surprise, at least William thought so, was the goat cheese stuffed dates wrapped in bacon.

While the hot items occupied the dining table, the cold

items were set up on the built-in wood buffet sideboard on the wall. The only things William had made were a couple of pound cakes, again using his mother's award-winning recipe. Geoffrey supplied the rest. Potato chips, dips, plates of cut vegetables and guacamole—everything a standard party needed.

The doorbell rang, and William heard Geoffrey greet the first guest. Even from the dining room, the rumble of Dan Harding's baritone was unmistakable.

William left the food and went to say hello. He stuck his hand out. "Dan, glad you could make it."

"William." Dan returned the handshake. "The witches here yet?"

"No. You're the first," Geoffrey said.

"Dammit. That always happens."

William grinned. "That just means you get to help yourself to the mac and cheese."

Dan's eyebrows went up. "You made your mom's?"

"Yeah."

"Point me to it."

William showed Dan to the dining room. As he watched Dan dig a heaping serving out of the big, square chafing dish, the doorbell rang again.

Just about everyone had arrived except the witches. William was starting to worry they wouldn't show. Geoffrey kept saying they would. He'd given the invitations to them personally, and they had said they'd be there.

The front door opened, and Matilda came in, followed by Hugh, who slouched behind her with his hands in pockets. Matilda chatted with Geoffrey, while Hugh found a chair in a corner and threw himself into it.

"Can I get you anything?" William asked.

Hugh sighed loudly enough that Matilda could hear him. She glanced at him then talked even louder, making a show of laughing at something Geoffrey said.

"Beer," Hugh said. "And keep 'em coming."

"Okay then." There was a steel tub of beers chilling in ice in the dining room, and William fetched him one.

Taking the beer, Hugh sighed loudly again, probably because Matilda was still in earshot.

"Got any light? This a lot of empty calories," Hugh said.

"No." William turned and walked away. He went up to Geoffrey and Matilda and jerked a thumb over his shoulder. "How much trouble is Hugh going to be?"

Matilda looked at Hugh and gave him a tight smile. He saluted her with his bottle. "None," Matilda said firmly. "He's going to get drunk, sulk the whole time, and then I'm going to drive him home."

"If that's all, fine. I just don't want to have to throw him out," William told her.

"You won't have to. We'll leave before then."

He nodded. As long as that was all that happened. But when did things ever turn out like people planned? William couldn't throw Hugh out yet, as he hadn't done anything, but it was the only means to guarantee that nothing happened.

The doorbell rang and William went to get it. He gave Hugh a last aggravated look then answered the bell.

There was a small crowd on the porch. Rosa and her three daughters, Consolata, Mary-Alice, and Juana, all dressed in their party best. This, in Mary Alice's case, was red velvet, a lot of buckles, and black lipstick.

"Come on in," William said.

"Thanks." Rosa handed him a big dish wrapped in an insulated blanket. "I brought tamales."

"Wow, thanks. You didn't have to." William took the still warm dish. He could smell the spicy pork and masa through the blanket. "I'll put these out."

"Are the witches here yet?" Mary-Alice asked.

William shook his head. "Not yet."

The girl sighed and frowned, resembling for a second, a miniature Hugh.

"Geoffrey said they'd come," he assured her.

"Fine." Mary-Alice drifted to the dining room to look over the food.

William followed with the tamales. He put them out on the dining room table. Sorry he didn't have another chafing dish, he put the tamales next to the mac and cheese that was already almost half gone. He heard a commotion in the living room and the front door banging open. William rushed to see what was happening, in case it was Hugh getting out of hand.

The party was spilling out onto the porch. Gasps of awe came from those who were already outside and those who were inside pushed forward to get a look at what the others were seeing.

William squeezed past Father Halloran, just in time to see the three witches land on his front lawn amid the twinkle of the Christmas lights.

Bruleé, the oldest, smiled and waved at everyone while Anglaise held back, her face stony. Caramel hid behind Anglaise and clutched her broom.

"Um, hi, everyone," Bruleé said.

Geoffrey stepped forward. "Welcome to your welcome party."

William went down the steps and shook hands with Bruleé. "And welcome to my home."

"It's lovely," Bruleé told him. Her voice dropped and she added, "Am I supposed to make a speech or something?"

She was looking over his shoulder and William turned. A wide-eyed crowd stared at the witches. William was suddenly embarrassed by his provincial neighbors. "No. I think they just wanted to see you land."

"Okay."

"Can we go in? I'm starving," Anglaise asked.

"Of course, come on," Geoffrey said.

William and Geoffrey escorted the girls up the porch stairs.

A man stepped up, hand out. "Dan Harding. I'm head of the Chamber of Commerce."

Bruleé shook his hand. "Pleased to meet you."

"You should join up," he told her.

Bruleé shifted her feet. "I don't know."

"We aren't exactly welcome," Anglaise said.

Dan shrugged. "We'll see."

"Thank you, anyway. We'll let you know if we stay in town."

The party drifted back indoors. Mary-Alice grabbed Caramel and took her to the buffet while the older two sisters mingled.

Anglaise heaped macaroni and cheese onto her paper plate. The dish smelled homemade, rich with cheddar cheese, and it had a golden crust of Parmesan. The party invitation had promised food, and so far the spread looked decent. All but the precut deli trays of vegetables and dip. She wasn't here for veggies, though.

"That's my mom's recipe," William said.

"You made it?" Anglaise glanced at him. She'd met William a few times and remained suspicious that he was interested in more than her cooking.

He nodded. "She won prizes with that mac and cheese. And the pound cake." He pointed out the sideboard. Two towering cakes sat on glass stands. "She did them up like regular cakes, so it was always a surprise for the judges. People expect a bundt pan or a loaf. But it works great for layer cakes too."

"Is it real pound cake?" Anglaise asked.

"It's real, all right." William nodded. "A pound of butter, a pound of sugar, and a pound of eggs in each."

She took another plate and went over to the uncut cakes. One was frosted in rich, dark chocolate, the other in what was either caramel or brown sugar frosting, judging by the light brown color. Anglaise picked up a cake knife.

"Which one is better?"

William pursed his lips. "Both? I don't know."

"Which one is your mother's favorite?"

He pointed to the light brown cake. "This one is special occasions only. It's—"

"Don't tell me," Anglaise said. She cut a generous wedge of cake for herself.

The tower of cake was three layers thick. Each layer could be considered a single cake unto itself. Instead of baking a thicker cake and slicing it into three layers, the cake had three cakes stacked one on top of the other.

Anglaise examined the cake texture. Dense and moist, definitely not a sponge and certainly not store-bought. The golden brown layers were separated by layers of generously thick filling, the same frosting that covered the outside.

She smelled the cake before tasting it. Butter, brown sugar, and burnt sugar frosting. Her fork met with resistance as she cut off a bite of cake, sure to get some frosting.

That first bite was everything the smell promised. The solid density of the pound cake melted into buttery nothing in her mouth. The frosting was a cooked frosting, harder to make than simple butter cream.

"So, you approve?" William asked.

Anglaise opened her eyes, unaware they'd been closed. "It's amazing."

She had to admit this was the finest pound cake she'd ever had. It was an entirely different species than the sticky-sweet, commercial loaves from the grocery store.

Bruleé instantly regretted arriving by broom after she saw everyone spill onto the porch like that. She was amazed Caramel didn't cast her *see-me-not* spell and fly back to town.

Maybe it was shock, but she was hoping it was because Caramel saw her friend and decided to stay. Either way, Caramel was inside with people. Bruleé watched out of the corner of her eye as Alyss fixed her a plate of tamales.

They couldn't move. Not now. It would be too cruel to tear Caramel away from the only friend she'd made since their parents died. Somehow, and Bruleé had no idea how, they had to stay in this town.

Bruleé hadn't told Anglaise, but she too had been trying to scry the future even as Anglaise had used her tarot deck. Bruleé peered into the depths of black tea, hoping to find out if they stayed in Midswich. She even used the ancient Chinese teapot her master had given her when she left San Francisco. The teapot had been used by generations of witches, and the magic had soaked into the clay.

The future, at least this one, was too fluid to predict. Nothing she did shed light on the darkness, and it didn't take magic to see that events would come to a head soon. Something would break. Either the protest or the witches.

Maybe this display of friendship boded well.

"Geoffrey's been singing your praises."

"Really?" Bruleé looked around for the green grocer. He was talking to the woman introduced to her as Rosa Ruiz, owner of the Mexican restaurant. Geoffrey kept glancing at the front door as if waiting for someone.

"Says your kind bring in tourists. Not to be too indelicate."

She felt her stomach tighten. "My kind?"

Dan nodded. "Witches. He says there's busloads of tourists who go on mystical tours to visit witches and what not. Like down in Salem."

"Is that why we're suddenly welcome?"

"Geoffrey makes a compelling case."

"So this is his doing." Bruleé wasn't sure how she felt. She wasn't about to be put on display like a sideshow freak, but Midswich was a tourist town. That's why she'd chosen it. It was a borderline theme park. She was counting on tourists to come to the teashop. Did it matter if they were there to see a witch? Those buses rolled through Boston, New York, and Salem all the time. The witches there had no problem catering to them.

"He thinks you'll be an asset."

"Well, maybe we'll find out." Bruleé was sorry she couldn't offer anything more optimistic. The past week had been emotionally racking.

Dan stuck his hand out. Bruleé looked at it for a second then shook it. "Welcome to Midswich," he said.

"Thanks."

Geoffrey kept one eye on the front door, the other on his watch. The hands were closing in on eight o'clock and still no Claire. He should probably give up.

Maybe welcoming the witches had been a bad idea. If he'd minded his own business, he'd be home with Claire right now.

The door opened and Geoffrey's heart squeezed.

Eddie and his date came in. He looked unsure to be just walking into someone's house, despite the big "Come right in" sign taped to the door.

Geoffrey waved them in. "Eddie."

"Oh, hey." Eddie grinned in relief. He presented the girl he was with. "You know Hillary, right?"

"I've rung up your groceries a few times—that wasn't an innuendo."

Hillary laughed. "No. I know."

"Are the witches here?" Eddie looked around.

Geoffrey pointed them out. "Come on. I'll introduce you."

He led Eddie and Hillary over to Bruleé.

"Bruleé, this is Eddie Piñero and Hillary…"

"Johanson," she finished for him.

"Nice to meet you," Bruleé said.

"You, too," Eddie said. "I've, uh, been meaning to go to the teashop but with the protest—"

"Don't let that stop you," Geoffrey said. "The food is to die for. In fact, the chef is here." He pointed to Anglaise, who was digging into a huge plate of macaroni and cheese a few feet away.

"She's young to be a chef," Hillary said. "Just a kid."

The doorbell chimed and Geoffrey jumped to attention. "I better get that."

He left the little group to themselves and hurried to the door. Hope twisted in his chest. Ringing the doorbell, despite the sign, was something Claire would probably do. From the corner of his eye he saw William also heading for the door.

Geoffrey put a hand up and William nodded, letting Geoffrey answer, even though it wasn't his house.

He pulled the door open and grinned broadly. The smile froze in disappointment. Flora Barton stood on the porch.

His smile melted. "Evening, Ms. Barton."

"Nice to see you too, Geoffrey."

"Sorry. I'm just hoping Claire will come."

"Fine, fine." She stepped in and looked around. "Good turn-out. Nice of you and William to do this."

"Thanks." He looked around too, pleased by the small gathering.

As soon as Flora spotted Bruleé, she excused herself, pushing past Geoffrey, and hurried up to Bruleé. "Good evening," she said.

"Flora. I'm glad you came."

"I brought someone," Flora said.

"A date?" Geoffrey broke in.

Flora fixed him with a searing glare, and he took a step back. "Not a date."

She turned back to Bruleé. "I was wondering if you could help me. Anne is in the car. It was all she could do to get down the stairs at our place. Could you help me bring her in?"

"Of course. Pardon me, Geoffrey."

"Anne? Isn't that your sister?" he asked. As far as he knew, Anne was bedridden with rheumatoid arthritis. Maybe it was a different Anne.

Bruleé and Flora went off. Bruleé headed for her little sister, Caramel.

The three women headed out.

F lora led them down the drive where she'd parked. Once Anne had seen the invitation, there had been no talking her out of going. Flora hadn't seen her so determined since they were little girls. For the past few days, she'd walked up and down the halls of their apartment building. The trick was the stairs. Flora helped Anne up and down the steps, one at a time. She could get down all right, but getting up was almost more than her still stiff and painful knees could manage.

Anne refused to be left home. She insisted the witches could and would help.

They reached Flora's car, and Flora pulled open the passenger's side door.

Anne smiled, weak and apologetic. "I'm afraid I have to impose on you," she told Bruleé.

"Nonsense," Bruleé said. "Give me your hands."

Anne held her hands out and Bruleé took them. The witch knelt down on the gravel drive and closed her eyes.

Flora looked at the silent Caramel. "Sorry for the trouble."

"I—it's okay," Caramel said. "B—Bruleé is h—happy to help."

"Too happy, if you ask me." Flora nodded at Bruleé. "At least make sure she bills me for this."

Caramel let out a sharp, high-pitched squeal before clapping her hand over her mouth. "I—I d—d—don't think she'll l—let me."

"Soft." Flora shook her head, but a smile curled her thin lips, anyway.

A full two minutes passed before Bruleé opened her eyes. She stood up. "That should help." She looked at Flora. "Do you have her walker?"

Flora pointed at the car. "In the trunk. I'll get it."

She opened the trunk and pulled out Anne's walker.

Bruleé and Caramel helped Anne get out of the car.

"I'm sorry to make you do this," Anne said. She gripped her walker and took a small, halting step forward.

"Nonsense, it's hardly a party without you." Bruleé waved away the comment. "How do you feel?"

Anne smiled. "Much more energetic."

Floral looked up at the house to gage the distance and frowned. Everyone had come out to see what was going on. A row of stunned faces lit by the porch lights gaped at Anne, who hadn't been seen in public in two years.

Father Halloran, Rosa, and Eddie crossed themselves, one after another. Flora's face burned at the attention.

Anne waved at them. "Hello! I've come to rejoin the living."

Slowly they walked up to the house, the party guests too stunned to leave the porch.

Anne stopped at the porch stairs—only five steps between her and the party.

Bruleé gave Caramel a nod, and by some agreement, they stood on either side of Anne, each one taking an arm.

Bruleé whispered the words of a spell.

<blockquote>

"Light as air
Float just above
Grounded care
Not too high
Just a hair"

</blockquote>

With a gentle touch, Anne's feet left the ground. Flora stared in disbelief as her sister's slippered feet floated. With little physical effort, Bruleé and Caramel guided the light-as-air Anne up the steps. Anne gasped aloud as she levitated, aided by the witches. Bruleé and Caramel gently set her down on the porch. Scattered applause broke out among the partygoers. Flora was tempted to turn around and go home, but with everyone focused on Anne, she couldn't. Besides, Anne had worked so hard to get here. She went up the steps behind her sister, just as the crowd swallowed Anne.

Geoffrey looked at Anne, eyes wide with disbelief. "How on earth?"

"Bruleé." Anne touched the witch's arm. "She's been helping me with the arthritis."

"Helping?" Father Halloran crossed himself for perhaps the third time. "It's a miracle."

"No. It's magic," Flora said.

"That's still a miracle," Father Halloran said.

"Whatever it is," William said, stepping between Flora and Father Halloran, "you're most welcome."

Anne giggled and hobbled in, surrounded by the amazed and well-wishing partygoers.

Flora hung back on the porch. She'd forgotten how much Anne loved attention. Not in a greedy way. There wasn't a malicious instinct in her. She just blossomed under attention, like a flower being watered. It had led her to marry that flattering fool, Gene, who divorced her when he found someone younger.

The two witches hung back too. Flora glanced over. Bruleé and Caramel looked winded. Bruleé wiped a thin sheen of sweat from her forehead with her hand.

"You better charge for this," Flora told Bruleé.

The girl looked startled for a second. "No. It's no problem."

"You're both all sweaty. It must be some kind of trouble."

Behind Bruleé, Caramel nodded as Bruleé shook her head. "Levitation is a standard spell, and the practice will do us good."

"Well, you don't sweat when you fly. It can't be that standard."

"Our brooms are infused with magic. They do the work for us, in a way," Bruleé explained. "Your sister isn't. Does that make sense?"

Flora nodded, even though she wasn't sure what Bruleé was telling her. Either way, it worked out to Bruleé not letting Flora pay. But who works at their own party? Tomorrow, Flora could go give Anglaise some money. Anglaise had sense enough to take it. Flora knew what Bruleé was doing—trying to build loyal customers by doing magic for free, but Bruleé didn't seem to know where to draw the line.

While everyone watched Anne walk up to the house, Matilda watched Eddie. She examined every interaction between him and Hillary—every casual touch, every laugh, every time their heads bent toward each other—trying to figure out how close they were. They hadn't been dating long, if that's what they were doing.

She hadn't spoken to Eddie since she'd brought cookies to his apartment. She'd broken their weekly lunch date with a text. Not that he'd protested or called her to find out what was going on, which is what she expected.

"This is amazing," Eddie said. His wide smile flashed on Anne then Hillary.

Matilda thought she caught the gleam of tears film over his eyes. Anne and Flora lived in the same apartment building as Eddie, and they all knew each other.

Over the rim of her plastic party cup of diet soda, Matilda watched Hillary. Would she notice Eddie's sentimentality? Hillary smiled at Anne and lightly shook hands with her as Eddie introduced them.

Hillary didn't notice a thing. Eddie pulled a tissue out of his pocket and, under the guise of blowing his nose, wiped his eyes. No one else seemed to notice but her.

Matilda looked over her shoulder at Hugh. He was still sulking in the chair he'd staked out for himself. And racking up quite the tally of beers. She counted four empties on the end table beside him and a fifth in his hand. Wasn't he excited even a little that Anne was walking again?

He saw her looking and he pointed to his watch, making a quizzical face. Matilda rolled her eyes and turned back to watching the party.

Father Halloran and Bruleé helped Anne to a seat on the couch, where she settled down, beaming at them.

Why did I even let Hugh come? He'd bitched and moaned and finally she let him accompany her, but she wished he'd just stayed home.

Matilda was going to have to break up with him. Their relationship was done. It's just that neither of them could seem to get the words out.

Consolata bounced over to Matilda. "Isn't it incredible? I can't believe Anne can walk." She lowered her voice. "Honestly, I wasn't sure she was still alive."

"Maybe people will look at the witches a little differently now."

"Hey, is their food as good as it smells?"

"Better." Matilda half listened, her mind far off, or at least about ten feet away.

Consolata dug her elbow into Matilda's side.

"Ow!" Matilda finally pulled her attention away from Eddie.

"It's good he finally found someone, huh?"

"Who?"

"Don't play dumb. Eddie."

"Are they really going out?" Matilda made an effort to sound casual.

"Jealous?"

And failed. "No. Just curious."

"Liar."

"I have a boyfriend."

Consolata waved at Hugh, who saluted with his beer bottle. "Who is getting drunk in the corner. Who disapproves of you going to the teashop. And who is not exactly the brightest crayon in the box."

"He's not that bad," Matilda said. She frowned. Why was she still defending him? Because she didn't want to be the one stupid enough to have wasted four years on him.

"Just sayin'," Consolata said. "As for them—" She pointed to Eddie and Hillary. "Make a move now, or forever hold your peace."

Matilda made a frustrated grunt and walked away. She heard Consolata snigger behind her, but it was all she could think to do. Any remark she made would dig her in deeper. Soon enough, she'd know if she was wasting her time with Hugh. The dream puffs should shed some light on their relationship. She headed for the food before Anglaise ate all the pound cake.

Hugh was well past buzzed and was heading straight for drunk. He'd have to hit the gym pretty hard to burn off the calories in this many beers.

Drunk was the only way he could stand to be in the same room as the witches. Already, half of Matilda's family weren't talking to her, while the rest kept coming to him, asking if he could do anything about her.

Since when had anyone been able to *do* anything about Matilda? As she so often pointed out, he wasn't the boss of her.

In their faces, he saw the same hope and assumptions in his own family's faces: the hope that Hugh and Matilda would settle down in Midswich. Hugh would follow in his father's footsteps and become mayor, and Matilda could raise their babies. They'd both get fat and become pillars of the community. Then, at last, dropout Matilda and slacker Hugh would be worth something.

He drained his fifth and sixth beers, setting the empties on the floor beside his chair. He was running out of space on the end table. At least, the more he drank, the hotter the blonde witch got. On a bad day, she was damn pretty. Now she was a Victoria's Secret model.

Hugh looked around for Matilda. He didn't see her. Maybe tonight didn't have to be a total waste.

The blonde witch breezed past, heading in the opposite the direction of the food. Bathroom break, probably. If his memory wasn't totally blown, there was a half-bath just off the kitchen.

Hugh stood up too fast and swayed on his feet. He looked at the collection of empties around his chair. A few of these could be taken to the garbage, and maybe he'd run into Blondie on his way back. He grabbed three bottles off the end table and headed in the direction of where he assumed the kitchen to be. What was Blondie's name? It started with a B. Baby would do.

The kitchen appeared at the end of a wood paneled hallway. Hugh tossed the beer bottles in the recycling and went back the way he'd come.

Jackpot! Blondie stepped out of the wall. Hugh blinked. Magic? No, the bathroom door was the same color as the wood paneling as the hall.

Hugh put on his most charming smile and went over to her, a little extra swagger in his step. "Hey." He nodded at her as he leaned against the wall.

The witch frowned a little and said, "Yes?"

"Did you fall from heaven or are you an angel?" He paused. "Wait, that's not right…Anyway, you are model-hot. Did you know that?"

"Oh," she said. "That's what this is. Am I supposed to forget that you have a girlfriend and protest my shop because, 'Oh, my God, he thinks I'm hot!'"

"If that helps, yeah."

She rolled her eyes. "Wow, you have the confidence of a much drunker man."

"I know, right?" Hugh slipped a hand around the witch's waist. He locked eyes with the V of her cleavage the frilly cardigan left exposed.

"So, what do you say, baby?" Hugh's hand migrated south to get a feel of firm butt cheek.

"Hugh!"

They both jumped.

Hugh looked up and saw Matilda and William. They were

clearing away plastic cups and cake plates. William looked at the ground, edging away from Matilda.

Matilda's cheeks pinkened. "You can take your hand off her ass."

Hugh yanked his hand away and put both of them up in surrender. "It didn't mean anything."

The witch elbowed him in the ribs. "I'm so sorry, Matilda," she said, her voice cracking at the end.

"It's not your fault, Bruleé," Matilda said.

"Bruleé." Hugh snapped his fingers. "I knew it started with a B."

Matilda handed the cake plate she held to Bruleé and grabbed Hugh's arm. "We're leaving," she said, dragging him down the hall.

"All right. No need to dent the merchandise." Hugh followed her, led by her iron grip. He turned back and waved at Bruleé, who gave him a nasty glare and spun around.

Claire pulled up to William's house, lips pursed at the two-story house decked out in Christmas lights. Close to a dozen cars sprawled across the circle drive.

She knew exactly who was here based on the vehicles alone. The group wasn't large, but it was influential. Claire saw the logo of Dan Harding's construction business on the side of a pickup. Geoffrey must have managed to suck Dan into the whole "witches are good" thing with his video presentation.

After receiving the invitation to the party, Claire had watched the video. She had to admit, he had a point about the witches bringing in tourism. But Pastor Austin also had a point.

What was to keep the town turning into a bunch of spell-reliant junkies?

Claire sighed and shut the engine off. How likely was the collapse of Midswich due to three witches? All week long, she'd been wrestling with these questions.

Geoffrey's surprisingly romantic invitation won her over, at least in part. Claire wasn't likely to lose her soul in one night and, as she kept reminding herself, the witches were just people. Meeting them couldn't hurt.

Claire went up the steps of the porch. Consolata waved at her from the railing.

"Hey, Claire," she said. "I didn't think you'd come."

Claire shook her head. "I wasn't going to."

"I think someone will be happy to see you," Consolata said in a singsong voice. "Geoffrey's inside. Go ahead in."

"Thanks," Claire said.

She opened the front door and poked her head in. The living room was crowded with partygoers. She saw Geoffrey over by the couch, talking to Flora. Claire's eyes widened and she stepped inside. The old woman on the couch was Flora's sister, Anne. She had to be. Claire hadn't seen her in ages. Last she heard, Anne was bed-ridden. Then how…

The witches. They must have healed Anne, or bespelled her.

"Claire! You came." Geoffrey ran over, enthusiasm shining on his boyish face. He almost kissed her then remembered they were fighting and pulled back.

"Is that Anne?" Claire pointed to her.

"Isn't it great? Bruleé has been helping her."

"How?"

"Herbal tea and healing sessions," Geoffrey said. "Come say hello."

He tugged her arm but Claire didn't move. "Is that safe?"

"You can't argue with results."

Claire gave him her most you-must-be-joking look, and she could see his enthusiasm wane.

"Come on, Claire, this is a good thing."

"How do you know? What if it's temporary? Or a gimmick? It's rheumatoid arthritis, right? That doesn't just go away."

"And it hasn't. Just talk to her. Talk to the witches."

Geoffrey's pull was more insistent, and he figured if she

didn't go over, he'd pick her up and carry her over.

"Fine." She sighed and went with him to the couch.

"Anne, you remember my wife, Claire?" Geoffrey asked.

Anne held out a crooked, gnarled hand. "Hello."

"Hello, again," Claire said. She shook Anne's hand, careful to keep her grip loose.

"Nice to see you again."

Claire gave the messy bun on Anne's head a professional once over. "Your hair's gotten so long."

Anne laughed. "I haven't been out much."

"You should have called. I'm sure we could've come to you."

"No need for that now. I can call for an appointment."

"We still live on the third floor," Flora reminded her caustically.

"Be sweet," Anne said.

"I hear you have the witches to thank."

"I do." Anne craned her neck, the move stiff, making her wince a little. "Bruleé, there you are."

Bruleé came in from the dining room, a thin slice of chocolate cake on her plate. She stepped over. "Yes?"

"This is my wife, Claire," Geoffrey told her. "Claire, Bruleé, our local healer, I guess."

Bruleé colored under the pink blush she already wore. "Not really. I haven't put in enough years for that."

"Then how do you know if what you've done for Anne is permanent?"

"Claire," Geoffrey said, voice sharp.

"No." Bruleé held up her hand. "It's a fair question. I'm working on her immune system to get it to stop attacking her joints. That should arrest the RA, but there is a chance it could return or revert."

"She told me this already," Anne said.

"Anne will take the spell tea I prescribed for as long as it helps," Bruleé told her. "The joints that aren't too damaged should continue to improve as long as she drinks it."

"Prescribe." Claire shook her head. "You aren't a doctor. And how can you just say Anne will be drinking your tea for the rest of her life? That's a rip-off."

"No, it's not," Flora said, speaking up for the first time. "Spelled tea is no different than the drugs the doctor gives her. Did you ever think she was going to stop taking the half dozen prescriptions the doctors gave her? Painkillers and immune suppressants? None of them have worked half so well."

Claire took half a step back. She wasn't sure what to say or what to think. The pills were science. That had to count for more than spells and tea. She forced a smile for the sake of politeness. "Well, it was nice seeing you, Anne. I think I better be going." Claire turned and walked stiff-legged back to the front door.

"Wait." Geoffrey caught up to her halfway across the living room. "Don't go. You barely talked to them."

He tried to touch her, pull her back. Claire dodged his hand. Geoffrey knew when to quit.

"Claire," he said, voice soft and plaintive.

"Just—I need to think, okay?"

She left and Geoffrey let her. Claire hated leaving him there. Hated crushing his hopes. His hopes for her. She couldn't just blindly accept the witches, but maybe she had been unfair. To Geoffrey's credit, he'd done research while she's just listened to Pastor Austin.

Claire got into her car and dug her cell phone from her purse. She dialed the pastor's number and prayed he'd pick up.

"Hello," Austin said.

"Pastor, it's Claire."

"Good evening, Claire. What can I do for you?"

She took a deep breath and scratched her forehead. What should she say? "I went to the witches' party. You heard about that, right?"

"Yes," he said slowly.

"Bruleé, the witch—it looks like she healed Anne Malone."

"What?"

"Anne is at the party. She can walk. Everyone is saying it's a miracle, but what if it's just snake oil? I mean, it could be real. I don't know." Claire exhaled.

"Are you still there?" he asked.

"I'm in my car. I left, I guess. I'm just sitting here."

"Claire," Pastor Austin said, voice soft. "If you want to go home, go home. The true nature of the witches will be revealed in time. If the healing is false, they will be shown to be liars."

Claire nodded. "But Geoffrey. What do I do about him?"

"Do you love him?"

"Yes."

"Focus on that then. Let God take care of the rest."

"Thank you, Pastor. I will." Claire hung up and started the car.

Austin's hand tightened on the phone receiver, knuckles going bone white before he put it down. The mantle clock said 9:40. Not too late to show up and see for himself the miracle the witches had performed. He looked at his clothes. A T-shirt and a pair of sweat pants. He'd have to go change.

He stood up. He could skip the work clothes, but he should at least put on a pair of jeans and a sport jacket.

Pastor Austin pulled into William's driveway. He hadn't been to the house much in recent years. Not since William's mother moved to Florida a few years ago.

At least he knew who he was facing now. But he could be civil as long as they could. His mouth tightened as he looked over the cars in the parking lot. He got out without bothering to lock the car. He wouldn't be here that long.

As he approached the house, two of the partygoers on the porch froze. Austin recognized Mary-Alice and the mousy witch. Mary-Alice glowered at him. She grabbed the witch and pulled her inside.

Just as Austin reached the stairs, Father Halloran and William stepped out.

"What are you doing here, Pastor?" William asked.

"Good evening, William, Father," Austin said as he

climbed up the porch. "I came to see the miracle."

"I'm not sure that's a good idea," William said.

"Terrible, in fact," added Father Halloran.

"We just don't want any trouble," said William.

"And what trouble are you expecting? Fist fights? Disorderly conduct?"

"General rudeness to start," Halloran said.

"Jon, be reasonable. Claire called, worried that the witches might be trying to pull a fast one on Anne."

"And you can go visit Anne tomorrow, Oscar. There's no earthly reason to have driven out here, except to ruin the party."

Father Halloran puffed up his considerable gut, straining his pants' button.

"Why not let him in?" cut in a voice behind William.

William and Father Halloran stepped aside, revealing one of the witches, the middle sister, Anglaise, unless Austin missed his guess.

"We've got nothing to hide. Magic healing is a proven fact."

"It may be fact, but it also depends on the skill of the witch. Too many desperate people are willing to pay for a cure, real or not," Austin said.

"Then come in and say that to Anne," Anglaise said.

William and Jon exchanged dubious glances. They decided to let him pass and stepped aside.

Austin entered the house. It had changed since William's mother left. The carpet was replaced by hardwood floors, and the homely cross-stitch on the walls replaced by modern art.

The room watched Austin. All the party guests had gathered, and the looks he was getting ranged from questioning to angry.

Austin was annoyed that they could all so easily turn against him for a bunch of witches. He had done nothing but try to counsel the community, with the aim of making it a better, healthier place to live. They all stared at him as if he was about to go off the deep end. He smiled at them all, making a conscious effort to turn the other cheek.

"Good evening, everyone."

A few people nodded at him, but no one returned his smile, except the new teacher from the middle school, whom he didn't know.

"Evening, Pastor," Anne said. With the help of her walker, she pulled herself off the couch and, with painful slowness, walked over to him.

Bruleé hovered at her side and Flora scowled over her shoulder.

"Anne, lovely to see you up and about." Austin pushed the words out, the effort to make them sound sincere had him sweating.

The witches had done something to Anne. Her little outing was certainly enough to impress the sympathetic and sway the undecided.

Anne beamed. "I can't tell you what a relief it is to be out."

Her smile was the nail in the coffin of his cause. He'd never be rid of the witches now. "I hear the witches are to thank for this," he said, staring over Anne's shoulder at Bruleé.

The witch looked back, her face frozen. Austin couldn't tell if it was anger or determination.

"I've been working with Anne," Bruleé said in a tight voice.

"We already went over this with Claire." Flora put a hand on Anne's shoulder. "Bruleé has helped, the drugs and the doctors haven't."

"That's just fine, Anne. Just fine indeed. Now that you're mobile, you can visit your doctor again. Show him what the witch did. I'm sure he's eager to see the results of the new course of treatment. What did he say when you told him you were trying a witch?"

"We didn't tell her doctor," Flora said. "None of his business."

"Oh," Austin said. "I hope you didn't quit your medications cold turkey. I hear that's bad."

"I'm still taking them all. I have herbal tea from Bruleé now, is all."

"Good. You've done your homework then, Miss Bruleé. I

can see Anne hasn't suffered any side effects from mixing homeopathic remedies with her course of drug treatment."

Silence and a number of uncomfortable looks met Austin's last statement. He smiled, a thin curl of triumph.

"You do have a list of Anne's current medications, don't you?" He filled the silence before anyone else could. "And cross-checked it for any reactions the meds may have with various natural substances. I am a big believer in herbs. A lot of people figure herbs are just herbs and don't treat them like medicine. But they can be potent specially when coupled with magic."

Flora and Bruleé turned red at the same time. Flora's brows knit as the color spread across her forehead. Bruleé looked at the Turkish rug on the floor and her hands twisted together. Austin couldn't believe it. He'd been pondering ammunition to throw at the witches the entire way over. He'd scored a hit with the first volley.

Flora hurled an accusatory look at Austin. "I forgot about the list, what with all the excitement."

"I've been so worried. I should have," Bruleé said.

"Stop it," Flora told her and grabbed Bruleé's arm to keep her from saying more. "It's my fault. I keep track of Anne's medications."

"Both of you shut up," Anne said. "I've been on the tea a couple weeks and nothing's happened. If I were going to drop dead, I would have already. I'm fine. I'm better than fine."

Bruleé sat down on the couch, still looking troubled. Flora tried to comfort her as she rubbed her back.

Austin held up his hands. "I just assumed the witch knew what she was doing. That's the only reason I ask."

"Spare me your concern, Pastor," Anne snapped. "You couldn't give two shits about me. You just want to get rid of the witches."

The room froze. For a second, Austin swore he could hear the puckering sound of everyone blinking.

"Bruleé, Anglaise, Caramel, Flora." Anne looked around and nodded at each one. "I'm tired, and I have three flights of stairs to get up at home. I'm sorry, but I think I'll need your help getting up them tonight. Let's go." With painful slowness, Anne inched toward the door.

Caramel held the front door for her, and Flora trailed behind.

Anglaise turned to Austin. "Well, you really know how to ruin a party, don't you?"

"It was a fair question," Austin said.

"You ambushed them," Geoffrey said, jabbing a finger at Austin.

"Yeah, what's your problem?" Mary-Alice went to stand by Geoffrey.

Austin looked around. The faint triumph he'd won faded. The faces gathered. Dan and William, Consolata and Eddie— all of them were angry.

He'd hoped to cast doubt in their minds. Get them to give up their blind acceptance of the witches. The plan had backfired. Austin cursed himself. Damnation was too good for him. He may have just secured the witches place in Midswich.

"I think you better leave, Pastor," William said.

Austin pulled himself out of the rage and despair threatening to suck him down. He forced his face to keep its mild expression. "Good night, then."

He nodded to the unhappy crowd. They didn't respond. He turned and showed himself out. Outside, he saw Flora's car crunching over the driveway gravel. A flicker up above caught his eye. The witches on their brooms flew above the car.

The childish urge to hurl a rock at them made his palms itch. His eyes actually swept the ground for one. There, a nice sized river rock under the gooseberry bush.

Austin exhaled and looked back at the sky. They were gone, disappearing behind the towering pines. He walked to his car and got in.

For a minute, he sat there, hands clenched around the steering wheel. Maybe they would listen to him. Maybe Anne's "miracle" wasn't so astonishing. Maybe he could still win. He rested his head on the steering wheel. All he'd done was make himself look like a bully and cement the good opinions of the witches' supporters.

Failure crashed him against the rock of self-loathing.

He started the car. This always happened. On some important point, he fell down and lost the trust of his flock. Other clergy, better clergy could have said something better. Convinced their people of the rightness of their cause.

His faith was strong. He tried hard to be a good leader and counsel the parish well. He'd met plenty of clergy who had given up, either on people or their faith. They'd checked out. Paid lip service to their office and nothing more. But Austin wasn't one of them, which made him wonder why he wasn't doing better.

P enelope hadn't been able to sleep ever since talking to Dani at the park. The thought that her only niece could fall into the same trap as her mother had never occurred to her. She thought she was safe. Even after the witches moved in, she thought Pastor Austin would get rid of them.

She didn't think the interference of a few fools who didn't know how dangerous the witches were would matter.

Not only had she been wrong, but sending the witches a real message had been left to her.

The idea of an alarm system was giving her second thoughts. She hadn't seen any stickers on the window of the teashop from a security company, so there probably wasn't an electric alarm. A magical one was possible.

Penelope stood in the alley behind the teashop. She held onto the crowbar as if it was the only thing anchoring her to the earth.

Midswich was the place people moved to in order to get away from crime. As far as she knew, only the bank and the gas station bothered with security alarms.

There could be a spell on the premises, though. Penelope had looked up spells online, and the two most common spells were "turn-the-feet" and "amber trap." The first would simply walk her right back out the door. The second would hold her frozen until the witches released her. If the "amber trap" had been cast, there was no way Penelope wasn't going to jail for breaking and entering.

Her leather gloves creaked as her hands strangled the iron.

She had to move before she chickened out and went home.

With a sharp inhale, Penelope wedged the crowbar between the door and the door jam. The metal squealed as she pulled back on the handle of the crowbar.

Penelope grunted. If she wasn't careful, she'd put her back out and the police could scrape her off the pavement.

A few more heaves on the bar and she heard the lock pop. The back door of the teashop swung open.

The shop was dark. The witches gone to that party William and Geoffrey were throwing. She'd been so angry when she heard about it, she'd broken one of Prince Albert's dog bowls. Then she realized the witches would be gone for the night, and she could give them what they deserved.

Her hands shook as she crossed the threshold. Penelope's jaw tightened and she cringed, waiting for a spell to take hold.

Three steps in. Four. Then Five. Nothing happened. Penelope breathed for a second while her eyes adjusted to the dark.

There was no spell. No "amber trap." She relaxed.

Penelope heard a bark. A jolt of terror froze her feet to the floor. They had a dog? Did she know that? She heard the tippy-tap of little paws coming down the stairs.

A pale, fuzzy blur ran at her. A Pomeranian, no bigger than Prince Albert, jumped around her, tail wagging. Penelope cringed in anticipation of a bite, but none came. She read the dog's body language in an instant.

The pom was friendly.

"Hi, sweetie," Penelope cooed. The pom yipped, the sharp barks loud in the silent kitchen.

"Shh. Settle down, sweetie," Penelope told it.

She searched the pockets of her black track suit. Surely there must be a doggie treat in one of them. She pulled a small peanut butter dog cookie from her jacket pocket.

The pom was all attention when it saw the treat. Penelope could just make out the quiver of a shiny, black nose.

"Want a treat? Want yum-yums?" She waved the treat and heard the pom pant in anticipation. "There you go." Penelope threw the cookie out the back door.

The pom shot out after it, lightning-quick. Penelope followed it, and shut the back door to keep the dog out. She slumped against the door and exhaled. Guilt cut into her when she heard the pom whine and scratch at the door.

Once she'd steadied herself, Penelope was ready. She had never been much of a vandal, and she wasn't sure where to start.

She went through the kitchen to the shop itself. Faint light came in through the gauzy curtains pulled over the windows.

There wasn't much to the shop. A few tables and chairs. An unlit bakery case. Penelope turned in a slow circle. Behind her was wall of teapots, each in its own cubby.

She could start there. Using the crowbar, she pulled one of the higher teapots down. The crash sounded like a gunshot in the empty shop.

Penelope froze. Cold sweat dampened her tracksuit. Surely that was loud enough to be heard in the police station a few blocks away.

Her heart thudded out the seconds, ticking off a minute sure as any clock.

Nothing happened. No siren wailed. No spell activated.

Penelope giggled with relief. She pulled a square teapot off the shelf and let it shatter on the hard wood floor. Then a floral teapot. A white one. A tall one, a fat one. They broke into pottery shards. Clay and porcelain. Her thick-soled tennis shoes crunched over the pieces. Cups and saucers followed the pots. The most delicate shattered to nothing.

When the wall of cubbies was almost empty, she turned to the tables. She yanked the tablecloths off, sending the silvery tea service to the floor. The tiered trays rolled away and the little pots for cream and sugar tumbled over.

The destruction fueled Penelope's anger. She thought she'd feel better sending the witches such a message. Instead, she kept picturing her mother. Her Hollywood starlet good looks. The smile she wore even as she lied to Penelope's face.

Clutching the crowbar like a baseball bat, Penelope headed for the kitchen. She tore down the pots and pans hanging over the kitchen island. The only thing her mother had been good for was being pretty.

Penelope opened a cupboard and swept the plates inside to the floor.

Spells had ruined her mother. Spells and vanity.

She beat the crowbar against a professional grade stand mixer, savaging it until the metal casing was dented.

Even her children's love wasn't more important than her looks.

Stainless steel mixing bowls clanged against the wall and refrigerator as Penelope threw them.

Why hadn't her mother loved her more than magic?

Penelope ripped open a tall cabinet. Jars of spices lined the shelves. Lavender, rock salt, rosemary, thyme, lemon balm, and a hundred others. The herbal mix made a perfume that washed over Penelope, and distracted her from anger.

A jar caught her eye. The pale contents glowed in the dark kitchen. The jar was airtight, lid held on with clasps.

Penelope squinted at the contents then blinked.

"Grampa Evan," she whispered. Marshmallows. She hadn't seen them for years, but her grandfather Evan used to make them. The square-cut marshmallows looked just as she remembered. She didn't think anyone made homemade marshmallows anymore. Everyone just went to the grocery store for those chewy, dried out fakes. Her mouth watered as the memory of soft, distinctly vanilla flavored treats came back to her. Penelope looked around. The kitchen was a mess. The shop, too. The witches were sure to get the message. She could leave now and rest easy, knowing they would leave. She grabbed the jar of marshmallows and headed for the exit.

The pom was sitting in the alley when Penelope came out. The dog wanted back into its home, but Penelope pushed the dog back with her foot and shut the door. She didn't want the little dog to cut its paws on the broken teapots.

Penelope looked around. She was still in the clear. No cops in the alley, no sound at all. Clutching the jar she hurried to her car parked three blocks away.

Matilda and Hugh drove in silence. She was hoping to make it home before he opened his mouth, but she could see the drunken gears turning in his miniscule brain.

"Hey, Mattie, I don't know what got into me," Hugh said from the passenger seat.

"About a six-pack, going by the empties," she said. Hugh only called her Mattie when he was trying to apologize for something stupid. She hated the name.

"It's just that that Bruleé chick is hot when I'm drunk, and you've been kind of a…um…distant lately."

Matilda filled in Hugh's pause with bitch. Distant being code for the same thing.

"Shut up, Hugh! Just stop talking," she snapped.

Whatever was left of his brain must have been working because he didn't open his mouth the rest of the ride home.

She pulled up in front of their house and got out of the car. Halfway to the door, Matilda realized Hugh wasn't beside her. She turned around.

With slow, careful movements, Hugh was trying to get out of the car. He stood up, tripped over his own feet, and face planted in the grassy median strip.

Matilda looked at the keys in her hand. It was Hugh's key ring. She could stomp inside and lock him out. That would show him the meaning of bitch.

"Little help here," Hugh said. He'd gotten to all fours, but couldn't manage the final phase of standing up.

The keys stabbed her palm as her grip tightened. Matilda went back to Hugh and pulled him to his feet.

"Thanks, babe." Hugh staggered, keeping upright only with Matilda's help.

As they neared the narrow porch, Hugh veered off and Matilda let him walk into the post framing the door.

"Ow!" Hugh bounced off the railing, and Matilda steered him to the door. She grinned at the audible whack when he hit the post.

"There you go," she said as she got the door open. "Almost home."

Hugh rubbed his nose. "You did that on purpose."

"You're drunk," she said. "But, yes, I did that on purpose."

Hugh didn't hear or didn't care. He leaned on her as she pulled him through the house.

Matilda dumped him on the bed. He bounced limply then curled up.

"Am I moving or is it the room?"

Matilda didn't answer. She sat down on the edge of the bed, letting out an exhausted sigh.

"I think we're done, Hugh," she said. For months, she'd been trying to work up the nerve to say those words, waffling about whether she should really break up with him. Worried about what people would think, and who she'd be without him. Once the words were spoken, she realized she'd been afraid for nothing. All she felt was relief.

Hugh's response was a gentle snore. Matilda dropped her head to hands.

"God, why are you so damn dumb?" she asked.

Hugh was out cold.

Penelope sat at her kitchen table staring at the jar of marshmallows.

When her mother was at her worst, she and her sister would spend days on end at Grandma and Grandpa's house.

Grandma Lydia was the family cook, but Grandpa Evan had a singular talent. Homemade marshmallows.

Penelope would watch entranced, the full fifteen minutes it took Evan to whip them with the eggbeater. He would stand there, in the Formica-clad kitchen, mixing and mixing until the simple combination of gelatin, sugar, and corn syrup turned into magic. He let her little sister pick the flavoring: vanilla extract, strawberry, orange, or mint.

Afterward, grandma made cocoa if it was winter, or chocolate icebox pie in summer. The marshmallows went on top of either one.

The kitchen timer dinged, startling Penelope. She was

pulled from her reverie by the milk close to scalding on the stove. She jumped up and added sugar and cocoa powder. None of that anemic hot chocolate from a package.

She stirred until the sugar dissolved. At her feet, Prince Albert whined, nose quivering, hoping for a treat.

"Sorry, sweetie, you can't have chocolate."

He whined louder but retreated to his doggie bed in the corner of the kitchen.

Penelope sat down at the table with her cocoa and opened the clasps on the marshmallow jar.

The strong, pure scent of vanilla wafted out. Penelope closed her eyes and inhaled deeply. Real vanilla, right from the bean. Not an extract. The perfume of it was intoxicatingly rich.

She took one of the marshmallows out of the jar. It was soft, soft as a pillow and left a dusting of powdered sugar on her hands. Penelope dropped it in her cocoa and stirred it in. Then, she took two more and added them. She watched them dissolve into a frothy foam on top of the cocoa.

She took a sip. Chocolate and vanilla coated her tongue.

She closed her eyes and, for a second, she was back in her grandfather's kitchen, sun gold and slanting through gauzy, lace curtains. The warmth of a family she didn't have at home.

Penelope opened her eyes. The cocoa was gone. She'd drunk it all. Maybe she should make another cup. No. Penelope let out a contented sigh. The events of the night caught up to her in a single, exhausting rush.

Her limbs felt too heavy to move, as if each arm weighed a hundred pounds. Penelope let her head rest on her arms. It'd be all right if she took a little nap.

The witches flew over Midswich, Bruleé in the lead. The cold night dried the sweat on her face but chilled the damp patches under her arms. She couldn't wait to get home and crawl into bed, even though it was barely 10:30.

All three of them had taken turns levitating Anne up three flights of stairs. Flora lectured Anne the entire way to their apartment about how she had imposed herself on the witches far too much and taken advantage of their generosity.

Bruleé tried telling Flora they didn't mind, but that made it worse, and she finally shut up.

Flora promised to pay them, and Bruleé insisted that an excuse to leave the party was payment enough. She had the feeling Flora would still add a few extra bills to the next payment on Anne's healing tea.

Downtown came into view, and Bruleé grimaced with relief, her fake smile faltering at the last.

Pastor Austin's words had dogged her since leaving the party. Bruleé had no excuse for failing to research the drugs Anne was on and look for interactions they could have with the herbs she'd prescribed. It was her good luck that Anne wasn't sick or dead.

She hadn't put anything in the tea that hadn't been used for generations to help arthritis, but Bruleé also hadn't finished her healing accreditation. She'd completed the classes but not the paperwork. When their parents died, she had dropped everything. Bruleé had intended to get back to it but never had. Now, a year had passed, she'd have to take refresher classes before she could file for her license. In the meantime, Anne's tea would have to stop. Bruleé's stomach churned with the idea of telling Anne and Flora, but she had to.

A sharp punch in the arm pulled Bruleé from her thoughts. Anglaise had pulled up beside her.

"You missed the house."

Bruleé looked below her. She was over the shops on the next block. She slowed her broom and turned around. Caramel was already touching down in the alley behind the teashop. Anglaise turned and dropped steeply into the alley.

As Bruleé got lower, the back of her neck tingled. Something was wrong.

Fraiche was out. Caramel held the pom while he licked her face. Bruleé remembered leaving him in the apartment upstairs. How had he gotten out?

She landed behind Anglaise, who stared at the *DELIVER-IES* door as if it was poisonous.

"What—" Bruleé saw what was wrong before she could finish asking. The back door was hanging funny on its hinges, the door newly battered.

Caramel made a high-pitched whine, the beginning of a sentence choked off by fear.

Bruleé turned her broom bristles up, ready to take out anyone who might be waiting. She looked at Anglaise, who nodded.

Anglaise turned the doorknob and pushed the door open a little. The injured hinges squealed in protest.

Broom ready, Bruleé rushed the room beyond. She swung the broom wildly in the dark just in case the intruder was still in the kitchen.

She froze when the lights came on.

The intruder was gone, but they had left devastation behind.

Anglaise swore behind her, an unbroken string of curses that went on for a whole three minutes.

Caramel cried. Her wailing sobs fighting for volume with Anglaise's rage.

Pots, pans, and mixing bowls were strewn all over the room. The cupboards hung open. Shattered plates dusted the floor, a snowdrift of pointed shards.

"The teapots!" Bruleé bolted.

She slapped the light switch and the fixtures overhead flared.

The cubbies on the wall were empty, all but the highest. The sales stock was gone, along with most of the teapots she served from. The special ones. Her own collection.

Bruleé's whole body shook as if from a fever. She was numb and cold and needed to sit down, but couldn't remember how to move.

"Son of a bitch! I'm calling the police," Anglaise said from very far away.

Bruleé blinked and looked around. Anglaise was behind the front counter dialing the phone.

In the distance, Bruleé could still hear Caramel crying. She should go comfort her. She should do something.

A hand touched her shoulder. Bruleé jumped and spun around. Just Anglaise.

"What did the police say?"

Anglaise shook her head. "You won't believe this but they aren't open."

"Then call the Musquash cops over! Call someone! We need a police report for the insurance, we need—"

Her voice choked off, throat too thick to speak. She wheezed trying to breath and realized she was hyperventilating.

Anglaise pushed her into a chair and put a hand on her back, murmuring something, and warm soothing energy washed over her. Bruleé's lungs opened, air rushed back in. She took a deep breath, head hanging between her knees, and breathed, basking in the calm magic of whatever spell Anglaise had used.

"All right, give me a minute. I can deal now," Bruleé said. She waved Anglaise off. "For heaven's sake, go do something with Caramel."

Anglaise gave her an extra pat and left without a word.

Bruleé sat there, her head in her hands. She should be getting the camera from upstairs, taking pictures, calling the insurance company. The list circled in her brain as she sat doing nothing.

The empty cubbies and shattered teapots were a silent accusation. She should have put spells on the shop to prevent burglaries. What fool just locked the door and left their livelihood unattended? She did.

In the kitchen, Caramel's sobs quieted, and Bruleé heard soft steps on the stairs. Maybe someone was getting the camera, doing what she should have.

Numbness paralyzed her. At some point, she'd have to get up, but not now. Just a few more minutes.

Anglaise came back, face drawn and gray. "Bruleé…" her voice trailed off.

"What?"

Anglaise had her full attention. Her sister was rarely at a loss for words, so if Anglaise wanted to say something, it must be bad. "I think…" She left the sentence unfinished.

"What is it?"

"The dream puffs." Anglaise's frown deepened, creasing her sharp features with worry. "I think they're gone."

"Gone?" Bruleé jumped up. "Gone, like how?"

"I don't know."

"Stolen? Did the jar break?"

"I don't know," Anglaise snapped.

Bruleé pushed past her and ran for the kitchen. She looked around. There was so much broken glass she couldn't tell if the jar of dream puffs was among the debris.

"We have to break the spell."

"If they dissolved, it's too late," Anglaise said.

Bruleé looked at the open spell cabinet in the kitchen. That was where Anglaise stored all her magical implements.

"Why don't you lock this?"

"Who's going to break in? Small towns don't have crime."

"Obviously someone did," Bruleé shot back.

They were arguing over spilled milk. Why didn't the spell cupboard have a lock? Why hadn't Bruleé set up security for the shop?

She pinched the bridge of her nose and took a deep breath. They were all frayed to unraveling.

"We need to at least try to break the spell. They may have just been stolen."

Anglaise nodded. "Okay."

Anglaise went upstairs to get Caramel. Bruleé heard her swear again then the fizzle of magic. Caramel must have locked herself in her room.

A minute later, Anglaise came down the stairs, marching Caramel in front of her. Caramel's eyes were red and she wiped her face on her sleeve. Bruleé was relieved to see her spell kit, a wooden case with leather straps Caramel kept her casting supplies in.

Bruleé was not relieved to see the dust on the case. She'd been neglecting Caramel's education. There'd been no time for her baby sister, and she was afraid to push Caramel too hard, so she just let it slide.

Pushing her doubts aside, Bruleé tried to think of something positive to say that wouldn't spook Caramel. "Thank you," was all that she came out with.

Caramel ducked and gave a shy, almost-smile. "I n—need m—m—more room."

They went into the shop. That had more floor space than the kitchen and apartment upstairs combined.

Bruleé and Anglaise cleared a space, picking up tablecloths and the metal tea service that had been dumped to the floor.

Floor cleared, Caramel blew the dust off her spell kit and pulled out a thick chalk. She drew a wide and near perfect circle on the floor. Bruleé was glad to see not all her skills had gone rusty and vowed to resume her sister's training as soon as things settled down.

There was an opening in the chalk circle and Caramel stepped through.

"I—I'll n—need both of y—y—you," she said.

Bruleé and Anglaise entered the circle and Caramel closed it behind them. She put the wooden case in the center and knelt to unpack it.

"S—set up the elements," she told them. Caramel handed Bruleé an abalone shell with a sage smudge stick in it. "Air," she said.

Anglaise received a squat, round candle that smelled warmly of beeswax.

"Fire."

Bruleé and Anglaise took their elements to the proper compass points, while Caramel set up water. She kept a bottle of spring water in the kit, and poured out a little in a shallow, silver bowl.

With a word, Bruleé ignited the sage. She blew out the flame and let it smolder. The smudge stick went into the shell, a curl of smoke rose off of it, joining with air and representing the element. Anglaise set the candle ablaze with the same starting spell, and returned to the middle of the circle.

The last element was earth and, for that, Caramel set out a

palm-size amethyst wand. They gathered in the center of the circle. Caramel sat down on the floor, Anglaise sat cross-legged, and Bruleé tweaked her skirt and sat neatly, making the third point in a little triangle.

Caramel dug into her spell kit and got the rest of the items she needed out: a ceramic-lined bowl that stood on three legs, paper, a pen, an athame, and a brown bottle with a handwritten label that read *Dragon's Blood.*

She handed Anglaise the pen and paper. "Write d—down the dream puff spell."

Bruleé always forgot that Caramel's stutter almost disappeared when she was casting. Maybe because they did so little spell and circle work together. More to fix. Somehow, in her effort to keep the family together, Bruleé had forgotten to actually do things with her family.

Anglaise wrote down the spell and handed it to Caramel.

"I need a little blood."

Anglaise grunted and held out her hand. Caramel made a shallow cut the length of a fingernail on her palm.

Caramel touched the paper to Anglaise's palm. A red stain spread on the paper. When Caramel judged there was enough blood, she took away the sheet of paper and put it in the ceramic cauldron. She opened the oil and poured a few crimson drops over the paper. "Join hands," she said.

They did so.

> "On the eve two days past
> A spell was cast
> Effects created
> The power now must be quelled
> Dream puffs meant to dream
> And share
> Now be dispersed
> Power broken
> Spell be lifted."

Caramel released Bruleé's hand and put the athame, point down, into the cauldron.

The paper ignited with a fierce, blue flame that climbed high above their heads. The flame snuffed itself out, leaving only a film of ash in the bowl.

Caramel poured a little more spring water in the bowl and swirled it around. She handed the bowl to Anglaise. "Pour the water out on the earth."

"Town square grass. I'm not going out to the woods tonight."

"Th—that's fine," Caramel said. She wiped away a section of the chalk circle so they could all exit.

Anglaise took the bowl and left through the front door of the shop.

"Thanks, again," Bruleé said. "You're the best spell breaker we have."

"I h—hope it h—helps."

"Me, too." Bruleé couldn't shake the sinking feeling that it was too late. Nothing else had gone right tonight, so why should this.

She saw the camera Anglaise had been taking pictures with sitting on the counter.

"You go back upstairs. I'll keep getting pictures and clean up the circle."

Caramel nodded and gave a bigger than usual smile of gratitude. She left with her spell kit.

Bruleé grabbed the camera and started snapping pictures of the broken teapots.

Her eyes teared up as she recognized the remains of specific pots. There was the blue Wedgwood that her grandmother had handed down. The gray shards of a ceramic elephant a friend had brought back from Thailand. The three hand-thrown pots she'd bought from an artist in Boston for resale. Her personally selected stock purchased from crafters and potters.

She brushed the tears aside and kept snapping pictures.

Chapter

atilda dreams. She is awake in the dream and somehow aware that this isn't her dream. She's not sure how this happened. The dream puffs she ordered should be at the teashop. Maybe the witches let them out or spiked the food at the party. She can't say.

The cheering crowd draws her attention. Matilda is somewhere—a town, a cross between Midswich and a tropical island with European style buildings.

There is a parade. Hazy people with soft edges cheer. Endless fluttering rose petals rain from a purple sky.

Matilda wades into the crowd. Is this Hugh's dream? Is he king of the parade on show for the admiration of adoring masses?

She pushes through the unresisting crowd that melts and shifts. She stands on the street curb in the front line.

The parade is mostly African animals—wildebeest, cheetahs, a group of lions, and African elephants the size of houses.

Atop the elephants are platforms, seats, and thrones, shaped like lotus blossoms. Sitting on the first throne is a woman in long, trailing, pink robes. The crowd screams gibberish as her elephant passes.

The next elephant bears a replica of Hillary Johnson dressed in leopard skins. She wears a glittering tiara that floats around her head like the halo of a Renaissance Madonna. She waves like the Queen of England. "You should totally come to Africa," she yells at the crowd.

Matilda snorts. If she had a rock, she'd chuck it at Hillary. She looks around, but no such luck. The stone pavers are secure in the dream streets.

What is Hillary doing in Hugh's dream? If anything, Bruleé should be here.

Matilda looks up at the next elephant in the parade. The rider is Consolata. Her black hair spreads over the back of the elephant like a blanket.

"How's your plan working out now? Loser," she shouts.

None of this is making sense. Wherever Matilda is, it's not Hugh's dream. Something must have gone wrong with the dream puffs. She hasn't even picked them up yet.

The last elephant goes by and Matilda's breath catches. Eyes wide, she stares at the final princess.

It's a version of herself. A more perfect version than she could ever imagine. Princess Matilda's hair is a lush fall of orangey-pink, the color of dawn, eyes like turquoise, and skin of glowing marble.

Matilda blinks at herself. Princess Matilda is ridiculous. No one could live up to that perfection. It's disturbing. Laughable. Flattering.

The elephant passes her, receding down the long boulevard faster than it should.

The parade is gone, except for the last elephant that keeps walking away yet remains in sight.

One last figure stumbles down the street, chasing the elephant—a clown dressed in rags. Rose petals cling to his legs and trip him every few steps.

The clown struggles to his feet, one hand reaching for the last princess. "Matilda! Come back, please!"

The real Matilda inhales sharply. Her eyes narrow and fix on the clown. "Eddie?" Shock tingles through her. Annoyance and anger spark and die in its wake.

Clown Eddie freezes. The makeup and ragged Pierrot costume are gone. He's dressed in his usual '50s hipster work clothes. He looks like he does at their weekly lunches, complete with book bag strapped across his chest.

He looks around. "Matilda?"

The parade is gone, spectators, gone, princesses disappeared. He and Matilda stand on a stone-paved European street with swaying trees growing from the sidewalk.

"How?" His eyes look as if they're about to pop out of his head they're so wide. "Are you real?"

"I'm real," she says.

"You shouldn't be here. This is my head." He's blushing, a brighter red than could ever exist in waking life.

"Something's gone wrong," Matilda says.

Eddie flops down, a puppet with cut strings, taking a seat on the curb. His head in his hands, he moans unintelligibly.

"What?" Matilda sits next to him.

"I'm so embarrassed." He kicks at the pavement with his heel. "You shouldn't be here. How'd this happen, anyway?"

"I think it's my fault," Matilda says. Her confusion and surprise give way to a warm feeling. "I asked the witches for something to get some insight on Hugh. I'm supposed to be in his dream. But I haven't even picked up the marshmallows."

"I have no idea what you just said."

Matilda shakes her head. "Doesn't matter. I'm here now." She doesn't add that she feels better than she has in months.

A breeze ruffles her hair and Matilda sees the ocean has come in. Gentle waves break against the stone street a few feet away.

"I'll never live this down," Eddie says. "I'm sorry."

"There are worse dreams I could have popped in to." She shrugs and laughs at the horrified expression on Eddie's face, the almost incandescent humiliation. "Relax." She nudges him with her shoulder. "There's worse things to be than a princess."

Eddie pulls his hat off and kneads it in his hands. "Can you just go?"

"No," Matilda says. "Not yet."

"Why?"

"I broke up with Hugh."

His head snaps up to face her. "Really?"

"Sort of. He was passed out, so I have to tell him again tomorrow."

"That's great! Or awful. Sorry."

"It's fine. I bet it's even mutual."

She watches the blue-green breakers rush over the pavement and recede. The sidewalk is now part of some kind of promenade, and there are antique cannons every few feet. The pyramid of iron balls stacked at their feet cast long shadows, even though the sun is high.

"So, you're not with Hugh anymore?" Eddie asks.

"That's the general meaning of 'breakup.'"

He nods and puts his crumpled hat back on. Eddie clears his throat then says nothing.

"Well?" Matilda elbows him.

"Well, what?"

She laughs at his shock. "Ask me, dumb ass."

"Umm…want to go out with me?"

"That's not how you ask a princess."

Eddie chuckles. "I'm not going to live that down, am I?"

"No, you're not."

"Would you like to go to dinner, a proper formal dinner somewhere nice?"

Instead of answering, Matilda leans over and kisses him. She feels him tense then relax and return the kiss. His lips are warm and dry, a nice change from Hugh's constant lip balm.

I can tell people our first kiss was in a dream, Matilda thinks. *Who else can say that?*

How Bruleé got backstage at a fashion show she doesn't know. Techno music throbs with palpable colors. She feels a slight pressure on her skin. Long, multi-jointed insectile women get dressed in clothing that looks made of foam and light.

A dream, she realizes. Cold fear numbs her hands. The dream puffs. Whoever broke the jar, or took them, has let them out. The dozen or so batch of marshmallows has found heads to inhabit. One being hers and whoever's dream this is.

It's too late, but Bruleé desperately wishes Caramel's spell had worked. They would be run out of town by angry villagers with pitchforks and torches for sure. The burning times maybe over, but no witch ever really walks safely.

"Awesome, isn't it?" asks a voice behind her.

Bruleé spins around. "Hugh?" Of all the dreams to end up in, it's the idiot drunk from the party.

He gives her a crooked grin. Small people, like tiny insect drones dress him in the strange dream clothes.

"New York Fashion Week," he says.

He gives her a wink and Bruleé rolls her eyes. He's no less smarmy in his dreams.

"I went down for it one year, snuck around the tents. I made it backstage to a Stella McCartney show before I got busted."

"Lovely. Did they put you in fashion jail?" Bruleé steps aside as a tall stick insect of a model brushes passed.

"No. They just tossed me out," Hugh says.

She sees a wistful longing tinge his handsome features. He looks like an advertisement.

"This is your dream," she says.

He snorts. "Duh."

"No. Your dream job."

"Duh, again."

Bruleé's lips purse. Frustration battles briefly with anger. She takes a breath. "So why aren't you pursuing modeling?"

Hugh looks like he thinks about that, brow furrowing as the gears turn. "Well, it's kind of off the wall, and plus I'm not gay, and plus my dad has some stick up his ass about me being mayor someday."

"But, are you happy?"

Hugh looks around. He basks in the sound and lights. His clothes float around him as if immersed in water. A smile tugs the corners of his mouth.

"I'm happy here," he says. His eyes open and fix Bruleé with his stare. "Did Matilda put you up to this? I think she wants to dump me."

"Not surprising," Bruleé mutters. "No, she didn't. This is a horrible, horrible accident for which we will pay dearly."

He shrugs. "That's cool then. I don't mind having you here."

Bruleé's teeth grind. "How big of you."

"Models, line up," a man with big padded head phones yells over the buzz of chaos and music. He claps twice and the models line up, according to some order already arranged.

In their faces, Bruleé sees shades of super models she recognizes from television, magazines, and billboards. There is a Heidi Klum clone, Giselle, Tyra, Kate Moss, and a dozen others. At least Hugh has put himself with good company.

"Come on." He grabs her hand and pulls her into line. "You don't want to miss the best part of the show."

She tries to pull her hand away but he has a solid grip. "No, I'm not dressed for it."

Hugh gives her a funny look. "Relax. It's a dream."

The models are moving. They disappear one by one behind a curtain. Bruleé quits struggling. "Fine. I might as well, since I'm here."

Hugh grins. "Atta girl."

Their turn comes up and Hugh puts on his model face: a blend of arrogance, bland disdain, and intensity that elevates his features to predatory god.

"You're really good at this," Bruleé says a little breathless. She may not like him but the man was undeniably hot.

He winks at her without changing expressions. "I know."

He pulls her through the curtain onto the runway. Flashbulbs go off. Or what Bruleé thinks are flashbulbs. The lights don't connect to anything. They float like fireflies, dim until exploding into life. Applause fills the air, but Bruleé can see no people.

Hugh's strut forces Bruleé to trot to keep up with him, but she has to admit walking the runway is a thrill. She wishes her clothes were a better match to the situation. She's wearing the skirt and cardigan from the party.

They reach the end of the runway and Hugh strikes a pose of perfect boredom. Caught up in the moment, Bruleé tries to copy him.

Hugh glances over at her. "Not bad."

She smiles. They turn and strut back alone on the runway. The other models apparently disappeared when they walked through the curtain.

The invisible crowd screams over the pulsing techno.

Right before they reach the curtain, Hugh grabs Bruleé around the waist and pulls her toward him.

"What are you doing?"

He grins impishly. "Going out with a bang."

He dips her before she can struggle. She clutches his shoulders afraid of being dropped. He leans in and gives her a kiss on the lips.

Bruleé tries to shove Hugh away, but his strong arms hold her firmly. At least he doesn't try to stick his tongue down her throat.

With luck, she'll wake up in the next three seconds.

The playground is unfamiliar to Anglaise, but then, any school playground would be. She was home schooled and her recesses were spent in the family's little backyard behind their Boston brownstone.

A huge Gothic school building, part cathedral, part prison, looms above. The building casts pointed shadows across the tarmac ball courts, jungle gym, and swing set.

The schoolyard is empty except for a clump of boys gathered in a circle.

Instinct tells her nothing good is happening. The boys cluster like dogs around a wounded animal.

An animal may be what they've trapped. She looks around for someone to help. Far off, she sees students and teachers, but they are too distant to see what's happening. Even if they were closer, they may not be of any use. Their backs are turned to the boys and they are still as pillars.

Anglaise chews her lip. She had intended to hide if she ended up in someone's dream. Not that hiding would spare her or her sisters the wrath of the town. But maybe they could've claimed they weren't affected by the dream puffs. People are touchy when it comes to other people, especially those with magic, roaming their heads. She figures the townies will feel better if only *they* swap dreams.

Anglaise waffles. Eyes scanning for a hiding place even as she clenches her fists, ready to free whatever the bullies have captured.

A cry goes up from the center of the circle. It's cut off by a whimper as one of the boys gives a swift kick. The boys chant in harsh voices, "Fatty fatty, two by four, couldn't fit through the bathroom door! So he did it on the floor, licked it up, and did some more!"

"Hey!" Anglaise yells. The word pops out without forethought or intent. The bullies look at her, their mean, pinched features rearranged with surprise. Committed, she trots forward. "Stop it," she tells them.

The rictus of surprise is frozen on their faces. They don't seem to know what to do. The dream creatures hiss.

Maybe this hadn't been such a good idea. Anglaise rolls up the sleeve of her chef jacket. "I said, get out of here." She manages to project much more menace than she feels. If she'd wandered into a bad enough nightmare, she may be the bully's next victim.

They scatter, fleeing into the shadow of the school and melt into the brick. Anglaise lets out her breath, relief easing the knots in her neck and stomach.

She looks at the ground. A fat, little boy in a dirty, short-sleeved shirt cowers on the ground. His hands are wrapped around his head and, even with the bullies gone, he doesn't look up.

Anglaise goes over to the boy. "Hey, kid, you're okay."

The boy doesn't move, except for the rolls of pudge that quiver with his silent sobs. She reaches out and touches his back. He starts, round face jerking up. Tears shine in his eyes and spill over his cheeks.

"I chased off those other kid…things," she says.

Instead of gratitude, the little boy looks at her with horror, mouth forming an O. The tears dry up, and his mouth presses into a thin, familiar line. "What are you doing here?" The boy stands up. As he stands he grows, the fat melting off. Pudgy fists become hard, lean knuckles. "Answer me!"

"Pastor Austin." Anglaise looks at him, shock, dismay, and a bone-deep sick feeling swamps her.

"I asked you a question!" he thunders.

The sky darkens and Anglaise risks a quick look around. The playground is empty. Even the distant figures are gone. She should have hidden, left Austin to his childhood torments.

"It's an accident." Anglaise backs up a few steps. She put her hands up and tried to remember if magic would work in a dream. "Someone broke into our shop."

"I don't care," Austin says.

"They stole the dream puffs. This isn't supposed to be happening!" Anglaise's voice rises in panic. She's ready to run if he tries to hit her. She thought clergy weren't supposed to do that sort of thing.

Austin breathes hard but he's stopped advancing on her.

"They let the Dreampuffs out or broke the jar," Anglaise says. "Either way, this is happening to a lot of other people."

The pastor frowns. He tilts his head to regard her from the corner of his eye. The school is now just a regular church. An elongated version of the one he preaches at. The sky lightens to dawn colors, pink and orange in neon streaks.

Anglaise's stomach constricts as she sees Austin relax. He smiles, a humorless slash of victory.

"You witches are going to pay for this." He rubs his hands together as if itching to lynch Anglaise on the spot.

"It's not our fault," She tells him and wonders why she bothers. "The dream puffs were made for a client. Whoever broke in let them out, somehow."

"You think that matters?" Austin levels a finger at her. His smile is gone. "How dare you spy on someone's inner life. I'll see all three of you stripped of power and in jail for this."

"You can't do that!"

"It's a violation of privacy."

"Dream swapping is common practice! Therapists, cops, lots of people use it."

"Not without consent," Austin hisses.

He has her there. But allowances are made for accidents. Dream swapping is common enough that when accidents do happen, it's little more than a minor misdemeanor. The dreams people trade are lucid so it's not a violation like telepathy and spy crystals.

The problem is, if Austin decided to press charges, who else in town would follow him?

A dozen people in town will find themselves in someone else's dream tonight. A dozen misdemeanor charges may add up to jail time. She wasn't sure.

Time to go on the offensive.

"Go ahead. See if we go to jail. But remember, I know why you really hate us, you hypocrite."

That remark washes away the glint of victory in Austin's eyes.

"Isn't that right, fatty-fatty-two-by-four?" Anglaise presses.

Austin turns white and so does the dream sky. Everything shrinks, the church, the playground, as if the walls are closing in. For a second, Anglaise thinks Austin is going to vomit. His lean runner's muscles twitch across his frame.

She pushes ahead, even though a bit of regret nips her conscience. "Your sin is envy, isn't it, Pastor? You don't hate us because we're witches. You hate us because we have a bakery. And, by God, if you can't indulge, no one should."

Austin's face is twitching now, too, a mass of ticks. Anglaise tries to take a step back and bumps an invisible wall that's as cold as glass.

She tenses, waiting for Austin to either punch her or have a stroke. Those seem about the only options he has left.

The glass bubble Anglaise and Austin are in shatters outward. They stand on bleachers, looking over a running track. Anglaise sees the rooftops of a collection of buildings, a college campus, judging by the mascot and varsity letters painted on the grassy field at the center of the track.

Running the track in fast forward is a tubby, younger version of Pastor Austin.

The current Pastor Austin drops to the bleachers as if his legs just gave out. He puts his head in his hands and makes a harsh, strangled noise that takes Anglaise a minute to place. A sob.

He doesn't cry more, but Anglaise swears she can feel deep, pulsing sorrow pour off him.

Below, young Austin continues running round and round, sweat beading and streaming over the creases of neck fat and elbow dimples.

"Just leave us alone, all right? You aren't the food police. We can't make people fat any more than a grocery store and I don't see you picketing the Dry Good candy aisle."

Austin looks at her, his face rising from his hands like an icy dawn. "I told you to get out."

"One of us has to wake up."

"How do I do that?"

"Will you even think about what I said?"

Austin stands, fists balled. "How do I wake up, witch?"

Anglaise steps back. She'd hoped she could win him over with reason but knew better before she opened her mouth. When he woke up, he was going straight to the police. Anglaise thought about keeping him asleep just for a few days. Just until she and her sisters could convince everyone the dreams were an accident. But that was illegal. Psychic kidnapping.

"Pain will wake you up, extreme fear…uh…those are the first two." Anglaise tries to think of the last couple ways to get out of the dream.

Before she can remember, Austin pitches himself down the bleachers. He falls slowly, his black cassock spreading out like wings. He has a martyr's flair for the dramatic, Anglaise thinks sourly.

Austin picks up speed as he falls. The bench bucks and tosses him as he hits the first one hard. He rolls down the stadium seating in a series of bone-crunching freeze frames.

Anglaise feels a tug at the center of her chest and she's pulled into the sky as it fades from blue to black. She is being returned to her own neglected dreams.

Geoffrey stands in the hollow space of the Dry Goods. He almost doesn't recognize it without the shelves, counters, and check stands in the front. But his great-grandfather had a picture taken, an old black and white photo, misty at the edges, of the store when it was first completed. Geoffrey recognizes it from that.

The light is white and flat. The dream could be in black and white, except Geoffrey holds his arms out. He's in color.

This isn't one of his restocking nightmares, where he has boxes and boxes to unload but can't find the right shelves to put the items on.

Geoffrey starts walking. He wonders why the dream feels odd. He is awake and aware and that's unusual for him. Emma told him all about lucid dreaming once, and he thought it was her usual New Age hokum, like chakras and crystals. But this feels exactly like what she described to him.

In the distance Geoffrey sees a figure. He's pretty sure it's Claire. Since she's the only landmark in the far too large interior, he heads for her. He walks a seemingly endless amount of time without Claire getting any larger, and he starts to wonder if this is his dream after all.

Tired of walking Geoffrey yells, "Claire? Is that you?"

The figure turns. And he's standing right beside her.

"That was weird." Geoffrey looks around. He didn't feel himself moving at all.

"What are you doing here?" Claire eyes him with suspicion, brows pulling into the crease in her forehead.

"What do you mean? Aren't I dreaming?"

"*I'm* dreaming," she snaps. "God, you would follow me, even here?"

"Well, I'm not here on purpose," he says.

They cross their arms in annoyance at the same time, and Geoffrey is tempted to laugh. He keeps it to himself, knowing Claire wouldn't appreciate the mirth.

"What's that?"

Something black behind Claire catches his eye. It's boxy and almost entirely blocked from sight by her body.

Claire keeps herself in front of the object. "Nothing," she says.

"Come on, let me see." The object is compelling for some reason. He can almost place what it is, but can't quite put his finger on it.

"No." Claire's voice is hard and flat. "It doesn't matter."

"It matters to you." Craning his neck, he leans over to the side.

Holding out her hands, Claire moves to block him.

"Is this to do with the witches?" he asks.

"No."

The something behind Claire begins to rock. Plinking music starts up, gentle notes that remind Geoffrey of a lullaby.

Putting his hands around Claire's waist, he lifts her aside.

Behind her is a black-draped bassinette. The cradle moves back and forth, with no one touching it.

Geoffrey's face crumples. He sets Claire down and hears her sigh.

"You still dream about having children?" The wind has gone out of him, and his words have a faint wheeze.

"Don't you?" Claire asks.

He reaches for the bassinette and pulls aside the gauzy fall of black fabric. The cradle is empty.

He sighs and lets go of the curtain. "I think about kids a lot."

"Why don't you say something?"

"It's easier to stay busy. And I guess I thought we'd given up."

"You mean I gave up. I'm the one that's infertile."

"That isn't your fault. We could try again."

"So I can bankrupt us?"

"No." Geoffrey takes her hands. "There are a lot of options. Adoption, or, if you'll keep an open mind, the witches might be able to help."

"The witches? What, spells and potions and voodoo?"

Geoffrey grins. "Voodoo works."

Claire punches his chest. "Be serious."

He smiles wider. "I am. When I was looking up information on witches, I did a search for witches and infertility."

Claire looks at him with narrow eyes, head cocked a little—just enough to drive home her suspicions. Geoffrey knows the look isn't as serious as she'd like him to think.

"Some of it depends on how good the witches are. But honestly, the odds aren't any worse than a fertility doctor, and they are a lot cheaper."

"You just want to keep the witches." She lets out a long sigh, resting her head against his chest. "I don't know. What if something goes wrong? You heard what happened at the party. Aren't they supposed to have a license?"

"I think Bruleé can get one. Anne is doing much better."

"What will Pastor Austin say?"

"If we can have a baby, do you care? It's now or never. I'm not going to be seventy at my kid's graduation."

He touches her shoulders and, running a hand up her neck and under her chin, tilts her chin to look at him. "Can't hurt to try?"

Her eyes pool with tears that grow and break, running down her face. "Maybe, or not. I—what if we have some mutant baby?"

"Then we get to join the circus."

Claire laughs through the tears and punches his arm. "Stop making fun of me. I'm serious."

"I'm sorry," he says, pulling her into a bear hug. "How 'bout this. We start the adoption process now, and think about the witches later. With luck, we'll have two kids before we turn fifty."

She says something, but it's muffled against his chest. He lets go so she can come up for air.

"All right," she says. Claire throws her arms around Geoffrey's neck. He lifts her off the gray tiles, spinning her around. Her giggles make him laugh.

"All right," she says again. "Tomorrow, we'll start looking for an adoption agency."

"And the witches can stay? And I get to quit sleeping on the couch?"

"We'll see," she says, but her smile tells him she's teasing.

"Hey, uh, while we're here," Geoffrey waggles his eyebrows.

Claire gives a slow, sexy smile, her tears dried up. "Why not, since we're here?"

Caramel is pretty sure she's in Fraiche's dream. Otherwise, why would Fraiche be the size of a horse chasing rabbits the size of ponies? What throws her off are the vivid cartoon colors of the landscape. She thought dogs saw in black and white.

She's also riding Fraiche. Caramel screams and giggles. Fraiche runs full tilt down a daisy-covered hill. She holds his collar while silky-orange fur whips around her.

The rabbits scatter in all directions, throwing up a storm of daisy petals that hang in the air.

"Faster, Fraiche," Caramel urges and he gallops harder.

In the back of her mind whispers a voice saying, this isn't right. She feels distantly that she failed and should feel badly. Caramel ignores the voice. Dreams are the only place she can ignore it. She wakes up with that voice in the morning and goes to bed with it at night. Only once in a while are her dreams anything approaching pleasant, and she means to take advantage of it.

A bark echoes overt the hills, and Fraiche stops in his tracks. The rabbits dart away and disappear. Caramel almost flips over Fraiche's head. She clings to his collar and rights herself. The daisy petals turn lazily in the air currents.

Fraiche's nose lifts, moist and twitching. Caramel takes a sniff herself, but there is no scent in the dream. She guesses it's because she's really still in bed, so everything just smells like her bedroom.

The bark comes again and Fraiche answers. His reply parts the daisy petals.

Caramel squints into the distance. On a far off hill she sees a black dot. She frowns. She wonders if the dream puffs are at work.

Fraiche arrows off toward the distant black dot and Caramel hangs on, knuckles white. She leans forward, trying to keep her balance on his neck.

The dot on the horizon hurtles toward them, resolving into a sleek, black Chihuahua.

Caramel says, "Aww," before she realizes someone is riding it.

Her hope that the dream is her own, crumbles, not that there aren't frequently other people in her dreams, but they usually aren't so clear.

The Chihuahua is closer and Caramel can make out the rider. The woman is Pastor Austin's staunchest supporter. Her gray-black hair, usually put up in a tidy up-do, flies out behind her, waving like a battle flag.

Caramel checks herself, making sure she's wearing clothes. She is. Thank the Goddess it's not one of those dreams. She's dressed in a puffy princess gown, almost the same cream color of Fraiche's fur.

The dogs bark, excited to be meeting someone new. The expression on the other woman's face shifts from elation to wrinkly distrust.

She looks down at herself, possibly checking to make sure she's not nude either. Lucky for both of them, she's wearing red, footie pajamas, like a little kid at Christmas. Not that Caramel's princess costume is any more mature.

Fraiche and the other dog perform the circular dance of dogs sniffing each other, while Caramel and the woman eye each other in silent distrust.

The woman breaks the silence. First her brown eyes spark with concern and fear, and something Caramel isn't sure of.

"You're one of the witches, right?"

Caramel nods. She tugs on Fraiche's collar but he won't budge. The black dog has his full attention.

"What are you doing in my dream?"

Caramel purses her lips. She doesn't want to talk to the

woman, but can't think of a way not to. "It might not be your dream." Her voice is soft but it carries through the thick air. At least the stutter is gone.

"Am I in your dream?" The woman's eyes wander from the dogs to the daisies to the sky above. So perfect and blue it looks like a mural.

"Or the dogs'," Caramel says.

"Why is this happening?" The woman focuses on Caramel, her gaze cutting into her. "Is this a spell? Are you trying to get rid of me somehow? Penelope Owens is nobody's fool, if that's what you're thinking."

Shaking her head, Caramel says, "It's the dream puffs. Our shop was vandalized and someone let them out."

Penelope pales. Her lips quiver. Caramel's eyes narrow as she reassess woman. She had been picturing the vandal as a movie villain. Some guy with a ski mask dressed all in black. Not a thick-set older woman who looks like she's never committed so much as misdemeanor.

The dogs, oblivious to Caramel's suspicions, shrink to their normal size. They chase each other in circles, through the daisies that have turned into plastic flowers.

"Prince Albert, stop that!" Penelope chases her dog around for a minute. He dodges her, darting off, slipping between her legs and jumping out of her hands. "That's a witch's dog, you shouldn't—"

"They can play if they want to!" Caramel yells. A real yell, one she can only do in dreams. Her voice drops. "Leave them alone."

Penelope freezes. She looks like she's waiting for lightning to strike or a fireball to be hurled.

"S—sorry." Caramel looks at Penelope's stricken face. The last thing she needs to do is give the old woman a heart attack.

The field of daisies shrink to a square room carpeted in Astroturf and plastic daisies. The far walls are painted like the sky. Fluffy, white cartoon clouds drift by.

Penelope nods curtly to acknowledge Caramel's apology.

In one wall of the daisy room is a window. Curtains of gauzy, off-white lace billow out caught on a breeze Caramel can't feel. The curtains wave and beckon like a friend calling her over. Caramel tilts her head as she studies the window. This is Penelope's dream, and she doesn't want to pry, but she wants to take a look in the window.

Penelope is nervously watching the two toy dogs romp in the plastic flowers. She looks like she's waiting for Fraiche to turn Prince Albert into a toad.

Caramel leaves the dogs under Penelope's watchful eye, ready to intervene if Penelope tries to do anything to Fraiche.

She goes to the window and looks in. Beyond is another room, a cozy kitchen styled in late '50s Formica. The walls are lemon yellow with sunny gold linoleum on the floor. A girl, about eleven years old, sits at the table. Her black hair is pulled into braided pigtails, a *Brady Bunch*-looking A-line dress, and saddle shoes.

Caramel glances back at Penelope, who is now looking at Caramel, a frown deepening the brackets around her mouth.

"What?" Penelope asks and goes over.

Caramel can't say anything. Her heart is pounding in her throat. Instead, she looks back at the girl.

A big glass jar, with an airtight lid held on with clasps, sits on the table in front of the girl. Inside the jar are distinct, square-cut marshmallows. And the jar is exactly what Anglaise uses to trap dream puffs. How could they be in Penelope's dream unless she was the one who took them.

The girl opens the jar and takes out a dream puff. She pops it in her mouth and slowly chews the sticky confection. Her expression is sad, brow wrinkled, mouth puckered with held back sobs.

Caramel glances two, then three more times, back and forth, between Penelope and the girl, as though watching a tennis match.

Penelope, the elder, turns redder with every second. Fury and shame war across her face.

Very delicately, Caramel edges away from the woman.

Penelope notices the slight movement and rounds on Caramel. She keeps one hand on the windowsill, clutching it as if it's all that keeps her upright. "Fine." She grinds the word out past clenched jaws. "I broke into your teashop. I wrecked it. I stole your stupid marshmallows. Go ahead and tell the cops. None of this—" She waves her hand through the air. "—is admissible in court! Do your worst, witch."

Dizziness almost sends Caramel to her knees. She feels a soft tearing in her chest, like someone gently cutting her heart into pieces. Heartbreak. She hasn't felt it since her parents died. Whatever else happens after they wake up, Tea Times Three and the life they tried to make in Midswich is over.

A sob hitches in Caramel's throat, a big hiccupping one that opens the door for more.

Even as her vision blurs with tears she sees the dream change.

Penelope is still talking, ranting about something Caramel can't hear over her own heaving sobs and the pound of blood in her ears. Prince Albert runs up to his mistress and paws her leg, looking worried. Penelope scoops up her dog and clutches him to her chest. Her eyes shine with tears, and Caramel can't imagine what she has to cry about. She's gotten what she wants. No more teashop.

The daisy room fades, sky blue walls crumbling, replaced with a towering building. Blank windows, row after row, look down on a grassy courtyard where Caramel and Penelope now stand. Behind Penelope, a woman in a hospital robe sits on a bench a few feet away. Fraiche sits at her feet, pom-pom tail wagging.

Slowly, rising from her subconscious, Caramel realizes Penelope is saying something important and she should listen.

"I'm glad this happened. Now you have to leave. And good riddance. You witches wrecked my family and destroyed my mother. She was a spell junkie. And I'm not letting you get your hooks into my niece! She won't end up like that. Not if I can help it." Penelope pauses to inhale.

Prince Albert's big, dark eyes glance from Penelope to Caramel. He looks more worried about his owner than defensive or angry. Normally, a dog will pick up on their owner's aggression. He should be barking at her from Penelope's arms. Instead, his eyes are pleading.

Caramel looks back at Fraiche. He sniffs the woman's slippered foot. The woman has black hair straggling over her shoulders, just like Penelope's.

"Danielle is too good to end up like that. Mom lied all, the time, right to our faces. She stole from my father, even from me and my sister. Stole from her own children! But Danielle has dreams, and she's worked too hard getting her life together for you to ruin it for her now!"

Caramel purses her lips. She has to say something to Penelope. Derail the rant. Thanks to Fraiche, Prince Albert, and Penelope herself, Caramel knows what to do. She just has to work up the courage.

"So don't you dare complain about injustice to me. I know how unfair life is!" Penelope pauses. Her breathing is hard, raspy with emotions.

Caramel inhales and takes a few steps back, unsure if Penelope will sock her or not with what she has to say. "You need to tell this to your mother."

Penelope blinks. "My mother's dead."

"Th—the memory of her is close," Caramel says softly. "T—turn around."

Penelope startles, as if expecting to see her mother's rotting corpse looming behind her. She whips around, noticing the woman on the bench for the first time.

"Mom." The word wheezes out of her in painful exhale. Penelope bends at the waist, as if she's been punched in the stomach.

"She never replies though. I never get close," Penelope whispers.

"Try again," Caramel says.

Penelope takes a few tentative steps toward her mother, halting a second with each one.

When Caramel is sure Penelope is out of earshot, she whispers a spell.

> "Loved one gone,
> Heart still longs,
> Answer my need,

> With truth to heed.
> No lies are left,
> No shame to hide,
> So mote it be."

Since they are in Penelope's subconscious mind, Caramel can strengthen Penelope's memory of her mother, allowing Penelope to talk to her and get the answers she has longed for, all these years. It's not as good as confronting her mother's shade, but it's close.

"Mom?" Penelope says as she nears the woman.

The woman stirs as if gently awakened. She turns her head toward the voice.

"Mom, is that you?"

"Penelope, you came," she says.

Caramel's breath catches. Penelope's mother isn't just pretty, she's stunning. Movie star beautiful. Caramel looks at Penelope again and wonders at the blood connection between them. Penelope must have taken after her father.

"Mom." Penelope swallows and Caramel can hear the lump in her throat. "I have to talk to you."

"Not now, dear. I'm doing my beauty regimen." Penelope's mother holds a cut glass vial in her hand. She pulls out the stopper and pours a drop out onto her fingertip.

Penelope reddens. Her hand lashes out, striking the bottle from her mother's hand. Serum and bottle go flying and the vial shatters on the lawn. Startled by the sudden move, Prince Albert leaps out of Penelope's arms. He runs over to Caramel, who picks him up.

"Stop it!" Penelope shouts. Her words ripple through the air, and Caramel can feel them prickle over her skin.

"What is it, darling?" her mother says.

"You. How could you do this to us?" Penelope points at the glittering shards of the bottle her mother held only seconds ago.

Her mother shakes her head. "I didn't mean to."

"But you didn't love us enough to stop."

"You never understood, Penelope."

Her mother pats the seat on the bench beside her. Penelope's eyes narrow suspiciously, but she lowers herself to the bench.

"My problem had nothing to do with how much I loved you girls or your father and everything to do with how much I didn't like myself."

"But—but you were beautiful, perfect," Penelope says.

"Not to me. People told me all the time I was pretty, but no one else on earth can tell you something about yourself enough to make you believe it."

"So it was just vanity." Penelope's words twist with bitterness.

"No, it was fear," her mother says. She sighs and tries to touch Penelope, but Penelope pulls away. Her mother's hand retracts. "Being told I was pretty was all I had. Without that, I didn't have anything else. So I started buying spells and I liked the results. I liked the attention, being fawned over and complimented. I kept buying more and using more."

"Did you even try to quit? Even once?"

A long pause goes by. Caramel holds her breath. She didn't mean to witness all this, but the buildings surrounding the courtyard are flat like photographs and she can't leave. She hugs the dogs, hoping that if the conversation gives Penelope some closure, she'll admit to the break-in. But Caramel feels like a spy, just sitting there, listening.

Finally, Penelope's mother says, "I wish I could say yes. But I didn't. Not until Lowell caught me."

"Why?" Penelope jumps off the bench. "Why not? Couldn't you see how much we were hurting?"

Her mother shakes her head. "I don't expect you to understand. I justified it a thousand different ways. None of them were good, but I didn't want to quit getting the spells."

Penelope shivers and bursts into tears. She buries her face in her hands.

Prince Albert squirms in Caramel's grip and she lets him go. He runs over to Penelope and stands on two legs, pawing her for attention. She kneels down and hugs the Chihuahua for all he's worth. Prince Albert licks her face, trying in his own doggy way to soothe her. The same way Fraiche has so often soothed Caramel's hurts.

"I hate you." Penelope sobs. "I hate you so much."

Penelope cries harder, as if a dam has broken. She sinks back into her seat on the bench.

"I know, darling." Penelope's mother puts an arm around her, and this time Penelope leans into her, head resting on her mother's shoulder, crying so hard, Caramel is afraid she'll throw up.

How long Penelope spends sobbing in her mother's arms, Caramel isn't sure. Long enough for Caramel to make another circuit of the hospital courtyard, looking for a way out. There isn't one.

As Caramel settles in the grass, she hears Penelope's sobs quiet.

"There, there," her mother says. She strokes Penelope's graying hair. "It's all right to hate me. I wasn't much of a mother toward the end."

Penelope raises her head. "What?" Her voice is raspy from crying.

"You should hate me. Witches didn't make me an addict. I made me an addict."

"She's just telling you to say that," Penelope says, but she doesn't sound entirely convinced of it herself.

Mother shakes her head. "This is your dream, your subconscious mind. You know the truth here."

Silence stretches out as Penelope thinks about her mother's words. At least Caramel hopes she's absorbing them. If Penelope will come forward when they wake up, tell everyone the dreams are an accident, then maybe Caramel and her sisters will survive.

"I thought I'd feel better," Penelope says. "If I could just talk to you, get you to say you're sorry—I thought that'd make everything all right."

"You knew I wasn't that sorry."

Penelope nods.

"But don't you feel better?"

With a sigh Penelope says, "I feel emptier."

"Good girl." Her mother hugs Penelope. "At least a bit of the hate has drained away."

Penelope doesn't move for a long time. Caramel's heart flutters with anxiety. Penelope seems calmer now, but she could still turn on Caramel. Still ruin the teashop in waking life.

A seemingly endless amount of time goes by, and Caramel could swear they've been asleep for days. She wants to get out of the dream, but Penelope has to wake up first.

Penelope's mother strokes her daughter's hair, and Caramel has to admit that this is the most peaceful she's ever seen the woman. Caramel is used to the wild-eyed protestor singing hymns outside the teashop and waving a sign that says *WITCHES OUT!*

Penelope sighs loudly. The dream shifts, and as she stands up, her mother disintegrates, blowing apart like a pile of autumn leaves. The flat backdrop of the buildings recedes and the grassy courtyard spreads out, becoming a park, and then an endless plain.

Caramel stands up. She doesn't move toward Penelope, can't quite get her feet to move.

Penelope gets off the bench. She turns to Caramel. "How do I wake up?"

Caramel hesitates. "What are y—you going to do?"

"Never mind," Penelope says. She pinches her arm hard, twisting the flesh.

Caramel feels something deep inside, like a string connected to her stomach, get yanked.

Everything goes gray—the grass, the sky, and then fades to black. Caramel feels herself falling.

Paris at night is magic. The sparkle of the lights, the Eiffel Tower a black silhouette against a starry sky that is too bright.

William sips coffee at the outdoor café where he'd made his home on his one trip to France. Inside the café, which for some reason looks just like his living room back home, a party is going on. The guests are all his friends from Midswich.

Grandma Betty steps out of the café. She's dressed as a waiter, vest and bowtie, with a long white apron.

"Grandma, why don't you sit down?" William remembers her complaining about her feet nonstop during the last ten years of her life. She had type two diabetes and didn't take care of it.

Betty has a tray of white demitasse cups, full of the achingly strong espresso he ordered in the mornings.

"No, thank you, Will," Betty says. "I didn't come to chat."

William slouches a bit in his wrought iron chair. Betty balances the serving tray on her hip in order to free up a hand. She sticks her wagging finger at him.

"You were thinking about giving that little white girl my pound cake recipe, weren't you?"

"Oh, my God, is that what this is about?"

"Don't give me lip, William." Her finger waves accusingly in his face. "And you know I don't appreciate taking the Lord's name in vain."

"Come on, Grandma. The 'fifties are over, segregation has ended."

"That pound cake recipe goes to your bride and no one else. And you are not marrying a white girl."

William frowns and rubs his forehead. "This isn't happening." As soon as he says it, he realizes it's true. He was in Paris three years ago, on a food and wine tour. And Grandma Betty died when he was ten. He's dreaming.

"Speak of the devil and he shall appear. Or she," Grandma says.

William looks up. She's looking across the cobbled street. He follows her gaze and jerks in surprise. The iron chair screeches on the pavement as he shoves away from the table.

Standing under a lamppost shaped like a Notre Dame gargoyle is Anglaise.

"I said what I had to say. You best take heed," Grandma Betty says. She puts the tray down and disappears in a puff of smoke.

"Grandma?" William blinks at the empty space she occupied a second ago. She's gone. At least for now.

He turns to Anglaise. Deep furrows etched by the yellow glow of the lamp score her forehead. There is something melancholy in the down turn of her mouth.

"You…uh…haven't been standing…"

"The whole time."

He feels a queasy rush of embarrassment shoot through him. "The whole time?"

Anglaise crosses the empty street and sits down opposite him. "This is a nightmare."

"Grandma Betty is from a different time—"

Anglaise waves him to silence. "Not that. I was hoping to wake up. Lay in a protection spell before angry villagers with torches come to burn the shop down."

"Why would they?"

"I'm actually in your dream."

"Yeah, I know."

She grunts and shakes her head. "No, you don't. I'm not a version of me appearing in your dream. I'm me and I'm in your dream."

William nods, as the full understanding leaves him speechless for a minute. "How?"

He leans over the table. He's tempted to poke Anglaise to see if she really is real, but realizes in a dream that may not mean much.

"Spell gone wrong." Anglaise props her elbows on the glass-topped table and holds her head in her hands. "Or not so much wrong as someone broke in our shop and let the spell loose."

"What?" William stands, his chair crashing to the pavement. "Are you all right?"

Anglaise looks at him, eyes round with surprise, jaw slack. She shakes off the look and her face tightens again. "I'm fine. They broke in during the party. We came home and the place was trashed."

"I'll bet one of the protestors did it." William pounds a fist into the palm of his other hand. "Call the police in the morning. Frank is usually first in the office. We'll figure out the culprit."

"William."

"I'd say Pastor Austin is the number one suspect but he was actually at the party. But not all of it."

"William!"

He glances down at her. "What?"

The look on her face stops him cold. Defeated, fearful.

"It doesn't matter who broke in. We're the ones going to jail."

"Don't be ridiculous."

"The spell that got out—" Anglaise takes a shuddering breath and William realizes she's on the verge of tears. "The spell makes people swap dreams. This is happening all over town."

"Oooh…" William's lungs squeeze out the word as a rattling exhale. He gropes for his chair and realizes it's on the ground. He pulls it upright and sits down.

Anglaise gives him a wry smile. "Jail is better than dead. If everyone is really angry, we may have to make a run for it."

"They won't be," William says. "More people like you than don't."

"No, more people are nervous than anything. This—" She waves at the shared dream. "—isn't going to make them feel any better about having witches in town." She finishes with an emphatic slap of the table, her voice high and quavery.

He reaches out, covers her hand with his, and squeezes it. "Things will work out, better than you think. No one's going to harm you."

"How can you say that?" Her words are hopeless, but she squeezes his hand in return.

"Because I won't let them."

He looks into her eyes, sees the doubt etched in every plane of her face. He wonders where her mistrust and pessimism came from that it should be so permanent. For a second, he wishes to soothe it somehow and wonders if he can.

A sharp rap on the café window startles him. William looks up and sees Grandma Betty inside. She shakes her head at him and wags her finger. He pulls his hand away from Anglaise as if she's scalding hot. Shame scours him. It was a knee-jerk reaction trained into him by Grandma Betty, but that isn't really her. He can make his own decisions.

William reaches out again but Anglaise takes her hand off the table.

"Look, my Grandma's from another time. I'm sorry about what she said before. Honestly. She's actually dead."

"It's not my business," Anglaise says and holds her hands up to stop him going further. "Can you just do me a favor and wake up?"

"How?"

"A sharp pain usually does it," she says.

"Like what kind?"

Anglaise sighs and William feels a sudden burst of agony in his shin."

"Ow! You kicked me!"

The lights around the café dim and William realizes he's starting to wake up.

"That's for Grandma Betty," Anglaise says. "All the people in your dreams are actually aspects of yourself."

"Come on, you can't hold my upbringing against me."

All around him, Paris is fading. The inside of the café is dark and empty. It looks like his living room just before he went to bed, the remnants of the party strewn about. Abandoned plastic party cups and paper plates occupy the coffee table and seat cushions.

"I might forgive you in exchange for the pound cake recipe."

William grins. "That's blackmail."

Anglaise smiles back, the first real one he's seen from her. "Take it or leave it."

"Let me sleep on that," he says just before she fades away.

Chapter 16

Someone had a firm grip on Bruleé's arms and her head bounced against the pillow as she emerged from a deep, dreamless part of sleep.

Her eyes snapped open and she fought off the grip. Anglaise's face, pale and wide as a worried moon, loomed over her.

"I'm up! I'm up!" Bruleé grunted as Anglaise finally let go.

The dream she had rushed back to her. It had ended when she'd smacked Hugh in the face for kissing her. Somewhere across town Hugh was waking up or fully awake or even getting dressed.

"We'll cast three protection spells!" Bruleé was on her feet in a single blur of motion. She looked around. Sure enough, there was Caramel, arms wrapped around her body and silent tears glittering on her cheeks.

"Caramel, back door, Anglaise, front door, I'll take the shop. Get your brooms out and keep them with you."

"Why don't we just leave now?" Anglaise asked. Her voice lacked the usual waspish sting and Bruleé wondered if she was looking for an excuse to stay.

Bruleé put a hand on Anglaise's shoulder. "I don't know where you've been, but my dream wasn't all bad. I think we have a shot at staying here."

"I d—d—don't w—want to go to j—jail," Caramel said.

"You two won't," Anglaise snapped. "I'm the one on the line."

"Just cast the protection spells," Bruleé said on her way to the bedroom door. "No one's going to jail."

Hugh woke up smiling. He hadn't felt this good in years. It wasn't just the stolen kiss either, but a sense of purpose he wasn't sure he'd ever felt.

He threw off the cotton quilt Matilda insisted on keeping on the bed and jumped up. His thoughts were a tumbled mess. Should he pack? He needed to close his bank account, but what time was it? There were a thousand things to do and sort out, but he itched to get on the road now. Throw some clothes in the car and just go.

Matilda. He looked down at her sleeping form. She was curled up in a ball, her back to the center of the bed.

The sight of her stilled him. He wondered if he was still a little drunk, because he felt suddenly sober.

He reached out to her then hesitated. Was she in someone else's dream, too? Would waking her up be harmful? He'd woken up just fine.

As if aware of his stare, Matilda stirred. She rolled over and squinted up at him. The bedroom was still dark, but enough light came in through the windows to see.

"What is it?" she mumbled. "Did you just get up?"

"Yeah."

Matilda sat up in bed and rubbed her eyes. "You passed out drunk."

"Sorry about that."

"You're still in your clothes, you know."

Hugh looked down at himself. Sure enough, he wore jeans and a wrinkled T-shirt. She'd taken his shoes and socks off for him, which was considerate, considering his behavior at the party.

"My clothes don't matter." He paced the room, heading toward Matilda, then changing his mind and going for the dresser.

"I just meant you should put your PJs on," Matilda said. "It's 4:30 in the morning."

"I'm not going back to bed." He pulled open the second drawer from the bottom of the dresser and took out his neatly folded stacks of T-shirts and jeans.

"Then what are you doing?"

"Packing."

A long pause followed, so long that Hugh turned around to make sure she hadn't fainted.

Matilda clicked on the nightstand lamp. Hugh flinched at the brightness but kept his eyes on Matilda's face. Was she sad? Angry? He couldn't tell because she looked so blank.

"Packing?" she echoed.

"I'm going to New York to live my dream."

"You have a dream?"

"Don't sound like it's so funny," he said.

"Sorry. What's your dream?"

"I'm going to New York to be a fashion model."

Another too-long silence stretched out. Hugh stopped taking his clothes out of the drawer.

"Just do it," he said without looking.

A cascade of giggles went up behind him. Matilda laughed so hard he could hear the bedsprings creak. Hugh stood up and turned around. Matilda had collapsed sideways on the bed, clutching her sides as she tried to stop laughing.

"Okay. Ha, ha," he said. "You can knock it off now."

Her fit slowed to a few gasps and she wiped away tears. Matilda straightened up, forcing herself to quit smiling. "Sorry. But a fashion model? Seriously? Aren't you too old?"

"That's only female models. Men have much longer careers."

"So sexist."

"But true," Hugh said.

He went over to her. "Come with me," he said.

Matilda's eyes widened a fraction. "To New York."

"Yeah."

"You're just asking to be nice," Matilda said. She smiled gently. "You don't want me there."

Hugh shrugged. For a second, he considered trying to come up with something to say to convince her.

She knew his hesitation for what it was. "I'm not leaving Midswich, and you know it."

"No, you won't," he said.

They looked at each other for a long moment. A deep sense of letting go passed between them. It was time they parted. Overdue, even.

"Friends?" Hugh asked.

"Friends."

Profound urgency woke William. His eyes popped open. He knew there was something he had to do or something awful would happen. What was it? Why couldn't he remember?

He stared up at the gray-black ceiling, the darkness of his bedroom unrelieved even by a stray beam of moonlight.

The urgency had followed him from his dream, but what was the dream about? Paris. Grandma Betty had been there. And...something else.

His eyelids drooped. The party had worn him out, what with Austin showing up and embarrassing the witches.

The witches!

William sat straight up as memory shocked him fully awake. Anglaise was in trouble!

He flung off the covers and leapt off the bed. The corner of a blanket caught his foot and William fell, face planting into a pile of clothes he'd left on the floor.

"Turn the light on, idiot," he said, getting up slower this time.

He switched on the bedside lamp. He'd been raised to be tidy with almost military precision, but if a man can't leave a few clothes on the floor, he can hardly be called a man.

William rubbed the ache from his nose. The clothes he'd chucked on the floor were from the party. No need to look for anything clean.

He pulled on the rumpled slacks and button down shirt. William skipped socks and ran out the door in his loafers.

Town was only a short drive—two miles at most—but William gunned the engine, slinging out of the driveway in a spray of gravel.

He had to get to the teashop. If Anglaise was right, an angry mob could be on the doorstep.

Geoffrey hovered between sleep and consciousness in a warm cocoon of satisfaction. He knew he was waking up, but he clung to the cozy feeling, hoping to linger just a few more minutes.

He pulled the blankets tighter around himself and rolled over. Rolled right off the couch, hitting the floor on all fours with an audible "thunk."

With a groan, he sat up. He forgot he was still sleeping on the couch in his den. Geoffrey pulled himself up with a corner of the desk and stretched out the stiffness in his back. He was getting too old to sleep on anything but a real bed. Once upon a time, he could sleep anywhere, even sitting up in a chair.

So much for the dreamtime afterglow. He tried to remember why he felt so good. Claire had been there. He knew that. Geoffrey grinned as bits of the dream came back to him. That certainly explained a few things.

As the rest of the dream came back to him, the smile faltered. Partly because he wasn't convinced it was a regular dream and, because if it was a dream, did he dare tell Claire about it? The fact that they didn't have children was a sore point with her. He'd always loved her, no matter what, but even that couldn't keep her from feeling like a failure.

Still, maybe the dream—if it was a dream—was a sign.

Geoffrey looked at the luminous clock on the wall. Almost five a.m. Claire would still be asleep. He decided to wake her up before he lost his nerve.

He opened the door of the den and froze. Claire stood there

just on the other side, hand raised to knock, hair disheveled.

She stared at him, eyes wide, and he was too surprised to do anything but stare back.

"What are you doing?" he said at the same time she said, "I had a dream."

They paused a heartbeat and said simultaneously, "You first."

"Jinx," they chorused then smiled at each other.

"I had a dream," Claire began again. "I was in the grocery store, but it was empty."

A burning cold shock snaked up Geoffrey's spine. "Empty except for a cradle, and then I showed up."

He could see a bolt strike Claire, too.

"H—how did you know?"

"It was really me, remember?"

"But how?" Claire insisted.

Geoffrey slapped the doorframe. "The witches!"

"They can't! I mean, can they just do that? Isn't it illegal or something?" Claire asked.

He thought hard about that. Geoffrey was no expert, but he would guess Claire was right. Forcing people to pop up in other people's dreams seemed like something that should require permission.

There was no way any of the witches were going to go out of their way to get in trouble, especially after Austin's snide commentary at the party.

"Something must have happened," Geoffrey said.

"What?"

"I don't know, but let's find out." Geoffrey took Claire's hand and pulled her down the hallway.

"We're in pajamas," she said.

"Doesn't matter!"

"But—"

"Come on, Claire. The girls can't help us get a baby if they're in jail."

Eddie sat in bed, cell phone in hand. Matilda's number glowed on the screen. His thumb hovered over the call button.

He wanted to call her. Ask her if that dream was for real, find out if it meant as much to her as it did to him. But she was home. Sleeping next to Hugh.

What if he was wrong? What if the dream hadn't been real and was just his fevered subconscious? Then what was he supposed to say? Ask her to cheat on Hugh? Ask her to break up with him?

Then there was Hillary. He wasn't really dating her. Not in any serious fashion. They hadn't even kissed yet. He gave her a peck on the cheek when he dropped her at her apartment after the party. He didn't want to hurt her. Hillary was very nice. But if there was a chance with Matilda, he had to take it or he'd regret it forever.

The cell rang, playing the ring tone he'd chosen for Matilda. Eddie jumped. He fumbled the cell and snatched it from the bedspread.

He looked at the flashing display, even though the song told him who was calling. Eddie's heart pounded against his ribs, threatening to break the cage of bone.

"Hello," he said as he answered.

"Are you awake?" Matilda asked.

Eddie scratched at his thinning hair, trying to smooth it down. "Is this a trick question?"

She laughed. "Depends, I guess. Did you dream what I dreamed?"

"Why are you calling?" His words sounded harsher than he wanted, but he couldn't stay on this roller coaster with her. He wanted an answer. Eddie rested his head on his knees as he realized, he hadn't even asked her the question yet.

There was silence from the other end of the line. Eddie thought he could hear a door close and Hugh's voice in the background.

"Matilda, I'm—"

"Hugh and I broke up."

Eddie's head snapped up. "Go on."

"He's leaving for New York to be a fashion model."

Eddie nodded. "I can see that. He's really good looking."

"Not you, too," she muttered.

"What?"

"Nothing," she said. "Can you give me a couple of weeks to sort through everything, clear my head?"

"I don't know," Eddie said.

"What do you mean? Are you really into that Hillary person?"

"No." *Now or never*, Eddie thought. If he didn't tell her now, he never would. "I've been in love with you for as long as I can remember. I don't want just a date or two. I don't want to 'see where this takes us.' I know what I want and it's you."

"God, Eddie, you sound like a chick-flick," Hugh said. Then he burst out laughing.

"Give that back," Matilda shouted in the background. "He just grabbed it from me!"

Sweat drenched Eddie suddenly, thoroughly soaking his cotton pajamas and dribbling into his eyes. Over the ringing in his ears, he heard the sound of scuffling over the phone.

"Guess I should been madder about all those lunch dates, huh?" Hugh had apparently retained possession of the phone.

Eddie could still hear Matilda grunting and swearing in the background. "Are you going to beat me up?" he whispered.

"What? No," Hugh said. Then he laughed again. "Although I totally could."

For a second, Eddie was stupid with relief, unable to from a thought or sentence. Hugh had never been a jock, despite his physique, but he had been a casual bully in high school, mostly limited to the occasional odd bit of intimidation or taunt. His saving grace was that he was the same to everyone, so no one was singled out and he was far too interested in himself, and girls, to put the effort in. But Eddie and Hugh had a shared past of awkward moments in which Eddie was usually doing his best to get away from Hugh.

"Thank you," Eddie said, his voice wavering in the middle.

"Nah," Hugh said. "We're grownups now. Plus, I don't want to mess up my face."

Matilda was shouting for the phone back, and before Eddie could think of a reply to Hugh, he said, "Anyway, here's Matilda back."

"I'm so sorry," Matilda said. "He just grabbed it from me when he came out of the bathroom."

"I think we should talk later," Eddie said. He didn't know how much of his confession Matilda had heard, and there was no way he could get the words out again. There was a sick, leaden feeling pressing on his stomach, and he needed to get to the bathroom.

"Yeah. I shouldn't have called," Matilda said. "Sweet dreams."

He couldn't help a chuckle. "You, too."

The cell phone beeped and went silent. Eddie put his head on his knees and took a few deep breaths. For a minute, he wondered if he was still dreaming, a continuation of the dream he'd shared with Matilda. The last few minutes had been surreal enough to qualify.

Eddie pinched his arm. Nothing happened. Awake then, he guessed. He wasn't sure if he should be relieved or not.

Austin jolted awake, dizzy from the sensation of falling. His arms and legs jerked to catch himself, but he was already flat on his back in bed.

He was perfectly awake when his eyes snapped open, the memory of his dream crystalline in his mind.

That witch! His hands balled into fists, gripping sweat dampened blankets. He lay in bed too furious to move, every muscle rigid.

How dare she spy on him like that? Enter his dreams without permission? Ferret out his secrets? No doubt she was looking for some form of black mail or bribery. A bit of information she could dangle over his head to get him to back down, so she and her sisters could stay and rot the town from the inside.

He wouldn't allow it. He would go now, confront them with what they'd done.

Austin threw off the blankets and leapt out of bed. He was at the bedroom door before he realized he was in boxer shorts and a T-shirt.

He went back to pull on a pair of sweats, a light jacket, and his running shoes. He dressed as fast as possible, as if now that he was up and moving, he couldn't stop. His body vibrated with righteous anger and only movement could expel it.

If he was going to make a coherent case against the witches, he needed his wits about him. If he were just a screaming hysteric, no one would take him seriously.

Austin jogged downstairs. He fetched his cell phone from its charger on his office desk. He didn't leave it on much, forcing people to call the house, but he had a few choice numbers on the cell, including the chief of police.

Pocketing the cell, Austin headed for the kitchen. His keys hung on a peg beside the mudroom door. There was little need of house keys in Midswich, but tonight Austin wanted to make sure the backdoor was locked when he left. Not that a locked door could keep the witches out. He just needed to do something to feel a little safer.

Penelope sat at the kitchen table, crying silently. The circle of light cast by the hanging lamp over the table wavered and blurred. She blinked, clearing the tears, and the light came back into focus for a second, until her eyes filled with tears again. The table was wet. A little glittery pool of droplets had formed. But she still couldn't bring herself to move. Not yet. At her feet, Prince Albert's comforting warmth leaned against her leg and he whined softly. She reached down with one hand and rubbed his head.

The dream was fresh in her mind. A swirl of emotions chased around and around in her head, some sharp and painful, others soft and uneasy.

For some reason, she wanted to call Danielle, assure herself that no harm had come to her niece. Her fear was irrational. Danielle was working the nightshift at the Fiddlehead Inn, a town away.

Maybe it wasn't fear for her niece but fear for herself that made her want to call. Or maybe Penelope just needed to hear a friendly voice. Danielle wouldn't be too busy. The graveyard shift at a small inn wasn't demanding. She might even be grateful for the distraction.

The phone rang. Penelope scrambled out of her chair, still stiff from falling asleep at the table. Danielle must be calling. She had sensed Penelope's pain and called.

Penelope reached the phone in the kitchen on the first ring, ripping the receiver off the wall.

"Hello," she said, relief cracking her voice. She wiped her tears off with the sleeve of her shirt.

"Penelope, it's Pastor Austin."

Everything Penelope had readied to say derailed. She was so sure it would be Danielle, she had prepared to apologize, tell her how silly their fight was, and how much she loved her.

Penelope's mental gears didn't shift easily. Guilt settled over her on hearing Austin's voice. Her stomach was icy-cold, even as her face flushed hot.

"Oh?" was the best Penelope could force out.

"The witches have done something terrible! They invaded my dreams, and who knows how many others? I'm sure it's illegal. We can be rid of them at last, tonight even." Austin's words tumbled out between heavy breaths.

"Really?" Penelope squeaked. She looked at the kitchen table. Spotlighted under the overhead light was the empty jar of marshmallows. There had been some left when she'd fallen asleep. Now it was empty. A snowy dusting of powdered sugar on the bottom and sides was all that remained.

"I'm headed to the shop now. I'm sorry it's so late, or early."

"I don't know," Penelope said, eyes fixed on the jar.

"I've already called Chief Hartwell, and he'll meet me there. I could use your support, Penelope."

She should say "No," go to her bedroom, pull the covers over her head, and go to sleep. If she did say "No," she'd have to explain why.

"I—I'll be there, just give me a bit." She looked down at her break-in outfit. "I need to change."

"Of course," Austin said.

He hung up and Penelope put the receiver back. She looked down when she felt a tug on her paint leg. Prince Albert looked up at her, head cocked as if asking what she was going to do.

"Stop looking at me like that," Penelope said. She hadn't thought she could feel guiltier, but looking into those soft, black eyes, a fresh pain stabbed at her.

Alyss was awake when the phone rang. She thought about getting up to get it, but she wasn't done thinking about her dream.

It wasn't really her dream though. She'd been in Morris's trailer, a place she'd never been in real life. Morris had been there, and they were both the size of mice. They'd been running from his giant brother, who chased them with a fly swatter. In every hole and crack they'd tried to hide in, there was a chunk of food that Morris would dive on and devour. Then his brother would find them again, chasing them to the next hole.

Was that really what Morris's life was like? She knew he had it bad, but it couldn't be that bad, could it?

During the dream, as they'd run and hide, Morris kept apologizing to her. He was sorry for how messy the trailer was. Sorry for his brother's temper. Sorry she was there.

It was very un-Morris-like. Of their little gang of goths, Morris was hardcore. Angry and violent, he got into fistfights with the jocks, fights he could win. He'd been expelled twice this year. Once in a while, if Alyss had too much time to think, she would wonder if it was just a matter of time before Morris brought one of the knives he owned to school.

Maybe she could talk to her mom. Get her to ask Morris to help out at the restaurant. He could get a meal and earn a few dollars he could hide from his brother.

God knows, Consolata was lazy enough, and Alyss didn't want to work there.

But any offer like that would have to be given in the right way. It couldn't sound like charity. Morris never took pity or accepted help.

The phone started ringing again. Or, it had never stopped. Alyss couldn't be sure.

"*Ai dios mio.*" Alyss threw off her blankets, padding barefoot to the phone in the hallway. "What?" she grunted into the receiver. "It's, like, four frickin' a.m."

"Rosa?"

"No, this is Alyss."

"Alyss, the witches are in trouble."

Cold shock put out her anger at the early call. "What? Who is this?" She still wasn't sure if it was a crank call. Nasty giggles could break out any second. The jerks at school were why she didn't give out her cell number. Once in a while, one of the worst tormentors realized that the Yellow Pages were online and would look up the house phone.

"It's William Shepherd."

"Mr. Shepherd?" Her doubt evaporated, replaced with concern. "What happened? What about the witches?"

"All over town, people are…trading dreams." His voice trailed off. "It may not be happening to everyone. I know it sounds insane—"

"No, it doesn't. It happened to me!" So that was Morris's dream life, a reflection of his waking existence. She shuddered.

"Austin was one of the dreamers. He's looking to get rid of them. I'm on my way to the teashop. I'm just in town."

"I'll meet you there!" Alyss hung up the phone and ran to her room.

She had to get dressed first. No way she was showing up in Halloween pajamas, orange with black bats all over them. Alyss grabbed underwear from the floor, figuring it was clean enough to wear for a few more hours. Then black jeans and a T-shirt.

In the hallway, Alyss hesitated. She wanted to just take off, but her mom might help the witches, too.

Alyss decided to try and wake the dead. She went to her mother's bedroom door and knocked a few times. Nothing. She opened the door and went in.

Rosa was under a fluffy comforter snoring softly, one foot sticking out of the blankets.

Her mom, Consolata, and Juana could sleep through anything. Not even the dozen rings it took her to answer the phone had awakened them.

"Mom." Alyss shook her mother's shoulder and, speaking in a normal voice, said, "Mom, wake up."

Still nothing.

Alyss shook harder and said louder, "Mom! Mama! Mama!"

She was just about to give up when her mom finally groaned and made a weak half-conscious swat at Alyss.

"It's not six."

"No, Mom. We have to help the witches." Alyss was losing her. If she didn't get her mon fully awake, Rosa would just fall back to sleep without ever having woken.

Alyss reached for the juice glass of water her mother kept by the bed.

"Mother of God, pray for us sinners," she cringed and dumped the water on her mother's head.

"Oh, shit, that's cold!"

Alyss smirked for half a second. Usually *she* was getting the lecture on not swearing.

"What the hell?" Rosa looked around. She was up now, bolt upright and scowling. "What is it?"

"Mom, the witches are in trouble. Mr. Shepherd just called."

"I didn't hear the phone." Rosa pulled the blankets off. "Why am I all wet?"

Alyss rolled her eyes. "You'd sleep through the apocalypse."

Slowly her mother's brain seemed to catch up on what Alyss was saying. "The witches are in trouble?"

"People all over town have been swapping dreams. Now Austin is going to get rid of them."

"I didn't swap dreams." Rosa frowned. "Are you sure about this?"

"Why would Mr. Shepherd lie?" Alyss didn't want to tell her mother she knew for a fact the dream swapping was real. She didn't want anything to change Rosa's opinion. It was one thing to support the witches, another to have your daughter mixed up with a spell gone wrong. "I don't care what you say, I'm going down to the teashop and see if they need help. Caramel's my friend," Alyss said.

Rosa smiled. "I didn't say you couldn't go. Go on. I'll get down there in a few minutes."

Alyss gave a single nod and ran for the door. In the hall, she remembered to shout," Thanks, Mom."

"No problem."

Bruleé sat at one of the round tea tables with Anglaise and Caramel. She had insisted on making a calming tea after they finished the protection spells. So far, she was the only one drinking it.

They sat silently among the rubble left by the vandal and waited. The waiting was hardest on Caramel. She looked greenish-gray. Her tea steamed in front of her, the mix of chamomile, kava, lemon balm, and lavender untouched. Even Fraiche was a quiet ball of fur on her lap. His liquid brown eyes scanned their faces.

Anglaise sat stiffly, hands clenched and propped on the table. Her leg bounced with nervous energy as she stared intently out the window. She looked ready to pounce and fight.

"So we just sit here?" Anglaise glared at Bruleé, eyes leaving the front window long enough to make her point and rub poison on Bruleé's doubts.

There wasn't a lot Bruleé could say. That was, in essence, her plan. Wait and see how angry the townspeople were. If they were in a forgiving mood, Bruleé could explain what happened. If not, their brooms were a few feet away leaning against the bakery case.

"We sit and wait," Bruleé said. She reached across the table and squeezed Caramel's hand. "I have a feeling we'll be all right."

The sound of tires squealing made them all freeze. Anglaise flicked another accusatory glance at Bruleé. This was it. The cops could be on their way to arrest them.

A car lurched to a sudden stop in front of the teashop. Anglaise jumped out of her seat. The chair hit the floor with a bang, and Caramel let out a strangled scream.

Anglaise grabbed her broom, and Bruleé could hear her muttering a power chant to gather and focus—energy she could turn into an offensive weapon.

"Anglaise, stop it!" Bruleé was out of her chair a second behind Anglaise, but it felt like minutes, her sister had moved so fast.

Anglaise was so ready to fight and run, she hadn't noticed the car that pulled up wasn't the police. No sirens tore through the night and no flashing red lights.

The magic Anglaise had called blazed in her hand, a ball of glowing white fire as incandescent as her rage. Bruleé felt like she was struggling through molasses as she trailed a few steps behind Anglaise, unable to catch up.

The car headlights died just as Anglaise charged through the front door.

"Stop it! It's not the cops!" Bruleé screamed.

Anglaise either didn't hear or didn't believe her. She kept going not even missing a step.

Bruleé cursed Anglaise, a string of incoherent swears and epithets. What was her idiot sister thinking? Attacking innocents with a ball of magic that would stun an elephant. The fact that she assumed the car was the cops made it worse. Assaulting an officer would get her jailed for life, if not worse.

A man got out of the driver's side door and Anglaise was ready to unleash the spell. The energy crackling off the baseball-sized orb singed Bruleé's hair.

Anglaise had lost control without knowing it. The spell was enough to kill a human. A dozen people, even. Bruleé gritted her teeth and felt her own magic surge up, firing her blood.

Just as Anglaise unleashed the spell, Bruleé recognized the driver.

William Shepherd.

Bruleé let her magic act subconsciously. She reached out faster than thought, pulling the energy ball aside just as William ducked. The spell curved away from William's shocked face and hit the pavement across the street. The concrete blackened and split, crumbling to dust under the force of the spell.

"William," Anglaise whispered, her voice dull.

Bruleé pulled Anglaise around to face her, shaking her by the shoulders. The only thing that kept Bruleé from slapping her was the look of shock and regret on Anglaise's face.

"Go back inside and drink the tea." Bruleé shoved Anglaise to the door. "And while you're at it, drink Caramel's. I'll deal with you in a minute."

Anglaise went inside as ordered. Her subdued acceptance told Bruleé she knew what she'd almost done. Bruleé shook her head and tried to calm herself. She was vibrating with rage. A mean part of her regretted not hitting Anglaise. The only time Anglaise curbed her temper was when she'd gone too far.

Bruleé turned back to William. He was hunkered against his car, staring at her. "What the hell was that?"

He stood up and looked at the crater in the sidewalk across the street. The lights on the sign for the Dry Goods lit it perfectly.

"I'm sorry. She thought you were the cops."

William gasped. "The cops?" He made a spluttery noise, searching for more to say, but only came out with a second, incredulous, "The cops?"

"Makes it worse, right?"

"Bonnie and Clyde worse."

"She won't get away with it," Bruleé said. "I'm sorry."

"Guess I shouldn't have come…" He turned to the teashop.

Anglaise was back at the table. She slugged down the calming tea in big gulps then put her mug down and picked up Caramel's. She drank it the same way, eyes never leaving Bruleé and William.

"So, why *did* you come?" Bruleé asked.

"To help. I ran into Anglaise in my dream. She said you might all go to jail."

Bruleé rubbed her forehead and sighed. "If I buried her in the woods, no one would find her, right?"

"What?"

"Nothing."

She was about to invite William in, when she saw a figure come around the corner, two blocks away. He was only briefly lit by the street lamp, but Bruleé would have recognized that scarecrow anywhere.

Pastor Austin.

"Oh no," Bruleé said.

"You should go inside," William said.

Austin was only a block away. He gestured wildly at them as he ran, a cell phone glowing in his hand.

"You!" he shouted.

Bruleé turned to William. "Just keep him busy a minute. I have to sort out Anglaise, then we'll be out."

William nodded. "Sure."

She headed back inside as William went to intercept the pastor.

Anglaise stood up as Bruleé approached. Two empty mugs sat in front of her on the table.

"What did you tell William?"

"Give me your hands." Bruleé ignored her question.

"You can't—"

"Hands, now. We don't have time for this," Bruleé snapped.

Anglaise hesitated. She looked young, petulant, and teary-eyed. Remorseful enough that Bruleé was tempted to change her mind. Then Anglaise thrust out her hands, palms up, and Bruleé's doubts cleared. She took her sister's hands.

"Power used
And ill abused
Bind and seal
Rune to limit
All magic talent
Until temper heals."

A glowing gold rune sparkled, one on each of Anglaise's palms. Bruleé felt a sharp tingle in her fingertips. The runes faded into her skin as Bruleé said the final words. The spell Bruleé had used was a broad power limiter. It cut Anglaise off from the majority of her magic, leaving her capable of only minor magics, nothing like the spell that had almost taken William's head off.

At least, that's what Bruleé hoped she'd done. She'd never used a spell like that before, and she was afraid she'd used a sledgehammer where a fly swatter would have done.

There were a dozen variations of the limiter spell, of differing strengths, easily tailored for any use. She just didn't have time to look them up, and the first one that came to mind was the strongest one she knew.

She could fix it later. Right now, Pastor Austin was right outside.

Bruleé let go of Anglaise's hands. "Are you all right?"

"Fine," Anglaise choked. She clenched here fists a few times, as if feeling for the runes.

"I'm sorry," Bruleé said.

Anglaise shook her head and grabbed her broom from where it leaned on the bakery case. "Let's get out there."

She didn't sound very enthusiastic, but Bruleé would take what she could get.

"Caramel?" She turned to her sister. "You can stay inside if you want. Just keep your broom handy."

"I—I—I—" Caramel said.

Outside, Bruleé could hear Austin and William shouting at each other. "Come if you can." She gave Caramel a reassuring smile.

Caramel still looked like she was about to hurl any second. If she did throw up, Bruleé hoped she made it to the bathroom. One less mess to clean up.

The friendly bell over the door tinkled as Bruleé and Anglaise stepped out of the teashop. She saw Austin freeze at the sound. His eyes narrowed as he sized them up.

Bruleé was surprised by the pastor's casual sweats and a T-shirt. Whenever she had pictured their last showdown, she always saw him in uniform. He didn't look very threatening, dressed for a morning jog.

William left off arguing with the pastor and stepped passed Bruleé to talk to Anglaise. "Are you all right?" he asked.

"Fine."

Bruleé glanced over her shoulder to see if they were holding hands. They sounded so much like a couple. But, no, William stood in the doorway with Anglaise, a respectable distance separating them.

"At last you show yourself." Pastor Austin thrust his cell phone at them and waved it in Bruleé's face.

"I wasn't hiding," Bruleé said.

Austin ignored her and went on. "I've called the chief of police, and he's on his way over here. You can't do that to law abiding people!"

"The dream puffs were an accident. I already told you." Anglaise was close to shouting. She strode toward Austin, broom clutched in both hands.

For a second, Bruleé wondered if she should take the broom from Anglaise to prevent her from clocking the pastor. She tensed, ready to spring, in case Anglaise started swinging.

"You just don't want to believe me." Anglaise stopped short of shoving the pastor, but had they been equal heights, they'd be nose to nose.

Bruleé blinked in surprise. With all they had to do when they woke up, trading dream stories hadn't been on the list. Drawing protective runes on the door jams had. Now she was sorry she hadn't asked.

"The police can decide how much of an accident it was when they get here," Austin said.

"You didn't have to call the cops, Pastor," William cut in. "No harm's been done."

Austin turned to William. "How do you know what harm's been done?"

"Anglaise showed up in my dream. All we did was talk."

Bruleé's eyebrows quirked, and she shot a questioning look at Anglaise, who was staring very intently at the empty space over Pastor Austin's shoulder.

"It's okay, William," Bruleé said. "Maybe we can clear this up with the police."

"There's no clearing up anything," Austin snarled. "I'm pressing charges!"

"You leave them alone," came a shout from the end of the block.

The group turned as one to see whom the voice belonged to.

Running down the sidewalk was Alyss. She ran in fits and starts, slowing a few times to a stumbling jog.

Everyone waited in patient silence. Bruleé wondered if the girl was going to collapse. Alyss came to a stop in front of the teashop and bent double for a minute, her breath coming out in hard pants.

"God, I'm out of shape," Alyss wheezed as she straightened up.

"Does your mother know you're out?" Austin asked.

"Yes, and she's on her way, too," Alyss said. "We support the witches." She groaned and clutched her side. "Wicked stitch, oh, man."

"That's from uneven breathing," Austin said.

Bruleé patted Alyss on the back, pushing a little magic into her. Just enough to soothe the cramp in her side.

"Thanks." Alyss was still winded, but at least she could stand upright.

"Thank you for the support," Bruleé said. "But the police are on the way. They'll have to decide what to do."

"What? No way!" Alyss glared at Austin. "Why can't you just leave them alone? They never did anything but help people."

"Really? Is that why my privacy was invaded as I slept?"

"How interesting could your dreams be?" Alyss shot back.

William snorted and Bruleé covered a smile with her hand.

"You're just a bully, like every other narrow-minded asshole in this town!" Aylss growled.

"Damn, girl," William whispered.

Austin's face reddened from the neck up, and his lips curled back from his teeth. Before he could say or do anything, Bruleé grabbed Alyss by the arm and pulled her toward the teashop.

"Hey," Alyss protested. She struggled, but Bruleé was used to wrangling uncooperative girls.

"Please, go inside. Caramel's having a hard time," Bruleé said under her breath.

She pushed Alyss through the door, waiting a second to see if she needed to add a locking spell on the door.

Alyss glared at her and then at Pastor Austin, but as she turned around, she saw Caramel, who stood up to meet her. The girls hugged and sat down. Bruleé sighed with relief.

"She can't talk to me like that," Austin's voice shook with rage. "I'm telling her mother."

"She's just a kid," Anglaise said. "She doesn't know—"

"You shut up!" Austin yelled.

"Any better is how I was going to finish that," Anglaise said.

What was going on? The whole showdown was spinning out of control, and everyone else seemed to have a puzzle piece she didn't. Austin was near incandescent with rage, Anglaise was being almost sensitive, and more people kept showing up.

"Ah ha!" Austin pointed up the street. "That must be Chief Hartwell."

A heartbeat after Austin spoke, Bruleé heard a distant car. The pastor certainly had good hearing. They turned as a group to look down the street.

A car turned the corner three blocks away. Bruleé couldn't make it out in the darkness. All she saw was a pair of rapidly approaching headlights.

The smug look on Austin's face faded a fraction as the car pulled in next to William's.

Geoffrey and Claire, still dressed in their pajamas got out of the car.

Bruleé wasn't sure which way this was going to go. She knew Geoffrey and his wife had been fighting over the teashop. Everything depended on who had won whom over to their side.

Geoffrey gave Bruleé a big smile as he and his wife joined the crowd.

"Claire, did you get my message?" Austin asked.

She shuffled and looked down at her pink sheepskin slippers. "Sorry, Pastor."

"That's all right, you're here now."

Her face pinched and she looked up at Austin. "No, I'm sorry. I changed my mind."

Bruleé felt something knotted in her gut relax. She gave a look of gratitude to Geoffrey and mouthed "Thank you."

He grinned and nodded.

"You changed your mind?" Austin said. "How could you change your mind in eight hours?"

"I'm sorry," she said again. "But—but it's personal."

"After what she's been doing to Anne?" Austin stabbed an accusing finger at Bruleé. "Dosing her without a valid license?"

"I'm close to my credits, only a couple refresher classes and a test," Bruleé said.

"I don't care," Austin roared. He turned back to Claire. "Did they do anything to you? Give you some potion to change your mind?"

"No," Claire said. She looked at Geoffrey.

"We shared a dream," he said. "I was in Claire's dream, and it reminded us of something. Something we gave up on."

"This uncontrolled magic running around town wreaking havoc is just what I'm trying to prevent."

"No, you're not," Anglaise said. "This has nothing to do with magic at all. Just be honest."

"What do you know?" William asked before Bruleé could get the words out.

"She knows nothing," Austin had gone from red to purple in the last few minutes.

Another car pulled up before anyone could say anything more. Again, Bruleé tensed, waiting for the cops to arrive.

Again she was wrong. Penelope Owens climbed out of the driver's side, Chihuahua in hand.

Whether it was the late hour or something else, Bruleé thought she looked miserable. Decades older than the fifty something Bruleé had her pegged as.

Austin looked relieved. Bruleé exhaled as his color returned almost to normal. He went to greet her. "Penelope, you're still on the side of God, aren't you?"

She nodded at him, but without much enthusiasm. "Pastor Austin."

"Do you know what the witches have done? The spell they unleashed to spy inside our minds?"

"That's not how dream puffs work," Bruleé said. "There are spells like that which are controlled but not dream puffs."

"You can tell it to Chief Hartwell," Austin said. "How do we know what spell you used? Take your word for it?"

He had a point. The dream puffs were made days ago, and since they dissolve in open air, there would be no evidence left. Even if Matilda told the police she paid the witches to make the dream puffs, they'd have to believe she wasn't lying.

Something Austin kept saying was circling in Bruleé's head. She only just thought of it when she thought of Matilda. The last name, Hartwell.

Bruleé turned to the supporters on her side. "Chief Hartwell? Is that any relation to Matilda?"

Geoffrey smirked. "You *are* new in town. He's her older brother. The Hartwells and the Kelleys control the town."

William pointed at another approaching car. "And speak of the devil."

The car flashed red and blue lights at the crowd, but left the siren off. Parking was getting scarce in front of the teashop and the chief of police was forced to park in front of Pickett's Antique Store.

A middle-aged man with auburn hair touched with gray got out. Bruleé could see the family resemblance immediately. He had the same keen eyes as his little sister.

Chief Hartwell had made only a token attempt to look official. He wore blue jeans and a police shirt, but the official looking belt around his waist had an empty holster, and he too was still in his slippers.

His look was anything but sleepy as he surveyed the group on the sidewalk and took careful stock of each of them before approaching.

Then the gears shifted. He put on a bland professional smile and came over to them, hand resting on the baton in his belt.

"What's the trouble here?" he asked the general assembly.

"It's the witches," Austin said. "I want to press charges for illegal spells."

"All right, let's hear from them." Hartwell looked at Bruleé and Anglaise.

"It was an accident," Bruleé said.

"Our shop was vandalized," Anglaise said.

The chief held up a hand. "One at a time, and start at the beginning."

Anglaise opened her mouth, but Bruleé stepped on her foot to shut her up. Anglaise shot her a searing look, but she closed her mouth.

"We were asked to make a dream swapping spell. A spell that is not illegal." Bruleé directed the comment at Austin, who ground his teeth but remained silent. "The spell is infused in homemade marshmallows that then become lighter than air. We had the dream puffs in a jar to keep them from escaping, but our teashop was broken into tonight. The jar with the dream puffs was either opened or broken, and the spell escaped. If let loose, the dream puffs dissolve in the air and find a person to settle into. Then you have people showing up in other people's dreams."

Hartwell nodded. "You clean up your shop?"

"No. I wanted the insurance people to see it."

"Let's take a look."

"You can't believe them," Austin said. "They could trash their own shop to cover the release of the dream puffs."

"We have photos, too. With the date and time stamp. We took them right when we got home," Anglaise said.

"How are we to know when you trashed the place?"

Anglaise took a step toward Austin, but William pulled her back.

"Their livelihood is the teashop," he told Austin. "They wouldn't wreck it."

"Insurance fraud," Austin said.

"Stop making accusations, Pastor. You need to keep quiet until I come back." Hartwell turned his best stern gaze on Austin, Penelope, William, and Anglaise. They all fell silent and held still.

He certainly has a knack, Bruleé thought. Maybe there was a touch of witch blood in the Hartwells.

Bruleé let him in the shop. She whispered a word to calm the wards on the door and stepped into the shop.

Alyss's eyes went wide when she saw Chief Hartwell. Caramel faded into the background as she used her *see-me-not* spell. "Don't arrest them! I won't let you," she yelled and jumped out of her chair. She held her arms side, trying to shield Caramel.

Chief Hartwell blinked twice but kept his face composed. Bruleé couldn't tell if he was angry or amused.

"No one's getting arrested. Yet."

"Caramel, run! I'll hold them off!" Alyss looked beside her. "Caramel? Did she already run?"

"She's still in the chair. Look hard," Bruleé said.

Hartwell and Alyss both focused on where Caramel sat. The *see-me-not* spell crumbled under too much scrutiny. Caramel didn't suddenly appear so much as become noticeable again.

"There you are," Alyss said.

"I didn't see her at first..." Hartwell muttered.

"Can both of you just sit down and relax?" Bruleé asked

Alyss sat and Caramel stayed visible.

Only Fraiche was unperturbed by the policeman. His pom-pom tail wagged a few times in greeting.

Bruleé walked Chief Hartwell around the shop. He took notes on the damaged teapots and kitchen equipment.

Again, he said little. Only nodded a few times and wrote in the little notebook.

"All right, I have what I need," he said as the tour ended. "Let's go back out there."

Hugh drove around the town square to meet up with Stratford Avenue on the other side. He'd been tearing through the empty streets, car stereo cranked to maximum. Slowing down to ten miles an hour to take the sharp corners was ruining his exit.

Once clear of town, Stratford turned into the highway and he could put on some speed again. Hugh hit the pause button on the CD player. No use wasting perfectly good Chemical Brothers on ten miles per hour.

Hugh turned back onto Stratford and pressed the gas. Before the pedal could reach the floor he noticed the flashers of a police car up ahead. His foot automatically jerked off the gas and eased on the brake. Had Paul set up a speed trap? The police chief didn't do that until tourist season or during one of Midwich's many festivals.

He looked past the flashing lights and slowed down even more. There were close to a dozen people milling on the sidewalk and the teashop was lit up like it was open.

As much as Hugh wanted to gun it for New York, every small town fiber of his being demanded he stop and see what was going on.

He pulled into a parking spot across the street, got out of the car, and hurried over. "Hey, Paul." He waved automatically before realizing he may no longer have favored status on account of dating the police chief's baby sister.

"Hugh." Paul eyed him coolly. "Come to join the fracas?"

"What's going on?"

"Good timing, Hugh." Austin pulled him over to his side of the sidewalk.

There were obvious battle lines drawn with Penelope and Austin on one side, and everyone else on the other.

"The witches have finally overstepped and invaded our very minds," Austin said.

"Oh, yeah, that," Hugh said.

He grinned at Bruleé and gave her a wink. She returned his efforts with a glacial, blank stare.

"So, you were a victim also," Austin said with apparent glee.

"Yeah." Hugh didn't want to disappoint the pastor, but he wasn't interested in whatever scheme Austin had going. Even a day ago, he would have been fine with getting rid of the witches. But a day ago, he thought he'd never be leaving Midswich. The petty concerns of the town had fallen away like a cheap suit, now that he was ready to embrace his dream.

"They're not so bad," Hugh said.

"What?"

"Let 'em stick around. Can't hurt tourism," he said.

Geoffrey nodded. "Right."

Austin's mouth gaped then snapped shut. "You were protesting with us just the other day."

"I'll be honest. That was mostly to piss off Matilda. Sorry, Paul."

"Not me you should apologize to."

The pastor turned back to the witches, accusation glimmering in his eyes. "What did you do to him?"

"You're joking," Anglaise said.

"Some kind of brainwashing to get him on your side, right?" Austin said.

"No," Bruleé said.

"It's not like that, Pastor." Hugh put a hand on Austin's shoulder to try and calm him, but the pastor shook him off.

"Then how is it you've all turned against me?"

Penelope cringed and took a step back, while Claire stared down at her fuzzy slippers.

"Bruleé just gave me the courage to pursue my dream," Hugh said.

"What dream is that?" Paul asked.

Everyone looked at Hugh, waiting for an answer. Hugh felt his resolve waver, the memory of Matilda's laughter fresh in his mind. Yet there was no way he could pursue his dream if he was ashamed.

He inhaled deeply and struck a pose. "Fashion model."

Silence. Hugh deflated. Maybe he wasn't good enough. Maybe he was too old and fooling himself.

Claire clapped a few times and then stopped when no one joined in. She laughed. "You have the looks for it."

Geoffrey shrugged. "Yeah, I can see it."

"Good luck," William said.

"Matilda in the car with you?" Paul asked.

Austin frowned. "So, you're leaving."

"Yes, I'm leaving, and no, Matilda isn't with me. We broke up. Mutually." He emphasized the last word in case Paul thought Matilda was home crying. "It was mutual."

"Come on, you have to be a little angry a witch invaded your mind," Austin pleaded.

"Lighten up, Pastor." Hugh slapped Austin on the back. "You'll live longer."

"Keep in touch," Paul said. "In case you're needed in court."

"Come on, it's not gonna get that far, is it?"

"I don't know yet."

Austin's face lit with hope at the words. The witches just looked stony-faced.

"There are regulations around magic I'll have to check up on," Paul added.

"Okay," Hugh said. He wanted to be on his way, but he didn't want to leave the witches.

Then he remembered his cell phone in the car. Hugh waved a final goodbye to the crowd as he jogged across the empty street.

He pulled the car door closed and grabbed the cell from its dash-mounted holder, pushing button one. The phone dialed Matilda for him. Hugh felt a small sting of jealousy and hoped she wasn't talking to Eddie. Not that he wanted her back. He just didn't want to be replaced so easily.

"Forget something?" Matilda said when she picked up.

"No," Hugh told her, "it's the witches. Your brother's down here checking them out."

"Which brother?"

"Paul. That dream thing happened all over town, and Pastor Austin wants them gone."

"I'll be right there. You still leaving?"

"I'm headed out now."

There was a pause on the phone that Hugh recognized as

Matilda wanting to say more. He started the car in the meantime.

"Hugh?"

"Yeah?"

"Good luck. I didn't say that earlier."

"Thanks." He smiled.

"Bye, again."

"Bye."

Hugh pulled out of the parking spot and hung up the phone.
On his way again. At last.

Once the policeman had left the shop, Alyss pulled Caramel to a table by the window for a better view. Caramel had
been doing her best not to look out at all. Actually, she'd been
doing her best not to throw up. Her stomach had been churn-
ing ever since she woke up, and now there was a feeling like a
brick in a washing machine down there. Something heavy,
spinning and spinning.

Bruleé's tea would have helped, but only she if could have
kept it down, and she hadn't been willing to try.

Alyss had managed to soften her anxiety. Caramel was
surprised to find she had forgotten what a comfort friends
could be. She'd only had two good friends in Boston, and
she'd cut herself off from them after her parents died. She
hadn't expected to make new friends.

Caramel squeezed Alyss's hand and instantly regretted it.
She was being too needy. No one liked needy.

"Don't worry," Alyss said and squeezed her hand back.
"Only Penelope's on Austin's side. Everyone else out there is
on *our* side."

Like a cold slap in the face, Caramel's anxiety returned.
She pulled her hand from Alyss's and hugged Fraiche. He let
out a whine to let her know her grip was too tight. Caramel let
go a little, absently scratching behind his ears.

Penelope was out there? Caramel leaned toward the window, peering around Alyss, whose face was glued to the glass.

There was Penelope. Same frazzled graying hair as in the dream. Her onesy pajamas exchanged for loose jeans and a light sweater. She hung a few steps behind Austin, keeping her eyes on the pavement.

Caramel chewed her lip. She should go out there. At the very least, she should have told the policeman that Penelope had broken in when he'd come inside.

She was afraid no one would believe her. It was her word against Penelope's. What chance did a witch have? Caramel could always make Penelope confess with a truth spell, but that wasn't likely to go over too well. She couldn't sit there, hoping Penelope's conscience kicked in, either.

Caramel had to go outside.

The thought made her nauseous. She looked at Alyss, then at all the people on the sidewalk who had come out to support the teashop. If Caramel did nothing, they'd have to leave town. Leave the only new friend she'd made in years.

"I—I—I—" she whispered.

Alyss turned. "What?"

"I—I n—need to g—go out there." Caramel's voice quavered.

"I think they're doing okay without you." Alyss smiled. "Hugh just left. No one else from the protestors has shown up. My mom is supposed to be coming. I bet she fell back to sleep."

Caramel stood up. "N—no, i—it has to be me."

Alyss climbed off the chair she'd been kneeling on for a better view. "Hang on. I'll come with you. Are you sure you're not going to barf? 'Cause if you do, I will. We might set off a chain reaction."

The image of everyone out on the sidewalk vomiting, one after another, flashed through Caramel's mind. She gave a faint giggle at the absurdity.

That small laugh buoyed her spirits. Her stomach settled a little, and she felt better than she had since waking up. "I—I—I'll be fine. J—just come w—with me."

"Of course."

Alyss grabbed Caramel's hand again and pulled her to the front door. The bell over the door tinkled as they joined the crowd outside the shop. Caramel should have used a silence spell because all eyes turned to her and Alyss. Even Penelope glanced at Caramel, face pulled down by guilt. Bruleé gave her a smile and a wink before turning serious again.

Caramel wondered if she should say something to Penelope. Maybe go talk to her. But she couldn't get her feet to move.

"…I'm just not sure, Pastor. We aren't well versed in magical law up here. These're the first witches in something like fifty years," Hartwell was just saying.

"Why can't I press charges now, and if the claim isn't legitimate, it doesn't have to go through?" Austin said.

"And that can still wait until morning," Paul said, his level voice rising.

"No it can't! How can I go back to sleep when they could invade my mind again?"

"The dream puffs are spent," Anglaise said.

"Says you," Austin snapped.

The police chief opened his mouth to reply, but the squeal of car tires cut him off. "What the hell?" he muttered to himself.

Everyone watched the new arrival. The car swung around the town square, going way too fast. The rear end fishtailed as it straightened out on Stratford.

The car screeched to a smoking halt in the middle of the road, a trail of burnt rubber marking the asphalt behind it. The door flew open with a rusty creak, and Matilda jumped out. She stomped over to her older brother, bathrobe flopping.

"Don't you dare arrest them, Paul."

Paul pointed at the aging Tercel. "You better get your car out of the road or I will cite you."

Matilda squared off with her brother, not even flinching at his threats, size, or official position. "They haven't done anything wrong. If anything, they helped us all tonight."

Caramel had the sudden urge to clap. Her hands twitched, but she kept one securely around Fraiche. Beside her, Alyss giggled. There was a chorus of agreement from Geoffrey, Claire, and William.

Matilda nodded and crossed her arms. "See, just like I said."

"The spying bitch didn't help me," Austin shouted. He froze and reddened. "I meant witch," he corrected himself.

"I think we all know what you meant," Anglaise said.

Alyss cut loose a braying laugh she smothered with her hand a second later. A fleeting grin twitched Caramel's mouth at both the pastor's slip and Alyss's need to hide her true laugh.

Paul coughed to get everyone's attention. "I will look into the legality of dream puffs for you, Pastor, but I don't know that it'll do you much good. The teashop was broken into and vandalized, which supports the claim that the spell was released by accident."

"Ha!" Matilda crowed. She hugged her brother who pushed her away immediately.

"Not when I'm on duty," he said.

Caramel saw Austin's face petrify with rage. His eyes bugged out, and she expected him to start frothing at the mouth. She clutched Fraiche, but he had finally had enough.

The Pomeranian whined and wriggled out of her arms, smooth as a fish. She thought he'd go to Bruleé or Anglaise, but instead he trotted over to Penelope. Fraiche sniffed all around Penelope's feet and pant legs, probably smelling Prince Albert on her.

Torn between going to rescue Fraiche from the other side and getting someone to do it for her, Caramel shuffled in place.

Penelope looked down at the dog and the tension in her face slackened. Fraiche's brown eyes stared up hopefully at Penelope, and he licked his chops.

Penelope knew what to do. She reached into her jeans' pocket and pulled out a broken dog treat. She dropped it and Fraiche snapped it out of the air before it hit the ground.

Satisfied, Fraiche darted back to Caramel. Penelope's eyes followed the dog, a thin smile breaking through the misery on her face. She looked at Caramel and their eyes met. Caramel tried to plead silently with Penelope. She could see the conflict in the older woman's eyes.

"Tell them," Caramel mouthed.

Penelope's face tightened and she looked away.

Caramel fought back a stinging wave of tears. Why was she so useless? Anglaise and Bruleé were arguing face to face with Pastor Austin, and Caramel couldn't even speak to Penelope. She lost the battle with the tears and gulped as the first hot, damp drops streaked down her face.

Since Penelope was a lost cause, Caramel thought about going back inside. She reached out for Alyss, but her friend was gone.

Not gone. Just a few steps away. Everyone was a few feet away. Chief Hartwell stood between Austin and Anglaise, as whatever argument they were having turned into a shouting match.

"I can file a civil suit and sue you for everything you have!" Austin roared.

"Go ahead! I'll have to testify in court about the dream I witnessed."

"Just what kind of dream was this?" Chief Hartwell asked.

"Seriously?" Alyss said.

"Not *that* kind," Austin said.

Everyone looked to Anglaise.

"It really wasn't bad," Anglaise said. "I don't know what he's ashamed of."

"You wouldn't understand," Austin shot back. "You couldn't."

"It does explain why he hates us," Anglaise said. "And it's not because we're witches."

"Shut up," Austin warned.

"You can't say that and not tell us," Geoffrey said.

"If the pastor sues us, I guess you can come to the trial."

Austin lunged at Anglaise, arms swinging. "Don't you dare, you witch!"

Caramel fell back, tripping on her own feet.

Austin's hand made contact with Anglaise's face, even as

Chief Hartwell caught him by the shoulders. The slap rang out—the clap of skin on skin ringing out in the cool night air.

Caramel hit the side of the teashop and slid to the ground.

Anglaise's head snapped to the side, but she hardly moved otherwise.

Fraiche barked in alarm, but for a long time there was only airless silence. Caramel heard the rush of blood in her ears and her heart pounded.

Everyone stood, unmoving as a painting, a Renaissance tableau captured in oils, a look of identical shock on everyone's faces.

Austin gasped and pulled back, remorse and horror twisting his lean features. It was almost pathetic. Caramel felt a twinge of pity for him. At least Austin knew things had gone too far.

Caramel looked at Anglaise and felt her stomach shrivel.

Judging by the faint pink mark on her cheek, Austin had barely made contact, but it was enough to set Anglaise off.

Naked rage lit Anglaise's face. Lucky Bruleé had noticed as well. She grabbed Anglaise, even as she tried to make a run at Austin.

Anglaise struggled against Bruleé's underarm hold, her fists punching air.

"Anglaise, stop it!" Bruleé said through gritted teeth.

"You wanna piece of me, fatty?" Anglaise shouted.

Austin jerked at the insult, his hands clenched, but he stepped back, regret and anger fighting for control.

Hartwell kept his grip on Austin, forcing him away from the rabid Anglaise.

"Stop it, stop it, stop it!" shrieked a voice.

Caramel looked around. At first she didn't recognize Penelope's voice, it was so shrill. Caramel pulled herself up and stood on shaky knees. She held her breath, waiting for Penelope's next words.

"It was me," Penelope's voice cracked. "I broke into the teashop and let the dream puffs out. I didn't know. I didn't know..." She covered her face and sobbed.

"Penelope?" Austin looked at Chief Hartwell and the policeman let him go. Austin put his arms around Penelope, letting her sob into his chest.

"That's a serious crime," Paul said.

"So, it's our turn to press charges," Anglaise crowed.

Austin glared at Anglaise. "You'd put her in jail?"

"Why not? That's where you'd like to see us. And don't think you're off the hook either." Anglaise almost broke free of Bruleé's hold, but William jumped in to help.

"Let go of me. I'm filing assault charges."

"You—I barely touched you!" Austin let go of Penelope. She staggered without his support.

Caramel's fingers knotted themselves into the fabric of the T-shirt she'd thrown on after getting up. She wiped the sweat off her palms. Her eyes went from Austin to Anglaise, darting back and forth.

Penelope's confession should have fixed things. Austin would lose leverage. Anglaise would quit being mad because the dream swapping was an accident. Then Austin would apologize for slapping her—he hadn't meant to—and then everything would be fine. The protest would fizzle, the teashop would stay open. Why wasn't any of that happening?

Caramel pulled on the hem of Alyss's T-shirt.

Alyss half turned toward her, reluctant to take her eyes off the spectacle, barely sparing Caramel a glance. "Yeah?"

"I—I—I know how t—t—t—to stop this."

"You do? Great." Alyss grinned. She put two fingers in her mouth and blew a piercing whistle. Everyone flinched and seven pairs of very angry eyes turned toward Alyss.

Caramel hid behind her friend and bit her lip to keep from saying "See me not."

"Everyone, Caramel has an idea. Listen up," Alyss told them.

There was no way Caramel could address that many people. She peeked over Alyss's shoulder. At least they weren't angry anymore. There was an even amount of doubt and hope on the faces of the crowd.

She had to say something to someone, though. Caramel leaned into Alyss's ear and whispered her idea.

Alyss nodded, listening patiently as Caramel stuttered. "Uh-huh…yeah, all right."

Caramel pulled back, shrinking back to a semi-crouch behind Alyss when she was finished.

"Okay, here's the plan," Alyss said. "Anglaise won't press charges for assault if Pastor Austin doesn't do his civil suit thing."

"What about Penelope?" Austin asked, suspicion dripping off his voice.

"Well, assault and breaking and entering cancel each other out. So no one presses charges."

Caramel tapped Alyss's shoulder.

"Oh, yeah, and the protest ends and the witches stay," Alyss added.

"I think the vandalism can remain unsolved if that were to happen," Bruleé said.

"What? No!" Anglaise sounded more dismayed than angry.

"Yes," William said.

Caramel crept out from behind Alyss. She looked at Penelope, who, for the first time that night, looked hopeful.

Paul held up his hands. "Now hang on. It doesn't work like that. We have witnesses to a crime and a confession in front of a police officer. I'm not sure I can just drop it."

"That's how small towns work," Geoffrey said.

"We can sort things out ourselves," Claire told him.

"That's only on TV, people," Paul said.

"Junior prom, Paul," Matilda blurted.

His eyes narrowed as he turned to his sister. "What?"

"Junior. Prom," Matilda said.

"How do you even…" He trailed off then answered his own question. "Amanda."

Matilda gave him a look of puppy dog innocence. "You'd be surprised what sisters share."

Paul looked over the group, scrutinizing Anglaise and Pastor Austin, the two troublemakers. Anglaise had deflated, but Bruleé and William had boxed her in. Austin had retreated to Penelope's side. He looked wary, but his color had almost returned to normal.

Caramel crossed her fingers and held her breath, hoping that Austin and Penelope would take the deal and that Chief Hartwell would allow it.

The chief's stony expression didn't change, but let he let out a sigh. "Fine," he said. "But all of you have to agree, and no one gets to change their mind next week. I am not filling out the paperwork for that."

Everyone on the witches' side cheered. Geoffrey and Claire hugged while Alyss clapped her hands. Matilda elbowed her brother, but the only response Paul gave was a purse of his lips.

Caramel's breath whooshed out, and her knees almost gave out. Fraiche wagged his tail, happy that the people around him were happy.

The only holdouts were Anglaise, Penelope, and Austin. As the cheers died down, everyone waited to see what they'd say.

Penelope looked at Pastor Austin, eyes imploring. He nodded and patted her shoulder, even if he didn't look happy.

"Agreed," he said.

Paul nodded. "And you?"

Anglaise crossed her arms and glared at the pastor.

"Come on." Bruleé nudged her.

Anglaise remained set.

"J—j—j—just say yes!" Caramel exploded.

Her voice was rough. She wasn't used to anything above a whisper. As soon as she spoke, Caramel was overwhelmed with horror. She backed away from the crowd, hands over her mouth. She wasn't sure what had happened. Why she'd yelled like that. Anglaise was just so stubborn.

"Sure." Anglaise coughed. "I agree."

Chief Hartwell gestured at Anglaise and Austin. "Shake on it."

They both looked at him as if he'd suggested eating poison.

"No," they said in unison then looked at each other with icy hatred.

"Okay, that's not going to happen," Hartwell said. "Can we all go back to bed now?"

An ear-splitting squeal echoed down the street, making Caramel start. Before she realized what had happened, Alyss grabbed her in a tight bear hug. Caramel was lifted off the pavement as Alyss hopped in a little circle. Her friend's joy was infectious, and Caramel found herself swept up in the emotion. She laughed, jumped, and let herself be carried away.

"You're staying! You're staying," Alyss cheered as she and Caramel bounced.

Alyss and Caramel came to a stop and Alyss let go of her. As soon as Caramel was free, she was tackled from behind.

Bruleé spun her around and hugged her so hard, Caramel was sure her ribs would collapse. As if Bruleé were squeezing an emotion out of her, Caramel felt something bubbly well up inside her and overflow.

She was happy, and so relieved that warm tears spilled down her face.

"We'll be okay," Bruleé whispered in her ear. "Thanks to you."

Finally, Bruleé let go and Caramel wiped her face with a shirtsleeve.

While Geoffrey, Claire, and William cheered, Austin remained glacial. He glared at the witches, Anglaise in particular.

Anglaise didn't cheer, but she didn't need restraining anymore. Caramel couldn't read her at all. She wasn't gloating or happy.

Then Caramel looked at Penelope. She smiled at her and mouthed, "Thank you."

Penelope looked startled. A second of hesitation and she gave Caramel an almost imperceptible nod, though her expression didn't change.

Austin put a hand on Penelope's shoulder. "Come on, let's go."

Penelope bit her lip and tore her gaze from Caramel. She nodded at Pastor Austin.

"Would you like a ride home, Pastor?" Penelope asked.

Austin sagged. "Very much. Thank you."

The cheers from Claire and Geoffrey went up again, louder

than before as the foe retreated. Matilda threw her arms around Paul and laughed.

Just before Penelope got in her car, she cast another nervous look at Caramel. Then her lips twitched in the faint impression of a smile.

Fraiche barked and waved his tail. Penelope looked at the pom and gave him a full grin that disappeared even faster than it had appeared.

"And I think everyone else should go home, too."

It was more order than suggestion, and everyone nodded in agreement.

Matilda hugged her brother once more. "Thank you, Paul."

His stony expression softened a fraction. "Go home, and drive slow. You already have nine points on your license," he said as he pushed her gently away. "Miss Ruiz?"

Alyss snapped to attention. "Yes, sir?"

"I'm driving you home."

She turned to Caramel. "I'll be by tomorrow with the guys. Wait till I tell them what happened."

"Th—thanks f—f—f—for coming," Caramel told her.

Alyss grinned. "Of course. That's what friends are for."

Chief Hartwell opened the passenger side door of his squad car and coughed softly. Alyss snuck in one last, quick hug then got in the car.

Caramel waved goodbye as the police car disappeared down the street.

Bruleé let out a whooshing exhale, bracing her hands on her knees.

Just as Caramel was about to see if she was okay, Bruleé straightened. She whipped her hair out of her face. "We made it! We're staying." She flashed them all a V for victory.

"Great," Anglaise said, voice flat. "I'm going back to bed."

She pushed past Bruleé on her way to the teashop door. She made it three steps before William caught her shoulder.

"Are you all right?"

Anglaise dodged his gaze. "I'm fine."

Her furtive look was one Caramel and Bruleé both recognized. When William looked at them for help, they both shook their heads. The best thing William could do now was check his concern and leave her alone. Caramel knew he'd get nothing more out of her except a string of cussing if he kept pushing.

On Caramel and Bruleé's silent advice, William let it go. "Okay. I'll be by tomorrow to see how you're doing."

"Don't bother." Anglaise kept her head down as she darted for the front door. She pushed through the shop and disappeared in back before Caramel could blink an eye.

"Does she mean that?" William asked Bruleé.

"I doubt it," Claire said.

"Yeah. No, she doesn't," Geoffrey agreed. "She just means, not right now."

Geoffrey grinned and elbowed William. "Gonna give up bachelorhood?"

"What? No! We only talked a few times."

Caramel giggled.

"What does that mean?" William asked.

Bruleé translated. "If she didn't like you, at least a little—" She held up a thumb and forefinger separated only by a fraction of an inch. "—she wouldn't even talk to you in the first place."

William nodded slowly. "Okay. I'll take your word for it. See you later." He shook his head and wandered back to his car.

With William gone, there were just four of them left on the sidewalk. The sky was just beginning to lighten to a predawn navy blue.

Bruleé yawned. "Well, I'm exhausted."

"Oh, sorry," Geoffrey said. "We won't keep you. But do you mind if we come back?"

"Of course not," Bruleé said. "Just give us a few days."

"Really?"

Claire dug an elbow into his gut. "Of course. You need some time after all that."

"All right," Geoffrey said.

Claire dragged him back to their car.

"Thanks for coming," Bruleé said.

They waved. Caramel waved back. She wanted to say something but, with the crisis over, she could feel her shyness creeping back. Fraiche spoke for her. He jumped up and down, barking with each leap.

Once they were alone on the street, Bruleé let out a sigh and put her arm around Caramel. "You are my hero," she said, giving Caramel a squeeze.

Caramel shook her head. She felt her cheeks grow warm with a blush. "N—n—no."

"Oh, yes, you are. Austin backed down, Penelope scuttled away, and we may just last till tourist season."

"Sh—sh—she's not so b—bad," Caramel said.

"Who? That Owens woman?" Bruleé cocked her head. "Well, I can take your word for it, I guess."

Bruleé steered Caramel back to the shop and she was happy to be led. Even the sight of the broken teapots on the floor couldn't squelch the bit of remaining happiness left over from knowing they were going to stay.

Epilogue

nglaise stood in front of the teashop. Bright June sunlight sparkled on the pavement beyond the awning. She hung back, sticking to the shade so the cheesecake she held wouldn't melt.

At 10 a.m., the streets were thick with tourists. Inside Tea Times Three, there was a line at the register. The shop didn't have near enough tables to seat the crowds, and most people had to get their orders to go. By ten-thirty, the crowd thinned out to almost nothing, not picking up again until four in the afternoon for high tea. The teashop was finally breaking even. On good days, they had enough profit to pay off some of the debt racked up during the first few months it was open.

Caramel was filling orders and ringing up customers as fast as she could, but she looked harried. The loose braid her hair was pulled into was coming apart and powdered sugar dusted her T-shirt.

Money permitting, they'd need to hire some part time help. Anglaise still wasn't sure if they'd made enough inroads with the community that anyone would work for them.

Bruleé, of course, felt everything was fine.

Pastor Austin had been true to his word, and the protestors evaporated the day after the dream puff incident.

Anglaise wondered what he'd told them. For some reason, word of Austin slapping her had never gotten out. Either by some mutual, unspoken agreement, everyone was protecting him, or Bruleé had done something. A spell to gently dissuade everyone from mentioning that bit perhaps.

She shifted the cheesecake to one hand and scratched her face. Austin's slap hadn't even left a bruise. The reddened palm print had faded after an hour.

A car horn honked, bringing Anglaise's attention back to the present.

Stopped in the middle of the street was William, his vintage Chevy idling.

"Ready?" he called out the window.

Anglaise didn't reply. She gave him a nod and headed for the car. Traffic was starting to pile up behind him, but there was nowhere for him to park. Every spot for blocks seemed to have a car with an out of state plate parked in it.

"Hey," he said as she got in.

Anglaise set the cheesecake on her lap and buckled the seatbelt. "Morning."

William got moving just as a chorus of car horns went off. He rolled his eyes. "New Yorkers."

Anglaise was quickly learning that "New Yorkers" was the fashionable swearword come summer in Midswich.

"Thanks for coming with me," Anglaise muttered. She kept her eyes on the chocolate brown top of the cheesecake in her lap. The cake box had a clear cellophane cutout in the lid to give a sneak peek at the contents.

She glanced sidelong at William to see his reaction.

He grinned. "I'm just surprised you're doing this."

So was she. Anglaise hadn't told Bruleé what she was doing, even though Bruleé had planted the idea.

"I don't want to, but I think I have to," Anglaise said. "Or something."

"No, it's good of you to try," William said. "I don't think I'd be so forgiving."

Shame spiked in her chest. William had forgiven her, or at least believed he had, for nearly taking his head off that night. Anglaise wasn't sure he fully understood what she'd done.

They hadn't met up for weeks after the dream puff incident and, when they did it was at the coffee shop in Musquash. Anglaise had been dodging William and making do with coffee from the Dry Goods. But until Geoffrey found the instructions on cleaning the cappuccino machine, the coffee was unbearable. She'd broken down and gotten on her broom, which she could barely control with her powers locked. Then she'd made the long, slow, wobbly trip to Mean Joe's one Sunday when all the baking was done.

She thought she'd be far too late to run into William, but there he was, at the counter, coffee in hand. Anglaise didn't even have time to duck out. He turned around as the door opened and spotted her.

Emotions flickered across his face like a slide show. Happiness, doubt, then fear and lastly, nervous hope.

He went over to her and invited her to sit down. Anglaise had intended to say no, but the word never make it out of her mouth. She didn't know what she'd said, could never remember, but she was soon sitting across from William at a quiet table in the corner.

She did remember the first thing he asked.

"Are your powers still locked down?"

"Yeah," she said.

William relaxed, shoulders sagging, his expression relieved. Then he wiped away the look with a smile and asked how she'd been.

They talked about nothing important before Anglaise made an excuse about having to get back to the teashop. He'd looked disappointed but didn't try to stop her.

Anglaise couldn't erase the image of his relief at finding out her powers were still cut off. Of course, he had every right to be scared of her, more than anyone in fact. She hated that she'd frightened William. She'd scared herself that night. But Anglaise knew Bruleé would unlock her powers eventually, and what would William do then? Right now she was safe. Normal.

A long, waiting silence brought Anglaise back to the present.

"Sorry, what?" She blinked. She'd been mindlessly staring at the cheesecake.

"I said I'm glad you called me."

Anglaise shrugged. "I don't have any other friends."

"Just friends?" William asked.

Heat rose in her cheeks and burned her ears. Anglaise turned to look out the window, pretending the parade of tourists leaving the historic Federalist-style courthouse had caught her eye.

There wasn't really a good response to the "just friends" question. Not right then. He was her only friend in town. Whether there was potential for more, she couldn't say yet.

"Anyway," William said, "I know you didn't need the ride. Thanks for asking, though."

Anglaise shrugged, glad he'd steered the conversation away from anything involving relationships.

"Flying sucks without my powers."

"Well, there's walking."

She laughed. Walking was never the first thing to occur to her. She hadn't done it much in Boston, and it was hard to remember Midswich was small enough that everything was in walking distance.

"All right," she said, "I just wanted moral support. And you know where Austin lives."

"That I do," William said. He took the next left and pulled up in front of a two story Tudor Revival house. Like every other house in Midswich, an obvious effort had been made to give it character. The flower garden in front could have come from the cover of a magazine.

Anglaise frowned at the house, the prettiness of the exterior at odds with what she knew of the resident. A notion that was ridiculous to its core. Why would Austin live in some hovel, just because she thought that's what he deserved?

"Garden much," Anglaise said sourly.

William chuckled. "Yeah, he does. Pastor Austin likes nature. The whole garden is organic."

She sniffed. "You don't get roses like that without a decent aphid spray."

"You're just delaying going in, aren't you?" He shut off the car and pulled the keys from the ignition. "I think it's a good idea," he said.

"What if he throws it in my face?" For some reason she wanted to make peace with the pastor. She didn't want his approval or friendship. It was something else.

Like the old saying, all she really wanted was to bury the

hatchet. If she could take their animosity down a notch, then maybe Anglaise could settle into the town. Move on. Make friends. Unpack the emergency suitcases she kept hidden under her bed.

"I don't think he will."

"That's not very convincing," Anglaise said.

"He'll slam the door in your face maybe."

"And still not helping."

"Just try. If this doesn't work, it doesn't work. Maybe you can try again later."

"No," she said. "There is no later."

"That's fine, but you still have to go up to the house."

"You suck at moral support." Anglaise pulled the door handle and shoved open the car door.

Behind her, William chuckled, but she ignored him and shut the door on the sound. She'd worked up the nerve to come this far, there was no use turning back.

All the stupid clichés people said to get other people psyched up ran through her head. They all sucked.

She marched herself across the sidewalk, running on sheer willpower, and stopped at the white picket gate.

William caught up to her. For a minute, they stood on the sidewalk, looking at the tidy house and garden overflowing with color.

"I could just leave the cake on the front step with a note."

"What happened to the girl who almost took my head off with a fireball?"

"It wasn't meant for you, and it wasn't a fireball," she snapped.

"It was meant for the cops, wasn't it, Gangsta?"

Anglaise snorted and let out a laugh. There was no way she should be laughing. Nothing from that night was funny. She had been ready to take down anyone who came for her. But any excuse to break the tension was welcome.

William held the picket gate open for her. "After you, Gangsta."

"That is not my new nickname," Anglaise said. "Or you can forget about even being friends."

His grin didn't falter as he waited for her to pass through the gate. He followed right behind her, and Anglaise heard the gate click shut.

The neatly edged walk, lined with bachelor buttons, felt like it stretched for miles. Somehow, without a word, William kept her feet moving, one step after another.

She found herself standing on the front stoop, a narrow circle of concrete in front of the red painted front door. Her hand extended, but stopped just short of the doorbell. She turned to look at William.

He nodded. "Go on."

Anglaise inhaled and pushed the doorbell. She heard the faint buzz of an old fashioned doorbell.

"Maybe he's not home," she said.

"I think you need to give him time to get to the door. One second might not be enough."

She sighed and waited. Anglaise tried out a smile, but couldn't get her face to cooperate so she gave up.

The click of the front door lock told Anglaise someone was home. Was he locking the door?

No such luck. The red door swung open. Austin's pinched face hovered behind the cracked door. She wondered if he knew a red door meant hospitality.

"What do you want?" he asked through the narrow opening.

Anglaise grit her teeth and raised the cheesecake. "I brought a peace offering."

"I don't eat…whatever that is," he said.

The door started to close and William darted forward. He wedged his foot in the door before Austin could shut it.

"Please, Pastor, just hear her out," he said.

Austin made a disgruntled noise in the back of his throat. "Fine," he said at last.

The door swung fully open, but his expression remained closed. He stood in the doorway, arms crossed, and didn't invite them in.

William pulled his foot back and nudged Anglaise with his elbow.

She took a half step forward and lifted the cheesecake higher. "It's a low calorie, low-fat cheesecake that also clocks low on the glycemic index."

Before Anglaise had decided to make something for Austin, she'd only had a vague notion of what all that glycemic stuff was. Now she could make pastries for a convention of diabetics.

Austin's disdain crumbled just the slightest, and he gave the cheesecake a second curious look. His mouth worked like he was chewing something sour for a second, or like he wanted to ask something but didn't want to look like it.

"Instead of sugar, I used an alcohol sugar, which has zero calories. Low-fat cream cheese. Carob instead of chocolate, because chocolate has added sugar, and the crust is made of almond meal. There's about a tablespoon of butter in the whole thing, and I doubt the entire cake gets much past five hundred calories, let alone a slice. And next time, I could try to make it with protein powder or something. But I don't know about that."

Anglaise shoved the cheesecake at Austin. He blinked at the cake in mute surprise.

"It's for you," William said. "Anglaise made it."

"There's no magic in it if that's what you think," she said.

"It's a gift," William added.

Austin didn't move. He was frozen in the front hall, stiff as the umbrella stand he stood next to.

A few seconds stretched into a few more. Anglaise felt her arms start to shake. "I can't hold this thing up forever. You want it or not?"

Why wasn't he moving? Was he too angry? That didn't seem right. He hadn't slammed the door yet, which seemed promising.

She had one last tactic to pull Austin from his shock.

"Fine. I guess I'll just throw it away."

"What? No," William said. "I'll take it. You can't just throw out food."

"Er—" Austin said. He defrosted quickly and stepped forward. "It's really low calorie?"

"It's not a trick," Anglaise said.

Austin pursed his lips. A thoughtful wrinkle furrowed his brow.

She wanted to snap at him, tell him she didn't have all day, but she forced herself to wait. Tried to will herself calm.

"I s—suppose I could try it," Austin said. "Seems a shame to waste it."

"Here." Anglaise handed him the cake box. "If it sucks, you don't have to eat it."

She turned to leave and pulled William around with her. The olive branch had been offered and accepted. Now it was Austin's turn to apologize, not that she expected he would.

Anglaise was almost to the gate when she heard the tentative clearing of a throat behind her. If it was William, it could wait until they got in the car.

William tapped her shoulder. "Hold up."

Anglaise turned. "What?"

He hooked a thumb back at the house. She looked where he was pointing. Pastor Austin had ventured as far as the little concrete stoop, hand raised for attention, and a constipated look on his face.

"Um…" he said.

Anglaise waited. If that "um" didn't lead somewhere quickly, she was leaving.

"Every August, the church holds a fair, and different organizations have bake sales to raise money. Some are for charity. Others, like the library, raise money for books. The high school clubs raise money for trips. You could pick a charity and have a table maybe. William can tell you more. The Chamber of Commerce raises money for a scholarship fund."

Anglaise wasn't sure what to make of the offer. She hadn't heard anything about a church fair, even though Bruleé had a big wall calendar with all the local festivals marked in red.

She glanced at William, who nodded emphatically.

"That sounds good," Anglaise said. "I'll tell Bruleé about it."

"All right then," Austin said. He offered an uncomfortable half smile then retreated into his house.

"Wow," William said. "No new businesses get invited to the church bake sale."

"Really?"

"That cheesecake better not make him fat."

She gave him a sour look. "That's not funny."

"Sorry."

"I'd never lie about food."

"So you would have thrown out the cake?" He pulled the car door open for her.

Anglaise paused. "I was pretty sure he'd take it."

"If he didn't?"

"It's made with carob, and Fraiche could have eaten it."

"Well, I'm glad he didn't get to," William said.

"I suppose if the cheesecake is too bad, we're out of that fair thingy."

"The man subsists on protein shakes and salad. I'm not sure he'd even notice if it was bad."

She smiled. "As a chef, I'm not sure that makes me feel better."

William reached out and put his hand on hers where she gripped the doorframe. The warmth of his skin sent a zing of electricity up her arm.

"Don't worry so much. Pastor Austin took your peace offering and offered you a spot in the fair. That's huge. He can't take it back and he's not going to."

"Thanks," she said. Anglaise was glad of the reassurance, but a little annoyed that William always seemed to home in on what was really bothering her, bypassing her words altogether. She slid her hand out from under his and got in the car. "I have to get back and get ready for high tea."

"Sure thing." William closed the door and went around to the driver's side.

The instant he wasn't looking at her, Anglaise let herself smile a big dopey grin she'd been fighting off since William had touched her hand.

She heard the click of the driver's side door and forced the smile back. "Are you going to be at Mean Joe's on Sunday" she asked.

"Yeah."
She smiled. "Good. I'll need a ride."

The End

About the Author

Ché Gilson is the author of several graphic novels including *Avigon: Gods and Demons* from Image Comics, and *Dark Moon Diary* from Tokyopop. Her short stories have been published online in *Luna Station Quarterly* issue 14 and *Drops of Crimson* (which is no longer operating).

She draws copious amounts of Pokémon fan art and is working on multiple novels including a contemporary fantasy about tea and witches, and two children's books. *Carmine Rojas: Dog Fight* (Black Opal Books, 2014) was her first novel.

http://spiderliing666.deviantart.com.

www.ingramcontent.com/pod-product-compliance
Lightning Source LLC
Chambersburg PA
CBHW060935120726
47910CB00002B/341